Marc Alexander had his first short stories published when he was fifteen, and became a full-time writer in 1972 of both fiction and non-fiction. He is an established writer of horror novels under a pseudonym.

D0519418

Also by Marc Alexander

Enchantment's End

Part the Fourth of
The Wells of Ythan

Marc Alexander

05197876

First published in 1992
by HEADLINE BOOK PUBLISHING PLC

A HEADLINE FEATURE paperback

10 9 8 7 6 5 4 3 2 1

ISBN 0 7472 3834 0

Typeset by Medcalf Type Ltd, Bicester, Oxon

Printed and bound in Great Britain by
HarperCollins Manufacturing, Glasgow

HEADLINE BOOK PUBLISHING PLC
Headline House
79 Great Titchfield Street
London W1P 7FN

For my father Ronald Alexander
whose long ago tales inspired
the Wells of Ythan

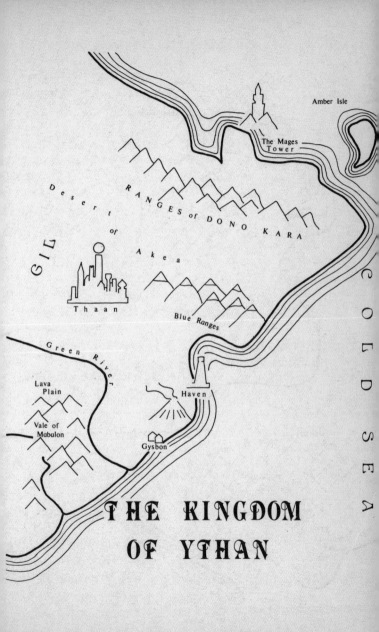

Amber Isle

The Mages
Tower

RANGES of DONO KARA

Desert
of
Akea

GIL

Thaan

Blue Ranges

OLD SEA

Green River

Lava
Plain

Vale of
Mabalon

Haven

Gysbon

THE KINGDOM
OF YTHAN

Enchantment's End

Part the Fourth of
The Wells of Ythan

Book One

PROLOGUE

It seemed like the irony — or the wrath — of the gods that at the moment I reached the end of the Pilgrim Path, which for a century had defeated the boldest hearts, the quest was lost. That moment will remain my most vivid memory for however much time the Mother grants before the Dark Maid touches my shoulder. My companions and I could not believe our shocked senses as we watched the precious water from the Wells of Ythan drain away, and with it our dreams.

If it had been merely a tragedy for myself and Krispin — and even the fool Ognam — it would have mattered little. But the loss of that water meant the evil force shadowing the kingdom, personified by the Regent, had triumphed.

We had travelled so far to find this final disappointment. For me the quest had begun when my home of River Garde, the castle commanding the River of Night which divided our Wald from the Outlands, fell to the barbarian Wolf Horde whose shape-changing leader treacherously murdered my noble father Grimwald VII, Hereditary Lord of the River

3

March. In vain I attempted to find the Lady Demara, my father's beautiful young wife, but I was sore hurt in the fighting and I found myself wandering in the forest almost witless. Yet I remembered my father's last injunction, that if River Garde should fall I must put myself in the keeping of Lady Eloira, Reeve of the High Wald.

When I recovered in her Peak Tower she revealed that, like my father, she was a follower of the Pilgrim Path, the secret brotherhood dedicated to the restoration of the Princess Livia. According to legend the Princess had lain in an enchanted sleep for a hundred years in some place beyond the ken of men.

Livia was the only child of King Johan XXXIII and her disappearance as a result of The Enchantment meant that when the good old king died soon afterwards the kingdom was left without a royal ruler. It was then that Ythan's Golden Age ended in chaos and in the uneasy order that followed, established mainly by the merciless Guild of Witchfinders, power passed to a line of Regents sworn to protect the Empty Throne until its rightful heir should claim it. In reality these corrupted rulers had little interest in protecting anything but their own vicious interests, and as time passed their power evolved into the malignity which spread through the realm like a canker through a once-fair body.

In the Peak Tower the Lady Eloira urged me to undertake the quest for the Princess and, believing that is what my father would have wished, I agreed. A youth named Krispin Tammasson would accompany me. An apprentice toymaker, he and his sister Jennet had been given shelter in the Peak Tower after their forest village of Toyheim was razed by the Wolf

Horde. I had little confidence that a lad with such a background would be the ideal squire-companion on such a mission but the Lady Eloira was adamant and, in fairness, I must confess that under the circumstances he proved to be more resourceful than I expected.

The Lady Eloira chose him because he was highly receptive when she entranced him with her pendulum and induced secret knowledge into his memory. He could only become conscious of certain aspects of this instruction under specific circumstances, an old Pilgrim ruse so that should the wayfinder be captured by the Regent he could not reveal the nature of the quest no matter what torment he might suffer.

After setting out from the Peak Tower with young Tammasson I deemed it my duty to attempt to rescue the Lady Demara from River Garde where she was held by the Wolf King. I am happy to recall that in this I was successful and with her maid Margan we escaped along the River of Night.

Alas, while encamped on an islet in the sinister Shallows I was the victim of a succubus under circumstances I still find too painful to pen. The result was that I was barely aware of my surroundings as we continued through the aptly named Land of Blight and paused at the ruinous City Without a Name. Here Krispin, thanks to guidance planted in his unconscious mind, retrieved a remarkable jewel known as the Esav from the image of some forgotten god in an ancient temple. As I say, I was in a confused condition at the time but I understand that he performed this task with some credit.

We continued downriver to the hidden Vale of Mabalon where among its quaint but hospitable

inhabitants my reason and strength returned enough
for me to continue the quest. It was decided that the
Lady Demara, who was carrying my late father's child,
should remain there in safety with her maid. Under
the circumstances it was an excellent choice yet I must
admit that I was more moved at our parting than I
cared to show.

With my companion I journeyed to mighty Danaak,
once known as Danaak the Golden, where instructions
emerging in Krispin's conscious mind led us to a
pleasure house owned by the Lady Merlinda who,
though a courtesan, was of impeccable lineage and,
like us, a secret follower of the Pilgrim Path.

It was her role to set us on the next step of the quest
which turned out to be the heretic city of Thaan where
we might learn the whereabouts of The Mage, a
sorcerer of such great age it was believed that at the
time of The Enchantment he knew where Princess
Livia was hidden. Our hope was that he would trade
this secret for the Esav.

While in the house of the Lady Merlinda we were
arrested by the Witchfinder-General and imprisoned
in a dungeon beneath the Citadel. Our fellow captive
was a jongleur named Ognam imprisoned for
ridiculing the Regent. Fate ruled that he was to become
one of our companions on the quest.

It was thanks to a young man named Gambal that
we escaped. It appeared that he was in the employ of
the Regent but had private reasons for wishing to flee
the city before some form of retribution fell upon him.
It also transpired that he wore the Disk of Livia –
the symbol of the Pilgrim Path – which explained why
he was ready to assist us. Through the use of an official
document he was able to lead us to a boat on the Green

River which flowed beneath the Citadel and by this means we escaped.

The hazard of our journey to Thaan was that the Regent had sent forth an army against the city because of the heretical views of its inhabitants who had never accepted that the All Father fell from grace and the Three Worlds were redeemed by his daughter, our Serene Mother. This meant that if we were to reach it first we needs must cross the Wilderness of Gil while the Regent's army took the ancient highroad to the north.

The efficient Gambal had arranged for us to be guided by a crook-backed caravan pilot known as the Hump who had a remarkable instinct for finding the way through unmapped terrain. He provided drongs and we set off across this terrible wasteland.

What a curious party we were — apart from myself there was a noble whore, a toymaker, a mountebank and the Regent's runaway Revel Master. Travelling with the Hump was a beautiful but curious creature named Silvermane who had the graceful lower limbs of a horse, and who obviously was deeply in love with our malformed guide. 'Beauty and the beast' we privately termed them but there is nothing as strange as the ways of love as, alas, I know only too well.

This is not the time to enumerate the perils we endured, suffice it to say that we did reach the heretic city and found shelter behind its walls just as the Regent's army began its siege. Here we were given audience by the leader of the heretics, an old man named Brother Mias, who helped us wonderfully despite the fact that his city was under attack. This was because the remote possibility of us succeeding in our quest could lead to the downfall of the Regency.

His scribes combed the Great Library of Thaan — the last repository of knowledge since the Witchfinders' scroll burnings — and just before the fall of the city a map was discovered. Torn from some ancient tome it showed a piece of coastline and an islet on which The Mage's Tower was built. Meanwhile Mandal, the Commander of the Regent's Host, endeavoured to cut short the siege by catapulting victims of the Red Death into the city. As the plague spread, infected citizens made a suicidal onslaught against their enemies with the purpose of carrying the contagion to them. It was an action deserving to be recorded as one of the great moments of history despite the fact it was undertaken by those of a misguided faith. I must confess that to me it was as noble as any heroic gesture in the tales told by minstrels in River Garde. But I digress.

During the heretics' counterattack my companions and I escaped the doomed city into the mines of the Drakenfel. Here we followed an underground river for untold leagues to a chasm which led us to the upper world and the Domain of Olam, a tiny enclave in the Desert of Akea. It had been secretly founded by an aristocrat at the time of The Enchantment to avoid the calamity that he knew would follow, and for three generations his descendants had lived there in ancient style. Though unused to strangers Mesire Florizan, the present lord of the domain, gave us his hospitality.

At this point the toymaker Krispin performed a service to the domain. The details are irrelevant here, suffice it to say that as repayment Mesire Florizan let us into one of his many secrets — the amazing relationship between the heirs of his House with a number of griffins who wintered in a desert valley before flying to the Cold Sea in spring to hunt the kraken there. He arranged for us to ride on the backs of the migrating creatures to The Mage's Tower, an experience so exhilarating that it alone was enough to make a lifetime worthwhile.

Four of us travelled on these fabled beasts — Ognam, Gambal, Krispin and myself — and when we reached the tower in the most desolate setting imaginable I must confess that our spirits sank in the shadow of its gloomy disrepair. When we found The Mage in his bedchamber we feared the Dark Maid had claimed him but by using the wondrous Esav we succeeded in reviving him.

Later he explained that most of the time his body lay in unnatural slumber while his spirit travelled in unknown realms. This was in keeping with the gramarye surrounding the tower which, like my companions, I found greatly disturbing, as indeed we found The Mage himself. For a time we could get no answer from him — perhaps he was weighing us up — though I cannot complain about the hospitality in the tower which had magically refurbished itself on his awakening.

In the meanwhile our fool Ognam had discovered a beautiful girl in an enchanted prison beneath the tower. It followed that he had to become infatuated by her, a most unsuitable occurrence as she was of a noble family whose estate, as she later told me, was on the Lake of Taloon. Later we feared that his reckless behaviour in releasing her would endanger the quest but this anxiety was soon eclipsed by the numerous difficulties that beset us.

Eventually The Mage consented to reveal the whereabouts of the Princess Livia in return for the

Esav whose magical properties he coveted. He gave us a flacon of water from the lost Wells of Ythan which would rouse her from her entrancement, and he arranged for us to travel to the Shadow Realm in a ship named the Amber Star. *Her amber-seeking master had found refuge with The Mage after most of his crew had been slain by corsairs the previous summer.*

I must say it was with great relief that we quit The Mage's Tower aboard this stout vessel. Far be it for me to write a single critical word against a great enchanter but the atmosphere of the place was so charged with magic that we were ill-eased during our stay. Several remarkable events occurred on our voyage south — an attack by krakens, Krispin's bespellment on a haunted island, a chase by corsairs and refuge in the port of Haven whose overnight transformation into a ruin left us bewildered. Yet it was a minor incident that was to have the greatest effect upon us, the rescue of two penal slaves from an open boat in which they had escaped. Short of crew, Shipmaster Danya was pleased to have them aboard and they worked with diligence.

When the Esav was handed to The Mage he gave me a needle, mounted in a box, which was made from a sliver of the Lodestone which geographers state is the pillar marking the world's end. This magical needle moved of its own accord, and by following its direction we would be led to Princess Livia's resting place. Thus guided by the Lodestone pointer we sailed down the coastline of Ythan and past the Mountains of the Moon which are the southernmost boundary of the kingdom. Beyond this lay the Shadow Realm, well named indeed because it lies under perpetual twilight.

The Amber Star *then took us inland along a perilous river until it was hewn asunder by a gigantic statue set to guard this strange region by ancient sorcery. Thanks be to the Mother we escaped without hurt and continued on foot to the base of the Mountains of the Moon where we beheld a gateway set in the cliff face.*

Our hopes soared at the thought that we were about to find the object of this long and arduous quest. Within we reached a chamber where, on what I can only describe as a couch of smoke, lay the most beautiful woman I have ever seen — the Princess Livia, heir to the Kingdom of Ythan.

It was a moment so filled with awe I have not the word skill to describe it.

When we had recovered our senses I prepared to awaken her and produced the flacon of water from the Wells of Ythan with which the sleeper should be bathed. It was then that hope withered through the blackest of treacheries.

One of the slaves we had rescued seized the shipmaster's crossbow and held us captive with it while his companion declared that he was a Witchfinder. These men had been deliberately set in our path by order of the Regent who, for obvious reasons, had as much interest in discovering the Princess as we. Proof of her destruction would end the hope of her return and I believe it was in the mind of the Regent to decree a new royal house with himself as its founder.

The treachery of these two men we had befriended was nothing to what followed. Gambal suddenly announced that he was the Regent's spy and it was through him that the Regent had followed the progress of our quest after he had pretended to engineer our escape from Danaak.

He spoke in view of a small mirror which he told us had acted as a magical window for the Lady Mandraga, the terrible crone who was Lore Mistress of Ythan and the power behind the Regent.

What followed filled us with even more bewilderment. The traitor Gambal said that even as he spoke she was probably watching us through this magical link. Then he spoke of his need to avenge himself upon her for a reason I did not then fully understand. And having admitted his betrayal of us with whom he had shared so many perils, he then betrayed his master the Regent and the Lore Mistress.

Without warning he plunged a dagger into the heart of the man with the crossbow. In his dying throes he fired the weapon. The bolt shattered the flacon of water and before our eyes this precious liquid, the only known element capable of restoring the Princess, drained away between the tiles.

No tutor of language, no learned scribe, no great minstrel could conjure the words to describe our despair.

— from the Memoirs of Alwald,
Hereditary Lord of the River March.

ONE
Livia's
Tomb

Krispin felt a sob tear his throat as the sparkling water from the Wells of Ythan flowed over the porphyry tiles, drained through the cracks between them and was lost for ever. Light from the wand he held turned the shards of the broken flacon into fragments of blue mirror. The only sound to break the silence came from the steps leading into the chamber in which the entranced Princess Livia lay on her couch of smoke; it was the dying sigh of Dikon sprawled with Gambal's knife protruding from his chest.

There was no movement. Both the followers of the Pilgrim Path and the agents of the Regent were stunned after so many shocks in quick succession – elation at the discovery of the Princess, the revelation of the Mute's and Dikon's sinister purpose, Gambal's admission of treachery and then his unexpected attack on Dikon whose crossbow bolt had shattered the vessel containing the miraculous fluid without which the beautiful sleeper could not be wakened.

They stood like an ill-assorted group of statues as the enormity of what had happened paralysed both mind and body; the fair young noble Alwald, Krispin the toymaker, Danya the weathered shipmaster, the jongleur Ognam, Gambal once the Regent's Revel Master, the beautiful but enigmatic Tana, and Edom the newly revealed Witchfinder whom the others had known as the Mute. Time passed but for the questers it could have been a minute or an hour as each was crushed by the knowledge of their failure at the very moment of triumph.

Ognam was first to awake from the stupor of shock. He flung himself on the damp tiles and struggled to raise one in the hope of catching even a few drops of the precious water that had trickled beneath it. In his red and green motley he looked like a bizarre burrowing animal as he struggled with broken nails and bleeding fingers, and Tana laughed hysterically at the sight and then dropped on all fours beside him.

Their efforts were in vain until Krispin unsheathed Woundflame and used the point of the sword to prise the square of purple-red stone. As it came away Ognam pressed his kerchief into the cavity to soak up any water but when he removed the cloth it was scarcely damp. With a curse he flung it into the shadows.

His cry released the others from their spell. Danya leapt forward and his massive sailor hands fastened on the Witchfinder's throat.

'You Potton-bred whoreson,' he gasped in his anger. 'You repaid my mercy aboard the *Amber Star* with black deceit, now I repay you.'

His fingers tightened. In his empurpled face Edom's eyes bulged from their sockets and his heels beat a soft tattoo on the tiles.

'No, Danya!' shouted Alwald.

The shipmaster ignored the protest. The Witchfinder's mouth was now a black hole from which his tongue began to swell. Alwald and Krispin each seized one of Danya's wrists and tugged until they were forced apart. Edom slumped to the floor and Danya stepped back with a dazed expression in his eyes.

'Enough blood . . .' Krispin began.

'We may need the Witchfinder,' Alwald said. 'If there must be revenge . . .' His eyes turned to Gambal who stood watching the scene from beside the body of his victim. Alwald put his hand on the jewelled hilt of his sword and flushed with anger he cried, 'Traitor! False comrade! If a man deserves death 'tis you!'

His sword flashed from its scabbard in the wand light and he advanced on the slim young man who watched with an ironical expression.

'It is of no matter if you kill me,' he said quietly as the point of Alwald's blade pressed the fabric of his tunic. 'I have admitted that I was a spy but on the other hand if it had not been for me . . .' He gestured to Dikon's body. '. . . you would be prisoners of the Regent doomed to face the Dark Maid in this tomb. Your quest would have been an even greater failure because the Princess would have been in the power of your enemy.'

'But as it is she must remain entranced,' retorted Alwald.

Gambal shrugged his narrow shoulders.

'I did not break the flacon. All that concerned me was to thwart the Lore Mistress and the Regent. It was something that burned within me since she caused the death of Lorelle.'

For the first time his voice became unsteady.

'I have avenged her and now I care not what

15

becomes of me. Plunge your sword into my heart if
you must.'

Alwald's grimace of anger changed to a look of
uncertainty but he kept his sword raised.

'It is true that you stabbed Dikon but that was for
your own end and does not excuse your treachery to
us, your friends.'

Gambal sighed as though beyond caring and said
wearily, 'I told you I am no traitor because I was
obeying the orders of my master the Regent from the
moment I came to you in the dungeons of Danaak.
If there was treachery it is you who are the traitors
– as Pilgrims you seek the downfall of the Lord
Regent, the lawful ruler of Ythan.'

'That tyrant,' muttered Krispin in disgust.

'Thousands are willing to serve that tyrant so who
was I to have questioned his ethics when I managed
to become his Revel Master. Then I would have
served the Demon Omad rather than work another
day in the slaughter halls. My own fate was all I
cared about, now it means nothing. Yet, as I said
while Dikon still held the crossbow, just as I learned
about love from Lorelle so I learned about
comradeship through our adventures together. If I
had not wanted to repay the Lore Mistress . . .' He
gestured to the small mirror which stood on a narrow
ledge set in the white marble. '. . . I would have given
you full warning when you found Dikon and the
Mute adrift off Gysbon.'

'You would have confessed all?' said Krispin.

Gambal nodded.

'Words!' sneered Alwald. 'Words come cheap with
a sword against your breast.'

'Sometimes truth flowers in the shadow of the Dark

16

Maid,' Ognam murmured but no one appeared to hear him.

'It matters not whether or no you believe me. It matters not what you do to me for it seems to me that all our hours are numbered. My only hope is that in the Citadel the Lore hag saw what happened here in her magical glass. That is my only care, all else that I cared about lies in a grove in the Domain of Olam.'

'Let him be, Alwald,' said Krispin.

With a look of contempt Alwald turned and sheathed his sword.

'Hold,' Gambal cried. 'Mayhap this will prove my despised words.'

He seized the small mirror from the ledge and held it up. The others recoiled. Instead of reflecting the interior of the chamber like an honest glass it showed a very old woman, her face demonic with frustrated anger, her eyes ablaze with hatred.

'Is that — the Lore Mistress?' gasped Ognam.

'Ay, even now Mandraga watches us from her lair in the Citadel,' Gambal replied. 'But no more, my lady!'

He opened his fingers. The mirror dropped to the tiles where it shattered into several pieces and each shard showed the same picture of Mandraga's contorted features. With a curse Gambal powdered the fragments beneath his foot.

Krispin held high the light wand he had taken from the eidolon in the City Without a Name and its cold light illuminated the Princess's resting place while Alwald and Ognam carried Dikon's body into the treasure hall and rolled it into the shadows.

'He was the enemy but you have to admire him,'

17

said Alwald straightening up. 'He had himself branded so we would believe him to be a runaway slave. It is a mystery why men such as he should serve the Regent.'

'The Companions of the Rose are in love with loyalty,' Ognam said.

They returned to the Princess's chamber where, in a corner, the still-unconscious Witchfinder lay bound with strips torn from his cloak.

Krispin could not take his eyes off the calm features of Princess Livia as she lay in her robe of yellowing samite on her couch of magical smoke that coiled within itself. Her calm features were identical to those of his beloved sister Jennet. The similarity was so uncanny that there was no doubt in Krispin's mind if the sleeper suddenly opened her eyes they would be the same deep shade of blue as Jennet's and if she spoke her voice would have the same soft but vivacious timbre. It seemed to the youth that it was impossible there was not some strange link between the two until he remembered that the Princess had become the victim of The Enchantment over eighty years before Jennet was born.

His thoughts were interrupted by Ognam.

'Come along, Master Krispin,' he said. 'It was you who found entry into this place, now we look to you to find the exit.'

'Do you think the great door has closed upon us?' Tana asked the jongleur, her hand on the red sleeve of his costume.

Once her touch would have made his pulse pound but now he merely moved back and answered politely, 'After we entered the passage it sounded as though that had happened.'

18

Krispin stepped into the long treasure hall which had been excavated from the living rock of the Mountains of the Moon and went to the head of the small party. The light that flowed without heat from the black tip of his wand glittered on gems heaped on stone tables and gleamed on silver objects piled round its walls, a vast hoard that none dared touch for fear of the sorcery they sensed in the dead air about them.

'Treasure all around her lies,
In her cavern cold . . .'

The words from the old children's rhyming game came into Alwald's head. Who was it who had said there was a grain of truth in every legend? Of course — the jongleur, after they had faced the horror of the dhrul in the Wilderness of Gil. Serene Mother, how long ago it seemed. He remembered pursuing the night walker with Krispin when it had made off with Gambal. Would that they had left him to his fate!

He caught up with Krispin.

'Keep watch on Gambal,' he whispered. 'He speaks glibly but I have no trust in him.'

Krispin nodded and led the way into the passage which ran from the treasure hall to the gateway set in the cliff. The others straggled behind him still dazed by the events of the last hour, and they only fully realized the danger of their situation when they halted before the bronze doors which towered three times the height of a man. There were no handles or bars or locks, nothing by which they could be opened.

Desperately they pressed their palms agains the cold metal with all their strength but they might as well have been heaving against the rock in which the doors were

19

set. While they fell back gasping, Ognam traced his bloodied fingers over the fine line where the two portals met but they fitted so perfectly that it would have been impossible to insert a fingernail let alone a finger. He stood back scratching his close-cropped head and even the jingle of his bells had a mournful sound.

'You opened them for us,' he told Krispin. 'Cannot you voice your chant and repeat the trick?'

'The words just came into my head when I held the Disk of Livia and I cannot remember them,' Krispin replied. 'But I shall try again.'

From within his shirt he pulled forth a chain on which hung the medallion with a spiral of runes incised on each side. Holding it in one hand he gazed at it in the light of his everlasting wand but to his dismay its runes inspired no solemn incantation as before.

'Nothing comes into my mind,' he admitted after several minutes. 'It seems I had only a spell for opening the doors. Mayhap the Princess would have known how to leave . . .'

As his words died he hunched his shoulders and then let them drop in a characteristic gesture.

'Put your mind to it,' said Alwald irritably. 'The old dame of the Peak Tower filled your mind with so much stuff you should be able to remember a simple spell.'

Krispin nodded and pressing the Disk of Livia against his forehead, he closed his eyes and strove with all his will to remember the words that he had found himself uttering outside the doors a short while ago.

All except Gambal watched him with tense expressions which reflected their fears of lingering death if the massive doors were to remain sealed. Tana had moved close to Ognam whose face was almost comical with its lugubrious expression. Danya gazed blankly at his sea-scarred hands with which he had almost brought about the end of the Witchfinder.

'It is no use,' Krispin announced finally. He had become red-faced with the effort of concentration, and he flushed even more with embarrassment as he sensed that his companions regarded him as the obstacle to the regaining of their liberty.

'Why did the Lady Eloira have to choose a simpleton for the wayfinder,' Alwald muttered under his breath; yet it was loud enough for Krispin to hear. An earthy retort formed behind Krispin's lips but he clenched them tight. Now was not the time to quarrel among themselves but he would make Lord Alwald eat his words some day. Some day! Trapped here they could only survive a few days at the most. Some day would never come for them.

'Let us return to the Princess,' said Ognam. 'We may as well look upon the wonder we have come so far to find.'

Without a word, Krispin began to walk along the passage with his wand held high, his eyes seeking some hidden entrance that they might have missed. Surely whoever created her cavernous resting place must have thought of an escape route in case some natural calamity blocked the doors.

'Is there some other way of waking Livia?' Tana asked.

'According to The Mage she will respond only to being laved in the Water of Life,' replied Alwald moodily.

On their return to the chamber they sank down to the hard floor and gazed at the still form of the

Princess as though at any moment she might awake of her own accord and lead them to freedom.

'I wonder if she dreams,' said Tana.

'Mayhap,' said Ognam, 'and mayhap we are only figments of that dream.'

TWO

Mistress
Urwen

Snow flurried down the ravine into the frozen faces
of man and drong alike. The nervous animals skittered
and the men cursed them and the cold that was bone
deep despite the padded garments they wore beneath
their chain mail. On either side, rock walls reared so
high only a ribbon of sky was visible, its louring purple
warning that night would soon descend upon the
Mountains of the Moon.

Leading the shivering column the standard-bearer,
a member of the élite Companions of the Rose,
struggled to keep the plain yellow banner of Ythan
from being snatched away by the wind which shrilled
imprecations at those challenging the solitude of the
ranges. Close to the banner, Captain Bors turned in
his high saddle to survey the straggling procession for
which he was responsible. Behind him rode a dozen
Companions of the Rose, their scarlet surcoats
embroidered with a distinctive black rose emblem,
escorting a drong-litter behind whose leather curtains
lay their master, the Regent of Ythan himself. A
detachment of foot soldiers stumbled after it, followed

by a number of drongs laden with the expedition's baggage. Bors shouted to the men to close ranks but if his words were not lost in the wind they were ignored.

He turned and peered grimly up the steep path. The ravine offered no refuge and he knew that before nightfall he must reach the plateau to which it led. He goaded his grumbling mount in the hope of increasing the pace by example.

'Captain Bors.'

He turned again to see a figure shrouded in a heavy cloak of dark green felt overtaking the Companions on a snow-dappled horse. Only a pale face with locks of rich red hair falling across the forehead beneath a fur hood proclaimed the sex of the rider.

'Mistress Urwen?' Bors responded.

Aware of her increasing importance he respectfully raised a hand which usually wore an iron gauntlet. Now it was protected against the bite of frost by one of the warm peasant gloves requisitioned at the final outpost of the hillfolk, a dreary cluster of habitations three days' march behind them.

Drawing alongside him, the young woman raised her voice above the voice of the wind, 'The Lord Regent is in great pain, and his anger grows apace. Cannot we make camp so he can rest in his pavilion?'

'This is no place to spend the night,' he answered. 'Soon we should reach the plateau, if there be any truth in the scholars' map.'

'They will regret their birthings if they are in error,' Urwen said grimly. 'We should have reached the Wells by now.'

'In high summer we could not have expected the storm that delayed us, mistress. And it is clear that

24

drongs are not ideal beasts for such mountainous work. Had the Lord Regent not been so secretive as to our ultimate destination when setting out from Danaak I would have brought mules.'

Sharply Urwen said, 'You do not argue the need for secrecy . . .'

Ah, Mistress Spy, if there be any truth in the rumour that our master will change from Regent to King it seems you already practise the haughtiness of a queen, thought Bors. Aloud he said, 'When one has served the Regent as long as I, life without secrecy cannot be imagined. And I do understand its present need, for if word of our master's true plight were to reach the ears of his enemies . . .'

His suggestive shrug rounded off the sentence.

'The Lore Mistress was in no doubt that when we reach the source of the healing water the Lord Regent's distemper will be cured completely,' said Urwen. 'Then his enemies had best beware. A new era is coming to Ythan.'

'As you say,' said Bors. 'In the meanwhile tell him that as soon as we find a place where it is safe to camp we will set up the tents.'

Urwen nodded and turned her horse. Bors watched her ride down the column to the litter.

'If you believe that old legend about the Wells of Ythan you may as well believe that the Princess Livia still sleeps after a century,' he muttered. 'But if the Regent thinks his cure lies in these mountains who am I to gainsay him. *Fealty Unto Death* is our motto — even if it means death by freezing.'

He looked anxiously at the sky, now considerably darker. 'I am going ahead,' he shouted to the standard-bearer. 'Keep the pace up.'

25

Soon he was out of sight of the column as the path twisted one way and then another. Rounding a corner of rock he was met by such a swirl of snow that for some moments he was blinded. He shielded his eyes with his hands and saw that the trail inclined even more steeply while the ravine walls diminished in height.

'Serene Mother be praised!' he cried.

Reaching the end of the ravine he emerged as though from a stairway. Before him lay a barren plain over which the wind drove drifting snow like writhing white serpents. Freed from the enclosing walls of the ravine, Bors saw rays from the departing sun shine through cloud rifts to illumine snow-draped peaks which rose in breath-taking majesty on the far side of the plateau.

An hour later the Regent reclined on a couch within the wind-plucked walls of his pavilion while outside in thickening dusk his men struggled to raise their tents and shelter the drongs. With her own soft hands Urwen prepared the evening meal over a charcoal brazier. 'Are you easier yet, my lord?' she asked. 'Has the potion worked?'

'There is less and less virtue in Mandraga's vile nostrum,' he grumbled. 'Pour me some Ronimar wine.'

Since Urwen had come to the Regent's attention he had changed almost beyond recognition. Then his bulky frame exuded power and his face, ruddy with good living, suggested geniality – until one dared look into his bleak eyes. Today the only aspect that remained of his former appearance was his glossy black hair cut straight across his sweat-dewed forehead. The once ruddy skin now had the hue and texture of parchment; his body was wasted and after Urwen poured black wine into a crystal goblet she watched with dismay the trembling of his arm as he raised it to his lips. His other arm was swathed in bandages, mercifully hiding the now hideous hand poisoned by the bite of a homunculus.

Urwen had learned through humiliating experience not to wipe the wine that had spilled on to his samite over-robe. As the virulence of his mysterious ailment increased so did the outbursts of petulance which had been utterly foreign to his cold nature a few weeks earlier.

Looking at the wreck on the couch Urwen had to remind herself of the Regent she had given her heart to — his aura of personal strength, his ruthlessness and convoluted cunning and — yes! — his cruelty. Above all she had admired his understanding of power which enabled him to rule the vast kingdom of Ythan. She remembered the way he turned Lord Odo's plot — in which her role as a spy had brought her to his notice — to his own advantage. And she recalled the orgiastic sensation she had felt when he had taken her to see his collection of automata and, for her benefit, had the mechanical executioner behead a priceless replica of the Lady Merlinda who, in her youth, had been one of his favourite mistresses.

For the hundredth time Urwen wondered if he would find a cure at the end of this secret journey or whether the legendary Wells he sought were in fact no more than a legend.

The Companion of the Rose who stood guard in the pavilion's canvas antechamber called through the heavy curtain, 'My Lord, Captain Bors awaits.'

The Regent heaved himself into an upright position and arranged a fur rug to cover his monstrously swollen arm. Unable to restrain herself, Urwen wiped

27

a dribble of wine from his chin. For a moment she thought he was angered but this time his lips twitched into the parody of a smile.

'Doubt not that you will be rewarded if I become a man again,' he murmured.

'I need no reward,' she answered.

'Enter Bors,' the Regent commanded.

The captain pushed his way past the drapes and stood in the soft light of oil lamps with a dusting of snow on his cape.

'The men have set up camp and the sentinels are at their posts,' he reported.

The Regent nodded.

'Sit down and get some heat into you.'

Bors seated himself close to a brazier and gratefully spread his hands over the charcoal.

'Tell me our position — how close are we to our destination?' the Regent said.

'If the directions prepared by scholars Quillion and Papen are correct — and I must say they have been so far — we are very close,' Bors replied. 'We must cross the plateau in line with three peaks that are taller than the rest. This will bring us to a pass and beyond that — the Wells.'

'How long will it take?'

'I saw the peaks before darkness fell and I should say we can cross the plateau in two or three hours provided there is no snowstorm — and the scryer predicts a clear day tomorrow. How long it will take after entering the pass I cannot say.'

'No matter. We will leave early with two of your most trusted Companions. The rest will remain camped here, the fewer who learn of the Wells the better.'

Bors nodded.

'My lord, there are wild stories among the troops as to the reason for this journey. I have seen to it the favourite is that you are making a pilgrimage to an ancient shrine dedicated to the Mother.'

'We will return to Danaak with the Companions only,' said the Regent. 'Have the soldiers dispatched to frontier regiments where their loose tongues are more likely to be mocked than believed. As for the scholars who found the secret of the Wells in Thaan's Great Library make sure that they will not be in a position to boast of their knowledge.'

'I understand. But what will be the explanation if − when − you return to camp with your old vigour?'

'What would you say, Urwen?'

'That the Mother answered your supplication,' she answered. 'Indeed if news spread that the Regent had been granted a miracle it would perhaps enhance your plans.'

'Good. In that case it might be best to let the troops babble in Danaak after all. If the scryer speaks true we shall set out at dawn. Now I needs must rest.'

'As you command, my lord,' said the captain, reluctantly removing his hands from the brazier.

When he had departed into the night the Regent slumped back on the couch.

'Tomorrow I may be whole again,' he mused. 'Yet this hard journey would not have been necessary had the alchemist not played me false by giving my elixir to the abomination he had created. Serene Mother! He looked upon that monster as his daughter.'

'Sealed in his tower Leodore has paid for his folly,' said Urwen.

'Someday I shall have the bricks breached to see how they both ended,' the Regent said. 'Yet it was pity that

Leodore forgot where his loyalty lay — forgot that it was I who saved him from the Witchfinders' cauldron — for he had his uses. One of his alchemies will give me more military power than any past ruler of Ythan.'

His voice faded with exhaustion.

'Save your strength for tomorrow,' said Urwen. 'I pray that this is the last time I shall need to do this to ease you.'

She produced a jar of unguent and then unwound the Regent's bandage until his ghastly arm and hand were exposed — livid, shapeless and with nails of horn, it proclaimed that the Regent was taking on the form of a homunculus.

THREE

Dawn
Flight

'And are you still determined to seek the Wells of Ythan?' asked the Hermit. 'The Wells that have been lost since The Enchantment?'

Despite his monastic cowl of raw wool and his fringe of iron-toned hair, his face appeared youthful in the honeyed light cast by a thick candle he had moulded from the wax of wild bees. Outside his grey tower, a weathered relic from an age time curtained from the memory of man, black night pressed on the Arkad Woodlands. A thousand thousand trees, each in gentle contact with its neighbours by root and leaf, sighed with corporate life and the acute ears of the Hermit sensed the forest's pain and dismay.

Opposite him sat the stranger to whom he had given the hospitality of his rough home. His high-cheeked features appeared to be ravaged by anxiety and grief despite the softening effect of the bees' flame.

'You say that only water from the Wells can save Silvermane, so I shall begin my search at dawn — if my wing will bear me,' the guest answered.

'Let me see if it needs more salve,' said the Hermit.

'It is a cure taught me by the horsefolk and its ingredients include Moon Bloom petals to dull pain and aloe which helps flesh restore itself — that is normal flesh of course. With your wing . . .'

He paused while a large pinion began to unfold through a slit in the stranger's jerkin. Normally it lay so neatly down his back that it would not attract notice unless he had removed his loose-fitting garments.

In the mellow light the Hermit watched with frank curiosity as the stranger moved his body to allow the wing to uncurl so that the upper edge, injured that day by a venomed arrow, was positioned on the table.

'Apart from bats, I have never seen a wing without feathers,' the Hermit said, 'but then I have never seen a winged man before.'

He peered at the place where he had removed the tip of the wing with a red-hot knife after the stranger had landed on the flat roof of the tower with a burden as unusual as himself.

'Are there others such as you?' the Hermit asked as he took a wooden stopper from a jar of dark, earth-scented ointment and began to massage it into the seared area with deft fingers.

'I know not,' replied the stranger. 'As a babeling I was found beneath a thorn tree by a caravan captain in the Wilderness of Gil. Then I had no wings and I grew up with a back so crouched that I was named the Hump. Always I believed I was a deformed human until a short while ago when the wings burst from my hunched back and with them came the inborn knowledge of how to fly.

'Of my forebears I know nothing. What I really am I cannot guess nor do I care. When I was a poor scorned thing I envied the birds who could soar away

32

from the world of harsh men. And now I have soared. For that I shall be ever grateful to the Mother, and for the fact that my new wings saved Silvermane and me from a thirsty death in the Desert of Akea. My prayer is that with these wings I shall save her again.'

He turned his head to gaze into the shadows where Silvermane, the girl with equine lower limbs, lay in restless slumber beneath a loosely woven rug on the Hermit's pallet.

'I well understand your desire to save the horsemaid whom it is obvious you love,' said the Hermit. 'But how do you think that you will find her cure? At my seminary, where I studied healing as well as Shrine ceremonial, we novices learned that there had once been Wells from which flowed the Water of Life. It was said that the kings of Ythan were anointed with it at their crownings but, with The Enchantment, they dried and their secret was forgotten.'

'That they are forgotten seems true enough,' agreed the Hump with a sigh. 'But my hope is they may still hold water somewhere beyond the ken of men. What else can I do but seek them? One gift I have always had and that is the ability to find my path in unmapped lands which is why I was sought as a caravan pilot. It was known along the trade routes that I could lead a caravan safely across a waste that none had crossed before. Somehow I just knew the way and now I pray the Mother that this gift will lead me to the Wells.'

He stopped and looked reflective as his inner eye was filled with a cumulation of wild landscapes he had traversed on the swaying back of a drong. His escape from reality was brief. Blinking open his weary eyes, he muttered, 'Master Hermit, you told me it is but a matter of time before the toxin in Silvermane will induce a death-like sleep and then death itself . . .'

'It would have been wrong to tell you other than the truth,' the Hermit answered. 'One of the horsefolk was brought to me last leaf-fall after he had been wounded by a poisoned arrow fired by a slave guard, and such was his fate. You I could save by simply cutting away the affected part but with Silvermane the arrowhead went deep and already the poison works in her body.'

'How long . . .' began the Hump and then could not utter the rest of the sentence.

'I cannot say,' replied the Hermit with pity in his voice. 'I lost my faith and fled the seminary before I was fully skilled in leechcraft but even if I learned all that could have been taught me I would still not be able to pronounce on a horsemaid. The one who was brought to me was conscious from one full moon to another, then lay in deepening slumber until the next, and then . . '

'At the most, I have two months,' muttered the Hump. 'Two months!'

For a moment he held his trail-tanned hand across his eyes, then raised them to the Hermit.

'And you swear that there is no other cure?'

'None that is known to me. The arrow poison distilled in Danaak has no antidote you may be sure — other than the Water of Life which ancient herbals stated was the panacea.'

For a while neither spoke. On the pallet Silvermane moved restlessly in her sleep. The Hump leaned over her and wiped her moist face with a piece of clean cloth soaked in an essence of forest flowers collected by the Hermit.

'Tell me, why does the Regent send slaves into the

Arkad Woodlands to axe the trees for charcoal?' the Hump asked as he returned to the table and the cup of wine that stood on it. 'Before the guards opened fire on us I saw vast gashes in the forest. Surely Danaak does not need so much charcoal.'

'Nor it does,' said the Hermit in gloomy tones. 'It is a mystery to me what use the tyrant could find for it, yet every week long trains of drongs loaded with the stuff leave for the capital. What I do know is that the Regent is bringing death to the woodlands and those that dwell in them, not only by the felling but by vast fires ignited by furnace embers borne on the wind. I have not the wit to fathom the language of the trees but I detect the mood of the forest in the soughing of its leaves, and the mood grows more and more fearful. The horsefolk are moving away from their traditional glades to the dim forests of the north.'

'I have known the dungeons of Danaak,' mused the Hump, 'and if their master has no mercy on men you cannot expect him to spare trees.'

'True,' said the Hermit. 'And it works the other way — you cannot expect compassion from those who glory in the deaths of wild things.' He gave an ironical smile. 'As a young man I valued compassion as the highest of the virtues. It seemed to me to be the answer to the malady of the world, and with that belief it was natural for me to become a shrine novitiate. Ah, there was none as dedicated as I, none more zealous in performing his offices — until the time came for me to assist the priest in his ritual when heretics were taken to the cauldron by the Witchfinders . . . Oh, the mob that watched! Even though they feared and hated the Witchfinders they jeered the victims in their throes because their doctrine differed from theirs. In that

35

moment the scales fell from my eyes. Only here have I found the tranquillity I needed for contemplation, but now the shadow I tried to escape is reaching to this far forest.'

He sighed.

'Forgive me,' he said. 'I prattle when your mind is full of fear for the horsemaid.'

'Silvermane and I believed that we could find peace here,' mused the Hump. 'I understand more and more what it is that makes men take the Pilgrim's Path.'

'Dreamers!' declared the Hermit. 'Well intentioned mayhap, brave certainly to risk the attentions of the Witchfinders, but dreamers!'

The Hump thought of the companions with whom he had travelled from Danaak to the Domain of Olam. They were followers of the Path and none struck him as dreamers but he said nothing. His host was the last man he would mistrust but like so many in Ythan who had learned that safety lay in silence he instinctively checked his words.

'Suppose the Princess Livia still sleeps in some hidden place as the folktales tell,' continued the Hermit. 'And suppose she is awakened — what then? How could she claim the Empty Throne when the Regent is all powerful. She would need a great army . . .'

'The people,' suggested the Hump. 'The people would want her on the throne — would want the return of the Golden Age that the land enjoyed under the royal house.'

The Hermit laughed bitterly.

'The people of Ythan lost their will long ago, and even if they had enough spirit left to defy the Regent the Witchfinders would make sure that no word of her revival reached them. But forgive me, my friend, I rarely have the opportunity to speak with one of my own kind and now I selfishly talk when you should be resting.'

In the candle light the Hump's eyelids drooped. His host spread rugs for him on the rush-layered floor and within a minute he was asleep. The Hermit shook his head at some inner thought, refilled his wine cup and went on to the roof of the tower to listen to the breathing of the night forest.

Some hours later the eastern darkness lessened with the false dawn and the Hump arose.

'It is time for me to go,' he said.

'Take this,' said the Hermit giving him a scrip of coarse hide. 'Traveller's bread and a sealed jug of wine. Keep it. If whatever gods there be favour you it can be used to bring back the water you seek.'

The Hump nodded his thanks. For a moment he stood over the slumbering form of Silvermane.

'She sleeps peacefully. There is no need to wake her. You will tell her why I have gone.'

'Of course. She will be safe here in the tower, of that you can be sure. I shall get word to her people and they can bring her their food and she will be cheered by speech in her own tongue.'

On the flat roof the Hump's wings unfurled, flexed and moved delicately to balance him in the dawn breeze that swept over the tree tops.

'Do you know in which direction you will go?' asked the Hermit.

'Of that I have no idea as yet. I can only rise and hope that if I keep the Wells of Ythan firm in my mind some instinct will guide me.'

In the semi-darkness the Hermit was aware of the

Hump's pinions rising high above his head and then sweeping down. His feet rose a little above the tiles; for a moment he hovered and bade the Hermit farewell then ascended, a fleeting shadow soon lost in a greater shadow.

As he rose his weariness and despair seemed to fall from him to remain earth-bound while his wings bore him upwards to the dark sky. This elation filled him every time he felt the upward pull of his wings proving he was still capable of this new-found miracle. Replacing the sensation of impotence he had suffered since bringing his wounded lover to the Hermit was the sensation of relief in taking positive action. He would find the cure for Silvermane or perish in the attempt.

As his wings beat regularly with a distinctive sighing sound he looked towards the horizon and saw that it was marked by a line of brilliant orange above which violet merged into indigo and indigo merged into black. And as he flew higher the darker shades faded to blue in which clouds streamed like rose-hued pennants. Directly below, the Arkad Woodlands still lay in night's shroud and the Hump realized he was soaring into the sunrise.

Soon the full glory burst upon him and he shone brightly in the high air.

For a moment he paused, his pinions constantly adjusting to ride the chill dawn wind. His mind was filled with the thought of the fabled Wells but no hint of direction came to him and all that his instinct told him was to go higher. Below, the night shadow retreated as the sun appeared over the world's rim and sent her light like a golden wave over the dark green sea of trees. It caught the pillars of smoke above the clearings to the south where armies of slaves were already hewing the forest and stoking charcoal furnaces.

The Hump continued to soar higher into the cold air than he had dared to venture before, rising with the sun until at last he was exhausted and hung on his wings like an eagle resting on air currents.

And then he saw them drifting towards him; huge semi-transparent globes from which hung long thread-like appendages whose writhing movements suggested uncanny life. Light striking their curved sides shot them with iridescence which made the Hump think of bubbles but while bubbles are innocent, the joy of children, these gave him a sense of menace. Perhaps it was because he thought he could make out vague, unearthly features — the lineaments of nightmare — marked on them as though they were vast floating heads. He remembered inflated bladders on which grotesque faces had been limned at village fairs.

There were six of them moving *against the wind* in a wavering line towards him. As they approached with unexpected speed their vast size became apparent, each as wide and high as the golden dome of Danaak's Great Shrine yet seemingly as light as thistledown. Their hanging tentacles coiled and uncoiled and swung lazily in his direction. And then his ears caught a soft sound like the cooing of distant doves and he realized they had a form of speech.

The astonishing sight of these rainbow-stained entities looming upon him seemed to hold the winged man as a rabbit is held by a serpent's gaze. It was only a soft touch on his neck that vitalized him. Jerking his head, he saw that others had approached him from the opposite direction. One, a huge opaline canopy, was directly above him and its long, suckered filaments caressed his skin as they sought to entangle him. The cooing became a crescendo of sweet and evil sound.

The Hump furled his wings and plummeted, tumbling over and over. He had glimpses of the globes becoming smaller and more transparent against the fresh sky with each rotation.

He opened his wings to check his fall and cursed in pain as it felt they were being torn from his shoulders. His descent slowed and then he was able to control his flight once more. Turning his face from the sun he glided south.

FOUR

The Clock
Strikes

The clock that chimed once a year prepared to strike.

Its case was worm-eaten, the dust of ages blurred its grotesque carving but inside, escapement and spring, cogs and spindles were as bright as when they had been assembled a century ago thanks to arcane spells that had been cast when molten copper and tin fused into the brass from which they had been crafted.

Its steady tock-tock, the only sound in the unlighted chamber, hesitated as gears began to mesh for a brief mechanical ritual: Time itself seemed to slow as with whirrings and clickings the clock commenced its annual celebration – for who dare claim that clocks, which mark the transmutation of future into past, are nothing more than enginery.

In a series of minute jerks a hammer raised, poised for a second as though figuratively drawing strength, then struck. A deep metallic note like a harbinger of doom echoed through the darkness and Tumbrul shuddered into wakefulness on his narrow bed.

'Not another year?' he exclaimed in a voice so

cracked and dry his throat might have been lined with rust. 'Not another year done and gone?'

In the darkness he fingered his beard which flowed down to his rounded belly.

'Heh, another year! How old am I . . . ? Cursed cobwebs,' he added as he sat upright and felt invisible filaments brushing against his skin. 'Ysldon might have done something about the twice-cursed spiders. It would have only taken a quick spell to get rid of them. They do not think, these magicians. Not practical. And he could easily have left me an eternal light but no! No! Here I am in the dark, covered with webs, and I cannot find my flint.

' "A great honour," he told me. "A great honour for your kind, Tumbrul. You will have your place in history as well as all the silver you can carry." Fine words heh, but he might have thought about the spiders.'

His long fingers — made longer by the talon-like nails sprouting from them — encountered the box containing his flint and steel beside the pallet. Sparks flashed, giving a series of brief glimpses of a small chamber with a vaulted ceiling and single doorway which held no other furnishings than Tumbrul's bed, the clock on the wall and a carved chest. After muttering some more, Tumbrul huffed on his tinder, a bead of yellow fire appeared and then lengthened above a thick candle.

The unwavering flame illumined the small subterranean chamber and its muttering occupant. He was a grotesque figure in his ragged jerkin and breeches of green velvet, about the height of a ten-year-old human child — a disgracefully corpulent human child. The area of his face not obscured by his grey-streaked

42

beard was a maze of wrinkles, his forehead bulged so that his head seemed too heavy for his body and the hairs on the pallid dome of his head could have been counted in a matter of moments. His nose was sharp and so remarkably long that when silhouetted side-on to the candle it looked like the beak of a wading bird. Despite his strange appearance he possessed one feature which would have prevented all but the most bold mocking it; his eyes glowed like a pair of emeralds when they reflected the light.

He ran his hand over his pate.

'Heh, every time I wake I am balder,' he complained in his rasping voice. '*He* could easily have done something about that. Not much to ask, to keep my hair, heh? Not much. Not much when one thinks of what he *has* done with his wizardry. But no good complaining, heh. Someday I shall have a palace and a room full of wigs. Mayhap in another hundred years.'

He sighed and lifted the lid of the chest from which he extracted a piece of headgear like a tasselled nightcap which he pulled on to his head as though to hide his gleaming scalp. 'And my nose. *He* might have done something about my nose. Could have easily made it longer. A touch of his wand, that's all it needed. But no. Oh well, to work, to work. At least I can have a look at what will be mine when I have done my task.'

From the chest he produced a pair of fine shears and then, holding the candle high in its tarnished holder, he left the chamber.

The resting place of the entranced Princess was lit by Krispin's wand, the cold light flowing from it shone

43

on Princess Livia lying on her couch and the lethargic forms of those who had attempted to rescue her from her ancient thrall. Edom the Witchfinder leaned against the wall with his ankles and wrists bound with strips of cloth. Though the Pilgrims were just as much prisoners as he, Alwald insisted on the binding for fear he might seize an opportunity to harm the Princess out of fanatical loyalty to the Regent.

Danya, Krispin and Alwald rested with their eyes closed after a great weariness descended upon them; Gambal lay back with unseeing eyes and pondered on the revenge he had wrought upon the Lore Mistress. When he realized that he was not going to be attacked by his erstwhile friends he regretted that the old camaraderie he had shared with them was a thing of the past. As the heavy hours passed this sense of loss was replaced by the thought that it mattered little because once the meagre provisions they had brought in their packs were consumed it would be but a short time before they felt the touch of the Dark Maid.

Ognam sat in the shadowed corner of the chamber, his short jester's staff which denoted his membership of the Guild of Jongleurs lay on his lap. Its carved head gazed up at him with a sly grin reminding him of the long-gone days when he had earned renown as a comic performer. He had seated himself in the corner to be alone with his thoughts but Tana had soon joined him.

'You do not mind?' she whispered.

When kindly Ognam shook his head she smiled, rested her head against his shoulder and closed her eyes in sleep. The irony of the situation struck the jongleur.

If the All Father fashioned men and women from his breath in the Beginning of All Things, as is preached in the shrines, he was a joker, Ognam thought to himself. *No sublime being would have used the world merely as a stage on which to play tricks upon his puppets unless inspired by perverse humour.*

He ruefully reviewed the recent events in his own life which mirrored this view, how he had met and fallen madly in love with Tana the mysterious prisoner he found in the grotto beneath the Mage's Tower. It had seemed to him, poor besotted fool, that she shared his feelings – until he smuggled her aboard the *Amber Star*. Once free it became obvious that she was no longer interested in him, especially as there was a possibility of her returning to her father's great demesne on Lake Taloon.

The realization of the impossibility of a young woman with such a background having romantic feelings for a strolling player had curdled his heart to the point where oblivion seemed preferable to the pain. It was in seeking to escape the world that he had a sudden and total shift in his emotions. He saw everything with a clarity that released him from the bondage of unrequited love. That was when the irony began. Tana remembered Ognam's courage in risking the Mage's wrath to free her and recognized qualities in him that she had overlooked before, this recognition being heightened by the fact he no longer gazed upon her with lovelorn eyes. He was polite but without interest in her, and she suffered.

Time passed in the chamber but it was no longer measured in hours or by dawn and dusk; here there was only heartbeat and hunger to mark its passage.

Once Danya started out of his green-sea reverie to exclaim, 'I heard a chime. I swear I heard a distant chime.'

'You were dreaming, shipmaster,' said Alwald. 'I heard nothing to break the accursed silence.'

'You must be right,' Danya agreed. 'It is true I was thinking of our night in Haven and mayhap it was an echo in my mind from that witched place.' He said no more but his words had brought Tana back to wakefulness.

'Ognam, what is it?' she asked.

'Nothing. Go back to sleep if you can.'

'We shall sleep long enough soon enough. Ah, how I wish we were back in my enchanted prison. Even though there were silver bars between us there was so much to look forward to, freedom, love . . .'

'Love?'

'Yes, Ognam, love. Did you not realize . . .'

'What I thought I realized I now realize was the realizing of something that could never be realized.' He dropped into his style of comic delivery, the fool apeing a scribe's use of words, the mountebank giving himself airs before the joke would rebound on him.

'Ognam, I grieve for the hurt I caused you on the *Amber Star*,' she whispered. 'I was a fool but freedom intoxicated me. I wanted to be a merry girl again.'

'And why not?' said Ognam. He looked at her perfect features and long glossy black hair which had once haunted his dreams and was saddened that her words meant nothing to him, words that a few days earlier would have been balm to his aching heart.

'But when you saved us in the Upas grove and kept up our spirits amid the phantasms my true feelings returned and I knew a great heart beat beneath your motley. And I hoped that if the quest was concluded here I could persuade you to escort me to Taloon and my father's mansion, though I know not whether it still stands after my captivity. If I found it in ruins it would have been no great matter if you were with me. Now I shall never see the lake again but you must know that I am not fearful because I can boldly face the Dark Maid beside you.'

In the shadow her slender hand sought his.

'Lady, you do me too much honour,' said Ognam formally. 'I am not what you imagine, no more than a vagabond player and if you do not see that now you certainly would have at your father's palace. Think of me as no more than a jongleur.'

As he spoke he saw that a ray from the light wand sparkled in a tear on her cheek. The sight of this spark suddenly filled him with pity, for he had known tears in his darkest hours, and his fingers closed on her hand.

'Dear Ognam,' Tana began but she stopped as a low grinding filled the chamber, alarming the company not because of its rasping timbre but because of its unexpectedness in this subterranean prison. They looked about them fearing that this sound heralded an earth tremor but this fear was replaced by another as an oblong section of the marble wall swung inwards like a door and in the space it had occupied stood an extraordinary creature, a pot-bellied, heavily bearded little man with a melon head and a nose grotesquely long and pointed.

Tumbrul stared back at them in equal shock.

'Serene Mother, a troll,' breathed Alwald.

'Troll! Troll?' shrilled Tumbrul. 'A black murrain on the scaly clod who dares call me that! I, Tumbrul, am proud to be . . .'

47

And then he realized that he had forgotten what he was.

'Not a troll anyway,' he concluded. As his indignation ebbed, excitement at the sight of the strangers made the dark blood pound in his veins.

'Return your sword,' he cried to Krispin who had Woundflame half unsheathed. 'If you be true questers you have nothing to fear from me. If you be false you have everything to fear from my blasting rod.' But even as he uttered these words he remembered that his hands were empty, that his blasting rod was propped against the wall beside his pallet – or was it with the besom in the closet?

'We – that is myself and Master Krispin here – have followed the Pilgrim Path across the kingdom from the High Wald to find Princess Livia,' Alwald replied. 'We are true questers.'

'That I can believe for how else would you be in her chamber,' said Tumbrul thankfully. 'At last my stewardship is at an end.'

He straightened and proclaimed in sonorous tones the statement he had rehearsed exactly ninety-nine times: 'In the illustrious name of Ysldon and the Royal Magi, I Tumbrul, son of Gorlag the Crafty, bid you welcome to the sanctuary of Her Highness Princess Livia, daughter of King Johan XXXIII and rightful inheritor of the Kingdom of Ythan. Know that I, Tumbrul, have been true to my avowed task of guardianship and now lay claim to my rightful reward when she is restored to Time Present. Let he who sought her stand forth.'

Despite his odd, even comical, appearance the speaker attained a brief dignity and Alwald rose to his

48

feet and approached the high threshold on which Tumbrul stood.

'Recite your name and lineage.'

Alwald complied with a certain satisfaction for such formality took him back to the ceremonial of River Garde.

'Now present the token.' Tumbrul intoned ritually.

'Token?' said Alwald. 'What token?'

'What token?' Tumbrul's voice became shrill again. 'How could you have evoked the gramayre guarding the cavern without the token, heh? Unless you be impostors . . .'

At the thought he drew back into the doorway.

'If we are impostors we are unintentional ones,' said Ognam. 'Some of us — myself being an example — did not actually set out in search of the lady who lies on the vaporous mattress but joined the quest at different times. Nevertheless we believed ourselves to be questers when Master Krispin gained access to this place with his disk . . .'

'Disk? What disk, heh?'

Krispin reached inside his tunic and brought out the coin-like Disk of Livia with its spirals of runic symbols. Tumbrul scurried forward, examined the disk eagerly and ignoring Alwald — to his ill-concealed umbrage — said to Krispin, 'Simpleton, you bear the token. Why did you not speak?'

'I . . .'

'Did not the runes on the disk inspire the incantation necessary to enter?'

'Yes, but when we tried to leave nothing happened.'

'I suppose it did not occur to you to hold the disk the other way round? One side is for coming in, the other for going out.'

At his words a murmur of relief rose from the others. 'My work is over,' he said. 'I have been custodian here since The Enchantment.'

'Then you must be over a hundred years old,' exclaimed Danya.

'Of course, but I have slept through every year except for the one day when I cut the Princess's hair . . .' He waved his shears. '. . . and dust the chamber.' He waved his brush. Then he looked at the length of Livia's hair. 'Always it is twice that length. Passing strange. The clock must have struck on account of your arrival. But I do not want to waste time now that it is restored to me. Proceed with the Awakening.Where is the water from the Wells of Ythan?'

'It is lost,' said Alwald sombrely.

'Lost! You say *lost*?' Tumbrul danced up and down in his rage. 'What sort of questers are you, heh? You cannot use the disk properly. You have no Water of Life to anoint the Princess. Buffoons! I have been awakened to meet buffoons.'

'I am the only one who deserves the honour of being called a buffoon,' said Ognam unexpectedly. 'And I caution you to listen respectfully to what we have to say after the perils we have endured or I shall crack my staff of office over your ugly pate.'

The effect on Tumbrul was remarkable. He nodded and sat peacefully on the step while Alwald gave a brief account of their adventures and how the flacon of precious water came to be spilled.

When he concluded Tumbrul said, 'A remarkable tale and one of much ill luck but all is not lost. The Wells are not impossible to reach.'

'You know where they lie?' demanded Alwald.

'I was told when I came here. And I know the Mountains of the Moon.'

'You will lead us there so we can bring some water back?' asked Krispin.

'To go and come back doubles the danger,' Tumbrul replied. 'Far better to take Her Highness to the Wells.'

FIVE

The Valley
of Yth

At dawn the small party set off across the plateau towards the three distant mountains beneath a cloudless sky testifying to the scryer's skill in weather prediction — the only form of divination permitted by the Guild of Witchfinders. Captain Bors was followed by two Companions of the Rose leading the drongs who bore the Regent's litter beside which rode the Lady Urwen. Inside, the Regent had the curtain of the litter drawn so he could gaze past the graceful neck of the leading drong at the trio of peaks marking his destination, the sight of which appeared to give him the strength to cope with the pain flowing from his infected limb.

In contrast to yesterday's progress they travelled easily across the flat terrain whose only flora was clumps of sere rushes and by noon they were approaching a gash-like pass in the mountain wall.

'So far the landmarks are correct,' Bors reported to his master. 'I doubt not that we will find journey's end beyond the pass.'

The Regent nodded as though the effort of speech

was too much for him and Urwen looked anxiously from his wasted face to that of the captain.

'Should we rest awhile to ease my lord?' she asked.

'Press on,' the Regent gasped. 'Do you not have the wit to see it is a race between me and the Dark Maid to the Wells.'

'I hear you, my lord,' Bors said ritually and signalled to the Companions to recommence the journey. Soon they were engulfed by the shadow which filled the pass and it seemed to each that it was not only the sudden cold after riding in the sunlight which caused a spinal shiver. From afar came a low groaning sound which was magnified by the rock walls.

'It is no evil spirit,' called Bors. 'It is a sound I have heard before in the Crystal Ranges, the grinding of an ice river that creeps down a mountainside so slowly that it mayhap takes a year to travel a league.'

'Why is the sky yonder so dark?' Urwen asked him.

'I have heard that dusk never lifts from the wild land beyond the mountains,' he replied. 'It is known as the Shadow Realm, a place where no sane traveller would enter, supposing he could cross the peaks.'

As they continued Urwen was reminded of the ravine they had climbed the previous day. This pass also sloped upward so that although the gap where it ended was visible they could not see beyond it. And when they did reach that gap the riders sat on their mounts too awed for speech.

Below them lay a valley walled by dizzy cliffs soaring to merge with the snow-mantled peaks. Apart from the grandeur of these precipices, across whose faces cruised black eagles, the valley itself was a marvel. Instead of being floored with rock and ice as would have been expected here, it was carpeted with green, the green of lush grass and the many-toned foliage of woods. And, though it was far below them, all caught the scent of flowers on the sharp air. And, though the sky above the western peaks reflected the gloom of the Shadow Realm beyond them, the valley itself was filled with bright light that held a warmth alien to such heights.

'It is like the Garden of Yth,' muttered one of the Companions, referring to an ancient legend that before the days of men there were bright beings who dwelled in a valley garden where flowers bloomed all year round and there was no sorrow.

'Mayhap it is the Garden of Yth,' the other Companion said.

'Do you not comprehend?' whispered the Regent who had forced himself into a sitting position in the litter. 'It can only be the Wells! The water from them makes their surroundings fertile. Hurry me to them.'

Bors and Urwen stood on the dizzy edge of the cliff, their eyes seeking a path to lead them to the verdant enclave below.

'There is no way down,' Urwen exclaimed in a voice of dismay. 'To have come so far . . .'

'Look,' said Bors. 'There does seem to be a track.'

She followed the direction of his gloved hand.

'It is no more than a fissure in the rockface. No drong could go down it, and the Lord Regent can hardly walk . . .'

'The Lord Regent will decide what he can and cannot do,' came an unnaturally high voice behind them. To their amazement their master had found the strength to leave the litter and follow them to the brink. Now he stood swaying so violently that Urwen seized his sound arm for fear that he would topple into space.

'Let us start,' he said. 'Rope me between the Companions in case I have a fainting spell.'

'But, my lord, I cannot see how far the track goes,' protested the captain. 'It may not reach the valley floor. Let me climb down first and see if possible.'

The Regent glanced at the shadows thrown by the peaks.

'There is no time for that,' he said. 'Am I going to lose Ythan to my enemies, to the plotters in the Citadel and the shrines, for fear of climbing down that path? By the Milk of the Mother, I shall reach the Wells or let the eagles pick my bones.' He turned to Urwen. 'As I speak I feel my body racked with change. I know that soon something monstrous is going to happen to me – so monstrous that even you will flee – unless I am cleansed.'

Shocked by the intensity of his words, Urwen looked into his ravaged face and saw that there was indeed a change in his features. The pallid lips had shrunk leaving his mouth a mere slit and – was it possible? – his nose was flattening so the nostrils were like holes in a mask while his eyes bulged from their sockets. A sob shook her, her lord and lover, with whom she had hoped to share the throne of Ythan, was being transformed into the likeness of the homunculus whose venom was his bane.

From under his cloak he produced a flask which he drained with a curse of disgust.

'I have finished all of Mandraga's vile potion,' he said. 'Mayhap it will give me the hour's strength I need.'

Behind them the two Companions finished tethering the drongs and came forward with a rope.

56

'I shall be the one linked next to you,' said Urwen. 'Then your fate will be my fate.'

'So be it,' said the Regent.

Several minutes later the roped party began to shuffle down the track which the keen eyes of Captain Bors had discovered. In places the path running diagonally down the cliff face was no more than three or four handspans in width. Only Bors in the lead looked ahead, the others pressed their hands against the rock which they gazed at with affectionate intensity. Once Urwen looked down to the valley and felt the pull of the earth, felt her head reel and her knees weaken until Bors, feeling the rope tighten with her sudden immobility, turned and grasped her wrist.

Perhaps it was due to the potion he had swallowed – enough to serve him for several days according to the instructions of the Lady Mandraga – that the Regent was managing better than they had dared hope. Sometimes he cursed when his limb, bandaged to the size of a bolster, rubbed against the rough cliff, but most of the time his only utterance was the rasp of his breath as he slid one foot after the other like his companions.

Although the path appeared to be a natural feature at first, after they had descended several hundred paces it turned into a flight of steps hewn in the living rock. The discovery brought a grunt of satisfaction from the Regent, not only because it made the descent easier but because it showed that in the past men had entered the valley.

'It must have been long ago by the way they have weathered,' said Bors. 'Before The Enchantment.'

'Let me rest a moment,' the Regent muttered.

He leaned against the rock wall, his eyes closed and

his chest heaving. The rope linking him to Urwen went slack as the young woman braved vertigo to mop the cold sweat glistening on his face.

'No man so afflicted could come down this cliff as you are doing, my lord,' she whispered. 'I admire you more in your weakness than when you had your strength.'

'I may reach the valley but I shall not be able to return as I am, nor would I want to. Soon . . .'

His words were cut short by a wild cry that resounded from the rock. Urwen turned her face and screamed. A black eagle, talons extended, beak agape, swooped towards them. One of its pinions buffeted her as it attacked with demonic fury.

Yudin, the Companion behind the Regent, slashed at the bird with his sword but before he could land a blow one of its talons clove his cheek and he collapsed at the feet of his master.

The bird whirled away from the precipice, hovered and again hurtled to the attack. The Companion who had brought up the rear covered several steps in a single leap. His sword struck the eagle across its outstretched neck as it sought to tear the Regent with daggered talons.

Black feathers swirled over the Regent and the eagle fell away with no more grace than a bundle of rags, but the Companion had no chance to savour his victory. Unable to regain his balance after the impetus of his leap, he teetered for a moment and then slid over the edge.

Snake-like the rope slithered over after him until it suddenly became taut. The Companion who was still kneeling with his hand to his gashed face gave a cry as it tightened about him and he felt the weight of his comrade dangling below. Despite his efforts to hold on to a step with bloodied fingers he was drawn towards the fatal edge.

Urwen gazed in horror. It was obvious that in a moment the second Companion would be dragged into the void, and after him the Regent. Below them the Companion made a vain attempt to get a handhold on the rock and then drew his blade across the rope. For a moment he swung wildly and then the final strand parted. With his limbs outspread like those of a starfish, and with his sword still clasped in his hand, he plummeted.

Yudin, sprawled half over the edge, rolled back to safety while Bors gazed down at the treetops far below.

'Let us get down these accursed steps,' gasped the Regent.

'Companion Bian was true to his oath,' Bors said slowly.

'Of course. If I return to Danaak his name shall be inscribed on the pillar of honour but now let us begone.'

When the four finally found themselves knee-deep in the sweet grass that carpeted the valley floor they beheld the broken body of the Companion caught in the upper branches of a hornbeam whose trunk was fluted with age.

'He is too high to reach,' muttered Yudin. He spoke with his palm held hard against his torn cheek. Bright blood oozed between his fingers. 'Yet burial is his right.'

'*The released spirit finds balm in the bosom of the Mother but those it leaves must continue the toil of the world,*' said Urwen, quoting scripture. 'There is a path leading through the trees. Help your master along it.'

The path that curved across a glade to vanish into woodland shade had been originally patterned with flat stones of different colours but time had mellowed their outlines and in place of mortar weeds sprouted between them. Yet its symmetry — like the steps hewn in the cliff — was an encouragement. Supported by Bors on one side and Companion Yudin on the other, the Regent of Ythan staggered on the final stage of his journey.

Suddenly his eyes rolled and spittle stringed his lips and he became dead weight on the supporting arms of his men.

'Should we let him rest?' Bors asked anxiously. 'He is close to swooning.'

'Rest — yes, rest,' murmured the Regent. He sank to his knees and then lay full length on the grass.

'Come, my lord, soon we shall reach journey's end,' coaxed Urwen.

Her words were ignored and Bors muttered, 'We can make a litter of branches but I fear that his life ebbs. See, he has lost control of himself and too often I have seen that on the battlefield not to know when the Dark Maid approaches.'

They stood above him in silence, helpless and ashamed of their helplessness. A sapphire-winged dragonfly hovered over the head of their fallen lord.

Yudin slowly turned from his stricken master and gazed into the wood, his interest so captivated that his hand slid from his face revealing the gash in his cheek through which his teeth gleamed.

'Listen,' he said. 'Surely it is a fountain.'

Urwen strained her ears and above the hum of her

pulse it seemed that she caught a sound suggestive of falling water.

'Rise, my lord, we are almost there,' she implored, but the Regent remained prone.

'I will make a litter,' Bors repeated, 'but I fear me it will be a task too late.'

Reaching down, Urwen grasped the Regent's swaddled arm and heaved with all her strength. His agonized bellow sent a flock of orange birds swirling out of the trees while Captain Bors instinctively clapped his hand to his sword grip.

Shocked into consciousness by pain, the Regent struggled weakly to roll over.

'I'll have you flayed,' he mouthed.

'On your feet if you would be Ythan's King,' shouted Urwen. 'The Wells are yonder.'

'The Wells . . .'

'The Wells! Have you lost the will to return to Danaak a whole man or did the homunculus poison your spirit as well as your body? Will you lie there in your filth or take the Empty Throne?'

The Regent drew a sobbing breath and nodded to Bors and Yudin. As gently as possible they lifted him to his feet and steadied him as he lurched forward.

SIX

The
Doll

Faithful Hans tugged his white moustache in his anxiety as he gazed down on the bed to which he had carried the Lady Eloira, Reeve of the High Wald. Beside him the equally elderly chirurgeon removed his fingers from her blue-veined wrist.

'Her heartbeat is faint but regular,' he pronounced. 'I do not think her life is endangered at this moment but . . .'

He did not need to finish the sentence. Both he and the steward were thinking of the great burden of years which their mistress bore.

'What was it that made her swoon on the roof?' the chirurgeon asked. 'Did she feel unwell before she collapsed or did she receive some shock?'

Not wishing to heighten the consternation of the Peak Tower's inhabitants Hans resolved to withhold the truth of how Eloira had untied the final knot in her ancestors' magical cord to conjure a spirit who she addressed as Tartak, and of whom she demanded a boon in arcane language that the steward found incomprehensible.

'I escorted her to the top of the tower to look over the mist and watch the sun set on the White Virgins,' he said slowly. 'Then she fell into a faint.'

'Since that accursed stranger — whose wounds I healed when she gave him refuge, may the Mother forgive me — murdered our watchman and stole the girl Jennet, the Lady Eloira has been of a melancholic humour,' said the chirurgeon while the Reeve's maid rearranged the coverlet of rare zaar fur over the frail form of her mistress.

'We can only wait,' he continued. 'Gill, inform me in all haste if there is any change — if her breathing becomes harsh or her eyes open.'

'Have you no potion for my lady?' demanded the elderly maid. 'She has given you a home and victuals for two score years and when she needs healing in return you can do nothing better than wait. Wait for what — the Dark Maid? No wonder you could not help poor Jennet find her rightful mind . . .'

'That will be enough, Gill,' said the steward. 'Master Chirurgeon is as concerned for our mistress as you.'

'If he was he would give her an elixir or a poultice or at least leech her.'

The chirurgeon shot her a look of disdain and stalked from the chamber.

'He will do his best,' said Hans reassuringly.

Gill snorted.

'I say we should send for her friend Piper. They say the Fey Folk have the power to heal which makes mortal physicians look no more than wart charmers.'

'Mayhap you speak sense but how would we find him now that the Wolf King is master of the Wald?' said Hans. 'But there is much I must attend to. Watch her well, Gill.'

The disgruntled maid nodded and seated herself on a stool by the bed with its fantastically carved posts, a long-ago tribute from the inhabitants of Toyheim. Hans was relieved to go to his own quarters for a restorative draught and rest. He was still trembling after the ordeal of beholding a being of terrible beauty materialize in a cone of lights.

Curse all gramarye! he thought as he reached for his special flagon. *I was mad to help the addled old dame!* And remembering her lying so small in such a large bed he burst into tears.

Meanwhile the Lady Eloira wondered why the snow crests of the mountains guarding the High Wald appeared blue in the afterglow. Then she realized she was looking at them through blue glass — the eyes of the beautiful doll she had cherished since childhood and which she had given to Jennet to calm her distress after the razing of her village. The Reeve's body lay motionless under the watchful gaze of her maid but thanks to the ritual she had performed she had been granted the power to transfer her animus to the doll.

Once she grew accustomed to seeing through glass eyes she felt a surge of relief as she focused on the face of Jennet who had placed her — the doll — on a piece of rock shaped like a diminutive seat.

'That is just the right size for you, Dolly,' she had said. 'Rest now. We are all very, very tired.'

The fact that Jennet appeared to be unhurt filled Eloira with a surge of relief. She found she could move her head, a most strange sensation, to look for the man who had abducted her charge. He lay muffled in his cloak in the shelter of a rock a dozen paces away.

Who is he? Eloira wondered. *He seems not to have*

stolen her to slake perverted lust, so what can he want with her?

Her thoughts were interrupted by Jennet who said in a little girl's voice, 'Dolly, it will be cold here on the mountainside tonight so I shall wrap you cosy in my shawl.'

At her words Eloira turned back to Jennet and her delicately painted mouth smiled her gratitude.

In the deepening dusk Jennet's eyes widened.

'Oh Dolly, for a moment I thought . . .'

'What are you saying?' called the man.

'I was just saying goodnight to Dolly.'

'Go to sleep now. Tomorrow we must find a path to the outside world if you want to find Krispin.'

'Goodnight, Master No-Name . . . Master No-Name?'

'Yes?'

'If you cannot remember who you are after you were hurt how can you remember about Krispin?'

There was a pause.

'Some things I have forgotten. Some things have come back to me. I remember all about Krispin. Now go to sleep like a good girl.'

Hearing these words Eloira was struck by the tragedy of this beautiful young woman whose mind had regressed to childhood. Now it was clear how the stranger had played upon the situation, persuading the 'child' to steal away from the Peak Tower on the promise he would take her to her beloved brother. And again Eloira wondered why.

The darkness thickened about them. From far away came a howl. Having heard such calls nearly every night of her long life in the High Wald, Eloira was aware that the ululating cry did not come from a wolf's throat. It was a nomad signal, probably originating from those members of the Wolf Horde who guarded the pass between the peaks known as the White Virgins. From forest-covered hills came a series of answering calls and the doll seated on the rock trembled.

The moon cast fantastical shadows about them when Eloira judged it safe to speak. Heavy breathing bred of exhaustion satisfied her that the stranger slept but what worried her was that the young woman seemed sunk in an equally deep slumber.

'Jennet,' she whispered.

Her voice was high pitched, almost squeaky, and exactly what one would expect if a doll were to speak, she thought.

'Jennet, open your eyes, my dear.'

Jennet's fingers holding the chubby porcelain hand of the doll tightened and she sighed in her sleep as though gripped by a dream.

Again Eloira spoke her name and this time her eyelids slowly opened to reveal eyes of dark blue whose whites reflected the moonlight.

'Dolly,' she whispered. 'You said my name.'

'Yes, but do not fear,' replied Eloira.

'I must be in a dream.'

'It may seem like that but I want you to listen to what I have to say.'

'A talking doll!'

Jennet's voice had lost some of its sleepy childish timbre.

'Not just a doll, my dear.'

Eloira had not considered how much to tell her. If she announced that it was the Reeve speaking it would

67

be too confusing for Jennet's childish mind and she might even be fearful of punishment for having run away from the Peak Tower.

'Is it — magic?'

'Good magic. Your Dolly loves you . . .'

'I am dreaming. Everything is strange. Sometimes in the last two days I feel I am no longer a child though I play the part . . .'

Her whisper died away.

'Tell me what happened, my dear, and I shall help you.'

'Oh, Dolly, am I going mad? Everything is so confusing?'

'Tell me and it will be less so.'

'He — the man they called Master No-Name in the Tower — took me away to find Krispin. We went through the forest and right up to the pass and there . . . but I do not need to tell you. You were with me all the way.'

'I was not magic then. Tell me what happened at the pass.'

'There were soldiers and suddenly they were attacked by wicked men in furs with black hair and yellow eyes and they swung great axes, and there was blood everywhere . . .'

Under her cloak her body shuddered.

'The Wolf Horde. They did not see you?'

'No. Master No-Name kept us hidden, but I saw the blood and I heard the cries and . . .'

'Yes?' The doll voice betrayed Eloira's tension.

'. . . and I knew I had seen men like them before, and seen blood and heard . . . but then there were cottages being set on fire . . . and they held Father Tammas and cut him right down the middle with an axe . . . and Dame Norbert . . . and . . . and . . . I ran out of our back door and across the yard with some of them chasing me but they forgot me when they caught the goose girl. All I know after that was sitting by the mere where I had seen the crystal bird until a man came and took me to a castle where the lady gave you to me but that was more dreamlike than talking to you now.'

'Do you realize you are not a little girl any more?'

'Oh, everything is mixed up. I seem to be neither child nor woman. I am tortured by memories I hardly understand and I know not why I am here.'

'Memories?'

'Memories I could not have if I was a child, the day of The Choosing, and Krispin.' A note of desperation came into her voice. 'Oh! I do fear I am going mad. Something happened when I saw the soldiers killed.'

'The change in you will surely be complete ere long and then you will once again be what you truly are. It was the shock of what happened at Toyheim that made you take refuge in the past but the second shock, of seeing the wolfmen again, is bringing you back to the present. Yet you still act as a child as when you wrapped your doll in a shawl.'

'But, Dolly, I did not want you to be cold,' Jennet answered and Eloira understood the conflict within her.

'*He* still thinks I live in childhood,' Jennet continued in her soft whisper. 'And I am letting him think so until I understand things better. He pretends to be kind but I have grown frightened of him.'

Her intuition is returning, too, thought Eloira. *But I must not panic her by telling her that he is a murderer.*

69

'You must get away from him, and I shall tell you how to get to the Peak Tower where your friends are.'

'It is Krispin I would see.'

'Krispin went on a long journey. You were the reason he undertook it, though I do not expect you to understand that for a while. How joyful he would be if he knew that you are returning to the present.'

'Tell me about Krispin . . .'

Her words were cut short by the urgent voice of the man.

'Who are you talking to?'

'My Dolly.'

'You are tired and should be asleep. And if you keep on talking to a doll you will be taken for a witch.'

'How do you know?' asked Jennet in her child's voice.

'I know all about witchery, little one.'

'Why?'

'Because I learned how to smell out accursed witchcraft and accursed necromancy and such evils in a big city called Danaak. Now go to sleep.'

Serene Mother! Could he be a Witchfinder! thought Eloira in panic. *How well he feigned loss of memory when he was brought to the Peak Tower. Did he come to spy on me and then recognize the likeness between Jennet and the portraits of Princess Livia? What a prize for him if he could deliver her to the Regent . . .* The thought of how the Regent could use Jennet — or at least her body — to put an end to any further questing for the Princess made Eloira sick with horror.

Only when she was sure that Master No-Name had fallen back into slumber did Eloira dare to speak again and then in a whisper that was low even for a doll's voice.

'Come, Jennet, you must come away from that man.'

'But he promised me he would take me to Krispin.'

'That was a false promise he made to a little girl. It would be impossible for him to find Krispin for he must be beyond the city of Thaan by now . . .'

If he lives, she added mentally.

'Then why does he want me to go with him?'

'There is no time to explain but soon everything will be clear to you. Come. Carry me down the slope to the forest. Once there I have no doubt we will be given help for I am a Fey Friend.'

An expression of puzzlement crossed Jennet's features. She was bewildered by everything but most of all the fact that Dolly could speak. It had to be all a dream — a dream that was often a nightmare — but soon she would wake up in her bed to the screech of Father Tammas's pump as Krispin doused himself in the yard. But until that moment she must live out her dream life. She climbed to her feet, adjusted her dress and clutching Dolly to her breast moved from rock shadow to rock shadow down the moonlit slope.

Eloira found the sensation of being carried thus extraordinary; it was as though the years had rolled back and it was she who was a child again.

Although she sometimes stumbled, Jennet made good progress towards the forest below as one would expect from a girl who had grown up in the High Wald.

'Soon be there, Dolly,' she breathed as the slope became less steep and she saw scattered trees rearing above them. From close by came the sound of a small cascade where a snow-fed brook leapt over the edge of a cliff.

'Which way now?' she asked.

'Follow the stream if you can find a way down,' said the doll voice of Eloira. 'Flowing water will lead us in the right direction.'

Cautiously Jennet approached the edge where the stream gushed into space and became an endless avalanche of silver droplets as the moon caught it in his rays. Shattered crags reared to left and right and several serpentine pines grew out of the cliff which plunged to black treetops far below.

'There is no path,' she said.

Before Eloira could reply there was the sound of a snapping branch and deep grunting. Jennet whirled round, screamed and dropped her doll.

Eloira was conscious of falling but there was no pain as she landed on a carpet of pine needles. For a moment she thought the Witchfinder must have followed them down; then as she turned her awkward little body over and sat up she saw a huge bear reared upright. In the moonlight its eyes were twin embers and the teeth in its slavering jaws ivory knives. It was a king of bears – Eloira guessed it might well be the fabled bear who held reign in a remote corner of the High Wald where no hunter would dare venture. Generations of Wald children had been thrilled by stories about him, the most common being that beneath his fur was a suit of golden mail. When upright he was taller than a helmeted warrior, his chest was a fur-covered barrel and his claws, darkened with dried blood, could disembowel a stag with a single blow.

He dropped on all fours and loped towards the paralysed girl, then reared up once more, snuffling and waving his forepaws in a vaguely human manner.

The Eloira doll climbed to her dainty feet and walked jerkily towards the beast.

'Run, Jennet. For the love of the Mother, run!'

At the sound of the shrill little voice the bear swung his great head and grunted in surprise when he saw the doll approaching him. He had never seen anything like it. It was far too small to be human, yet it was certainly no animal. What would it taste like?

Eloira's words and the bear's change of interest freed Jennet from her paralysis. She fled and the bear did not appear to notice. Down on all fours again he moved towards the doll, sniffing the air, jaws agape.

Eloira turned and ran wildly. The bear roared with what another bear would recognize as laughter and moved after the scurrying figure. For some moments he enjoyed the game, gambolling just behind the quarry to terrify it into greater effort, and then he paused. There had been a human. She had vanished. It was the human he wanted. The little running thing that had no life scent had tricked him. Rage filled him. He did not want to play with it any more. His cry of anger echoed from the peaks above and died far over the forest below. He swung his paw. Cruel claws caught the doll and hurled her in a high arc beyond the precipice.

SEVEN

The Sun-in-Splendour Company

Tumbrul placed his lanthorn on the porphyry floor of the chamber so that the others would not be left in darkness when Alwald and Krispin followed him with the light wand.

'Your light is so much brighter than mine,' he complained and added in his sour style, 'Why in the name of the Three Worlds could I have not been left with such a device. Not much to ask of an enchant. . .' He clamped his lips midword and led the way along the passage that lay behind the secret door.

Unable to resist warning the two Pilgrims, Gambal called, 'Be not too trusting of that earth runt.'

'Advice on trust comes ill from you,' retorted Alwald.

'As you will.' Gambal shrugged his narrow shoulders. Holding his wand outstretched Krispin followed the ludicrous figure of Tumbrul while Alwald brought up the rear with his sword drawn. Soon their sense of balance told them that the floor was sloping downwards. Dust rose in clouds from beneath their feet.

'You have not been sweeping here of late,' said Krispin lightly.

'Not in the agreement,' Tumbrul retorted. 'And if you think you have the right to make remarks as though I, Tumbrul the . . . er . . . am some scullion you can shift for yourselves.'

'You mistake my friend's meaning,' Alwald interposed hastily. 'He was comparing the immaculate condition of the Princess's chamber under your care with this passage that is obviously not.'

'Heh,' said Tumbrul.

They reached an oaken door and from his belt Tumbrul unfastened a key two handspans in length and struggled to turn it in the bronze lock. Finally the tongue screeched back and the door swung open to reveal a long hall. Alwald was filled with a chilling sense of awe such as that he had experienced when the Lady Eloira had taken him into her ancestral crypt. Like the vault in the Peak Tower the cold air of this place had not known movement for decades, but what startled Alwald and Krispin was the thirty granite slabs on which lay shrouded forms just as Eloira's uncoffined ancestors had been laid for their eternal rest.

'Why have you brought us to a tomb?' Krispin demanded, his hand on Woundflame's grip.

'Tomb? What tomb?' retorted Tumbrul. 'This is no tomb.'

'Then what are those?' cried Alwald gesturing to the supine figures.

'This is the Hall of Warriors,' said Tumbrul as though explaining something to a witless child. 'Those *corpses* are Princess Livia's bodyguard or will be when they are summoned back to Time Present.'

He gestured to the end of the hall where, on a slab much larger than the others, lay a man taller and broader than the others.

'Barlak,' said Tumbrul as though the name was explanation enough.

Behind this stone bier was a long table loaded with empty dishes and drinking vessels. Above it, suspended from the rock ceiling by a rusty chain, was a huge battle horn bound with bands of blackened silver. As Krispin raised the wand for better illumination the shadows along the walls dissolved to reveal piles of antique weapons.

'Like Princess Livia they were entranced at the time of The Enchantment,' Tumbrul explained with a touch of proprietary pride. 'While a Princess needs the Water of Life to restore her these rough and ready fellows are easily wakened. It would be better for them if it had been otherwise but it would require tuns of water from the Wells to bathe such a troop. Now, Master Disk-wearer, get on with it.'

'How . . .' began Krispin.

'How? Did you never hear folktales? Any child would know what to do.'

'The battle horn,' said Alwald. 'You are supposed to wind it.'

'It would be best if it were done by Lord Alwald who is accustomed to the hunting field,' Krispin told Tumbrul. 'I must confess that horn-blowing did not come into the training of an apprentice toymaker.'

Alwald stepped up to the suspended instrument, filled his lungs to bursting and put his lips to the mouthpiece. As the first deep growling note issued from the throat of the auroch horn Krispin was relieved that he had passed on the honour to his companion, realizing that a series of splutterings like a clover-bloated drong would have been the best he could have produced.

With his cheeks bulging like a wind god Alwald continued to blow so that the sound that had begun deep and majestically rose until it reached the pure high note of a huntsman's horn ringing through a forest. It echoed through the hall, where black spiders fled from the slabs, and along the passage so that those in Livia's chamber started in surprise and apprehension.

Alwald swung the horn away on its chain. Even while its dying note still hung in the dead air Krispin saw a movement on one of the slabs. A cobwebbed hand rose, fingers opened and clenched; cocooned knees were drawn up and a breathy sigh was heard.

As silence returned Alwald leaned against the wall with his chest heaving as one who has run a league.

'Your horn-blowing appears to have awakened the dead,' said Krispin as he watched apprehensively the figure on the central slab rise to a sitting position and claw frantically at the clinging spider thread that enveloped him. To the two Pilgrims the sight was an uncomfortable reminder of when they had been enveloped by filaments of Upas trees.

From the shrouded head came an angry muttering which, as the grey web was torn away, became increasingly audible and angry.

'. . . no talk of pox'd webs when we agreed . . . call himself a magician and he could not lay a spell to keep whore-whelped spiders out . . . and as for that misbegotten dwarf . . .'

As handfuls of sticky web were tugged away the warrior within gradually materialized. He wore a spiked helmet decorated with a Sun-in-Splendour emblem and beneath it they saw rugged features, scarred forehead, a large ugly nose, broad cheekbones and a black unkempt beard flowing over his mail-covered chest. His glittering eyes roved the hall and he bellowed at Tumbrul, 'Are you paralysed, Potton turd? Pull this spider web off me or by the Demon Omad I shall have my spear up your fundament so fast you will sneeze sparks.'

Krispin could not help laughing and Alwald said, 'What a poetic sentiment after a century of slumber.'

Noticing Krispin and Alwald the big man said in a more moderate voice, 'Pardon, Sir Questers — for I take it you are such — I would be shamed if you thought my words were directed at yourselves. My wrath is merely for this twist-gutted trollson who has been too lazy to keep us free from whore-humping spiders.'

'It was not in the agreement,' Tumbrul argued as he reluctantly picked at the grey threads.

'I'll give you agreement!' shouted the warrior with a resurgence of anger. 'I'll ram your reeking agreement so hard down your throat you'll shit vellum and piss ink.'

'He does have a military turn of phrase,' Krispin murmured to Alwald admiringly.

Throughout the hall other curses were rising as on every slab festooned figures struggled to free themselves from the fine strands that had enmeshed them over the years. When the first warrior swung his greaved legs over the side of his bier slab Tumbrul said formally, 'Captain Barlak, it is my duty to present to you Lord Krispin of River Garde and Master Alwald Toymaker who have braved the Pilgrim Path for the sake of the Princess Livia . . .'

'Lord Alwald,' whispered Krispin.

'Krispin Toymaker!' hissed Alwald.

'Good sirs,' continued Tumbrul turning to them, 'I name you Captain Barlak who with his warriors is in thrall to an ancient agreement to protect Princess Livia upon her awakening.'

Barlak nodded.

'Is she awake?'

'Not as yet,' said Alwald guardedly. 'There is a difficulty . . .'

'Excellent,' Barlak boomed, pulling more cobwebs from under his helmet. 'We will have time to feast as was promised in the agreement.'

He glanced over his shoulder at the long table and a strange luminosity began to envelop it. Misty objects appeared which soon materialized into smoking cuts of beef and enormous dishes in which fowls and geese steamed as though they had been rushed from ovens instead of conjured up by a century-old spell.

As the halo round the table faded and the hot smell of food overcame the stale air the warriors moved unsteadily from their slabs with their eyes alight in their colourless faces. They wore identical tunics of chain mail and the rayed sun symbol, and when each reached the table Barlak clapped him on the shoulder and greeted him by name. As soon as they seated themselves they reached for the jugs of ale and flasks of wine.

'Here's to the old Sun-in-Splendour Company!' they shouted clashing their tankards. 'To its living and dead and he at its head!'

'Join us, you heroes of the quest and let us see if your drinking is equally heroic,' boomed Barlak. 'Here

80

are viands from the Horn of Plenty and drink from the Bottomless Pitcher as in the old sagas.'

'We thank you, Captain,' replied Alwald hurriedly, 'but we have hungry companions and would take meat to them.'

'As you will, my lords,' said Barlak as he reached for the leg of a roasted goose. When Alwald and Krispin had piled two trenchers to overflowing with bread and meats they returned along the passage to their companions, Tumbrul following with a pitcher of wine in each hand.

'This place gives me the same unease as The Mage's Tower,' said Krispin. 'Did you see how the flambeaux on the walls began to flare when you left with the light wand? And those men – who are they and who enchanted them?'

'I care not as long as I am soon in the Mother's clear air again,' said Krispin. 'I am weary of this quest that never seems to end. Always there is a new task before us. Now it is a journey to the Wells of Ythan – if they still exist.'

Their return to the Princess's chamber was welcomed by expressions of relief and a barrage of questions as the trenchers were passed round and Tumbrul filled their leather wine cups.

'What about our doleful friend?' asked Ognam nodding to the bound Witchfinder.

'Let him sup air,' growled Danya. 'If it were the other way round the best Witchfinder hospitality you could expect would be the cauldron.'

Ignoring him Ognam went over to the prisoner and held out a piece of meat for him to bite.

'Tell me,' he said as the man chewed hungrily, 'why are you a Witchfinder?'

'To serve the Mother,' he replied between mouthfuls.

'But the Mother is merciful and that is not a word I have heard applied to your guild.'

'We have no mercy on evil. It has been our role since The Enchantment to ensure obedience to the Queen of the Three Worlds . . .'

'. . . and the Regents.'

'Of course. The temporal power of the Regency complements the spiritual power of the shrines. After the fall of the All Father the Serene Mother became omnipotent and therefore to question what is ordained is to blaspheme.'

'But has it occurred to you that those who believe the All Father never fell from grace may be right and the shrines and your guild mistaken? After all no men have heard a voice from the heavens or seen letters of fire proclaiming who is right.'

'You question the Divine Will!' cried the Witchfinder and he spat out lumps of half-chewed meat rather than swallow something befouled by the hand of a heretic. 'Your words are a blasphemy.'

'But if, as you say, the Serene Mother is omnipotent she ordained that I should speak these words and therefore she must be a blasphemer herself.'

The Witchfinder turned his head away and began to whisper the One Hundred and Forty-four Adorations to protect himself from such heresy.

Ognam returned to his corner and Tana refilled his wine cup.

EIGHT

The Wells
of Ythan

The path led Urwen and the swaying trio behind her into a broad grassy clearing in which stood a balustraded terrace of white and grey marble. In its centre they saw the gleaming dome of a rotunda supported by slender columns, while at intervals along the parapet stood graceful stone urns trailing creepers with flowers of scarlet, turquoise and royal purple. Down the middle of the terrace rainbows trembled in the glittering spray of fountains.

'The Wells of Ythan,' Urwen breathed.

The sight of the sparkling water gave the Regent a final surge of strength. Shrugging away Captain Bors and Yudin, he tried to mount the semi-circular steps leading up to the terrace. A moment later he stumbled. Urwen took his good arm and together they ascended. When they reached the marble paving they felt the refreshing coolness of water about them and saw that apart from the fountains the terrace contained several wells lined with greenstone ashlar as well as ornamental pools and shell-shaped basins into which water gurgled from vessels held in the stone hands of graceful statues.

The Regent began to pluck impatiently and uselessly at his bandages.

'Allow me, my lord,' said Urwen, returning to her submissive role. As she unwound the malodorous linen she saw that an old man in a black broad-brimmed hat and an equally dark cloak was sitting on a bench in the shadow of the rotunda. His face reflected great age – and authority that the years had not dimmed. It was a stern face except for the lips; they held a suggestion of humour as though the old man was party to a secret jest.

The Regent watched him while Urwen continued to uncoil the bandages but he remained seated and silent.

'Serene Mother!'

The exclamation came from Captain Bors as the last bandage fell to the tiles. Even Urwen, accustomed to dressing the Regent's arm, recoiled at the way it had changed since they had left camp early that morning. Before, the hand had been bloated and misshapen, the arm rope-veined and swollen but it had been recognizably human. Now it was something else, something outside the breed of men as though the limb of a demon had been grafted on to him. What had once been fingers twisted as though they had life independent of their host; the skin of the arm was now like that of a long-drowned corpse. Here and there it was rent under the pressure of the swelling but it was not normal flesh that was revealed but something dark and *rippling*, and even the freshness of cascading water could not lessen its charnel stench.

With sudden intuition Urwen pulled open the Regent's tunic and clapped her free hand to her mouth. The infection had spread from the arm to the breast and she remembered his fear that the toxin in his blood

84

would transform him into a replica of the soulless being that the alchemist had manufactured.

And when the Regent opened his mouth to cry out she saw that his strong square teeth had become pointed.

'Quick, he must be bathed,' she said but Bors had turned away sickened and Yudin slumped on a marble seat with his torn face in his bloodied hands.

'I bid you welcome to the Wells of Ythan.'

The old man approached them with the aid of a long staff. His voice was soft yet clear and when he reached them Urwen was surprised to see his height equalled that of the Regent.

'You have come with little time to spare,' he said. 'The water of the Wells is known as the Water of Life but it will only cure while there is life. To restore the lifeless would usurp the divine nature. Lady, take your changeling to that pool and let him lie in it.'

'Do you know of whom you speak, old man?' demanded Bors.

'I have a good idea of those who might come here,' he replied, 'but fear not, the Wells heal all — the water has no sense of morality.'

They helped the Regent across the marble floor to steps leading into a circular pool. He almost fell in his eagerness to immerse himself and when he was waist deep he lay back, his unaffected hand gripping a bronze ring held in the sculptured jaws of a griffin, and floated.

Urwen and Captain Bors sank on to a bench while in the background the Companion Yudin bathed his face in a scalloped bowl.

'What will happen now?' Urwen asked impatiently.

The old man leaned on his staff and said, 'If you

have come so far for a miracle, allow it to unfold. Watch and you will see soon enough.'

If there was a hint of mockery in his brilliant eyes it was hidden by the shadow of his hat brim.

'May I ask who you are?' said Bors in a voice of professional respect.

'A man should have the freedom to ask anything though if he gets answers is another matter. My name is long forgotten and matters not. It is enough that I was known as the Guardian of the Wells.'

He looked along the terrace with its plumes of spray and drifting fountain mist and smiled to himself. 'A small domain but unique.'

'What do you guard it against?' asked Bors.

'Fallen leaves,' replied the Guardian and he gestured to the rotunda where a besom leaned incongruously against a pillar of rare stone. 'And misuse.'

'Forgive me, but a man of your years as a sentry . . .' began Urwen.

'The Wells are outside the natural laws and need no physical safeguard. It is those who come here I try to protect.'

'From what?'

'The truth.'

'But . . .'

A jubilant shout cut through the plash of falling water. They turned and saw Companion Yudin gazing at his reflection in a pool.

'Look at me, look at me,' he cried, turning his face to them. 'It is true — the Wells are miraculous.'

The Guardian ignored the man's excited words but Urwen and Bors stared at him in wonderment. The gaping wound in Yudin's cheek had vanished as though the eagle's talon had never touched it. The skin was tanned and healthy without a scar and it seemed there was a light in his eyes that they had not noticed before.

'The relief,' he cried as he explored his face with his finger tips. 'Imagine what some flasks of this wonder water would mean on a battlefield, Captain.'

Bors nodded without speaking. Few are granted the opportunity of beholding a miracle and he was too awed for words. Urwen's eyes turned to the floating body of the Regent. Gone from his breast was the corpse-like lividity; the skin beneath its renewed shadow of dark hair was as she had known it before the unnatural infection had spread from his hand.

Seeing Urwen's eyes upon him the Regent raised his arm. From a swollen parody of a human limb it had returned to its normal size, the rents that had disclosed the noisome flesh had healed. His hand was still a gauntlet of inflamed flesh, the horn that had replaced the nails gleamed like the claws of a hunting animal but as she watched the hand shrunk so that knuckle and joint and palm line reappeared and the terrible horn tips dissolved until they were nothing more than normal nails.

The Regent found his footing on the steps beneath the water and stood up to his full height. Urwen saw that the pallor which he had concealed with rouge when he had made rare public appearances was replaced by his usual ruddy complexion, his lips had regained their sensuous colouring and when he drew them back in a smile of triumph his teeth shone like new ivory.

'My love, you are whole again,' murmured Urwen taking his transformed hand as he stepped from the pool.

'I feel a strength in me as never before – and

the pain has vanished,' he said. 'Yet I tremble.'

'Rest,' said the Guardian. 'Such rapid healing puts strain on both mind and body.'

The Regent sank with a sigh of satisfaction on to a bench and gazed at the prismatic colours glowing in the fountains.

Bors said, 'Master Guardian, I have long been troubled by an old hurt, especially at the time of the rains . . .'

'Immerse yourself,' said the Guardian. 'The blessing of the Wells is for all who find them.'

'If that is so, why are they so hard to find?' asked Urwen while the captain removed his outer garments, his shirt of mail and his baldric, and plunged into the water.

'For generations without number the Wells have been a mystery to men, for only those with enough belief to seek their healing discovered their healing,' answered the Guardian. 'After The Enchantment most of what had been written about them was destroyed in the scroll burnings and public talk of them was enough to be condemned to the cauldron by the Witchfinders. To the folk of Ythan they changed from mystery to myth.'

'As a child I heard it said by my grandmother that they grew from the tears the Mother wept at the fall of the All Father,' said Urwen.

'I heard that they once watered the Garden of Yth,' added Yudin.

The old man smiled.

'There is always a drop of truth in an ocean of legend,' he said. 'But truth is an even more difficult thing to find than the Wells because it is hard to recognize when it is found.'

'Is it true that it can be found in your Wells?' asked the Regent.

'They are no more my Wells than the sky is owned by the birds that fly in it,' said the Guardian. 'But there is much more to them than mere healing.'

'Does truth dwell here?'

The Guardian nodded.

'Then I would know it.'

'You would find the price too high, Lord Regent.'

'What is the price? An eye, as some legends tell? The knowledge of the hour when the Dark Maid will come?'

'Truth is not prophecy, it is far more terrible. The price is the burden of knowledge of what life is instead of what you believe it is.'

'That does not sound so terrible.'

'No? Then it is something to which you have not given thought.'

'You play with words, old man.'

'Why should I do that, Lord Regent?'

'To give mystic importance to these healing springs and thus to yourself as their self-appointed custodian.'

'Such a vanity requires those who would be impressed by it and you have learned that the Wells are far from the world of men.'

The Regent grunted.

Captain Bors emerged from the water and said, 'For the first time in years my shoulder is free from the nag of an old Cimmerii arrow wound.'

'Sleep now,' said the Guardian. 'You are safer here than you are in your citadel. No men, Fey or animals will harm you, for peace reigns supreme in this valley.'

'Tell me, Master Guardian, was it the Garden of

Yth?' asked Yudin who was losing the military timbre from his voice.

'If you believe so, my son.'

'But you said . . .' began Urwen.

'Rest now for your journey back.'

The Guardian smiled his wry smile at them and turned to the rotunda.

'Old man, I shall want casks in which to take away some of this Water of Life,' said the Regent imperiously. He nodded to Yudin. 'Your words were true when you spoke of its use on a battlefield. Every Companion will carry a flask of it on his baldric and the Black Rose company will be invincible.'

'That I could not permit,' said the Guardian gently. 'Be content that you will return with hurt healed.'

He walked into the deep shadow within the pillar supporting the dome.

'I like the old dotard's use of the word "permit",' said the Regent. 'This water will become the best weapon in my armoury. It will buy allegiance where silver would fail, it will make the next king of Ythan a miracle worker in the eyes of his subjects.' He laughed. 'It must be the water of youth as well as healing for I feel a strength surge within me I have not known for years.'

'But the Guardian . . .' began Bors in a faraway voice.

'His guardianship is at an end so see to it he is suitably rewarded for his devotion to the Wells.' The Regent drew the flat of his hand across his throat but the captain's eyelids had closed. A soft snore issued from Companion Yudin where he lay on a bench.

Urwen seated herself beside the Regent.

'You alone have not entered the water,' he said.

'Have you no pain of which you would rid yourself?'

'My hurt ended when I saw you emerge a man again,' she replied.

'In Ythan I shall emerge as king,' he said. 'My dynasty will fill the Empty Throne for a thousand seasons.'

He turned to her.

'You have proved your worth to me. Ask what you will. Mandraga can have little time left despite the potions with which she snatches moments of youth. Would you be Lore Mistress of Ythan as well as its queen?'

Yes! Yes! thought Urwen, but aloud she said softly, 'You must know what I want, Lord Regent.'

She stood before him and while Bors and Yudin slumbered on she unclasped her cloak and then, while the Regent watched with brooding eyes, she removed the rest of her garments until she stood naked before him.

'Now,' she whispered. 'Under the fountain.'

He rose and together they walked into the glittering spray.

When the four opened their eyes they beheld a firmament of stars blazing with diamond fire above. The valley grass was soft beneath them but of the Wells of Ythan there was no sign.

NINE

The Fall
of Lasgaad

Moonlight glimmered fitfully on the high gabled roofs
of Lasgaad as the wind flowing from the Outlands
drove streamers of cloud wrack across the midnight
sky. The crumbling town stood astride the ancient
highway that wandered from the range-girt Wald to
the far capital of Danaak.

Once Lasgaad had been prosperous with a large
caravanserai within its massive walls and its folk lived
well on the trade that passed through its high arched
gates. But that was before the caravan trade dwindled
and grass sprouted between the paving of the highway.
Slowly the town sank into decay. Woodworm pocked
the gates. When stone fell from the ramparts there was
no silver, or will, to repair them. Within those
ramparts the folk cursed the Regent whose taxes had
killed their trade but they kept their eyes downcast
when the black coach of a Witchfinder lurched along
their rutted streets.

This night they had more to fear than unexpected
charges of heresy, apostasy, necromancy, scroll-
concealment, rune-reading and the rest − tonight

sentries shivering between the merlons crowning the walls kept their eyes on a row of sparks spread across the plain, the campfires of the Wolf Horde.

The morning before, a detachment of men from the Tempest Legion, who had been engaged in collecting tax from the miserable hamlets on the plain, goaded their exhausted drongs into the market place. After he had ordered the bell of the main shrine to toll a summoning, Captain Lod announced that the barbarians who had captured the Wald earlier in the year were now swarming through the Pass of the White Virgins.

'I am ordered by Companion of the Rose Karik to hold this town until the Regent sends reinforcements,' he continued. 'From this moment all citizens are under military orders and anyone caught leaving the precincts will be executed. At the noon gong males over twelve seasons will assemble here with whatever weapons they can devise. Old men and womenfolk will immediately begin work on the fortifications.'

And so the citizens drilled and toiled and watched the horizon with anxious eyes. Their apprehension was increased the next day by the arrival of peasants who had fled from the approaching menace. Each new arrival had a more horrific tale to tell though in realiy their only contact with the enemy had been the sight of a distant dust cloud as the nomads advanced at the tireless trotting gait of their steppe ponies. Another omen, which in normal times would have been greeted with secret joy, was that the chief Witchfinder deemed the situation such that he must consult the Witchfinder-General in Danaak. The sight of his funereal vehicle rolling down the pot-holed highway deepened the fear that all felt in their hearts.

At sunset the folk of Lasgaad crowded the ramparts to see a haze of dust glow briefly golden in the west. The Wolf Horde had arrived and when dusk fell scores of cooking fires flickered half a league away.

Standing on the steps of the principal shrine, Captain Lod attempted to encourage those townsfolk who were not guarding the walls.

'The enemy are barbarians who normally roam the Outlands to hunt aurochs,' he declared in his parade-ground voice. 'They are without discipline and are unusued to civilized warfare. They may excel at the quick skirmish but they have no idea of mounting a siege as there are no towns in the Outlands. They are without siege engines and if we stand firm they will soon slink off as they have no concept of a prolonged campaign. Meantime you can be assured that an army from Danaak is marching to our relief at this moment.'

Veterans of the Tempest Legion caught each others' eyes and winked with soldierly cynicism.

'He forgets to say that the Mother-cursed Potton turds are Mother-cursed werewolves,' whispered Master-at-arms Guth to the trooper beside him.

'I have heard some knaves are spreading rumours that the nomads possess supernatural powers,' Lod continued. 'Such stories are not only absurd but heretical. Anyone caught repeating such foolishness will join those who did not heed my words of yesterday.'

He nodded to the end of the square where in the glare of flambeaux the bodies of men who had attempted to flee Lasgaad revolved slowly beneath a communal gallows.

Without speaking the crowd melted away. Soon afterwards the throb of drums reached the town.

*   *   *

With his crimson wolf-skull sceptre set up behind him, the Wolf King was a fearsome figure in the leaping firelight. Before him his lieutenants squatted on mats of auroch hide. Their yellow eyes reflected the flames as they raised their bone goblets of wine pillaged from the cellars of River Garde. In the centre, the shaman in a wolfskin robe stood with upraised arms and recited a tale of the bygone when Ruak the shewolf birthed a human child in her litter a hundred generations back and thus became the Great Mother of the nomad people.

While the chanted words continued, a tall man in a tunic of chain mail appeared from the shadows and stood beside the Wolf King's seat of piled saddles.

'Watchman Affleck,' growled the King. 'You pleased . . . you have your way.'

The man who had been the Regent's spy in River Garde, and who had opened its gates to the barbarians, shrugged and said, 'My way is best, Wolf Lord. It is true that your army could by-pass Lasgaad but if you are to overwhelm Danaak your men should know what it is like to fight against men behind walls.'

'I agree,' said the Wolf King. 'Bloodspill good . . . my wolflings need fight. You tell me . . . how we take town.'

'You won River Garde because it was believed that you could not cross the River of Night,' said Affleck.

'Regent tell us how.' The Wolf King laughed. 'Soon he be sorry for that.'

'It is also believed in Ythan that barb . . . that men from the Outlands do not attack after duskfall,' Affleck continued. 'In Lasgaad they will not expect you to begin the assault until the sun is risen. Surprise them, Wolf Lord, by attacking tonight.'

'Perhaps,' said the Wolf King. 'Men ride all day. Men weary but if Wolf-in-the-Sky agree . . . we attack. If Wolf-in-the-Sky not show himself we wait. Now, Watchman . . . you listen until story ends.

'As the Wolf Lord wishes.' Affleck sat cross-legged beside the Wolf King. He was tired of travelling like a nomad and tired of the nomads who were ruled by superstition, yet he knew he must continue his uneasy role if he was to win the prize of River Garde.

The shaman's saga ended and the Wolf King spoke to him. To Affleck, who had been trained as a spy in Danaak and had witnessed – and envied – aristocratic life, each man appeared as barbaric as the other. Both were dressed in wolf fur, the shaman's robe being decorated with feet and tails of the totem animal while the King's headgear was the mask of a wolf which he wore far forward so that from some angles it appeared as though he had a wolf head. Seeing this, Affleck shivered, the Wolf King was feared as a shape-changer and Affleck had reason to know that it was no exaggeration.

He wondered yet again if he had made a fatal error in betraying his master the Regent by urging the King to lead his horde against Danaak, and then the vision of the fair castle dreaming over its reflection in dark water returned and soothed his doubts. As for the Regent, he had learned from the last courier to enter the Wald that he was the victim of some mysterious malady and by now might even be laid in the Vault of the Regents beneath the Great Shrine.

The King returned to his seat and the shaman produced a hoop across which a piece of auroch gut was tightly stretched. When he rapped this with his knuckles it gave forth a drum-like note. Beating out a slow rhythm he began a foot-dragging dance round the fire. From outside the circle other gut drums took up the measure and several men in shaggy skins came and shuffled after the shaman while nomads gathered from all directions to stand beyond the circle, their coarse features slowly taking on unexpected expressions of ecstasy.

'Shaman ask Wolf-in-the-Sky for sign,' the Wolf King told Affleck. 'If we get sign . . . fight tonight.'

The drumming and dancing continued monotonously, only broken when the shaman threw back his head to utter a howl which to Affleck's acute ears was exactly like the howl of a timber wolf in the forest of the Wald. When this happened the nomads would gaze up into the sky with tatters of cloud flowing across it and each time it seemed the cloud wrack had lessened. When Affleck followed the gaze of the warriors for the final time he saw that the sky was clear and ablaze with stars. The Constellation of the Griffin glittered in the north while directly above the Star Bridge was a path of cold light. Never had he seen starshine so bright.

The drumming stopped.

Silence. Then a vast intake of breath.

It seemed to Affleck as though there was a shadow moving across the Star Bridge. Its shape was visible only because its darkness briefly extinguished the cold points of light behind it, and that shape was *animal* . . .

'The drumming has stopped,' remarked Master-at-Arms Guth unnecessarily.

'You should thank the Mother that barbarians do not attack after nightfall,' said Captain Lod. 'They will be resting now and I reckon we can expect them after sunrise.'

'And I hope we can expect reinforcements as well,' muttered Guth. 'That Companion of the Rose will surely have raised the alarm by now.'

Captain Lod said nothing but inwardly he doubted the possibility of outside help. The military courier who had brought his last dispatch from the distant capital had told him privately how the Regent's main army had fallen to the Red Death on a campaign against the heretics of Thaan. Until the Regent recalled the frontier companies and new men were conscripted there would be no force capable of defeating the barbarians. It was up to him and his men to hold back the horde for as long as possible, a daunting prospect when he considered the state of Lasgaad's defences.

Where he stood on the western wall with his master-at-arms a watchtower that had collapsed years ago had never been rebuilt. It left a gap in the upper part of the rampart below which a mound of rubble provided a ramp for sure-footed foemen. The gap had hastily been blocked with furniture confiscated from nearby houses. Lod had detailed half the Tempest detachment to guard this weak point during the day, the rest being dispersed among the ill-armed men of the town to stiffen their defence. Now most of the defenders slept, taking advantage of the belief that the nomads only fought during the daylight hours.

'The campfires are going out,' reported the Master-at-Arms, and looking across the plain Lod saw that the sparks of light that marked the enemy encampment were vanishing even as he watched. Normally he would have expected them to fade gradually as their fuel turned to ash but now it looked as though they were being extinguished deliberately.

'Have the men stand-to, Guth,' he said. 'Mayhap I was in error about barbarians not fighting at night. Something strange is going on out there.'

As though to confirm his unease the moon emerged from behind a wayward remnant of cloud and the captain saw what appeared to be a shadow lengthening over the plain, a shadow created out of the dust flung up by the hooves of steppe ponies.

'To arms! To arms!' shouted Guth.

Curses and commands rippled round the walls. A cracked shrine bell began to clang the alarm and men still dazed by sleep appeared on the ramparts grasping a variety of weapons to take their places behind the crumbling merlons.

They were still arriving when the first wave of wolfmen approached, leaping with acrobatic ease off their galloping mounts and running towards the walls with their long-hafted axes held aloft. Swaying above the sea of heads were a number of poles on which were mounted wolf skulls. The foremost of these was painted red and was the crude standard of the Wolf King himself.

A few arrows flew from the battlements but it would have taken companies of archers and sling-bowmen to have halted the onrush. More effective were the pieces of masonry the defenders hurled down when the enemy was directly below them. Some managed to mount the debris from the fallen watchtower but Captain Lod's troopers drove them back with their spears from the makeshift barricade above it. Several men stood ready with lighted torches to fire the wooden furniture if the howling nomads won a foothold on it.

'Ho! the Tempest! The Tempest for ever!' shouted the regular troops as they thrust and parried but this battlecry was their last act of defiance. Through the scrambling ranks of the enemy appeared a man clad entirely in wolfskins with a wolf mask on his head. His guttural voice rang above the din of battle: 'Bow to the Wolf-in-the-Sky and you live.'

'Up your flaming Wolf-in-the-Sky!' Guth shouted and seized a javelin to hurl it at the Wolf King. But the missile never left his hand. Before his disbelieving eyes a change came over the enemy; his wolf mask seemed to merge into his head, his face lengthened into a muzzle and his furs were no longer loose but his actual coat. Yellow eyes blazing and jaws wide, he sprang over the barricade and as he bore Guth down his fangs tore his throat.

Behind him similar dark shapes were leaping over the jumbled furniture. A torch was thrown into it by a trooper a moment before a barbarian axe clove his brow. Flames began to dance and the reek of singed fur hung in the air but enou . wolfmen gained the ramparts to drive the panicked defenders before them.

During this diversion the nomads below were able to approach the city gates and soon a hundred axes were smashing into their decayed planking. Within moments a stream of barbarians flowed beneath the arch and the massacre began. Buildings blossomed into flame and by the ghastly light townsfolk peering fearfully from their upper casements saw strange figures moving in the streets below, some were axe-wielding men but the others . . . the others were the dark forms of enormous wolves. And while the men sought maid and matron to suffer their battle-fired lust, the wolves sought the hot flesh of the vanquished.

Few lived to tell of the rape of Lasgaad. Among those who managed to escape amid the bloody confusion was Captain Lod. His right arm hanging useless after an axe blow, he reeled through a postern gate and set off along the ancient Danaak road. Behind him columns of ember-bright smoke rose skywards and his ears were filled with the screams of the Wolf Horde's victims.

It was not only fear that drove him from the doomed city, he knew it was his duty to warn the Regent of the supernatural powers of the outlanders who had entered the kingdom.

TEN

The Blasting Rod

Holding the Disk of Livia at eye level, Krispin concentrated on the reverse side to that which had enabled him to pass through the pylon gate into the caverns. As had happened then — and when he had materialized the black boat by the River of Night — words of which he had no understanding streamed into his mind and these he found himself declaiming before the bronze doors.

Nothing happened.

His companions exchanged apprehensive glances and then turned to Tumbrul with expressions of doubt.

'Keep going,' he hissed. 'Invoking magic is not like pulling the spigot of a water butt.'

As Krispin continued to recite his arcane litany, there was a slight movement in the air about them, a flexing of unseen energies, and then the ponderous sound of stone grating on stone. Down the middle of the doors appeared a golden line of light which, as the gap widened, eclipsed the silvery radiance of the wand light. The onlookers raised their hands to shield their eyes as upon them burst the glory of the sun rising above the Mountains of the Moon.

Krispin's words died away and he and Alwald led the others half blindly beneath the pylon's colossal lintel. To the west, the sky appeared dim and louring with the perpetual twilight of the Shadow Realm, to the east, snow-mantled peaks glittered against a sky of soft blue. And after their long trek through the shadowed land, followed by the gloom of the caverns, the effect of light and colour on the Pilgrims was to give them a surge of hope that memory of so many past disappointments failed to dampen.

They were followed into the light by Tumbrul and the Sun-in-Splendour warriors who not only looked deathly pale from their years in total darkness but from the celebration that followed their revival. A wine-sweat glistened on their brows and their hands trembled on the hafts of their weapons. Barlak wore the great hunting horn that had awakened him and his fellow sleepers across his broad back and each man carried a pack. Some contained food salvaged from the feast, others held precious objects taken from the treasure chamber which the Princess would need on her return to Ythan. But no pack was as heavy as the sack that Tumbrul carried over his shoulder, crammed with a selection of treasure that was the reward for his century of custodianship, and which had taken him long and delightful hours in choosing.

The last men-at-arms to emerge bore a silvered litter on which the Princess lay beneath a canopy of spider silk lace. When Tumbrul had produced it from some cavernous store Krispin had helped to lift her on to its mattress filled with swan's down, and the sensation that it could have been his sister Jennet who he was supporting so overwhelmed him that for some time he was afraid to speak for fear his voice would betray his emotion. Alwald, who had seen Jennet at the Peak Tower, was also amazed by the resemblance between her and Livia and he wondered mightily.

Tumbrul, his eyes bedazzled like the others, gazed westwards over the plateau and then at the towering ranges.

'I think we follow the cliff northward for half a league,' he said finally. 'Then we should come to a path leading up into the high mountains.'

'Are you sure of that?' demanded Barlak with the irritation of one who has drunk his night away. 'We are in no mood to march up mountains if you only *think* you know the way.'

'I was given directions a long time ago, but the more I look the more certain I become of the route,' replied Tumbrul. 'As this is the very last act of my agreement you can be assured I have no wish to prolong my time with disagreeable soldiery.'

While the warriors formed up round the litter, Danya said, 'What about him?' He nodded to where Edom the Witchfinder stood with his wrists still tied behind his back. 'A bolt from my crossbow would rid us of the nuisance in the blink of an eye.'

'Hardly merciful, shipmaster,' Ognam murmured.

'I was merciful when I took him aboard the *Amber Star* and by way of repayment he planned to leave us to die of hunger. A kraken bolt is a mercy compared to what our fate would have been.'

'I shall not give you satisfaction by pleading for my life,' said the Witchfinder. 'Do what you will.'

Danya unslung his bow and tensioned a bolt whose envenomed point was protected by a leather sheath.

'The pleasure of revenge would be fleeting, remorse

might be a more enduring companion,' said Ognam stepping casually between the shipmaster and the prisoner.

'Step aside, fool,' cried Danya. 'I shall have no more remorse over putting a bolt in his belly than I would have in shooting a kraken.'

'Fool you say but not such a fool as the fool who calls me a fool and thinks blood can be spilled without staining the spirit,' retorted Ognam.

'Enough words,' snapped Alwald. 'I was trained in the honourable profession of arms in River Garde and no man-at-arms who followed our black banner would slay a prisoner — so unstring your shaft, good master Danya.'

'Then may I say, Lord Alwald, the more fool you,' muttered Danya but he lowered the crossbow.

'You were right,' said Barlak in his rusty voice, 'but decide what is to be done for we may as well begin our march as wait here.'

Alwald nodded to Krispin.

'Cut his bonds.'

Krispin drew Woundflame and parted the rag strips.

'Now go, Witchfinder,' Alwald ordered. 'Keep away from us because I vow there will be no mercy the second time.'

'Either way it will be death for me,' Edom muttered. 'Who can survive in these uplands without food?'

He walked a discreet distance and then stood working his fingers as the circulation returned to his hands.

Tumbrul, weighed down by his sack, and holding a quaintly carved rod in his left hand, set off over the reed-like grass that grew beneath the frowning cliff. The litter followed with its escort while the others straggled behind it with Gambal in the rear. After some time the Witchfinder began to follow, careful to remain beyond crossbow range.

An hour later the party reached a spot where the cliff gave way to a slope, caused by an ancient landslide, up which a track zigzagged through boulders that lay strewn in all directions.

'The path leads to the Wells,' declared Tumbrul. 'Follow it and it will take you past those three peaks to a valley . . .'

'You speak as one who does not intend to guide us there,' Barlak growled.

'There is no need for me . . .' began Tumbrul but when he saw the look in Barlak's bloodshot eye he grumbled to himself but led the way up the slope.

When dusk descended upon the Mountains of the Moon the travellers found themselves on the remains of a road that had been cut in the rock in olden times. Once it had been paved for chariots but the frost and rain of unnumbered seasons had left it merely a broad track curving into the mountains. Even Tumbrul knew nothing of its history except he was sure that it had once led to the Wells of Ythan.

At one point it broadened with a sheer drop into the gathering gloom on the left while to the right a rock-strewn slope of shale rose steeply towards the nearly invisible peaks. Some blocks of dressed masonry lay scattered about and there were remains of a low wall along the outer edge of the road.

'Mayhap in bygone days there was a pilgrims' inn here,' said Barlak. 'It is a good place to spend the night.'

The last relay of litter-bearers gratefully lowered

their burden and Tumbrul supervised the erection of a light covering to protect the Princess from the night airs. Packs containing treasure were piled beside it, sentries were posted and the company settled by the ruined wall which provided shelter from the everlasting west wind. Krispin set about making a small fire with sticks torn from thorn bushes and, when flames began to flicker beneath its pungent smoke, food was brought out. A feeling of contentment stole over the travellers after their arduous day.

'How did it come to pass that you and your men were enchanted?' Alwald asked Barlak as wine from last night's feast was shared out.

'To you it may sound strange but much of the detail is like something half remembered from a dream,' Barlak replied with unusual gravity. 'That is the effect gramarye has upon men's minds; it makes memory like something seen through the bottom of a glass. I do remember that my lads — the Sun-in-Splendour Company — had been dispatched to defend a town by the sea.'

'Who was the foe attacking it?'

'Men who came in ships. The sea seemed to be covered with enemy vessels and we were outnumbered beyond counting.'

'Ay, outnumbered we were,' said the man beside him. 'Five hundred of us had marched to defend the quays and man the trebuchet below the light-tower.'

'Barrels of naphtha it fired and set several of the Sea Kings' ships ablaze,' added another.

'Sea Kings!' exclaimed Barlak. 'It was the Sea Kings we fought that day. When they sailed into the harbour the sound of their arrows filled the air like flights of geese.'

'And the name of the town?' cried Danya who like the other Pilgrims was held by the story. Barlak rubbed his scarred brow and then admitted, 'At this moment all I remember was the fighting.'

'There was blood everywhere,' said the first warrior. 'We lopped off their heads as they climbed the seawalls until the water changed colour.'

'A red tide,' agreed the second. 'But much of that dye was ours.'

'Once they gained the quays there was not much of the old Sun-in-Splendour left,' Barlak continued. 'For every one of our axes there were ten of theirs and we retreated into the big square that opened on to the waterfront to make our last stand with honour. The townsfolk were behind us with pitchforks and hammers, even kitchen cleavers, for they would not quit the place they loved so dearly. Soon there was a rampart of dead across the square and the sky was darkened by smoke from houses that had been fired until the sun was like a silver coin above us.

'As I speak it comes back to me, the clash of arms, the wailing of the wounded — for in truth warfare is a very noisy business — and the battle chants of the Sea Kings.

'And then it happened. All that was left of the force good King Johan had sent to protect the port was no more than you see before you this night and we had but a few moments of life left. Suddenly everything seemed to become misty as though we were in a waking dream, and we lowered our weapons with weariness but none struck us and the cries of the folk died away in wonder.'

'What happened then?' demanded Ognam with a professional story-teller's enthusiasm.

'I strive to remember clear,' Barlak replied. His men too appeared to be trying to focus on something floating just beyond the edge of memory, then one cried, 'That was when we heard the voice.'

'Ay, the voice,' his comrades agreed.

'It was a mighty voice,' continued Barlak, 'deep as the dying note of Grand Johan in Danaak's Great Shrine and it was all about us. And without the need to be told we know that it was the voice of a mighty wonder worker.'

'And what did this voice say?' asked Gambal whose interest in the story caused him to break his silence for the first time in hours.

'It addressed us as heroes and offered to strike a bargain with us — if we would serve the Princess Livia as her future bodyguard the town would be saved from the Sea Kings by being removed from Time Present. It may sound strange but we had understanding of what was meant and we were happy to swear oaths on our honour and by the binding of our spirits.

'Then the town began to dissolve so that all that remained were ruins; the cries of its folk became fainter as though they were borne out of our ken.'

'It was a miracle,' said one of the warriors. 'Everything remained misty while our strength returned.'

'Then the voice ordered us to march and it was the strangest march I have ever known, for it was as though we were shadows marching through a shadow-land, and time had lost meaning and fatigue was unknown,' Barlak said. 'At the end of that weird journey we found ourselves here in the Mountains of the Moon. There was a man in a black gown waiting for us beneath the pylon whom we knew to be the enchanter, and he explained the agreement and led us to the hall where you found us.

'And then a weariness descended upon us so heavy that it was almost impossible even to raise a finger, and when we lay down we felt we could sleep for a hundred years – as it seems we have, according to Master Tumbrul's reckoning.'

A silence fell as it does at the end of a good tale. At last Krispin asked, 'Was the name of the port Haven?'

'So it was,' exclaimed Barlak. 'Ay, Haven.'

Fatigued by the long day's travelling the company, apart from the sentries, soon drifted into sleep to dream of the land of might-have-been, of dead hopes and unfulfilled joys and innocence betrayed . . . dreams that thankfully would fade from memory when the sleepers awoke. Sitting with his hand on his precious sack, Tumbrul's head sank so low that the tip of his elongated nose rested on his bulging paunch and his dreams were of deep cavernous halls whose flambeaux reflected on bright silver and which were filled with the strange music of his folk – but of those folk he could find none.

Suddenly a shout from one of the sentries banished these night phantasms. On their dazed awakening the travellers followed his outstretched arm with horrified eyes. Harsh moonlight made every detail clear – the dark figure on a ridge high above, a huge boulder rolling down the scree towards the litter in which lay Princess Livia.

'Save the Princess!' shouted Barlak and seizing one of the long carrying poles he struggled to pull the litter out of the path of the flying boulder. Others sprang to his aid. The litter was raised and moved at a run but not fast enough for the warrior grasping one of the rear poles. His scream drowned the splintering of the handle as the boulder struck him and hurled him off the road into the void beyond.

'The Witchfinder!' Danya gesticulated to where Edom was about to dislodge another boulder.

'Your crossbow!' Alwald shouted.

As the shipmaster fought to tension it with over-eager fingers a grotesque figure scrambled up the slope with one hand clutching a short rod. The others gaped, unable to believe that Tumbrul was capable of such agility.

Up and up he went, sometimes on all fours, while above him the Witchfinder rocked the man-sized stone to and fro.

Tumbrul was only a dozen paces from the enemy when the boulder was over-balanced. As it bounded down the incline he jumped aside, lost his footing on rock debris and came tumbling head over heels after it.

On the road the travellers scattered as the rock flung up a storm of embers from the fire before crashing through the remains of the ancient wall.

When Danya raised his crossbow he saw Gambal racing up the scree to where Tumbrul sprawled. As Gambal was in the line of fire the shipmaster's finger hesitated on the trigger.

'Take my blasting rod,' gasped Tumbrul. 'It knows the enemies of the Princess. Touch him with it.'

Gambal looked up at the Witchfinder and seized the intricately fashioned rod.

High on the ridge Edom ran to where he had positioned the third boulder while the travellers were sleeping. Now he used all the weight of his slight body to roll it after the litter that the warriors were bearing away. Suddenly he saw Gambal scrambling up amid slides of shale and without hesitation he sent the boulder thundering down on him.

Gambal, clambering on his hands and knees, saw it grow until it blotted out the night sky. He tried to twist out of the way but it caught his left arm and tossed him to one side. For a moment he lay in agony, then he saw the Witchfinder seize a piece of rock to dash out his brains. The danger gave him the strength to regain his feet and stagger upwards as the Witchfinder flung the fragment at him.

Gambal sank to his knees as the missile struck him in the chest, forcing the breath from his lungs.

'You, traitor, I would kill above all,' cried Edom and he seized another stone. 'May this be Dikon's revenge!'

Summoning the last reserve of his ebbing strength, Gambal flung Tumbrul's blasting rod at the man poised above him. It struck the Witchfinder full in the face, and his face began to *glow*. The rod fell to the ground and was consumed by the heat of its own making.

Those below watched in sickened fascination as Edom's head became incandescent, the fiery heat spreading down through his body as the redness of the forge travels through an iron bar in a smithy. For a moment the Witchfinder capered on his ridge festooned with fire, a column of sparks spiralling above him; then the body dwindled away before their eyes, the fire died and all that remained was a cone of ash.

ELEVEN

The Necropolis

It was the Night of the Fools when Garn decided to run away from the house into which his parents had sold him. He knew that if he was caught it would mean being sentenced to the mines, but he felt even that would be preferable to having to satisfy the strange whims of Master Black. The last boy who had received the attentions of the house's richest customer had been so hurt he had lain in a swoon in the garret for ten days before the Dark Maid took him.

Mistress Joy who owned the house had taken careful note of the wounds on the pallid body before it was taken to the charnel pit, not out of concern for the departed lad but in order to claim compensation from Master Black. And tonight Master Black was returning. Garn was fearfully aware of this because Mistress Joy had brought the costumes that Garn and the girl who was to be his partner would have to wear for the night's entertainment — Master Black had a great sense of the theatrical.

He was known as Master Black by reason of the colour of his dress and the fact that none of the children had seen him without his black leather mask which was similar to that which was worn by members of the Executioners' Guild. It was rumoured — with a shudder — by the inmates of the house that he was turnkey in the Citadel whose imaginative nature craved for more satisfaction than the routine treatment of the Regent's prisoners provided. There was no dressing up in the smoky halls below the Citadel's foundations.

'I'm going to run,' Garn muttered as he fingered the fur costume he had been ordered to wear.

Aldis, whose value to Mistress Joy was her soft fair hair and virginal expression, laughed mockingly.

'How?' she asked and nodded to the barred window through which the noise of the approaching festivities could be heard.

'There must be a way.'

'You will get used to it, Master Black and all. The trick is to yell and make out you are more hurt than you really are. At least he is no worse than old Wilk who used to come here for his little games.'

'Serene Mother, I would rather be in the mines.'

'You get better fed here — as long as you are pretty. Come on, Garn, get dressed or you'll feel the whip even before Master Black arrives. I shall try and keep him interested in me seeing it is your first time. Not that I would do that for anyone else.'

'I am not going to hide behind a girl,' Garn declared.

'You do not know what you will do before the night is out,' said Aldis sombrely.

Beyond the barred windows the citizens of Danaak threw themselves into the delirium of the one festival that had survived The Enchantment while the boy waited in terror for the arrival of Master Black. The other inmates, whose services would not be required until after the house's habitués had witnessed the crowning of the Fool King, avoided the white-faced Garn and Aldis as though they feared to be contaminated by the evil luck that awaited them.

The arrival of Master Black heralded a nightmare. Afterwards Garn could hardly recall the strange games that he forced them to play, his anger-lust growing with each mistake they made, but he did remember that when Master Black began to punish them for their so-called disobedience to his shrill commands Aldis took more than her share of flagellation in order to spare him.

What shocked him out of his pain-shot daze was Master Black thrusting a whip into his hands and ordering him to use it on the girl.

It was then that a sudden icy sensation of knowing exactly what he must do filled him. He raised the whip and cracked it against the leather mask, and while it did no physical harm it did at least startle Master Black. He turned to avoid a second blow and Garn leapt from behind, looping the lash round his neck. Feeling the plaited leather against his throat Master Black gave a yelp of alarm but those in the house knew to ignore such cries when guests were enjoying themselves.

The cry became a ghastly choking sound as the makeshift garrotte tightened. Master Black, whose lack of height was made up for by girth, made a grotesque figure as he lunged about the room in an endeavour to shake off the boy hanging from the lash that crushed his windpipe. Behind the slits in the executioner's mask his eyes started from their sockets. He fell, his heels drumming the floor while his fingers

117

plucked uselessly at what had been his instrument of pleasure.

Several minutes after the body had gone limp Garn let go the whip and looked up at the speechless Aldis.

'We are going to run,' he said but she did not seem to comprehend. He found her dress and pulled it over her welted body, gently put her shoes on her blood-spotted feet and wrapped her in Master Black's cloak. Suddenly realizing that the silence might seem odd to Mistress Joy, he threw back his head and emitted a howl. He then turned to Master Black himself and, when he unbuttoned the corpse's costume to find the key to the chamber, he noticed a silver emblem of a cauldron attached to a neckchain.

A Witchfinder!

Master Black was not a turnkey after all. Garn had killed a Witchfinder! And as he donned the black garment he grinned savagely as he thought of the retribution that would fall upon the mistress of the house from the Guild of Witchfinders.

Taking Aldis by the hand he unlocked the door. In the passage outside, the child who was stationed there to relay any request Master Black might make to further his satisfaction was curled up in exhausted sleep. In the city the noise of the carnival was reaching a crescendo and Garn guessed that the inmates of the house not professionally engaged would have their faces pressed against the window grilles to watch the fireworks celebrating the mock coronation.

Lifting the robe to prevent himself tripping, he continued down a flight of stairs with Aldis following like a somnambulist. At the doorway the porter, who had been celebrating the festival with a flask of liquor known to the poor of the city as Widow's Balm, merely muttered drunkenly as the black-garbed couple vanished over the threshold.

In the narrow street, above which high-gabled houses leaned towards each other as though wearied by their antiquity, the boy and girl followed the crowds. Every few moments the scene would be lit by a garish wash of coloured light from exploding rockets. In doorways harlots waited for custom with their skirts waist high, at corners tumblers pranced amid flares, and everywhere masked revellers danced and scuffled.

In a square overlooking the Green River, Garn and Aldis leaned against the stone parapet with heaving chests. Below, the water was streaked with mauve, orange, emerald pyrotechnic reflections.

'You have ruined everything,' gasped Aldis. 'We have nowhere to go and if you get caught . . .'

Behind them a fight started between some soldiers and a humpbacked man, and a couple of packmen joined in on his behalf.

'Come,' said Garn.

'Where?' Aldis asked suspiciously.

'To the Tombs. We will be safe there.'

She looked doubtful but he seized her hand and led her away.

To the west of the city, beneath the sheer walls of the Citadel, stretched the old walled necropolis where for generations merchants, burghers and aristocrats had been interred in tombs reflecting their worldly success. Since The Enchantment, this city of the dead had become neglected; weeds choked its paths, wild vines obscured once-illustrious names on marble monuments, and mausoleums suffered the embrace of wind-sown trees.

With neglect the necropolis became the domain of

outcasts — the madman, the thief, the fugitive and the beggar found sanctuary among its tombs. The more daring tunnelled into vaults and plundered sarcophagi and found shelter behind the bronze doors of mausoleums. The gates to the necropolis were bricked when ragged bands of tomb-dwellers, nick-named ghouls, stole into the world of the living after nightfall to rob and rape. Priests from the Great Shrine intoned an interdict upon the place and poisoned food was set out — and ignored by the hungry. From time to time a company of nervous guards was sent to patrol the avenues with orders to kill the human rodents on sight but none knew the secret ways of the necropolis like its inhabitants and most outcasts survived.

It was to this no-man's-land that Garn brought Aldis. They climbed through a breached wall as dawn was lightening the sky and found themslves face-to-face with a band of young ghouls who had taken advantage of the carnival madness to try their luck in the city.

'Who have we here?' demanded the muscular leader named Murt who stood a head taller than Garn. 'Little spies or little runaways?'

'We have come from the house of Mistress Joy,' answered Garn evenly. His words provoked hoots of laughter.

'You have not paid me my fee, little whore-boy,' sneered Murt. 'Everyone who comes must pay a crown for protection against the bad people who prey on such as you.'

'I have not a copper coin let alone a crown.'

'Then I shall have her,' said Murt pointing at Aldis. 'You can take her back in a few days . . .'

For the second time that night Garn launched

himself against an enemy. The ghoul was unused to resistance in his victims and was completely unprepared. He stumbled backwards, tripped and fell to the paving with Garn on top of him. Murt writhed and would easily have thrown Garn off had not the boy seized him by the ears and thumped his head down on the paving. Again and again he brought the bully's head against the cracked stone until his eyes rolled and his body went limp.

Garn tugged Murt's dagger from his belt and leapt up to face the rest of the ghouls.

'Tonight I killed a Witchfinder,' he hissed. 'And this will prove it.'

With his free hand he produced the cauldron medallion which he had wrenched from Master Black's bruised neck. 'Leave us be or . . .' He nodded to Murt who lay supine with bubbles forming on his lips and who, when he revived the next day, was to remain a simpleton for the rest of his short life.

'Find yourself a tomb,' said one of the ghouls, looking contemptuously at his unconscious leader. 'And if you want to join us . . .'

Still holding the dagger, Garn shook his head and taking Aldis by the hand led her down an avenue lined with mourning trees.

Recognizing that the couple were outcasts like themselves the ghouls followed and with the camaraderie of the damned took them to an empty vault where they could rest.

As the weeks passed, Aldis gradually lost her terror of the place. They too became ghouls, dwellers of the crypt, who lived on what Garn managed to forage on raids into the outside world. And like others before them, they gradually came to value their new surroundings, the grieving statues that guarded the entrance to their marbled dwelling, the air of peace which hung over the semi-wilderness and above all the fact that for the first time in their short squalid lives they enjoyed a sense of freedom.

Their mausoleum was far grander than anything either had known before. Little by little they turned it into a home with a lamp, some utensils, makeshift furniture made from coffin boards and – their most prized possession – a brightly coloured rug that Garn had stolen from the caravanserai market. At night they curled up together under a collection of rags in an empty granite sarcophagus which had been hewn for a hero of a long-forgotten war. But though they lived closer than most husbands and wives, and though a feeling of love gradually grew between them, there was no question of lovemaking as they lay in the heavy darkness of their tomb – the likes of Mistress Joy and Master Black had destroyed all physical desire.

One morning they were awakened by the sound of stone scraping stone and by the dim light that filtered through the coloured crystal panes set in the dome of the mausoleum they saw one of the heavy flagstones slowly rising. Aldis held back a scream with her hand, Garn reached for his knife and, terrified that a real ghoul was about to appear, they peered over the rim of the sarcophagus.

The slab slid to one side and a man's close-cropped head appeared, blinking in the dim light. He climbed out and when he stood upright there was a dignity about him despite his filthy clothing and grey stubble. The watchers held their breath while he leaned forward and lifted a ghastly caricature of a human out of the opening.

TWELVE
The
Woodcutter

Fulk sat cross-legged at the edge of the clearing in which a circle of hoarstones glimmered faintly in the starshine. Other men waited in the shadows for the moonrise but apart from coughing and hawking, the mark of those forced to live without proper food or shelter, they held their silence. Across Fulk's knees lay his heavy woodman's axe and his hand moved rhythmically up and down its blade with a whetstone. Honing his axe was second nature to him; it had irritated his daughter Hildi that when he returned from the forest he could not rest as other men but would sit sharpening the blade which he always complained had been blunted by the day's work. Only when it was razor keen was he satisfied enough to put a sheath of goose-greased leather over the shining edge and pick up the bowl of stew Hildi had prepared for him.

Each evening she would say, 'I serve your food hot and you eat it lukewarm. Could you not whet your axe *after* supper?' And always he would reply, 'You and I owe our living to this axe. It has to be treated with respect for it is the finest-wrought blade in the northern Wald and each day it becomes worn in our service. Therefore its pride must be restored as soon as possible.' And she would say, with a toss of her pretty head, 'I should say that we owe our living to your strong arms rather than an old axehead.' And he would laugh and have the last word. 'I could not tear down trees with my strong arms alone.'

To the east the sky began to lighten above the ranges and then the moon rose like a prodigious pearl between the White Virgins. His chill light threw the surrounding trees into tangled patterns of black and silver and illumined the circle of stones known as the Coven and the tall Wish Stone in the centre.

A murmur and then a mutter rose from the men in the shadows as they saw two figures appear beneath the megalith; one was a tall man in the tattered uniform of River Garde, the other a girl in a white kirtle whose comely but modest features were framed between twin black braids. This was the inspired virgin they had risked so much to see — the Wish Maiden.

She stepped forward and raised her arms rather like a priest in a shrine giving the blessing after the Adoration.

'Hear me!' she cried. 'It is not long since I first stood here to proclaim my message that I am the one chosen to lead the men of the Wald to victory over the savages who desecrate our forest by the spilling of children's blood and the shaming of women. When I first spoke it was asked of me what I, a simple maid, could know of warfare and in truth I had to answer that I knew nothing but I had received a vision in which I was commanded to rally the dispossessed.

'Since then the truth of that vision has been proved. My lack of martial knowledge was made up for by the good soldier Wode who for many years served Lord Grimwald in River Garde. As you know, we have had success against the enemy. It is no longer just the bodies of rivermen and foresters that turn our trees into gibbets. Many is the head of a wolfman spiked by forest paths to strike fear into his fellows. And most of you will have heard how we burned the bridge across the River of Night.

'But such forays are not enough. We must strike into the heart of the horde, and for our plan we need you to join our band. Here is your chance to avenge your dead dears, your burned homes, your ravaged daughters . . .'

Serene Mother, if only it were that simple, thought Fulk, and his hands trembled as he gripped the haft of his axe. He no longer heard the Wish Maiden; once more hateful pictures rose from his memory to play the old human game of self-torture.

Since the death of his wife from the ill birthing of their daughter, Fulk the woodcutter had lived deep in the forest many leagues to the north of River Garde, so deep in the forest and so far from hamlet or village that when the Wolf Horde invaded the Wald he decided it was safer for him and his daughter Hıldi to remain where they were. He knew that the nomads, accustomed to roaming over their treeless steppe, had little liking for the woodlands and would not penetrate them unless they were confident of slaughter and loot for their pains.

And while most of the Walk folk abandoned their homes, Fulk and Hildi continued their usual life. Now, poised on the brink of womanhood, she tended their timber-built cottage as well as any goodwife, and she was so merry that she kept his spirits high when others

125

in his position would have brooded on the injustice of life. But since the invasion he never ventured far from home, and most of the day she could hear the pok-pok of his axe.

Over the last few days a change had come over the girl which greatly perplexed Fulk. He knew the time must have arrived when there was much that he should explain to her yet he could not find the right words. It was a woman's task to explain womanly things. How could he, a simple woodcutter, tell his beloved daughter about mating without sounding coarse, and disgusting her? And yet if he did not the shock of the change from girl to woman could be equally alarming if she did not know what to expect.

While she brooded or laughed and joked unnaturally he found no answer to his dilemma. Each day he swung his heavy axe as though he had anger against the innocent trees he cut and tried to think of the right sentences to tell her when he returned home. But when he ducked his head to enter the door the words fled from his mind and he found solace in using his whetstone.

It was the day before yesterday when the world that Fulk had created for himself and Hildi in the deep forest had come to a sudden end. As usual he had risen with the sun and at the cottage door she had handed him the home-baked bread and the home-curdled cheese just as she had a thousand times. And he kissed her as he had a thousand times and strode off with his axe on his shoulder, singing under his breath about snow-white roses that grew underneath a cottage window.

It was noon when he sat on the trunk of a tree he had just brought down to eat the bread and cheese when a ragged stranger emerged into the glade.

'Greeting if you come with a good heart,' he said in the traditional welcome of the forest folk.

'My heart may be good but my belly be empty,' replied the stranger. His beard was as matted as his hair and his eyes had a feverish glitter.

'Then eat,' said Fulk.

Without a word the man devoured the bread and cheese and then spoke his gratitude. 'I had forgotten the taste of good bread so long have I lived on berries which turn my fundament into a sluice.'

'You have come from the south?'

'Ay. I was a tanner until the Wolf Horde sacked my hamlet and I took to the woods. Been working my way north since.'

'Then you will find it safe here,' said Fulk. 'It is too far from River Garde for those plainsmen to venture.'

The tanner gave a bitter laugh.

'If you think that you are deluding yourself. Often during the last week I have hidden up trees or lain in bracken to escape bands of wolfmen. They spread further and further in search of loot and young slaves. I could not believe it when I heard your axe blows and then saw you sitting as calm as though Grimwald still ruled in River Garde.'

'They are close?'

The fugitive nodded.

'They are all around us.'

'Then I must go to my home . . . to my daughter. Good luck, tanner.'

Fulk hurried through the trees, his heart uneasy. He blamed himself for putting his daughter in danger. He had been so sure that they were safe in this remote tract of forest, but now it seemed he might have been in terrible error. It was with relief that he strode into the clearing in which his cottage stood looking as neat and normal as ever. The flowers that his daughter had planted bobbed brightly and her caged bird sang so blithely it must have forgotten its long-lost freedom.

He called her name, expecting her to come to the door with a smile of surprise on her face at his unexpected appearance. But his call died away among the trees and when he hurried indoors he found no sign of her but saw that the kitchen crocks had not been cleaned from breakfast.

Anxiously he looked about for some sign, and then noticed that her basket was missing. She must have taken it to gather mushrooms or pick wild apples.

Outside he set out on a trail which he guessed she was likely to have followed but he did not call her name again for fear there might be marauders within earshot.

Serene Mother of the Forest, may she be safe, he prayed mentally as brambles clutched his leggings as though eager to hold him back and slender branches sprang into his face. He felt choked by a panic that he had not known since the day he had heard his wife shriek above the mumbling of the midwife.

He plunged through a screen of bushes into a small grove where in the past Hildi had come to pick ripe redberries — and for a moment his heartbeat faltered.

She lay as though asleep on a bank of soft ferns. Her long hair covered part of her face so that he could not see whether she was unconscious or dead. Her skirt was round her waist and her legs lay wide revealing dark down that he had not ever imagined in connection with his little girl. As the blood surged through his arteries and his face burned crimson at the sight of her

128

semi-nudity, he felt a voyeur's guilt but this was immediately replaced with despair.

She had been raped, but was she alive?

His question was answered as her unbuttoned bodice rose and fell and she sighed as though in sleep . . .

Until that moment his eyes had noticed nothing but her spreadeagled body, now he saw that she was not alone.

Deep both in shade and fern lay another, a young man with black hair cut straight across his forehead and features which, while undeniably pleasant, bore the broad-cheeked cast of a nomad. His wolf-fur jacket was open, his breeches undone and his arm was outstretched through the fronds so that his fingertips rested on Hildi's palm.

A heartbeat later Fulk stood above him, his axe raised for the stroke that would split the smile of the barbarian who lay asleep after his foul crime.

Before he could deliver the blow his daughter leapt up beside him, her hand caught the sweat-polished oak of the axe haft.

'No, Father, no!' she screamed.

Fulk lowered the axe and gazed at her in bewilderment, relieved that she was unhurt but uncomprehending her words.

'Turn away,' he muttered. 'It will take but one stroke.'

'Father, Father, you do not understand!'

On his bed of fern the young nomad opened his yellow eyes. For a moment his lips curved into a smile at the sight of the girl, but only for a moment as the tall form of Fulk came into focus. He jerked into a sitting position and pushed himself further back into the fern, desperate to get clear of the heavy axehead which flashed in a sunbeam slanting through a gap in the overhanging foliage.

The woodcutter tried to raise the axe again but his daughter clung to it with both hands.

'He has done nothing wrong,' she cried. 'I love him. We love each other.'

Fulk stepped back in sickened astonishment.

'You have given yourself to . . . to *that*?'

'I love him,' she repeated stubbornly. 'He is not as you think. He is kind . . .'

'But how . . . ?'

'We met some days ago when I went along the path to pick redberries. He was lost in the woods.'

'And each day, while I have been at work, you and he have been coupling?' Fulk's rage was terrible.

'If you wish to call it that. Some might have a more gentle word for it because he is the love of my life, and it matters not where he comes from. All we want is to be together.'

'My daughter . . . with a beast!' Fulk breathed, and tears of shame coursed down his tanned cheeks. He shook the girl free and raised the axe but the nomad having wrenched his belt tight through its buckle leapt to his feet. He reached out his hand to the girl who sprang forward to grasp it and together they fled through swishing ferns.

Fulk raced after them to the edge of the glade where a root caught his foot and hurled him to the ground. The skin of his forehead was rasped away by the rough bark of the tree and for several minutes he sprawled before it dazed and bloody. Then he wearily set off through the trees in futile search for the fugitives. It seemed his hatred for the nomad was matched by that for his lewd daughter who surrendered her maidenhead to the first young male who had come her way — and not even a youth of the Wald but a shape-changing barbarian!

For the rest of the day and all through the night Fulk blundered about the forest, anger roaring in his brain to a point of madness. But the only living creatures he found were squirrels who watched him with wide eyes from the high branches and deer who fled down their secret trails.

The sun was high on her path the next day when he stumbled back to his cottage to find it a pile of smoking embers.

The tanner's warning had not been false. A marauding band of the enemy had chanced upon it while he was plunging like a madman after the hapless couple. As a matter of course they had looted it and then set the thatch alight. One glance was enough to tell Fulk there was nothing left to be retrieved. He put his axe over his shoulder and began the long journey south, knowing that all he wanted from now on was to kill wolfmen. Of his daughter he dared not think.

Now he returned to the present, to the clear voice of the maid as she stood dwarfed by the Wish Stone exhorting the men of the forest to join her band. Some, having seen that this person who had become a living legend was no more than a slip of a girl, walked half-ashamedly into the forest but several approached her and the tall man beside her. Leading them was Fulk.

'You look a likely warrior,' she greeted him. 'Will you follow the Wish Maiden into battle?'

He nodded.

'All I want is to hew the barbarians as I once hewed trees,' Fulk declared.

The soldier Wode looked appraisingly at his

powerful frame, his arms with muscles swelling like ropes beneath bronzed skin and the great axe which gleamed cold in the moonlight.

'Welcome, woodcutter,' he said. 'The Wish Maiden and I have been waiting for one such as you.'

THIRTEEN
The Burden of the Years

All the long day and all the long next day the Pilgrims toiled along the upward path that wound ever deeper into the Mountains of the Moon. Although recovered from their awakening debauch, the warriors appeared to find the carrying of Princess Livia's litter increasingly arduous. Times taken between the changing of bearers became steadily shorter, but Krispin and Alwald and their companions were so immersed in their own thoughts that they paid little attention to the men marching behind them or to Tumbrul who stumped on ahead.

After the twilight of the Shadow Realm and the perpetual night of the caverns, the clear mountain light and vivid blue of the sky, emphasized by the dazzling purity of the snowy peaks towering ahead of them, was joy to the travellers. Those who had sought the sleeping Princess strode forward in the renewed belief that, having brought her from her resting place, the quest would soon be completed — provided that the peculiar creature Tumbrul had not misled them.

What would happen when their obligations were fulfilled was something that none could predict; they knew what they wanted but how this might be achieved was a different matter. Alwald's wish was to return to the remote Vale of Mabalon and the Lady Demara; equally Krispin wanted nothing more than to go back to the High Wald and the girl who meant the most in his life, and at this stage both young men tended to ignore the fact that the whole breadth of the kingdom separated them from those they loved.

Gambal's thinking was much sharper than that of the others. He pondered on the possibilities that would be presented if Princess Livia did ascend the Empty Throne of Ythan. As time blurred the outlines of what had really happened in her chamber he might yet profit from the fact that it was his knife blow that had saved Her Highness's life, and surely the least he could claim for such an action would be re-instatement as Revel Master in the Citadel. When he earned the enmity of his three fellow questers and had then plunged the blade into the heart of the Regent's agent he'd had no thought of the future. At that moment there was no future, only the present dedicated to avenging his lost Lorelle.

When Dikon had fired the crossbow in his death throes and the precious water from the Wells of Ythan had ebbed away, his moment of elation was followed by a sense of anti-climax. The revenge he had dreamed of since they had left the Domain of Olam was no longer something to be looked forward to, no longer a thought to inwardly cherish but something that was over and which the tyrant Time would take further and further from him just as it remorselessly distanced him from the presence of Lorelle. But now, walking painfully up a stony path in this awesome region beyond Ythan's furthermost frontier, he experienced the return of his old ego – the Gambal who in Danaak had escaped the horrors of the subterranean slaughterhouse into which he had been sold as a young boy.

Now he recalled with bitter satisfactoin how by his wits alone he had replaced old Wilk as Revel Master and then had won the confidence of the Regent himself. He was suddenly confident that those wits would serve him as well in a future that was full of possibilities. The first step was to re-establish his old footing with his companions whose goodwill might be useful, for while the destruction of the Witchfinder had won their grudging respect it had not done anything to renew their old comradeship. He began to address his nimble mind to this problem.

'And what will you do when the quest is over?' Tana asked Ognam as she walked beside him with aching limbs and a determined smile. Ever since they had emerged from the great doorway set in the pylon she had contrived to be close to him. With his natural kindliness overcoming the antipathy that replaced his obsessive love for her following his sighting of the crystal bird, the jongleur humoured her and was now carrying her pack with his own.

'I know not,' he replied. 'Firstly, the quest may be further from ending than we guess, and secondly I have reached the stage in my life when the future is of far less importance than the present. At the moment I am content to put one foot after the other.'

He became thoughtful for a moment as he remembered the sense of peace that the vision of the wondrous bird had given him, and how the things he had striven for in his vagabond career had suddenly become as petty as the playthings of childhood when recalled in the mature years.

'But Ognam, you must have some idea of what you want,' Tana persisted.

He shook his head as though coming out of a reverie.

'I expect life will go on as before,' he said with a smile. 'The open road. Singing for my supper. A comic turn at village weddings, a tumbling act at carnivals until my joints get too stiff . . .'

'Oh, Ognam, that sounds dreadful.'

'Not to a jongleur, lady. Ythan is a place without joy, and if I can win a smile or a laugh or even an amused jeer, it is a tiny victory against the shadow . . .'

'But surely that may change with the return of the Princess,' Tana interjected. 'And what has happened to your dream of becoming a poet again? I still remember the verses you gave me that night in Haven.'

'Mere doggerel,' Ognam murmured.

'You cannot say that. I know that you meant them heartfully then − would that you meant them now.' She sighed. 'I know I hurt you after we left The Mage's Tower. After unmeasured time in my lonely prison I became intoxicated by freedom, by space, by the people on the *Amber Star*, and I felt like a young girl again with nothing in her head but dancing and foolishness and − yes, I admit it − flirting, but it was a passing thing. Ognam . . .' Her tone became tinged with anger. '. . . you should have realized that and been patient if you had any understanding of me at all, if you really cared for me.'

Ognam, remembering how his passion for the beautiful raven-haired girl had sent him wading into a mere in search of oblivion, was filled with an impulse to laugh followed by a sense of sadness for lost hopes.

The land of the might-have-been is a doleful land to contemplate, he thought and was relieved when a shout from the rear halted both the party and his musings.

'Ho, Lord Alwald, stop for the love of the Mother,' Barlak called. The companions turned and realized by the distance separating them that the warriors carrying the Princess's canopied litter had halted several minutes earlier while they had continued to ascend the track. The litter had been put down and the bearers appeared to be standing in a circle.

Sensing from the tone of Barlak's voice that something was greatly amiss Krispin and Alwald hurried back and pushed aside men who stood as though they had been magicked into statues. Before Krispin looked down at what lay in the centre of the circle he was startled by the expressions on the faces of the warriors opposite him, men whose whole lives had been the profession of arms and who must have experienced the shock of battle many times. But now there were only expressions of fear and revulsion on their hardened features. Then Krispin looked down and saw for himself.

On the ground lay a warrior who Krispin knew by the nickname of Firewort, a tall muscular man whose beard flowing over his breastplate had been of a redness that put Krispin's auburn locks to shame; now it was ash grey. His huge hands, still gripping the haft of his war axe, appeared to have lost their flesh so that it was fingers of little more than bone that encircled the polished wood. And his face . . .

Serene Mother! Krispin's inner voice exclaimed. *What has happened to his face?*

The once luxuriant hair above his brow was now no more than straggling white tufts, the brow itself was etched with furrows that seemed bone deep. Eyes that were of piercing blue when Krispin last saw them had become glaucous while the skin of the face was wrinkled like that of someone who had lived far too long beyond the mortal span.

The withered lips drew back and through a web of mucus the man tried to speak but all he achieved was a pitiful babbling. And, even as his fellows watched, the ageing process continued before their eyes; lines deepened, flesh shrunk, the skeletal hands lost their grip on the axe haft and waved in pathetic supplication. From the throat came an agonized rasping as the bony chest rose and fell in a desperate struggle for air.

Several of the men watching made the Sign of the Mother and their eyes turned from the object at their feet to Barlak with an unspoken question. For a moment he tried to avoid their gaze. Then one whispered, 'As leader you have shown such mercy on the battlefield.'

Barlak nodded reluctantly, drew his sword from its wooden scabbard and stepped forward. Krispin and Alwald turned away from the grotesque scene, but Barlak did not need to bring down his blade on the neck of his comrade. The heaving chest was suddenly still, the rasping ceased and with a tremor the remains of the warrior lay still, opaque eyes turned sightlessly to the sky.

For long moments there was silence, then Barlak said, 'The hundred years he lay in the cavern have overtaken him . . .'

'But the sorcery!' muttered one of the men.

'It would seem the sorcery is losing its power,' Barlak continued. 'Have we not felt unnaturally weary this day.' He looked at the back of his hand, then held it up. 'It was not mottled like this when I awoke this morning. We are all ageing, my friends. Mayhap the fate of Firewort will be the fate of us all.'

'Should we not return to the cavern, perhaps the sorcery remains strong there,' said a warrior who, like the others, was scrutinizing his hands.

'There was no mention of this when we made our agreement in Haven,' said another.

'Ay. What about the promise we were given?'

'Nothing is certain in the world, not even sorcery it seems,' Barlak answered. 'What matters is that we made a vow. We must be true to it for as long as we are able for we have little left except our honour.'

'What about the honour of the sorcerer?'

'I cannot answer for him,' said Barlak. 'I have always been a simple soldier and I know naught of gramarye but I do know that I made an oath and it is still my duty to serve Princess Livia. I shall carry her litter until the Dark Maid greets me, and I only pray the Mother that Her Highness shall reach the Wells before that happens. Together in the past we have faced barbarians and outcasts and corsairs for the honour of the Sun-in-Splendour Company and the Royal House of Ythan, let us attempt this final act for the Princess with equal honour.'

'Well said,' muttered one man. 'Better to die full-harnessed in the open than skulking in a cave.'

'Then let us go to it,' said another, 'There is white in your beards I did not notice before and I feel the weight of years on my back.'

The companions stood apart and watched while the warriors built a cairn of stones over the desiccated remains of their comrade. His axe and helmet were left on the topmost stone and then the Princess's litter was raised once more but the men could not stop themselves taking furtive glances at the backs of their hands and at the faces of their fellows.

For the rest of the day the party continued its slow ascent into the mountains. Although none of the warriors suffered anything as dramatic as the fate that overtook Firewort there was no doubt that they were visibly ageing. From one hour to the next their spines bowed and wrinkles spread, and before long it was necessary for the travellers to help them to carry the litter. Yet though they felt the ebbing of their strength they kept grimly to their task, even the most enfeebled pathetically grasping the litter handles in order to keep their vow to the last.

When the sky turned to amethyst and the mountain snows were momentarily dyed cerise by the sun before she descended out of view, the party halted gratefully at the entrance to a pass between two soaring peaks. The warriors collapsed with their backs against cold rock, too weary to open their packs for food, and it was only after Krispin had coaxed a meagre fire into life and a leather wine bottle had circulated that they stirred themselves to eat.

'I have heard that you can make music with your staff, Master Ognam,' said Barlak. 'We would take it as a favour if you would pipe for us.'

The other warriors nodded, their heads now grey, white or bald.

'It is a long time since we heard a merry tune,' said one. 'And I'll wager we are not likely to hear one again unless the Dark Maid sings us a lullaby as some say when she comes for children.'

There was laughter at his words.

Ognam picked up his staff that was decorated with a replica of his own head at one end. This staff, which had been presented to him when he joined the Guild of Jongleurs long ago, was hollowed and pierced with holes like a pipe. Soon his fingers were twinkling over them to produce a tune so lively that to everyone's astonishment Tumbrul jumped to his feet and began a stamping dance that became so wild it took him into the stick fire and for a moment he cavorted amid a swirl of sparks.

The warriors tapped their gnarled fingers to Ognam's rhythms and Tana gazed at him with admiration shining in her eyes. Then, as the fire burned down, he changed his style to play a simple melody that was both melancholic and tranquil. When the last notes died away Barlak said, 'Play no more, for I would sleep with that music in my head and if it is to be the last I hear it will be well enough.'

The others muttered agreement and Barlak continued, 'It makes me look back and wonder at the passing of the years and the things I left undone. There will be no great monument to such as we, no lines about us in bards' lays, there are no women to weep at our passing . . . and yet, by the Serene Mother, we have seen wonders that few men have witnessed and we have kept faith.'

'Ay!' chorused the others. They turned to each other

and clasped tremulous hands and then rolled themselves in their blankets. When the dawn came three did not rise at Barlak's quavering command for them to fall in.

FOURTEEN

'Alas,
My Daughter!'

The tunnel ended in a blank wall. To the three men who had followed it through the Citadel's doleful nether world it seemed like the final penalty for incurring the wrath of the Regent.

The leader of the trio was Mandal, once the Commander of the Host, who had followed his master's orders to catapult plague victims into the besieged city of Thaan. This action had brought about the end of the heretics but the infection had also destroyed the Regent's army with the result Mandal was disgraced and consigned to a lingering death in the Cage mounted high on the outer wall of the Citadel.

With him was old Leodore, who had engineered Mandal's escape from the humiliating contrivance in which the Regent's dying enemies became spectacles for the mob below. At the behest of the Regent Leodore the Alchemist had worked in secret at his arcane calling, but after he had achieved the greatest goal in alchemy, the creation of artificial life in the form of a pair of homunculi, he too had earned his master's fatal displeasure.

Supported by these two was Lord Odo whom they had literally plucked from the dungeon he had shared with rats and madness since his attempt to seize control of the kingdom. Foolishly he had endeavoured to win the Companions of the Rose to his cause and force the Regent to drink a poison draught without reckoning on the fanatical loyalty of the Companions. They had kept the Regent informed of the plot from its inception to the point when Odo's moment of triumph turned to one of terror and left him desperately babbling the names of his fellow conspirators.

'Is there no way forward?' asked Leodore in a toneless voice.

He was stricken with grief at the loss of the creature he called Titi, the female homunculus for whose sake he had deceived the Regent. Blood had been her nourishment and it was blood she craved when she plunged into Lord Odo's dungeon to sink her spike teeth into the neck of a turnkey. But the violent death throes of her victim and Odo's insane screaming had terrified her and, unable to climb up to the open grating by which she had entered, she vanished through the dungeon doorway into the Stygian night of the lowest galleries.

Leodore would have leapt down and followed her had not Mandal held him back.

'There is nothing you can do,' he hissed. 'You could not find it — her — in the dark corridors and you would be captured within minutes.'

Sobs racked the old man but he knew that Mandal spoke the truth. After the Regent had ordered the sealing of the entrance to his tower he had slowly starved and he knew that he no longer possessed the strength to climb down into the dungeon let alone chase after the panic-stricken creature.

Meanwhile in the foul cell below, Lord Odo had continued his clamour.

'Wait, we do not want them searching for us,' muttered Mandal. He lowered himself to the sodden straw below, pushed the oaken door back into place and then shot its massive iron bolt. Seizing the turnkey's lanthorn, he had paused to look at the crouched figure of Lord Odo chained to a central pillar in such a way that it was not possible for him to stand upright or to sit down. Hardly anyone of the Regent's court would have recognized the aristocrat who had been a member of the Regent's Council; his liced hair hung to his waist and, beneath the rags that encircled his loins, his shanks were covered with ordure and festering sores resulting from the bites of prison rats.

Mandal was struck by the thought that if they managed to reach the outside world Lord Odo might be of some value. The notion was vague and he did not have time to pursue it; it was an instinct rather than a plan but he often acted on instinct.

Taking up the gaoler's keys he tried them one after another in the lock that held Odo's chains to the massive staple set in the stone column. The fourth fitted and a moment later the prisoner, deprived of support, fell to the straw screaming his fear of the rats that infested it.

Mandal threw the gaoler's cloak over his shoulders, then propped the turnkey against the pillar and encircled him with the chains so that nothing would seem amiss in the dark cell if a guard was to glance through the spyhole.

'Help me lift him up,' Mandal called to Leodore

and, startled by the fact that Odo weighed little more
than a half-grown child, he raised him until the
alchemist was able to help drag him into the passage
above. Mandal passed up the lanthorn, heaved himself
up through the aperture and replaced the rusted grille.

'I fear there is little that can be done for him,' said
Leodore as Odo leaned against the rough-hewn wall
and whimpered to himself.

'But mayhap he can do something for us,' replied
Mandal. 'Let us press on.'

He moved down the passage supporting the docile
prisoner.

For a long moment Leodore remained by the grille.
He felt his old heart was breaking at the loss of Titi
and he had no wish for Mandal to see the tears that
were creeping down his cheeks. He knew that to
Mandal the homunculus was an abomination; no one
could ever understand what her creation – and that
of the male whom the Regent had hurled into the fire
– had meant to him. By creating these creatures from
his elixir he had fulfilled his greatest ambition as an
alchemist, indeed he had achieved what members of
his esoteric profession had attempted for generations
without success.

What he had not expected after their fashioning was
the sentiment he felt for them. Never having fathered
children, Leodore regarded them with a father's eye
and after the death of the male he was determined that
the female should survive. But by secretly giving her
the elixir he had prepared for the ailing Regent he
sacrificed everything. And now the only homunculus
in the world was lost in the labyrinthine hell below the
Citadel. For a while she might exist on the blood of
some of the human denizens of this subterranean

146

world but in the end it must be her fate to be hunted down by dungeon guards. And what made it more pitiable was that despite being a parody of humanity she knew human emotions – especially fear.

'Alas, my daughter!' he murmured.

Mandal had turned and hissed for him to follow and, like a somnambulist, Leodore obeyed.

Sometime later they reached the wall of ashlar marking the end of the passage.

'There must be a reason for this,' Mandal mused after the initial shock. 'No one would go to the trouble of cutting a passage of this length if it were not to lead somewhere.'

He held up the lanthorn to examine the slabs that made up the roofing. The one directly above him was not of the usual roughly trimmed stone but smooth marble. Leaving Leodore to support Lord Odo, he pushed against one end and slowly, finger-breadth by finger-breadth, it began to tilt on an unseen pivot. The more he pushed, the counterbalancing of the slab made it easier and suddenly it swung upwards like a trapdoor.

Cold air struck Mandal in the face as he struggled to raise himself through the opening.

On his entry into the chamber above he saw he was in an oblong room with polished walls lit by coloured light shining through stained crystal set in the dome. In the centre of the chamber was an open sarcophagus and he realized he had entered a tomb.

It seems I have stumbled from one nightmare into another, thought Mandal. He bent over the trapdoor and called to Leodore to help him lift Lord Odo through. When the skeletal figure appeared he rolled

147

himself into a ball, murmuring softly about rats and someone named Urwen.

Leodore followed and Mandal lowered the slab back into place.

It was then that Mandal became aware of two ragged figures crouched in shadow behind the sarcophagus, a boy and a girl who were about to enter young adulthood. He was handsome, she pretty and both had long unkempt hair. On being noticed the girl gave a cry. And no wonder! With his face covered with grime and his clothing stained with the blood of the warder, Mandal knew he must appear like some graveyard stalker rising from a crypt, and as for Odo . . .

'Be not alarmed, I am no vampire,' he said soothingly. 'Nor is there any need for that, young sir,' he added as he saw that the boy held a dagger. 'I pray you tell me where I have emerged.'

'In our tomb,' said the girl who was partly reassured by hearing a human voice issue from the apparition.

'In the City of the Dead,' added the boy. 'If you have come to rob we have nothing of worth for you, and if you have come for her you will feel my blade in your cod.'

'The City of the Dead,' repeated Mandal showing no concern for the boy's words. 'So you must be ghouls?'

The pair nodded reluctantly.

'Then have no fear,' Mandal continued. 'I am an outcast like yourselves. I have escaped from the Citadel by means of a forgotten escape tunnel that comes out here. Before that I was in the Cage.'

'It was you I saw one day when I went into the city,' said the boy. 'You were once Commander of the Host.'

Mandal nodded.

'No more. I fell foul of our Lord Regent for following his orders at Thaan. Now I am a fugitive with these two friends who, like me, know what it is to suffer at the hands of our master.'

'Are you hurt?' asked the girl.

'The blood? It is not mine but that of a turnkey I am thankful to say.'

The boy nodded to the girl. The bloody proof of a slain dungeon keeper reassured him that the stranger was on the same side of the Regent's law as himself.

'I am Garn and this is Aldis,' he said, putting away the dagger he had taken from Murt when they first entered the necropolis.

'Who are your friends?'

'One is ill from being in the dungeons too long and he wanders in his wits.'

Garn laughed.

'That is nothing unusual in the City of the Dead,' he said. 'We just laugh and tease them, and run from those who have killing rages. We seal them up in their tombs if we can.'

'You need food,' said Aldis. 'You are welcome to what we have.'

'My thanks. Even a few crusts would be as welcome as a banquet,' replied Mandal.

'We can do a little better than that.' And from a box in a corner the girl brought out bread, cheese, dried fish, smoked meat and fruit which she divided on to rough platters. And with a triumphant grin Garn produced a flask of wine.

'It *is* a banquet,' said Mandal. 'Never has food looked so delicious. How . . . ?'

'Garn brings it,' said Aldis proudly. 'At dawn he

goes beyond the wall and he steals from the stalls in the caravanserai.'

'It is safest there,' said the boy. 'There is so much bustle that I am less likely to be noticed. I have never lived so well as I have here.'

'It is the first home I have ever had,' added the girl simply. Mandal marvelled at the different aspects of life he had encountered since his fall from favour, and his mind went back to the old witch with whom he had shared the Cage.

When Aldis served the food, Mandal could not restrain himself from snatching his share but Leodore soaked some bread in wine and gently fed it to Lord Odo before he ate.

'I am grateful to you but why have you treated us so well?' said Mandal when he could eat no more.

'In the City of the Dead outcasts are brothers,' said Aldis.

'And you were Commander of the Host,' said Garn. 'It would not be unlikely for you to revenge yourself upon the Regent for there are many who would follow you in revolt. And if you should succeed you might remember this day.'

'You have wisdom beyond your years,' said Mandal. 'And should that come to pass you will not be forgotten, my word upon it. We need shelter until the old man regains some wit and strength. He was a great noble whose disappearance was a mystery, and if I can secretly restore him to his family I may receive the help I need.'

'Nearby is an empty vault where you can stay and I shall bring you food,' said Garn.

'Tell me about the City of the Dead,' Mandal said as he savoured the wine which though sour was the best he had ever tasted.

'It is like a real city. The finest tombs were built on an avenue a league long, better than houses they must have been when the dead were still brought here. From this avenue run other avenues with tombs like this one, and from them run alleys where lesser folk were buried. In the old days there were gardens and trees but now everything is overgrown so that in parts it is like forest.'

He went on to tell about the many hundreds of outcasts and fugitives who had found their way into this haven to be nicknamed ghouls, and the thieves and cutpurses who used its hiding places and the rival bands that fought against each other and how there was a king of the city but he had not seen him. And he described how from time to time mounted guards would come from the Citadel to round up outcasts for the slave caravans or the Hall of Execution but few were caught because the soldiers feared the ghouls once they were within the necropolis and they would not leave the grand avenues.

'They try to stop us from going into Danaak by posting sling-bowmen at the gates but there are many secret ways through the high wall that was built all the way round the cemetery,' Garn explained.

'And tell me what news there is in the world since I was put in the Cage,' Mandal asked.

'It is said in the wineshops that the Regent may claim the Empty Throne for himself when he returns from his progress,' replied the boy. 'And it is told in the caravanserai that the Wolf Horde captured the town of Lasgaad and now they travel along the old caravan route to Danaak. Gossips say the army that could have routed them was lost at Thaan . . .'

'Or on its return in the Raven Pass,' muttered Mandal.

'. . . and how the only man who could have defeated the horde was Commander Mandal.'

'And yet I was jeered in the Cage.'

Garn laughed and said, 'And in the caravanserai I heard a tale I like very much. Some merchants saw a flying man. Yes! He had great wings and was heading south over a wilderness. What freedom!'

Book Two

When the bird of crystal flies
Across the world in summer skies . . .

When the hero's horn is sound
To wake the sleepers neath the ground . . .

When the prowling wolf is slain
Before he reaches Danaak's plain . . .

When the usurper would be crowned
And Ythan's Wells are double found . . .

Then will Ythan's path divide
For good or evil to decide
Which fate her future will unfold,
An age of shadow − or of gold.

— from *Prophecia*
by the Sage Omgarth

ONE
Ysldon

For two days the party continued to follow Tumbrul through passes and often along a path that was little more than a fault running across dizzy rock faces. For the last afternoon they struggled over a snowfield which exhausted the enfeebled warriors so much they could barely drag themselves along and several more died as the result of the unnatural old age which had fallen upon them. It was left to Krispin, Alwald, Ognam and Danya to carry the litter shoulder high to keep it clear of the snow — Gambal had not recovered sufficiently from the hurt the Witchfinder had inflicted upon him to take a turn.

When dusk gathered they found a place sheltered from the keening wind among great boulders that had rolled down from the peaks in bygone times. As they settled, Tumbrul, who had been scouting ahead, returned with his gash-like mouth set in a triumphant leer.

'I knew I was right, I knew I was right!' he chanted. 'What a wonderful guide am I. The valley we seek lies ahead. In the morning we will descend into it and there we will find the Wells and be freed of our vows.'

If he had expected acclaim he was disappointed. Everyone was too weary to be excited by his news and the most he got was quavered threats from the warriors that he had better be right or else . . .

There were no more sticks for a fire and no piping from Ognam; the travellers were eager only to roll up in their blankets and plunge into the sleep of exhaustion. Yet Barlak, now a rheum-eyed shadow of his old self, still ordered the least affected men into watches to stand guard over the Princess during the cold night.

When the sun rose the words of Tumbrul were remembered with more enthusiasm than they had received the night before, and once the bodies of two more warriors had been laid to rest among the rocks − there was no strength left for cairn-building − they set out after the dwarfish figure of their guide. By midmorning they came to the lip of a great valley. Its walls were of sheer rock that rose towards three great peaks rearing above it like snow-draped sentinels. Below them, black eagles glided on limpid air but what seemed so remarkable was that the flat floor of the valley was covered with variegated greens of grass and foliage. And as the travellers stood lost for words they felt the valley's warm and fragrant air caressing their faces.

'If the Wells do truly contain the Water of Life then this is surely where they are,' Ognam murmured.

'I believe you to be right, Sir Jongleur,' said Gambal so pleasantly that Ognam gave him a surprised glance. 'It is beyond natural law for such a fertile enclave to exist so high amid ice-bound ranges so there must be a mystic element here.'

'Are we going to stand and look all day or are we going to seek our destination?' Tumbrul demanded. 'I was told that there are two paths leading into the valley, one at the east end and one at the west. The eastern path is hazardous but the one at this end is much easier, no doubt because those who cut it knew that it led only in the direction of the Shadow Realm from whence Pilgrims might venture.'

'If you think this one is easy I should hate to have to go down the other,' muttered Krispin who had never lost his fear of heights. Seeing the expression on his face, Alwald gave him an ironical smile as much as to say, 'You may have played the hero in the past but look at you now!'

'Let us go down without delay,' quavered Barlak, 'for I fear my time is short.'

Tumbrul, his sack of treasure still over his shoulder, led them to where the path began. Cut in the rock, it appeared to be just wide enough for them to carry the litter and the questers wondered whether it had been hewn for such a purpose. The warriors, now two-thirds of their original number, shuffled down with trembling hands pressed against the rock wall to support themselves, followed by the rest of the party who prayed this would be the ending of the quest.

As they descended deeper into the valley they were conscious of a delightful sensation with every breath they took, a scent that the four questers had not experienced since they walked in the gardens of Olam. It was the green smell of growing things, grass and wild flowers and trees bearing blossom. And the air that bore this admix of perfumes grew warmer by the moment, bringing relief to the old men who had been in their prime a few days before.

After half an hour they reached the valley floor, stepping from the rock knee deep into grasses over which butterflies hovered in a silent gavotte. From a nearby copse came the silvern note of a bellbird.

'Paradise,' mumbled Barlak and it seemed that the wrinkles beneath his dim eyes were wet. 'Mayhap there was truth in the story of the Garden of Yth . . .'

'Heh, this is not time for fables,' Tumbrul scolded. 'Let us follow the path through those woods.'

Barlak tried unsuccessfully to straighten his bent back and, in a voice that briefly regained a hint of its old authority, he ordered, 'Form up and try to look like a royal bodyguard.'

His men, some using their weapons as crutches, shambled after Tumbrul while the travellers bearing the litter followed behind. Even as they walked through the insect-humming trees one of the escort dropped to his knees, his face a ghastly parody of age, and rolled dead into the ferns bordering the path.

'Close up,' Barlak cried in a cracked voice. The gap was filled and the strange procession continued at its funereal pace.

Before long the trees thinned out and the company saw before them a vast stretch of greensward in whose centre stood a magnificent terrace above which fountains sparkled amid rainbowed mist.

Alwald exclaimed in astonishment.

'We have seen it before!' marvelled Ognam. 'In the Wilderness of Gil!'

'Serene Mother, can it be the same?' Krispin murmured. 'How can that be?'

Gambal laughed.

'To think we drank from the Wells of Ythan and did not know it,' he said.

158

Bewildered and yet conscious of a rare dreamlike atmosphere about them, they advanced towards the steps that led to the opening in the balustrade. In the middle of the terrace, just as the questers remembered, pillars of brightly veined marble supported a cupola from whose shadow appeared an old man wearing a dark robe and a hat whose broad brim concealed most of his face. He leaned on a long staff and yet there was something about him that suggested that such support was not strictly necessary.

He advanced to the top of the steps and stood regarding the awed party.

'Pilgrims, welcome to the Wells of Ythan,' he greeted in a voice that was deep and clear and made the listeners feel that while it was the voice of one steeped in wisdom there was a thread of amusement in it. 'I have been long expecting you.'

'Master Ysldon!' cried Tumbrul and he threw himself on to his knees, the precious objects in his sack clashing as he did so.

Ysldon! thought Krispin. *Ysldon!*

It was a name he had heard uttered by The Mage, and it was not only the name that came back to him but the figure of Ysldon — the same figure that had appeared on the Amber Isle to save him from the disembodied spirit of Shath.

The old man smiled down at the grotesque little figure of the guide.

'Greetings, Master Tumbrul,' he said and, descending the steps, he walked to where the Princess's litter stood. He lifted the canopy curtains and gazed down at the young woman who lay as still as an image on a tomb.

'All is well,' he said, dropping the curtain. He turned

to Tumbrul. 'You have kept the covenant faithfully. You are free to go where you will with your reward.'

Tumbrul bowed his head in respectful acknowledgement.

'And you, Barlak,' the old man continued. 'I see you are returned to Time Present.'

'But not for long, Mesire Ysldon,' replied Barlak in a faint voice. 'As you see Time Past has caught up with us. Many of my company lie dead by the mountain trail and age weighs so heavily upon our shoulders that our lives can only be measured in hours. Yet we have escorted the Princess Livia as was agreed and if we can do no more it is not to our dishonour.'

The old man inclined his head.

'Be patient, my old heroes, while I have words with these Pilgrims who crossed Ythan and beyond, who have braved hardship and survived perils outside the belief of most men, to succeed where hundreds failed in reaching the Abode of the Sleeper, and bring her here to be awakened.' His low vibrant voice filled Krispin and Alwald with a warm sense of achievement unknown to them before this moment.

'Come and rest,' he said, gesturing for them to ascend the steps. One of the warriors was so unsteady on his legs that the old man gently took his arm and led the small procession the final few paces to the Wells of Ythan.

As he reached the top step, Krispin felt the hair at the nape of his neck rise as though recalling some incident from a previous reality. He really had seen the terrace with its fountains and pools and bubbling wells, its nymph-like statues pouring endless water from ewers and its satyr heads spouting water into sculptured bowls when he and his companions were near dead of thirst in the Wilderness of Gil. They had wakened to find it vanished and believed they had been granted a mystical experience, a miracle without explanation so special that afterwards they rarely found words to discuss it. Yet here were the same wells hundreds of leagues from the wilderness.

The Princess's litter was placed in the shade of the rotunda and all seated themselves on stone benches supported by carvings of fantastical beasts. The old man stood with his back to the sun, a silhouette with a thousand dancing prisms from a fountain making an aureole behind him.

'My name is Ysldon, the Guardian of the Wells, and long have I waited for this moment,' he began. 'Most of you have seen me before. You men from the Sun-in-Splendour Company knew me at the siege of Haven; you Pilgrims will remember me from the desert, and you and I, Krispin Toymaker, met again on an isle in the Cold Sea.

'And you have seen me in other guises that you did not recognize, but of that we will talk later. Suffice it to say that I have had full knowledge of the long and arduous trail that has led to what you believe is the conclusion of the quest.'

Alwald opened his mouth to say something but Ysldon held up his hand.

'All in good time, Lord Alwald,' he said. 'First hear me out. When you and Master Krispin left the Wald you understood that the object of your journeying was to discover the resting place of Princess Livia and revive her. Did you ever ponder on what would happen if you succeeded? Or were you content with the thought that once Livia drew breath you would be free to resume your lives again? Did you consider how the

161

Princess would be returned to her rightful throne?'

He fell silent. The only sound was the continuous splashing of water.

At last Alwald said, 'I suppose we thought that once the Princess was awakened — and most of the time it seemed unlikely we would ever find her — it would be the task of those dedicated to her cause, the followers of the Pilgrim Path, to see she regained her rightful place.'

'Excellent,' said Ysldon with a note of humour. 'And if you think that you were correct, where are the Pilgrims who will lead her to Danaak? The only Pilgrims I can see are sitting before me.'

Krispin felt his heart sink as he guessed what the Guardian was leading up to.

'Having come so far, having braved the Land of Blight, the dungeons of Danaak, the siege of Thaan, the underground river of Varah, the Desert of Akea, the Cold Sea and the Shadow Realm, it would be an evil joke if the quest ended in failure after all.'

'But how can that be?' asked Krispin, gesturing to the litter. 'We found the Princess and we brought her here to be revived. Is that not enough?'

'You know in your hearts that the quest does not end here,' replied Ysldon. 'The quest ends when that sleeping girl becomes Queen Livia of Ythan, and unless you agree to take her to those who would be her subjects there is no purpose in wakening her.'

Again he paused. From the elation of having found the Wells, a weariness fell upon the hearts of the companions. It seemed they were bound to a task that would never be ended.

'Your magicianship,' said Ognam bravely for there was an air of authority about the Guardian that did

162

not encourage argument, 'from what I have learned on my recent travels with Lord Alwald and Master Krispin I know you were famed as the greatest of sorcerers, indeed it was your dread seal that was on the flacon containing the Water of Life that we carried from The Mage's Tower to the Princess's resting place. And so to a simpleton like myself it seems that it would not be beyond your powers to magick Her Highness to Danaak in the twinkling of an eye and set her on her throne with her crown on her head and — and turn the Regent into a toad.'

Ysldon smiled a cold smile and shook his head.

'The last thing you are is a simpleton, Master Jongleur,' he declared. 'And I understand your desire for me to wave a wand or chant a spell for it to be as you say, but you do not understand the nature of magic. If it could be as you wish there would have been no need for The Enchantment or for the quest. Should you have the courage to continue along the Path, I shall explain much of what puzzles you now.'

The fountains splashed. The warriors drooped on their benches in deathly fatigue; the others waited for the inevitable question and only Gambal knew how he would answer — unless he accompanied the Princess to Danaak he had no hope of becoming Revel Master at her court. Ysldon began to speak of Ythan and the evils besetting it which the companions had experienced for themselves — treachery such as brought the Wolf Horde into the Wald in order to bring down the hereditary rule of Alwald's family, the extortion that forced good folk to become outcasts or slaves, the horrors of the dungeon hall and torture chamber, the Guild of Witchfinders employing terror to shackle men's spirit and the menace of a ruler who saw the Red Death as an ally.

'It was written long ago by the Sage Omgarth that at this time Ythan would have a choice of destinies,' Ysldon continued. 'It may follow the darkening path of the regency or turn to the path of goodwill with the return of the monarchy. The fate of the kingdom is poised in the balance and fate has given you the chance to weigh the scale against the tyrant. Your fellow Pilgrims living in secret throughout the kingdom would envy your opportunity to complete what you have valiantly achieved so far.'

He extended his hand to where Krispin and Alwald sat side by side and into the toymaker's mind came an image of razed Toyheim so real he could smell the smoke of burning houses. Into Alwald's mind swam a vision of the nomads surging across the River of Night after his father had been murdered by their werewolf king and as with Krispin the mental picture was stronger than the world about him. They returned to reality to hear Ysldon asking who would continue the quest by serving the Princess after she was restored to Time Present.

'What say you, Master Jongleur?'

'I will,' replied Ognam quietly.

'And I!' declared Gambal.

'And I,' sighed Alwald and Krispin in the same breath.

Ysldon nodded his satisfaction.

'In that case we need no longer delay,' he said. 'Lord Alwald and Master Krispin, it falls as your due to awaken the Princess. Take her and immerse her in yonder pool.'

They lifted her in her time-yellowed robe and

tenderly carried her to a pool lined with chalcedony
and down steps to the water that bubbled from a well
mouth in its centre. The others watched in silence,
even the aged warriors hobbled from their benches
to the edge, as Krispin holding her ankles and Alwald
supporting her shoulders lowered her into the water.
Her golden hair floated free about her face and then
at a word from Ysldon they allowed her to sink
beneath the surface.

TWO
The
Return

Danaak — once known as The Golden — lay in a haze
of summer heat. A languor had fallen upon the city
huddling about the enormous rock upon which the
Citadel raised its soaring towers. Its squares were
deserted; most of the boatmen who poled their high-
prowed craft on the river that dissected the city from
north to south dozed in the shade of graceful bridges,
the narrow passages between the gambrel-roofed
houses were no longer thronged and the noon gongs
of the shrines had a drowsy tone. On the ramparts
ringing the city, watchmen yawned openly and an
unusual quiet even hung over the caravanserai which
was the hub of the old trade routes radiating over the
kingdom.

In the City of the Dead, the old walled necropolis
that covered a quarter of Danaak's area, the outcasts
who normally sheltered in ornate mausoleums dozed
among the creepers that shrouded the vistas of sculpted
marble. It was not only the heat that produced this
languor but the knowledge that the Regent was still
away on his mysterious progress.

167

High in her apartments in the Citadel, Ythan's Lore Mistress the Lady Mandraga gazed at the mirror suspended between two pillars but, though the silvered crystal distorted her reflection into that of a beautiful young woman, her mind was lost in a maze of memory, of secret sorceries and the deadly intrigue that had brought the present Regent to power.

The present Regent . . . As she thought about him her involuntary sigh disturbed the incensed silence of her chamber. She did not need the reports of her spies to be aware of the curious change that had taken place in the city like the deceptive stillness before a tempest. She sensed that beneath its sullen surface flowed dangerous currents that would merge into a tide of revolt unless the Regent returned to demonstrate his authority and root out those who plotted against him.

The question that plagued the mind of the Lore Mistress was whether he would return whole, cured of the bane caused by Leodore's alchemic creature, or would the venom in his blood claim his life before he reached the mysterious Wells of Ythan. Of their existence the Lady Mandraga had no doubt but were the directions found in the Great Library of Thaan reliable?

So far the Witchfinders had done nothing to interfere with potential rebels; only names supplied by their army of informers had been recorded according to the instruction of the Regent before he departed on his 'progress'.

The Lady Mandraga had no idea how that 'progress' fared as it had been agreed no courier would return to fire speculation or give warning to conspirators. She could only wait, breaking the tedium with hired lovers when she was able to briefly resume the youthful form that appeared in her mirror thanks to her long and secret search for the Elixir of Life.

It was an almost imperceptible tremor in the air that roused the sentry at his post above the watergate of the Citadel, where the Green River emerged to flow through the rich orchards and pastures that lay to the south of the city. The airy vibration was repeated, then came at regular intervals like a drumbeat so distant it was felt rather than heard.

Could it be the drumbeat to which oarsmen heaved on their sweeps?

The man strained his ears until he was deafened by the roar of his own pulse but still he was aware of the rhythmic disturbance in the distance. He knew it was against the law for a merchant's barge or a passenger craft to use a rowers' drum, this method of maintaining speed over long distances was reserved for the black vessels of the Witchfinders and the Regent's barge. With his mind fixed on the traditional reward of a silver crown for the first sentry to alert the garrison to the return of the Regent — and a flogging if it proved to be a false alarm! — the man waited as long as he dared and then fearful that some other guard might recognize the far-off beat, he ran to his commanding officer.

Within minutes the tenor of Danaak's life changed completely. The plain yellow banners of Ythan broke out above every tower and iron ceremonial trumpets, so heavy and long they were mounted on tripods, began to blare a throaty fanfare of welcome. Not to be outdone Archpriest Mattan ordered Grand Johan, the bell of the capital's Great Shrine, to be rung in hypocritical jubilation. A detachment of Companions of the Rose clattered down to the quays with their red

169

surcoats flying and Witchfinders in their black robes were suddenly visible among the crowds that ancient custom forced into the streets.

'The Regent returns! The Regent returns!'

The crowd of idlers in the Square of Punishments forsook the free entertainment to run to the banks of the Green River.

'The Regent returns!'

As the words rolled over the City of the Dead its denizens woke from sun-sodden slumber to slink into crypt and mausoleum like ragged ghosts, for who could say what new dangers would come in the wake of Ythan's master.

'The Regent . . .'

Officials, merchants, burghers and courtiers who had waxed rich under the régime harkened to the clamour in their mansions and palaces lining the Green River, and in each luxurious residence there was the scurrying of menials as masters and mistresses adorned themselves to greet the dispenser of the favours they enjoyed. Flags were unfurled above their rooftops and outdoor braziers of incense were ignited to sweeten the air for their master.

'The Regent . . .'

The cry penetrated the stews and drinking dens, and in foul alleys strumpets and cut-purses winked at each other in anticipation of the business the official celebration would bring. In garret and cellar, men and women who had talked conspiracies felt their blood chill; it was one thing to champion freedom while the tyrant was away and another when he would be back in the Citadel with his élite guards, informers, assassins, Witchfinders, dungeon masters and executioners.

But all who heard the increasing clamour, whether idealistic young scholar or fawning official, wondered the same thing — what would the Regent's barge be bearing? Before his departure, wild rumours had circulated about his health — he had been touched by the Red Death, he had lost his wits, he had turned into a blood-drinker . . . Who or what would be returning to rule their lives: a moribund cripple, a madman, a dhrul?

When the watchman on the Citaldel's highest tower saw a procession of craft appear round a distant bend in the river and recognized the Regent's gonfalon above the bows of the leading boat he gave a signal which was followed by the releasing of hundreds of vividly dyed doves. As they swirled above the city like a whirlwind of confetti, the Lady Mandraga entered her palanquin and, escorted by a dozen Companions of the Rose, was borne to the old royal quay where the nervous successor to Gambal supervised the unrolling of carpets. Musicians prepared for the traditional paean of welcome by tuning lyres and rebecks, testing tabors and timbals and blowing notes on bombardons, serpents and flageolets.

Almost as soon as Mandraga emerged from her curtained litter, the Witchfinder-General descended from his black coach and the Archpriest appeared. Beneath the border of his golden robes his bare feet proclaimed holy humility as he followed a path of rosewater sprinkled by handsome neophytes.

Both men inclined their heads to the Lore Mistress as custom demanded and beneath her veil her bloodless lips twitched in response.

'How you would like to see another in my place,' she murmured and her thoughts turned uneasily to the flame-haired spy Urwen who, since the Regent's illness, had become both his mistress and nurse.

A distant murmur of voices suddenly increased to low thunder and the leading barge glided between the crowded quays lining the river banks. As it drew closer, the Lore Mistress gave a sigh of relief as she saw the Regent standing boldly beneath his fluttering standard in the prow. There was no trace of the sunken cheeks and ashen skin that she remembered from his departure and the voluminous cloak that he had worn to hide the swathed monstrosity that had been his arm was thrown back to allow him to raise *both* arms as though invoking a blessing – or curse – upon those crowding the banks.

The initial shouting died to an awed silence as the Regent's state of health became clear. Now there would be no more rumours of cursed maladies, no suggestion that he was suffering the ravages of silver skin or blood bane – if anything he appeared more robust than before. For this the Lady Mandraga felt an uncharacteristic sense of gratitude, tempered by the sight of Urwen standing behind the Regent with Captain Bors.

The following reception afforded the Regent, in which the Lore Mistress played her ritualistic role with amazing vitality for one of her years, took over an hour. Then, when he had embraced the members of the Regent's Council, saluted the dignitaries in order of importance, received the blessing of the Archpriest and accepted the traditional scroll of allegiance from the Guild of Mendicants he muttered two words to the Witchfinder-General, 'Arrest them.'

Moments later the Witchfinder-General hurried from the sombre Great Hall to issue his instructions

172

and Witchfinders, escorted by men from the dreaded Nightwatch Company, moved through the city in search of those whom spies and informers had reported for subversive sentiment or activity.

With the ceremonial completed the Regent retired to his apartments where he waited with Urwen for the arrival of the Lady Mandraga. There was a restlessness about him that reflected his regained strength; he paced the chamber with a goblet of black Ronimar wine in his hand while Urwen reclined on an ivory couch and watched him with possessive eyes.

When the Companion of the Rose guarding his door admitted the Lore Mistress, Urwen only half rose to greet her, a lack of courtesy that was not overlooked by the old woman who was reassured by the ex-spy's lack of subtlety.

'I am overjoyed that you found the Wells and that their water is still the panacea,' she told the Regent as she seated herself and rested her withered hands on the crosspiece of her crutch. 'Already I hear there is talk of a miracle in the city.'

'The shrines will be quick to exploit it,' he said, 'but it can do no harm, on the contrary. The water was in fact miraculous beyond belief.'

'And you have brought me the promised flask?'

'I regret it was not possible.'

Mandraga uttered an imprecation that made Urwen flinch. The Regent explained how they had awoken to find that the Wells and their mysterious custodian had vanished. As he spoke she fought to hide the disappointment seething within her and was haunted by the thought he might be lying to her.

'And now, lady, tell me everything that has taken

place since my departure,' he concluded. 'What of the Pilgrims?'

Mandraga glanced in Urwen's direction.

'She stays,' said the Regent shortly. 'As the regency is to become a monarchy she must be aware of everything if she is to play a part in it.'

To the old woman his words seemed to hang in the perfumed air as she realized their underlying meaning.

So Ythan is to have a queen as well as a king, she thought. *And doubtless you see the role superior to that of Lore Mistress but I may yet have a surprise for you, Lady Urwen.*

Aloud she said formally, 'As you wish, Lord Regent. Did you hear news of the Wolf Horde on your return journey?'

'No. We travelled without stopping by day or night through the southlands. Tell me.'

'Two weeks ago a Companion named Karik brought me word that the Wolf King had led his barbarians out of the High Wald. Since then I received word that Lasgaad has fallen to them. I have kept this news as secret as possible until your return, though wild rumours have travelled the caravan routes.'

'It may be I was unwise to use the nomads to destroy Grimwald of River Garde.'

'From what Companion Karik saw at the Pass of the White Virgins your spy Affleck was lending encouragement to the Horde. But he is not the only dealer in treachery.'

The Regent gave her a sharp glance of inquiry.

'We shall talk of that in a moment. I believe it is the Wolf King's desire to fight a holy war on behalf of his Wolf-in-the-Sky. With our main army lost to the Red Death at Thaan our hope might lie with the Commander of the Host.'

'But I sent him to the Cage before I departed the city.'

'He escaped,' and Mandraga related how he had vanished leaving only a bundle of rags behind.

For a while the Regent gazed into the dark depths of his wine while Urwen watched him anxiously.

'If Mandal is still alive in Ythan he will be found, and when he is he will long for the comfort of the Cage,' he said finally. 'As for the Wolf Horde we have no need of the likes of him, thanks to old Leodore . . .'

His voice trailed off as he became immersed in his thoughts.

'And what other tidings?' he asked suddenly. 'You spoke of treachery but I can tell you that all the mice who played while the cat was away are being rounded up at this moment.'

'The traitor I had in mind was your Revel Master Gambal,' Mandraga replied. 'When the Pilgrims reached Princess Livia's resting place . . .'

'Where?'

'I could not say except somewhere in the Shadow Realm. All my mirror showed me was a chamber with Livia lying entranced in the centre.' And she went on to describe how Gambal had stabbed the Regent's agent.

'Why should he do that?' Urwen asked.

Mandraga hesitated.

'Mayhap he saw greater personal advantage through such an act if Livia was revived.'

'And mayhap it was an act of revenge for the death of that heretic novice you destroyed through your will,'

175

said the Regent harshly. 'To think we almost had the Princess, that we might have ended the dangerous myth for ever but now she will remain an inspiration to those who would overthrow me.'

Urwen sat with downcast eyes but inwardly she rejoiced at the Regent's angry tone to the Lore Mistress, something that would have been unthinkable a few moons ago. Clearly the old hag's influence upon him was waning. And she would see to it that when the electrum crown of Ythan was placed upon her lover's head Mandraga was no more than a legend.

'Has your mirror told what has happened since?' he demanded.

'The mirror has remained blank,' Mandraga admitted. 'But it is not quite the end of the story, my lord. I pray you to come with me for a short while.'

She hauled herself to her feet with the aid of her crutch and led the way to her own apartments. Here they were admitted by one of her mute servants and the Regent and Urwen followed her up a staircase that spiralled to the upper chambers of her tower. Several times the old woman had to pause for breath, her face seemingly drained of blood in the shafts of light that shone through the lancet windows set at random in the masonry.

At length they reached a bronze-studded door.

'Here may lie the answer to the question of the sleeping princess,' said Mandraga as she slid back a panel covering a spyhole. 'Take a good look, my lord.'

The Regent stepped up frowning and stooped to put his eye to the aperture. For a long moment he gazed into the chamber beyond.

'Livia!' he breathed at last. 'You have the Princess Livia!'

THREE

The
Awakening

Slowly and with great gentleness Krispin and Alwald allowed the body of the Princess Livia to sink for a moment in order for her to be completely immersed in the limpid water, then they raised her so that her face was above the surface. Her golden hair spread about her head like a tangled halo, her robe floated loosely about her and — was it a trick of the light reflecting so brightly from the pool? Krispin wondered — the faded samite out of which it had been sewn was returning to its original pristine condition.

Apart from the murmurous splashing of the fountains and the far note of a bellbird in the woods, silence enveloped the Wells of Ythan as though the spirit of nature held her breath in expectation of some wondrous happening. As he stood waist deep in the pool steadying the Princess, Krispin felt his fatigue slough away as a serpent sloughs its skin to reveal a revitalized creature. His foot no longer ached from a stone bruise that had caused him to limp, tired muscles tightened with latent strength and he was filled with a sense of well-being such as he had not known since the commencement of the quest.

His sensations were not merely physical; there was something magical in the very air about him — not the disturbing kind of magic that had oppressed him and his companions in The Mage's Tower but a force redolent of life and wonder that reminded him of some happy childhood dream.

As he watched the Princess seeming to float between himself and Alwald he saw her breast rise and fall. Alwald lifted her head higher from the water. Her eyelids trembled and when they opened Krispin was not surprised to see that they were of the same luminous blue as Jennet's.

'. . . child,' she murmured drowsily. '. . . where . . . the child . . .'

The rest of the travellers stooped over the pool edge in their eagerness to watch every detail of the revival of the young woman who unknowingly had had such a vital effect upon all their lives. Tana sobbed openly while tears from the normally irascible Tumbrul plopped into the water like fat raindrops; Ognam grinned more broadly than he ever did in a carnival caper and the aged warriors turned their wrinkled faces away to hide their unmilitary emotion.

For a long moment the Princess's eyes closed again, and when they opened for the second time she was fully awake. Looking up she saw Alwald's face above hers and stretching up her arm to touch his cheek she said softly, 'My errant knight, thou hast ended my enchantment at last. Tell me thy name that I might bless it.'

'Alwald . . . Your Highness,' he stammered. Then, as Krispin released her ankles and he raised her to a sitting position on the steps that led down into the pool, he remembered the etiquette of chivalry and added, 'Alwald, son of Grimwald VII, and Hereditary Lord of the River March.'

'Not a prince?' said Princess Livia innocently. 'Ah well . . . And who be those good folk looking so solemn and tearful?'

'They have followed the quest to find you, Your Highness.'

'Then I must give them my thanks.' Suddenly a look of perplexity crossed her face. 'But what am I doing in a pool? I believed I should wake in a chamber beneath a mountain.'

Krispin was intrigued by her slightly archaic mode of speech, realizing that the language of Ythan would have altered since she had last spoken it.

Ysldon moved to the top of the steps and raised his right arm in a gesture of greeting.

'Princess Livia, only issue of King Johan XXXIII, Dame of the Crystal Mountains, Keeper of the Sacred Lamp, Defender of the Shrines and Maid of the Black Rose, I, Ysldon, Guardian of the Wells of Ythan where you now find yourself, welcome you to Time Present.'

She gazed up at his figure, a dark silhouette against the rainbow spray of the fountains.

'Oh, Magus, it be good to see thee,' she cried. 'How long is it since I was entranced?'

'One hundred years.'

Her head drooped and she buried her face in her hands.

'Alas, all that I knew hath gone. My father and my . . .'

'Ythan remains and has need of you.'

'Always thou thought first of Ythan, Magus,' she

said with a hint of petulance. Looking up, she caught sight of Tana. 'Ah, lady, thou must tell me what is being worn in Danaak. My gown must be so out of fashion I be ashamed.'

'I fear I can be of no help, Your Highness,' Tana replied. 'Like you I have been out of the world.'

'Help me, sir knight,' the Princess said to Alwald. 'I cannot sit thusly all day long.'

Taking her soft white hands, Alwald raised her up and helped her to mount the steps. Water ran from her clothing like drops of quicksilver so that when she stood on the terrace it was almost dry. To Krispin it was amazing that she was capable of walking and then, remembering his own renewed energy, he understood that the miraculous water had made her century of entrancement seem of no more account than a night's sleep.

At the top of the steps she bowed to Ysldon and then kissed Alwald on the mouth.

'If I remember the folktale aright that is the traditional reward for he who waketh the sleeper,' she said. Alwald flushed, though whether with pleasure or embarrassment Krispin could not tell as he waded to the steps.

'A jongleur,' the Princess cried, catching sight of Ognam's motley. 'My father's jongleur could pipe most merrily. Dost thou also make music?'

The bells on Ognam's cockscomb hood tinkled as he bowed his head to signify that he did.

'Then pipeth a reel to celebrate my return from a hundred years of night.'

Ognam bowed again and taking his hollowed jester's staff he began to play a tune that teased the feet of all who heard it.

'Dance with me, sir knight,' cried the Princess and she seized Alwald's hand. 'And you who hath quested for me.'

She gestured to Tana to take Alwald's other hand and Gambal joined the chain until his injury pained him. Seeing Tumbrul close to her the Princess linked the fingers of her free hand with his and then, with Ognam keeping pace with them, they danced laughing down the terrace steps to the greensward. Butterflies rose like clouds of flower petals to escape the feet of the merrymakers.

On the terrace Ysldon said, 'The Wells are for all.'

Holding his injured arm Gambal descended into the pool while in a tremulous voice Barlak ordered his palsied company to immerse themselves 'at the double'. Ysldon watched from beneath his wide hat brim as Krispin helped Barlak down the steps into the water and then steadied those who tottered after him. When the last warrior lay back in the water he climbed out and stood watching the distant figures dancing in a circle round Ognam.

'In my time I have seen much that is wonderful,' Krispin said. 'Yet I did not expect it to be like this.'

'And how did you expect it to be, Master Krispin?' asked Ysldon standing beside him.

'In truth I do not know, though I suppose I expected something more solemn.'

'Ah, the music and cavorting. It is a natural expression of joy. Remember that although Livia has long been entranced she still has the heart of a girl whose life was filled with courtly foolishness.'

'It seems to me that after the Amber Isle I am greatly in your debt,' said Krispin and, remembering how the Princess had addressed Ysldon, he added, 'Sir Magus.'

In the shadow cast by the broad brim of his hat the old man smiled and said, 'Shath had waited long for a victim but he chose wrong when he thought you would be the means of his return to the world. I could not permit my enemy that.'

'And I was also thinking of how the Wells appeared to save us in the Wilderness of Gil,' added Krispin. 'At the time we did not recognize them for what they were. Looking back it was like a dream and I still do not understand . . .'

'There has always been a dreamlike quality about the Wells for mortal men,' said Ysldon. 'It is because they do not completely exist in Time Present. Of course you do not comprehend how they could appear in the wilderness and yet be here; there is that in their nature which allows them the possibility of moving not only in Place but Time, of following the skein of chance as ordained by the All Father when he created the Three Worlds. Thus I was able to will them into your path when it seemed that thirst and weariness would bring your pilgrimage, so bravely begun, to an untimely conclusion.'

Krispin sighed. He could see the Wells, had been renewed by their water, was speaking to their mysterious custodian and yet he failed to grasp fully what he was being told about them any more than he had understood the gramarye of The Mage.

'You wonder why my magic did not come to your aid at other times when you were endangered on the quest,' said the old man, now leaning on his staff.

'I wonder how that living here among these mountains you knew about the quest at all,' Krispin replied.

'I became aware of it when you found the Esav in

the City Without a Name. Such was the potency of the Jewel from the Stars that its removal did more than bring buildings tumbling down, it created a tremor in the aether that told me something far out of the ordinary had begun. From then on I followed your progress with great interest and some admiration, not all the time of course, because my place is here, but enough to be aware of how the quest fared.'

'But how . . . ?'

'When you and Lord Alwald crossed the ranges from Mabalon did not an eagle circle above your path, and when you sailed from The Mage's isle did you not see a great fish in the skerries? Thus, and in other forms, did I watch the course of the quest.' Seeing Krispin's look of astonishment he laughed. 'If that barbarian king of the Wolf Horde can become a wolf at will, shape-changing is a mere nothing to a magus.

'The reason I did not aid you with sorcery when you were endangered on your journeying — blast the stone giants with lightning bolts or shrivel the kraken with cold fire — was because the nature of the quest was that it had to be accomplished by mortal folk without the aid of High Magic otherwise the challenge it presented would not be fairly met.'

It would not have worried me if the challenge was not fairly met, thought Krispin. *A little helpful magic in the dungeons of Danaak or when I met the water horse would not have gone amiss.* Aloud he said hesitantly, 'We did have the use of a magical boat when we began the quest.'

'I am talking about High Magic,' said Ysldon with a touch of asperity. 'Not Fey conjuring.'

He might have said more but the sounds of laughter and shouting broke the calm of the terrace. In the pool

Barlak and his warriors were gazing at each other with expressions of dawning delight as colour returned to white beards, wrinkles vanished and hearts that had pained once more beat with a strength that set pulses racing.

Barlak stood up in the water and his chain mail which had been tarnished by the passage of the years now shone like newly minted silver.

'It grieves me that my comrades who we left on the mountain paths could not have been restored like us,' he said as he ascended the steps. 'If we brought them to the Wells . . .'

'I too regret their passing especially as it was I who entranced you all,' said Ysldon, 'but there is nothing that can be done for them. The Wells will cure ills and hold death at bay but once the Dark Maid has made her claim their power is naught. It is the All Father's First Law.'

Barlak shrugged.

'Each man has his death awaiting him and there is no escaping it,' he said. 'All of us would have been slain by the corsairs at Haven if you had not bargained with us to serve you.'

'It is the Princess you serve,' said Ysldon. 'And that service is far from over because she will need a bodyguard in the days ahead.'

'At least we will have the strength to protect her properly,' said Barlak and he yawned.

Krispin felt pleasantly weary and leaned on the balustrade; over on the grass he saw that the dancers were lying in a circle around a recumbent Ognam as though sleep had overtaken them even while they danced.

'Forgive me, Sir Magus, but I can hardly keep my

eyes open and yet there was much that I wanted to ask you,' he said.

'You will remember from the time you bathed in the Wells before that slumber follows fast on healing,' Ysldon told him. 'Rest now, there is nothing in the valley that can harm you or your companions.'

'But, remembering the last occasion, may I ask if the Wells will be here when we wake up?'

'Assuredly. And your questions, or most of them, will find answers. Now join your friends in sleep.'

Krispin looked about him. Shipmaster Danya, his back against one of the pillars that supported the cupola, was snoring gently; the warriors were laying themselves down on the tiles with their heads resting on their arms.

Am I dreaming all this? wondered Krispin as he stretched out on a bench, but before the answer came he had plunged into dreamless sleep.

FOUR

Danaak Nights

It was a busy night in the Hall of Execution as it was a tradition in Danaak that executions, other than the special pageants of punishment arranged by the Witchfinders, took place after sundown. The entrance to the hall was through a gloomy gargoyled arch in the Citadel's wall. Prior to The Enchantment it had been used merely as a fodder store for the royal drongs.

Lit only by flambeaux, the hall appeared in keeping with its dismal purpose. At the far end was a broad platform on which were mounted three posts the height of a man. By each of these stood a leather-masked executioner holding a black cord of plaited spider silk. To one side of the platform stood several young men wearing the traditional black-and-white chequered masks of those apprenticed to the Guild of Executioners; on the opposite side, on a gilded throne, sat a priest who at the appropriate moment would administer spiritual comfort to the condemned by asking if they repented. It was a rhetorical question as each victim had a wooden ball forced into his mouth

– nicknamed 'the apple' – before being brought into the hall to ensure that in his last moments he did not utter treasonable sentiments.

The body of the hall was filled with the relatives of the prisoners and idlers taking advantage of free entertainment. High on the walls on either side were boxes from which rich, privileged and noble men and women enjoyed strange satisfaction from watching the death throes of their fellow mortals. It was not unusual for the spectacle to inspire erotic excitement, especially among the more jaded voyeurs of death, and therefore the boxes were discreetly curtained.

In one such box the Regent sat with Mandraga the Lore Mistress beside him. For an hour he had been watching the garrotting of those who had been unwise enough to speak against him while he had been absent from the capital.

'I wish to see one more and then I shall give audience to your young Witchfinder,' he said. 'The next prisoner is the merchant Azrul. In the past he had dealings with the lamented Odo so perhaps that is where he got his treasonable ideas. A note was sent to the Witchfinders denouncing him for making defamatory statements about you, my lady.'

'The note was probably sent by a rival merchant.'

'Of that I have no doubt. That is the beauty of denunciation – it provides employment for the Witchfinders and, as the wealth of the condemned is confiscated, an excellent source of revenue.'

'What did he say about me?' Mandraga asked.

'An obscene suggestion that you have perverted appetites.'

'That is nothing to the rumours that have circulated about you of late, Lord Regent.'

'At least the stories about me inspire fear rather than sniggers — and therefore respect.'

A drumroll heralded the arrival of Azrul the merchant, his cheeks bulging under the pressure of the apple, between two Citadel guards. He was dragged to the middle of the stage where apprentices seized his arms from behind and jerked him back against the centre post. The master executioner intoned, 'By the Law of Ythan and the authorization of the Ancient and Honourable Guild of Executioners I do hereby end your life as one not fit to enjoy the beneficence of the Lord Regent against who you most foully plotted treason.'

While the priest stepped forward to play his part in the charade wagers were swiftly laid among the onlookers as to how long the prisoner would take to die as defined by the waterclock. It could be a period of several minutes though it was known that if the executioner was bribed sufficiently by his victim's kith he would shorten the agony to a few seconds. Alas for Azrul no one had approached the master executioner with silver, as became evident when he flicked a cord across the merchant's throat and tugged it so that the back of his head struck the post.

Silence fell upon the hall as the regular spectators appraised the ghastly sequence with experienced eyes, noting the spasms that shook the body, the blackening of the face and the bulging of the eyes as the cord slowly cut deeper and deeper.

'So perish my enemies,' said the Regent when the body was dragged to the trapdoor that opened on to a chute leading to the river below. Here was moored a black barge which carried its cargo of corpses to an unknown destination. This boat figured terrifyingly in the imagination of Danaak's children when their mothers used it as a threat to curb bad behaviour.

'The Witchfinder Mordan waits in my chamber,' said the Lore Mistress as she struggled to her feet with the aid of her T-shaped crutch.

They left the box while an apprentice executioner threw sawdust over the spot where the merchant had died of the black cord, as the expression was, and escorted by a Companion of the Rose and the Regent's Avenger, they made their slow way to the Mandraga's tower. Here the Regent sat in a chair of intricately carved Upas wood while one of her mutes poured him a goblet of black Ronimar wine. Another mute ushered in a frank-faced young man in a black robe on the breast of which was embroidered the silver symbol of the Serene Mother.

'This is Master Mordan who brought the girl Jennet from the High Wald,' announced Mandraga. 'Since their arrival both have remained in this tower, as such was the import of his mission I deemed it should remain secret until your return.'

The Regent nodded and turned to the Witchfinder.

'You have done well, young man,' he said benignly. 'And you will not find me ungrateful. Tell me about it from the beginning.'

Mordan tried to moisten his lips but found that his tongue was dry. He had rehearsed what he was about to say over and over but now that he was in the presence of the dread ruler of Ythan his confidence dried with his saliva. The Lady Mandraga nodded to her mute and wine was poured for him.

'I was dispatched to the High Wald with a detachment from the Nightwatch Company by His Righteousness the Witchfinder-General,' Mordan began. 'My task was to arrest the Lady Eloira on a charge of necromancy.'

The Regent nodded. Thanks to the terror inspired by dungeon rats Lord Odo had babbled of Eloira's devotion to the Pilgrim Path.

Mordan, gaining confidence from the rare wine and the Regent's expression of encouragement, told how his party had been attacked by a band of dispossessed Waldmen led by a girl who fought like a Battle Maiden in the old tales. After being wounded he was overlooked as dead and knew nothing more until he regained consciousness in the Peak Tower, the home of the old woman he had come to arrest.

'I feigned loss of memory,' he explained, 'and while I was regaining my strength as a guest in the tower I glimpsed the girl Jennet and recognized her likeness to old portraits of Princess Livia. And I was struck by the thought, Lord Regent, that if I could bring her privily to Danaak it would possibly be of advantage to you.'

'And to yourself, no doubt,' said the Regent with a smile of understanding that made the Witchfinder's hopes soar. 'Tell me about the girl.'

'There was something amiss with her mind,' he said and explained how Jennet had withdrawn into childhood after the destruction of her village.

'That made it easy for me to lure her away from the Peak Tower,' he continued.

'How did you achieve that?'

'I pretended I was going to take her to her brother whose absence was a sadness to her.'

'And by the strange ways of Fate that brother is one of the Pilgrims who reached the real Princess,' said the Lady Mandraga.

191

'Say on, Witchfinder,' said the Regent.

Mordan warmed to his story of how he had lured Jennet from the Peak Tower.

'It was my plan to take her to the Companions of the Rose who guarded the pass leading from the High Wald, so we could have had a fitting escort to Danaak, but we reached the outpost only to see the Wolf Horde treacherously overwhelm it,' he said. 'This meant that I had to find a way over the ranges which was far from easy. Apart from the problem of the perilous terrain, Jennet was becoming suspicious. After the shock of seeing the nomads again it seemed that at times she was less childish and I had more and more difficulty in reassuring her that our journey really was to find her brother. One night in the forest she actually ran away while I slept.'

'But you got her back.'

Mordan permitted himself a soft chuckle.

'She had not gone far when she was chased by a bear. The fright of this sent her running back to me, for I was the only one she could turn to for protection, and after that she seemed to be quite childlike again. I finally found a path that led us through the mountains and down to the plain beyond where, not wishing to encounter the wolfmen, we trekked south living on berries.'

'How did you make the journey to Danaak?'

'We came to the cottage of an old man who was better off than the others we had passed. He had a horse and there was food in his larder, and he provided us with both — and needful silver which I found in his pallet.'

'At the point of your knife, no doubt,' chuckled the Regent.

'We came at last to a highway and I was able to hire a closed coach at a wayside inn, and we were driven to Danaak without anyone seeing the girl.'

'Excellent,' said the Regent. 'At the moment secrecy is of the utmost importance as I am sure your nimble mind can appreciate. It is for that reason I must keep you in the Citadel, not that I think you would utter an indiscreet word but if you were in the city you would have to report to the Witchfinder-General and . . .' Here the Regent gave a deep sigh. '. . . my enemies are to be found everywhere. They would show you little ruth if they suspected you had done me this great service.'

Mordan drew in his breath at the Regent's words. Could he be implying that the Witchfinder-General was suspect? If the Guild was to be purged at least he, Mordan, had proved his devotion to the Regent and . . . He felt dizzy at the possibilities that must lie ahead.

The Regent said, 'Doubtless you are still weary after your journeying so I shall have you conducted to your resting chamber. You will find the view remarkable.'

He clapped his hands and the Companion of the Rose entered.

'Captain Bors, take Master Witchfinder to the place appointed for him.'

'The course of Destiny turns in our direction,' the Lore Mistress said when they were alone. 'You are whole again and you have someone who could be passed for Princess Livia.'

'If she were dead,' mused the Regent. 'It could be announced that she had been discovered in some remote spot but after the century-long entrancement her body could not stand the awakening. And so all could see that she really was dead I would build her a wondrous mausoleum with a crystal sarcophagus, a perpetual reminder that Ythan's royal line had died out.'

'Or you could marry her.'

'What? Lady, at last I fear age is dimming your wits.'

'Take her as your wife. If you are going to become the monarch what could be better than to have a real queen — or so folk would think — as your consort.'

The boom of the midnight gong rolled from the Citadel in an expanding wave across the sleeping city. Picketed drongs in the caravanserai grunted uneasily; in the shrines acolytes raised their eyes from the flames that flickered before the statues of the Mother and even in the houses of joy there was a break in the music, a pause in the coupling as the menacing sound penetrated barred windows and thick draperies.

To many, the voice of the Citadel gong was like the voice of doom. Traditionally, it was only sounded when there was a threat to the kingdom, its original purpose being to keep the guards on the ramparts wakeful, but now it was a reminder that somewhere beyond the great Plain of Danaak the Wolf Horde was advancing inexorably.

Day by day rumours of the invasion had grown and festered, and the rich and favoured quit their country estates for the safety of Danaak's towering walls. But what most alarmed the citizens was that there were no visible preparations to halt the barbarians. Only the Witchfinders were more in evidence, the sight of their black-hooded robes adding to the unease that hung like a miasma over the city.

In her high tower the Lady Mandraga crouched in a chair before the mirror suspended between silver pillars. Her face was ghastly white and her hands trembled as she poured drops from a phial into a winecup to hold back the exhaustion which threatened to overwhelm her frail body. The air of the chamber was thick with herbal incense fuming from bowls on bronze tripods while, on the floor, archaic symbols had been limned in her own blood. In one corner a water-driven incantation wheel repeated its supplication to unseen forces. Candles moulded from wax that had more to do with the Hall of Execution than the hive guttered in lamps secretly reclaimed from the once-forgotten Cavern of the Sorcerers that lay beneath the earliest foundations of the Citadel.

The mirror merely reflected the strands of smoke drifting before it. Since it had shown Gambal's act of revenge it had not responded to Mandraga's command to reveal the fate of the Pilgrims. Now, at the Regent's insistence, she was performing an arcane mirror spell in order to raise the desired vision without the aid of the linking hand mirror that Gambal had smashed.

'What demon's kitchen is this?' demanded the Regent as he entered the chamber in a robe of dark velvet. 'You told me that by the midnight gong you would know if you could make the mirror obey you. The gong has sounded.'

Ah, Regent, how your tone has changed since you regained your health and that spy-whore wormed her way into your cold heart, thought Mandraga wearily. *You reek of her musk when in the old days you would have been facing your enemies.* Aloud she said, 'The ritual has just reached its completion, according to the *Scroll of Reflections*. Within minutes we shall see if it has succeeded but whether it be success or failure this night has cost me dear.'

'It would be unlike you to fail,' he said presently and though on the surface his words were complimentary Mandraga felt they contained a subtle implication that if the mirror did not produce the result he wanted it would be because her powers were waning. She quickly banished the thought in order to devote all her concentration to the remainder of the rite.

Rising to her feet with the aid of her crutch she uttered an evocation in Old Ythan. Immediately the mirror became a kaleidoscope of shadow patterns that she and the Regent watched with breathless concentration. The grey shades became tinged with sullen colours – the green of darkest ivy, sombre brown and dark earth red – which coiled and split and reformed at great speed. Then the colours flowed into each other and they were no longer patterns but images from nightmares briefly glimpsed; the face of an imp, a seething mire, a monstrous beast.

Image after image appeared as though the mirror was proving its resistance by this meaningless display. Then the luminosity faded until the polished crystal was as black as starless night.

The Regent turned his leonine head to the Lore Mistress but she ignored him as her voice rose to repeat the incantation and this time the words filled the chamber with a vibrance that suggested a youthful throat. He saw what had been glimpsed in the past and inspired hushed rumours – the outlines of Mandraga's body became blurred so that at one moment he was looking at a stooped beldame and the next at a beautiful young woman. And it was the young woman's voice that commanded the power inherent in the crystal to do her bidding.

The lamps dimmed and for some moments the mirror remained stubbornly void, then became filled with whirling motes which coalesced into a candle-lit scene.

'Livia has been awakened,' breathed the Regent.

The mirror showed a long table at which a diverse collection of people sat with their faces turned to an old man seated at the head, his face hidden by the large brim of his hat. Beside him, beautiful in the gentle light, was the Princess Livia. In the background the same glow was caught a hundredfold in falling drops of water that had been flung high by a fountain and behind that, little more than a black silhouette against a starry sky, was a graceful dome supported on slender columns.

'She is identical to the girl Witchfinder Mordan brought us,' whispered the Lady Mandraga. 'If Livia was to die, none could gainsay that we had the true Princess in our keeping — as your bride.'

'And at least we know where she is,' said the Regent. 'I recognize the Wells of Ythan. She must have been carried there to be revived by the Waters of Life.'

As they continued to gaze at the mirror the vision it held rippled from time to time as though the glass resented being forced to portray this image.

'So those are the Pilgrims,' the Regent mused. 'The one beside the Princess must be the son of Grimwald, but who or what is that long-nosed freak beside the jongleur? It would make a good addition to my collection. Serene Mother, to think that motley crew succeeded where so many failed. Would that I could hear their speech.'

'When I saw Gambal thus portrayed I took meaning from the movement of his lip,' explained the Lore Mistress. 'Look, Lord Alwald speaks of a journey on the morrow . . .'

Her words were cut short by a sharp report and a crack crossed the mirror from side to side; the vision of the feast faded and once again the glass reflected incense smoke.

'Are you satisfied, Lord Regent?' gasped the Lady Mandraga.

'I thank you,' said the Regent. 'At all costs Livia must not enter Ythan for many would rally to her. Keep the wench Jennet content in her chamber and secure from conspiracy. Meantime the Pilgrims must be destroyed. I shall dispatch my most trusted guards under Captain Bors who will remember the route to the Wells.'

'Even if he leaves tonight the Pilgrims will be gone before he reaches the ranges. I know another way.'

Wearily she crossed to an iron chest. This she unlocked and from it lifted a flat box containing rows of identical toy soldiers which once might have been carved and painted for the children of the wealthy.

Another night in Danaak; another reverberation of the midnight gong floated over the restless city. In the dungeon hall beneath the Citadel the giant capstan revolved slowly as a hundred near-naked wretches chained to its massive beams pushed to the encouragement of whiplash and curse, its shaft turning gearwheels and cranks to work mysterious machineries below.

In her tower the Lady Mandraga sat at a table on which two score miniature soldiers were set out like toys in a boy's game, only in this case the figures vanished one by one as she laid her finger on them and whispered an imprecation against those she would harm.

In another chamber the Lady Urwen turned a key in the massive lock on her door despite the fact that a Companion of the Rose was on impassive guard without. She opened a casket, once a valuable tool of her trade, containing a number of phials in velvet-padded racks. She removed one containing a fine blue powder and hid the casket away before hurrying to join the Regent.

In yet another chamber, where bars across its casements were in contrast to its comfort, Jennet lay on a couch covered with rare sandhart furs. The moon, dissected by the bars, threw his cold light upon her and was reflected in her tears. But not even a sob escaped her to break the silence she had held since her arrival at the Citadel.

At a gateway in the city ramparts leading directly from the Citadel the iron portcullis was raised to allow a hushed procession to emerge on to the broad highway that curved to the west. It was led by the usual company of knights with pennons hanging limp from their lances in the sultry air. Behind them rode a standard-bearer holding the yellow banner of Ythan, and after him came a company of Companions of the Rose escorting the Regent's coach drawn by a team of matched drongs.

It was followed by a mounted detachment of slingers, there being no place for foot soldiers in a column that had to travel many leagues a day. A convoy of wagons followed loaded high with cases, canvas-shrouded mangonels and men skilled in working these engines of war. Finally came carts filled with provisions and military supplies guarded by more mounted troopers.

Apart from the screak of wheels and the melancholic protests of the drongs, the company moved away in silence but already the few nocturnal travellers who had witnessed the departure from the shadow of the city walls were scurrying to spread a variety of rumours – the two most popular being that the Regent and his court were fleeing the capital or that he was leading forth a secret army to take the Wolf Horde by surprise.

FIVE

The Feast
of Friends

It was seemingly distant music that made Krispin open his eyes; not the gleeful sound of Ognam's pipe but music of a more majestic nature that came from instruments he could not recognize. Among its harmonic strands was entwined the voice of forests given tongue when a high wind passes over them, the murmur of mountain rills and the rhythmic surge of the sea which was still fresh in his memory from his days aboard the *Amber Star*. The effect was to give him the feeling of being uplifted as a feather floats on an upward current of air.

For a long while Krispin was content to lie on his marble bench, his mind filled with the music and his eyes filled with the sky that was rapidly darkening to indigo as the sun followed her course behind the peaks. After entering the pool of healing water and the long sleep that had followed he was enjoying a sense of dreamy well-being that normally was known only to those addicted to Moon Bloom petals. But soon, as his random thoughts coalesced, he was gripped by an exciting idea.

The sight of Princess Livia had vividly brought the image of his beloved Jennet to mind. When he had watched the Princess dancing with the others in a circle round Ognam she could have been Jennet dancing with the lads and lasses of Toyheim at the midsummer festival. And then it struck him that if the Wells of Ythan had revived the Princess so completely after her bespellment surely their water could cure Jennet from the cloud that had descended upon her mind.

The more he considered it the more convinced he became that he had found the key to bring her back from the shadows to her proper self. He would hide a flacon of the precious water in his pack when they returned to Ythan and then find his way to the High Wald and Jennet. As for the quest and the establishing of Princess Livia upon her throne, he would leave that to the likes of Alwald and the true followers of the Pilgrim Path. He had fulfilled his obligation to the Lady Eloira now that the Princess had been revived; his loyalty lay solely with Jennet especially as a possible cure for her malady was within his reach.

As he continued to gaze upwards the indigo deepened to velvety black and the Constellation of the Griffin, that familiar skymark he had wished upon as a child, glittered to the north. A hand was laid upon his shoulder and turning his head he saw Gambal outlined in the soft light that shone from the rotunda.

'I have been sent to rouse you,' Gambal said. 'A feast awaits.'

'A feast?'

'When I awoke a long table was laid, with lamps of perfumed oil burning. I doubt not that it is the work of gramarye rather than mortal hands but here I do not find discomfort in the idea. It seems that in this valley lies the peace of the world.'

Krispin nodded and sat up yawning. At the far end of the terrace he could see the table as Gambal had described.

'I should like to take this chance to say a word,' said Gambal, seating himself upon the bench. When Krispin did not respond he continued in a low voice, 'I well understand how you and the others must feel about me after I . . . after I told that I had been the Regent's spy.'

Krispin had no wish for such a conversation and made no reply. 'It was through the Regent that I escaped a life so *disgusting* that you, who grew up in the sweet air of the country, can have no inkling of what I suffered. Therefore it was natural for me to owe him loyalty,' Gambal went on. 'It was only later, when the evil ways of his régime became clear to me, that I decided to shift my loyalty to those I had been deceiving.'

'I thought you said it was because of the death of Lorelle,' said Krispin.

Gambal nodded hastily.

'Of course. It was the way in which she was driven to her death that opened my eyes. But the good that came out of my grief was that if I had not realized the true nature of my master and his accursed Lore Mistress you and your friends would still be languishing in the caverns.'

'I suppose so,' said Krispin doubtfully. 'The others are taking their places at the table.'

'Hear me out.'

'Why?'

'You owe it to me because you and Alwald saved my life in the Wilderness of Gil.'

In spite of himself Krispin looked puzzled at this piece of logic.

'I want you to know that although we were on different sides for much of the quest, there was never a moment when I had personal ill feeling towards you or the others. Indeed, for the first time in my life I tasted the pleasure of comradeship.'

Reluctantly Krispin nodded his acceptance of these words.

Gambal said in a tone in keeping with the innocent cast of his features, 'If you accept what I say I beg you to tell the others of the sincerity of my feelings towards you all.'

He rose quickly to his feet, brushed the back of his hand against his cheek and walked away congratulating himself on having persuaded Krispin, the most simple-hearted of the company, to heed him.

Mayhap we misjudged him, Krispin thought as he left the bench. *No one can fully know what hurts another feels or how they make him act. My fault is that I pass judgement too easily. I never made proper allowance for Alwald when his ways peeved me yet he had lost home and loved ones just as I. Serene Mother, grant me more understanding.*

The table was loaded with hot yeasty bread, steaming tureens, platters of roasted fish and meats, glowing fruits and glass vessels whose wines shone ruby and pale gold in the lamplight. Dark-robed Ysldon at the table head motioned Krispin to take the seat next to him and opposite the Princess beside whom Alwald sat. Ognam was next to Krispin and beside him Tana's dark beauty was a perfect contrast to the radiant fairness of Livia. Gambal was seated opposite Tumbrul and Danya, and the rest of the table was taken up by the warriors still exultant at their escape from unnatural old age.

The Magus looked down the double row of his guests and tapped a goblet with his horn-handled spoon. Conversation faded with the clear note it gave forth and he said, 'Not only is this feast in honour of Princess Livia, but for all of you who have made tremendous journeys, not just in distance, like Lord Alwald, but through Time like Barlak and his brave men-at-arms . . .'

'And me,' interjected Tumbrul.

'. . . to join together tonight in celebration of an event of vast importance in the history of Ythan – the ending of The Enchantment.'

He paused and around them the mysterious music rose to a triumphant crescendo. When it subsided to a haunting background melody Ysldon continued, 'Now let us break bread and drink wine together, and while you eat I shall endeavour to give the explanation you deserve after your efforts to reach the end of the Pilgrim Path.'

He paused again while they ladled soup into bowls and glasses clinked as wine was poured, and when all were served he continued, with his hat brim as ever shading his eyes. 'It delights me to see that, thanks to the Water of Life, you have so well recovered from your travails. Although this valley has been near forgotten since the wars that followed The Enchantment ended the freedom to travel, and the Guild of Witchfinders proscribed knowledge of it, the Wells have continued to flow with their healing free for anyone who comes to claim it.'

205

'Anyone?' Alwald asked.

'Anyone,' replied Ysldon. 'Before The Enchantment, prince and pauper, priest and cutpurse, whoever had the faith to make the arduous journey were given healing here. Since then few have sought the Wells and fewer found them, though it was but a few days ago that a man with a vile complaint reached the valley in time for his life to be spared. It was the Regent of Ythan.'

'The Regent!' The name was repeated in simultaneous astonishment. 'The *Regent* was allowed . . .'

'It was not a question of being *allowed*. The Wells are for all, they have no reckoning of good or evil but only truth which lies in their depths. As for me, I am merely the Guardian of the Wells and it is not for me to say who may bathe.'

For a moment Ysldon's eyes seemed to sparkle with ironic amusement and they guessed he was understating his role.

'Lord Magus, where is the enemy now?' demanded Alwald.

'He has returned to the capital where, from what I overheard, he proposes to change from Regent to King. It would seem, my dear Livia, that you have been found by your questers just in time.'

She lowered her head in agreement, her eyes fixed on her platter.

'What puzzled the Lord Regent was when he woke from the slumber that follows immersion he found only grass where the terrace had stood,' continued Ysldon with a chuckle. 'Doubtless you were equally puzzled when you woke in the Widlerness of Gil, Lord Alwald. He had underestimated my wits and was not too discreet in his plan to have my throat cut.'

206

'But with your powers . . .' began Alwald.

Ysldon shrugged.

'It was enough for the Wells and I to disappear — our materialization on the Isle of Elfaine made a pleasant change — rather than unnaturally alter the course of events by smiting the ruler of Ythan. And this is a matter on which I would speak for it must seem passing strange to you who have suffered so many perils on the Path that I did not come to your aid with incantation and spell, and why I do not magick Her Highness on to her throne with the Regent in chains at her feet as Master Ognam suggested. The answer is that such conjuring would ruin the purpose of The Enchantment.'

Knives were stilled on platters, goblets paused between board and lip as Alwald and his companions wondered if at last they were going to learn the answers to questions that had beset them on their journeying, questions that The Mage had avoided answering.

'What do you know of The Enchantment, toy-maker?' demanded Ysldon, turning to Krispin.

'Little more than that which is told in a folktale, Lord Magus,' he replied. 'That a hundred years ago some wicked sorcerers entranced the royal lady here and hid her away — as we found to be true — and that her father Good King Johan failed to find her and died of a broken heart, after which Ythan's golden age ended in chaos.'

'And?'

'Nobles fought for power and common men turned against each other. Witchfinders grew powerful by destroying those they accused of sorcery, even to weather-making, for it was their claim that it was through gramarye that Ythan lost its royal line.'

'And?'

'And out of the confusion grew the Regency which was an excuse for tyrants to rule the kingdom as custodians of the Empty Throne.'

'And in your village, Master Krispin, or in your castle, Lord Alwald, did you have any idea why The Enchantment should fall upon the royal house?'

Krispin shook his head but Alwald said seriously, 'My nurse told me that it was the revenge of an ugly . . . uh . . . of an old . . . of an enchanter who desired the hand of the Princess in marriage but her father rejected him.'

Beside him Princess Livia suddenly giggled and put her hand to her mouth.

'As a child I heard it was the work of a Fey who was not invited to the Princess's name-day feast,' volunteered Ognam.

'It was a poisoned needle,' said Danya, his face creased as he tried to recall the mythology of childhood. 'Or was it a poison draught? — the deed of a jealous stepmother.'

'Such ridiculous tales!' exclaimed the Princess. 'I never had a stepmother and could thou imagine *me* sewing?'

'Those stories were from a much older time and while they once had a grain of truth behind them, they have nothing to do with the charming young woman who sits on my right hand,' said Ysldon. 'The true reason for The Enchantment was that the age of High Magic was ending. Have you ever wondered what it was that gave Ythan its golden age?'

'It was ruled wisely by a long line of good kings,' said Danya.

'That is the belief but it is not the whole truth —

not that I am saying that Her Highness's ancestors were not good men. No, it was the effect of High Magic. Do you understand what I mean by High Magic?'

'We know of gramarye,' said Alwald. 'No one could stay in The Mage's Tower and not know about that.'

'Gramarye is to High Magic as apple ale is to rare wine. And it was High Magic that gave Ythan its peace, prosperity and power.'

As he spoke, Krispin remembered The Mage saying something similar and he leaned forward, eager to catch Ysldon's softly spoken words.

SIX
High Magic

'Listen.'

The Magus Ysldon held up his hand in the style of a sagaman.

'To begin at the beginning I must go back to the days when the Kingdom of Ythan was founded by a nomad chief named Johan,' he said. 'This man had been dispossessed of his lands beyond the River of Night by savage strangers who appeared out of the trackless region once known as the Home of the Winds. Those of his folk who survived the unexpected onslaught he led into the Wald but it was no place for mortal folk as in those days the Pottons still had their underground palace there.

'Johan and his followers marched to the Pass of the White Virgins and down to the wild country beyond which held as many perils for them as the Wald. At last they reached a fertile plain in the centre of which an enormous rock formation rose out of the earth and here Johan decided to stay. He built a fortress on the rock to protect his people from attack by the rulers of the petty kingdoms that were scattered across the plain, and over the next few generations it was enlarged into the Citadel under whose shelter grew the city of Danaak.

'When he had established himself Johan I, as he came to be called, defeated his awkward neighbours one by one and absorbed them into his territory, and so Ythan was born. Johan's royal descendants continued to push back the frontiers until it became the vast kingdom it is today.'

'How was it that Johan was so successful when he had not been able to hold his original demesne?' Alwald asked.

'You touch the gist,' said Ysldon. 'Johan had inherited a passion for wizardry from his forebears and when he began to build his fortress he offered hospitality – and later his hand – to a sorceress in return for her power to safeguard the new realm, bring victory to his campaign and protect him and his descendants with a special conjuration. But the enlargement of his territory was not always difficult because the populace of some kingdoms hanged their rulers and petitioned Johan to accept them as his subjects.'

Krispin asked why.

Ysldon explained that once you entered Ythan the grass grew more lush, the beeves carried more weight, the fruits of the trees were more plentiful and the sweetness of the wine was stronger.

'It was all due to High Magic,' he said. 'It was even believed that the highest towers of Johan's fortress were not made by hand but raised in a single night within a cloud of black fog. As to the truth of that I cannot vouch, but I do know that the foundations of mighty Ythan could not have been laid by a mere band of refugees, no matter how determined they were, without spellcraft.

'Johan's successors continued to keep on good terms with sorcerers who became obsessed with the idea of a perfect state in an imperfect world. Under royal decree a College of Magi was founded to study the nature of magic – until then those who practised sorcery had little idea of the powers they invoked – and the head of the college was given the title of Magus Royal and became the king's chief adviser. In my day I was Magus Royal to Johan XXXIII.'

Ysldon paused thoughtfully and wet his lips with amber wine.

'For centuries Ythan was a blessed land. If pestilence came, even the Red Death, High Magic – the most powerful and noble manifestation of gramarye – banished it. If reivers dared to raid within its frontiers from the Outlands, the king's army was shielded by High Magic and every royal arrow struck like an elf-bolt. If crops failed, the Magus Royal performed a rite and corn burst forth more golden than before and vines sagged beneath the weight of their fruit. If there was sorrow High Magic softened it and if there was joy it was heightened.

'Ah, fortunate were they who were birthed in Ythan in those idyllic days. Never was a realm so favoured. Her argosies plied the seas for rare viands and perfumes, her highways thronged with caravans laden with rich merchandise from the four corners of the kingdom, and those who laboured were well rewarded not only with silver but secure homes. Music was heard everywhere and the poet more honoured than the man of war.'

'A golden age indeed,' sighed Ognam, remembering

213

how he had heard something similar in The Mage's Tower. 'Few today would know the difference between a hexameter and a cithern.'

'But why did such a glorious epoch have to end?' asked Alwald who, like the others, had forgotten food while he listened to Ysldon's melodious voice.

'The golden age became senescent with the decline of High Magic,' he replied. 'For generations sorcerers who supported Ythan's Kings believed that the power of High Magic would be attainable for ever, nor did they have reason to suspect otherwise while their invocations continued to work for their own advantage and the commonweal. Only after I was admitted to the College of Magi did we perceive the terrible truth that High Magic was finite and, having been tapped for so long, its potency was waning.

'Each time a spell was cast the store of High Magic was diminished even as taking a cup of wine from a tun lessens the amount it contains. Realizing this, some sorcerers strove to preserve the precious element but others, thoughtless of the future, perversely squandered it on personal aggrandisement and, despite my efforts as Magus Royal, the College of Magi was riven with dissent. The actual ending of the golden age began with a visitation of the Red Death when no spell of enough potency could be raised to protect the folk of venerable Leymark from its bloody embrace.'

He stopped speaking and his eyes clouded as scenes of long-ago horror returned to his inner vision.

Tana said, 'Lord Magus, I do not understand. You tell us that magic was at an end. Yet there was still sorcery, for was I not abducted by it to The Mage's Tower?'

'I am talking of High Magic, lady,' replied Ysldon. 'Magic that could move mountains, tame seas, build empires and make those who mastered it believe they were gods – its inherent evil burgeoned because they forgot they were yet mortal men and women. In comparison the magic you have seen, my friends, is conjure magic, the dregs of a great elixir, and even those dregs are fast fading. Soon there will be no magic left in the Middle World other than that which is part of place or artefact, such as an enchanted spring or a becharmed sword . . .'

Krispin turned his face away, not wishing to meet Alwald's eye in case Ysldon's words would reawaken their argument over the ownership of Woundflame.

'But to resume my story,' said Ysldon. 'It became clear to me and some of my brother adepts that soon Ythan would depend solely on the efforts of its people, a dire prospect because, from the sweeper to the king, they had no concept of life without High Magic supporting them in the background.

'Of course the change did not come within a day or even a year which gave me and a few mages whose knowledge was almost equal to mine time to make preparations. We consulted the prophecies of the Sage Omgarth whose rhymes confirmed our forebodings. Yet, while we conferred and studied arcane lore in the hope of lessening the disaster, life in Ythan – apart from where the Red Death reigned – continued pleasantly enough. The peasants danced on the village greens and the nobles in their halls, and in Danaak hardly a day passed without some merry diversion.'

'We had lovely masques,' sighed the Princess.

'Despite the lovely masques, evil was becoming

215

manifest within the kingdom, not only with pestilence and blight but in the hearts of men, especially those who recognized the portents of decay and sought to profit from it. Worst, I fear, were the magi who, sensing the decline of their power, used what remained of High Magic for their own ends. One sorceress conspired to end the line of kingship by magic . . .'

In the warm light Krispin noticed a tear stealing down the cheek of Princess Livia and, as Ysldon continued to speak, her features became so distressed he was filled with pity. So far the Princess had said remarkably little and now he understood how she must suffer by waking up to find everything she had known was now in the past, her family and friends dead, her whole world changed. Looking at her he could imagine that it was Jennet reliving her heartbreak.

'What would it avail a sorceress to end the royal house, Mesire Magus?' Ognam was asking.

'It was to open the way for her young favourite to become the new master of Ythan in the upheaval that would follow,' Ysldon explained. 'There was no point in her harming King Johan because his days were numbered so she called a curse down upon his only child. It was a traditional curse of entrancement, well known through the Sleeping Beauty fable. She used it because of the old protective spell that had been laid upon the royal family which made it impossible to bring death to one of its members without suffering equal retribution.'

The Princess lowered her face into her hand.

'I regret the pain my words may cause,' said Ysldon turning to her, 'but you cannot escape such memories if you balance them with the thought of what is to be gained.'

She inclined without speaking and he continued, 'The malediction was cast in some secret place far from Danaak and it was only when Her Highness fell asleep in the middle of a rout that I began to understand the danger in which she lay. To the despair of the court physicians she was more and more frequently overtaken by periods of deathlike sleep until she fell into the trance which, because it did not end her life, held no threat of retribution to she who laid the curse. As a victim of such enchantment Livia could not inherit her father's crown.

'There was nothing that even I could do to halt the malaise though with my understanding of such bespelling I knew that as time passed it would be possible for her to be awakened − not by a kiss as folktales tell, but by being laved with water from the Wells of Ythan. I secretly planned a place where she could rest safely until such an event might come to pass, and this I explained to her before she fell into the final trance. Then myself and a few loyal magi drew upon what remained of High Magic to create a cavern chamber beyond the remotest border of Ythan with protective enchantments set upon the path leading to it through the land that became the Shadow Realm.'

'The apparitions that sought to turn us back!' exclaimed Krispin.

'It was so.'

'And the colossus that cleaved my fair ship in two!' muttered Danya in suppressed anger.

'That too, Shipmaster, but I think you may yet lay your hand on the tiller of a vessel more remarkable than your *Amber Star*. But to continue with my story. By means magical the Princess was brought to the

217

Mountains of the Moon and laid in her chamber with Barlak's good men as her guard. Alas, because the glamour that preserved them down the years faded with the wane of High Magic their true ages overtook them.'

'We do not hold you to blame, Lord Magus,' said Barlak. 'Had we not agreed to your bespellment our bones would have bleached among the ruins of Haven.'

'The taking of Haven out of Time Present was my last use of High Magic,' continued Ysldon. 'Of course I can still conjure but it is like the play of babes compared to my erstwhile powers. Once Livia lay safely upon her couch of smoke I walked to this valley and as the last Guardian of the Wells had been called by the Dark Maid I took his place.'

'So Her Highness was hidden away to preserve her from her enemies,' exclaimed Ognam in understanding. 'It is the other way round to what I heard as a child.'

'To preserve her from her enemies, and the folly and bloodshed that followed the death of her father. But there was another reason. We who spirited Her Highness away knew from the prophecies of Omgarth that the bright day of Ythan would become darkest night. As suspicion and persecution, plague and famine cast their long shadows over the kingdom the glorious past would become no more than a myth. Without the royal line, with priests interested in naught but robes and rituals, and with Witchfinders instead of teachers, there would be nothing left to remind folk that better times were possible, nothing to inspire them to resist the yokes of tyranny. Nothing, that is, except a belief that somewhere lay a Princess of the old blood who, if she could be wakened, would herald a new and better age. And despite the efforts of the Regents and the Witchfinders who feared that some day she might return, the legend of the Sleeping Princess survived.

'She was a beacon of hope in the darkness, and braving persecution men and women sought to find her along what they called the Pilgrim Path. Down the years hundreds perished in the search, for the quest itself was a testing – only when Pilgrims appeared with enough natural resource as well as courage to find her would the kingdom be deemed ready for her return.'

Ysldon smiled gravely and bowed to his guests – a gesture that filled Krispin and Alwald with secret pride.

'For that reason we decreed that no remnant of High Magic, other than what might be encountered naturally, might aid those who had undertaken the quest.'

'But when we were in the Wilderness of Gil . . .' Ognam began.

'That was not High Magic,' said Ysldon sharply. 'It would not have been the first time the Wells had appeared to ease the distress of travellers.'

Ognam wisely said no more.

'You, my friends, have met the challenge of the quest not a day too soon,' Ysldon resumed. 'To quote Omgarth's *Prophecia* the destiny of Ythan is about to change for good or ill according to whoever triumphs in the forthcoming conflict, and the outcome is beyond prediction because this era of Time Future is unformed. All we can glean is that the kingdom will be affected as much as it was at The Enchantment and once its course is decided so it will be for generations.

'The truth of his words is proved by the flight of the crystal bird across the face of Ythan for the last three seasons, a portent of change as it was at the time of The Enchantment.'

'The crystal bird!' exclaimed Krispin and Ognam together.

'Once I beheld it, before I began the quest,' Krispin continued excitedly. 'What is it and from whence does it fly?'

'Even I cannot say where it begins its aerial voyage,' replied Ysldon. 'In olden times some believed it came from beyond World's End, others that it appeared from Time Future. As to what it is I can only say it is a miraculous harbinger and its flights prepare the wise for prodigious upheaval. It shines with the glory of the All Father or . . .' Ysldon's tone became ironic, 'in this enlightened age should I speak of the glory of the Serene Mother?'

There was a silence and then Gambal, speaking carefully as though at pains not to give offence, said, 'Lord Magus, I am puzzled, for logic tells me that the creator of the Three Worlds must know the future as well as the past, for all of Time must be as one to him. Therefore, as the future is already defined, what is the purpose of us trying to alter it? Who are we to think it possible to change the design laid down at the Beginning of All Things?'

'Ah, there is a thinker at my table,' smiled Ysldon. 'Since the First Time sages have pondered that question. I say that your argument would be logical if there was only one future but there are a myriad futures ahead of us. According to the most ancient of scriptures — now out of fashion with the shrines, I believe — when the All Father looked upon his creation it came upon him that because Time was a part of it as much as the earth upon which we sit or the Star Bridge above us, he knew the form that everything would take in the future, that there could be nothing unexpected — and that he had sentenced himself to boredom for eternity.

'So in his wisdom he caused his final creation to come about which some call Chance and others Chaos, and which removes all certainty so that even the deity — whether father or daughter — has no knowledge of which particular path of all the countless paths of destiny will be followed.'

'If that be so,' pressed Gambal, 'how could the Sage Omgarth prophesy future happenings?'

'When he looked to the distant future he could only prophesy changes and, thanks to Chaos, not what they would lead to. Nearer to his own time he could predict accurately because the chain of events was already in progress. We only live in the present, by the time we move into the future it is the present, but to a seer like Omgarth the line between future and present was blurred and therefore he had an inkling of what was about to happen before ordinary mortals.

'But enough. It is long since I entertained and I have no wish for this evening to be solemn. Listening to me you have let your broth and meats cool . . .'

He waved his hand and steam rose again from bowls and on trenchers meat sizzled once more in its own fat. Talk began, awkward at first but livening as goblets were raised and drained and the music — the Music of the Spheres, Ysldon called it — rose to accompany the flying words and increasing laughter.

Suddenly Alwald had an uncanny sensation that he was being observed by some unseen watcher. He turned and looked into the fragrant darkness but nothing stirred and he put it down to his imagination. At the same time Krispin shivered as though a goose had walked over his grave.

SEVEN

Fire
and Flame

To and fro, to and fro the whetstone caressed the edge of the axe blade that had already been honed to the sharpness of a new razor. Through the cave entrance Fulk the woodcutter could see a line of firs with the moon balancing upon their jagged points. Behind him the cave widened considerably and here the followers of the Wish Maiden sat in quiet groups round charcoal braziers which burned without giving off smoke that might catch the attention of a nomad patrol. Fuel for these stoves presented no difficulty as there were many dispossessed charcoal burners in the Maiden's ranks.

Occasionally one of the men would glance at the solitary figure and wink at the others; they admired his strength and skill with an axe but they found him a loner, a man whom it seemed impossible to befriend. There was an element in his gloomy silences that embarrassed the men who all carried burdens of grief. Without even speaking he reminded them of things they sought to keep hidden in the attics of their minds. Only Wode got on well with him, saying to the Wish Maiden, 'Watch that man, my love. Solitary he may be but I feel in my bones that one day he will perform us a great service.'

She laughed and kissed him as she did when they had a chance to be alone together in the forest; in the company of her devoted Waldmen she was the virginal prophetess who, with her respectful lieutenant Wode, had enabled them to strike back at the invaders of their forest home. Since Wode had thrown his lot in with her the numbers of men drawn to her cause had multiplied several times over. And after every successful foray — such as the destruction of the bridge over the River of Night — more came to follow the girl who claimed to be inspired by the ancient spirit of the forest.

Wode instilled into these recruits the need to be as ruthless as their enemy.

'Fire must be fought with flame,' was his watchword and it was demonstrated by poles planted beside forest paths on which were impaled barbarian heads. It was such stern methods that had won Fulk over, and tonight Fulk would have his first taste of blood-letting.

To and fro hissed the whetstone.

Two figures appeared against the moonlit cave mouth, the slender silhouette of the Wish Maiden and the thickset form of her lieutenant. This had been one of the nights when, under the protection of Wode, she went to a lonely place to commune with the elemental source of her inspiration. Now that she was returned Fulk could see that her eyes were unnaturally bright and her expression was one of remembered elation.

The spirit has moved her, thought Fulk and, after putting the whetstone in his scrip, he ran the edge of his axe blade down his hirsute forearm and was satisfied to see that it left a strip of skin as smooth as the Wish Maiden's cheek, giving substance to the story that he used his axe as a razor.

A leather curtain was hung across the entrance, boar fat candles were lighted and the Wish Maiden sat among her veterans with a looted goblet of spring water while Wode, a tankard of apple ale in his hand, remained standing.

'Tonight is propitious,' he declared. 'Tonight we are going to strike such a blow against the Potton-spawned horde that it will be told a hundred seasons hence.'

There was a murmur of eager anticipation.

'Until now only Brindal has been privy to our plan, not because we do not have full trust in you but, as you well know, no prisoner of the nomads can keep his silence once he has been consigned to the Pit.'

Heads nodded in bitter agreement.

'Listen then,' continued Wode. 'Tonight we are going to capture River Garde.'

There was an indrawing of breath at the boldness of the announcement — and its apparent impossibility.

The Wish Maiden held up her hand.

'Fear not,' she said in her usual calm tone. 'The venture is not as mad as it sounds. Think of what success would mean. With one great deed we would win the key to the Wald.'

'And the black pennants of the River Lords would fly again,' said a riverman who in happier days had supplied fish to the castle kitchens.

'This time there will be new pennants over River Garde,' said Wode. 'The days of the River Lords are gone. Grimwald is dead and who can say what happened to his son.'

'A fowler saw him sailing downriver to the Land

225

of Blight,' said a goatherd. 'And he had the Lady Demara with him.'

'Ay, it is told he freed her from River Garde with her maid Margan,' added a forester.

'And it is also told that he went off to seek the Sleeping Princess,' said another, the humorist of the band whose words were rewarded with laughter.

'If he be mad enough to enter the Land of Blight we shall never hear of him again,' Wode said. 'After we take River Garde it will have a new mistress and the pennants will be white for our maid.'

Realizing the import of his words many of the men grinned their approval but others looked doubtful.

'We fight to avenge ourselves on wolfmen, not to set up new dynasties,' muttered one.

'Fear not, Goff,' said Wode quickly. 'Someone must hold the castle once the Wald is free to stop the return of our enemies and who better than she who has led us against them.'

There was a chorus of agreement which faded as each man considered the enormity of what Wode was suggesting. It was one thing to ambush nomads in the forest where they had the advantage of having spent their lives as woodsmen but to attack a high-walled castle that had only fallen once, and then through treachery, would be a daunting task for an army with siege engines — and suicide for such a ragged band as they.

Wode sensed their misgivings and said, 'Since the Wolf King led his men over the ranges there has only been a small garrison there, and no doubt a discontented one, for the barbarians are dispirited away from their steppes.'

'Mayhap they be,' a forester muttered, 'but if the

castle was empty it would still be nigh impossible to scale its walls.'

'True, but that makes our foes less watchful. Do not forget that for many years I served with Grimwald's guards and the place has few secrets unknown to me.'

The girl rose and faced them.

'My brethren, of all who have suffered in the Wald you are the ones who have fought back and your valour has made the name of the Wish Maiden the bane of the wolfmen,' she said simply. 'Call upon that valour once more and none will dare cross the bridge or ply the river without our permission.' And she went on to explain Wode's plan to bewilder the enemy before the main attack was launched. He knew of a secret tunnel that led under the castle to a well that was only used in times of emergency as fresh water from a stream was normally preferred. It was believed that young Lord Alwald had used this passage to rescue the Lady Demara and as a result the nomads sealed the wellhead by cementing iron bars across it.

'Although no man can pass that grille it will not bar flame,' the Wish Maiden said. 'For many nights now Wode and Brindal have ventured along the tunnel to pour skins of oil into the well where it lies on the water. Once lit it will roar up the shaft like a blaze up a chimney and set fire to the armoury above, and that is when we shall strike. As for entry into the castle that will depend on the skill of our good friend Fulk.'

She moved the leather curtain. A pale luminosity indicated that the moon had slipped below the pines.

'It is time for us to set out,' she said. 'As always, anyone who does not have faith in what we are about to do may remain behind without dishonour.'

As one, her followers rose to their feet and reached for their weapons.

The castle of River Garde loomed huge against the starshine.

The Waldmen crouched beneath the boughs of the trees that grew almost up to its eastern wall, each wondering what the next hour would bring and if he would manage to play his part in Wode's daring plan. Few lights showed above the battlements which gave them hope that the castle was lightly garrisoned after most of the horde had ridden west to carry their terror beyond the White Virgins.

Wode and Fulk stood a little way from the others beneath a pine whose head towered above the other forest trees.

' "Old Grandfather" we used to call it,' whispered Wode. 'It must be nigh on sixty paces high, certainly long enough for what I have in mind if it falls right. What is the very fastest you could chop through it?'

In the faint starlight Fulk eyed the trunk professionally and then spread his arms against its sticky bark.

'Such wood is very soft compared to oak or ash and I rarely bothered with it when I worked in the forest,' he said quietly. 'But this was rightly called "Grandfather" and its girth makes up for hardness. When I was a-cutting wood all day long I learned to pace myself so that my strokes were as telling at sunset as when I began in the morning, so working like that I reckon I would bring it down in under half an hour.'

'But if you worked as though your very life and the lives of your comrades depended upon it, how long?'

'Mayhap ten minutes, if I got the cut right so it

would break under its own weight when I reached centre.'

'Do better than that and your name will become a legend. Old Grandfather will be our ladder if you position it so its top branches rest on the wall beside that turret.'

'It will not be easy in the dark.'

'There should be light enough when Brindal fires the oil.'

Fulk nodded and, taking a whetstone from his pocket, he began to stroke it along his axe blade while he peered at the bole of the pine and planned his strokes.

Suddenly the breeze carried an outburst of uncouth cries and all eyes turned to River Garde where a gigantic tongue of flame gushed from the armoury roof.

As its ruddy glare thrust back the shadows the Wish Maiden cried to Fulk, 'Woodman, work as you have never worked for the sake of the Wald.'

He needed no urging but spat on his palms, took up a position in front of the tree and swung two strokes in such rapid succession that it was impossible for those watching with indrawn breath to follow them. A huge chip flew free and the scent of resin rose from the wound.

A down-stroke, an up-stroke, another wedge of pinewood flew into the dancing shadows. It appeared to Wode that the blurred axe was eating the tree as rivulets of sweat glistened on Fulk's face and his chest heaved in rhythm to his grunted breathing. And when one of the flying chips opened his cheek he did not pause for an instant in his whirlwind performance.

Cries continued to float from the castle where the

flames leapt even higher and a firmament of red sparks drifted over the forest. The alarm bell began to toll.

Fulk jumped into a new stance so as to attack the tree from a different angle. Old Grandfather creaked his protest as the blade sliced deep into his heartwood and his branches trembled in despair.

A dozen more blows and Fulk backed away. With a continuous groaning the tree began to tilt. The wood surrounding Fulk's great V-shaped cleft splintered and with this last restraint gone the giant pine slowly toppled just as the woodcutter had planned so its top branches were caught on the battlemented wall.

Wode was the first to leap on the still-trembling trunk. He was followed by foresters who had climbed trees after birds' nests almost as soon as they could walk and they were followed by the less sure-footed rivermen.

Fulk sank to the soft earth with his heart pounding agonizingly and his blood roaring in his ears. His fight for breath had dried his throat so it felt scalded but he thought triumphantly that even if his heart were to burst he had brought down Old Grandfather in less than half the time he had told Wode. When he looked up he saw that the Wish Maiden was among those clambering up the angled trunk and picking up his axe once more he followed.

Wode crashed out of the upper foliage and jumped through a crenel on to the wall. By the flames leaping from the armoury's woodlined roof he saw a couple of nomads racing towards him with their long-handled axes raised. As the first one came within striking distance he suddenly lunged with his two-handed broadsword so that the warrior transfixed himself upon it with the momentum of his charge. With an expert heave he catapulted the screaming man into space and, brandishing his crimsoned blade, shouted, 'First blood! First blood!'

Seeing more Waldmen appear on the wall the second nomad turned and raced down a flight of stone steps to raise the alarm among the confusion that already reigned. Wolfmen began to abandon their chains of leather buckets to seek their weapons when with cries of 'The Wald! The Wald!' a party of ragged foresters sprang down the steps and began to maim and kill before they realized what was happening.

Joined by the Wish Maiden and several of their followers, Wode raced along the familiar walls and down a stairwell at the barbican where with one tremendous sweep of his sword he decapitated the gateman. The head, still wearing a wolf-skull helmet, blinked at them from the paving while they frantically unbarred the gates.

A roar of triumph went up as more Waldmen surged beneath the arch and followed the blood-spattered Wish Maiden to the armoury square where a battle raged amid blazing debris.

Although the nomads fought with their inbred desperation many were past their prime and within half an hour most of the garrison lay dead on the cobbles. While some Waldmen tended their own wounded and laid out their dead decently – the bodies of the barbarians were hurled into the flames – the rest began a terrible game of hide-and-seek with the survivors.

Fulk raced from square to square, along passages and up tower stairs in the hope of finding the young wolfman who had lain with his daughter. To him the nomads looked alike and twice he thought his axe had brought him revenge only to be disappointed when he looked into the faces of his victims.

Hand-in-hand with Wode the Wish Maiden ran along the ramparts intoxicated by victory and laughing as her followers dragged out the enemy from their hiding places to be flung from the walls or – after the Pit and its ghastly contents were discovered – to be driven into the roaring pyre.

By dawn the armoury had burned itself out, the wine of victory had been drunk and from watchtower and turret streamed white pennants. They were not the only sign of the Wish Maiden's triumph, a score of spiked heads leered from the barbican. Fire had been fought with flame.

EIGHT

Snow
Wraiths

'Underneath my dear love's casement
From its bed a black rose blows,
There my heart remains in bondage
Through summer shine and winter snows.

'My heart now hangs upon the thorn,
The rose lies on her breast this morn . . .'

So sang Ognam as he shrugged his pack into position.
'My heart now hangs upon the thorn,' chorused
Krispin and Danya less musically than the jongleur but
no less cheerfully. The travellers − even Tumbrul −
were filled with rare optimism and goodwill. None
could remember feeling so strong, and at this moment
Barlak and his men could hardly recall the sensation
of their unnatural ageing. Even grief for comrades who
had succumbed to it had faded to the philosophic
resignation that would have been felt if the same men
had died in a professional passage of arms. The dead
had gone to the arms of the Mother, the world was
waiting for the living.

233

Beneath the cupola Ysldon and the Princess spoke long and quietly together and Krispin, having completed his musical contribution, sat apart from the others. He was nervous of catching the eye of the Magus in case his face should reveal guilt — an echo of a childish fear that had frequently gripped him at Dame Nobert's school in Toyheim. The night before, after the rest of the company had fallen into heavy slumber following the feast, Krispin had filled an empty wine flask with water that spurted from the mouth of a stone satyr.

This morning the flask was hidden safely in his pack yet he was uneasy. Although no prohibition regarding the water had been issued, he felt instinctively that if he had asked permission of the Magus to take some away he would have been refused. Now he was anxious to get the farewells over and be on the journey once more, and his apprehension increased when he saw Ysldon beckon to him and Alwald.

'Tumbrul will lead you through the ranges until you find the trail leading down into Ythan,' he told them. 'There he will leave you for his own realm.'

'Where is that, Lord Magus?' Alwald asked.

'Underground. Unhappy Tumbrul, he fears he may be the last of his kind and though he may value treasure above all else I doubt if it will bring him solace.'

'And after he leaves us?' asked Krispin, relieved that the Magus had made no reference to the secret in his pack.

'Now that you have accomplished the quest for the Princess the prohibition on certain sorcerous assistance need no longer apply. Therefore I shall use some of the power left to me to arrange an easy passage to your

234

destination in Ythan. Once you are aboard the white barge you will be safe, though after that I can promise nothing.'

'Where is our destination, Lord Magus?' Alwald inquired.

'A place where those loyal to the Path may begin the restoration of the Princess. All will be clear in the fullness of time.' (Alwald afterwards remarked to Krispin that it was a characteristic of practitioners in the art of gramarye to retain an air of mystery rather than give straightforward answers.)

'Will you return to Danaak if the Princess is enthroned?' Krispin asked.

'My place is here,' replied Ysldon. 'The day of the high magician is long over and I know of only one other from the time of The Enchantment. Your old host The Mage owes his long life to the fact that most of the time his body rests like a bear in winter while his spirit travels outside of Time Present. My interest still lies in the contemplation of this world and it is due to living amid these miraculous fountains that my span has been prolonged. Sorcery had nothing to do with it because the Wells are beyond that, just as they are much more than a source of healing water. Truth lies in their depths, and for the mind of man it can be the most perilous commodity in the Three Worlds — and the ultimate reward. When I am finally ready for the ordeal through many seasons of preparation I shall seek it.'

Carried away by thoughts beyond the understanding of ordinary mortals his voice faded and Krispin and Alwald stood in embarrassed silence for several minutes.

'You must leave now,' the Magus declared as with

an effort he returned to the present. 'Each hour is precious if Ythan is to be saved from the ever-growing power of Regent and Witchfinder. Come, my friends,' he continued in a brighter voice. 'Farewells should be brief if the journey be long. Regret the parting but treasure the meeting.'

Standing at the head of the terrace steps he held his staff in one hand and made a cabbalistic sign with the other as each of the travellers bade him goodbye.

'Remember, you have achieved more than you realize,' he said when it was Krispin's turn but Krispin thought little of the words in his relief at leaving with the flask undetected.

They followed Tumbrul over the daisy-scattered grass to the woods where they turned to see the Guardian of the Wells standing against the flying rainbows of the fountains with his arm raised in a blessing, then he was lost to sight as they entered the dappled shade of the trees.

Tumbrul strutted ahead with several of Barlak's men close behind; the Princess walked beside Alwald and the others followed with the remaining warriors forming a rearguard. All strode out with a zest that was obviously the effect of the Wells. Krispin noticed that even the cloth of his tunic and hose appeared as though it had been newly woven; the colours of Ognam's motley were no longer faded and the mail of the men-at-arms shone silver.

With this sense of renewal came merriment. The warriors sang snatches of camp songs last sung a century ago while the others chatted like children being led to a treat rather than a handful of Pilgrims bound for the territory of their all-powerful enemy. Even Danya, who had tried to conceal his mournful feelings since the loss of his ship, grinned reminiscently as he recounted seafaring yarns to Gambal who encouraged him with appreciative smiles and sympathetic noddings.

This light-hearted mood ended when Tana looked up and gasped with revulsion. Cradled in the upper branches of a tall hornbeam was a body partly wrapped in a red surcoat. Beneath its helmet, empty eye sockets gazed incuriously down upon them though the lipless mouth leered a ghastly welcome.

'Serene Mother!' several breathed and made the protective gesture.

'By his coat he was a Companion of the Rose,' said Gambal. 'He must have fallen from yonder cliff.'

With dismay Krispin followed the line of his outstretched arm to a track that wound up the dizzy precipice marking the end of the valley. He joined the others in making the sacred sign.

As the party toiled up the cliff-face, those who had recoiled from the skull's grimace now regarded it as an ill-omened portent. Although the sun continued to pour warmth and light down on the verdant valley, the sky directly above had taken on a leaden cast that reminded Krispin of the sky that loured over the Cold Sea. Soon a strong wind whirled cruising eagles like autumn leaves and chilled the travellers with cold borne from the snows of the three peaks dominating the western end of the valley.

'Hurry!' screeched Tumbrul above the wind. 'We must be off this path before the storm breaks.'

Path? thought Krispin as the others drew further and further ahead of him. *Path! How can that little monster call this crack in the rockface a path?*

By the time Krispin hauled himself over the edge of the cliff under his companions' impatient gaze, lightning was flickering round the heads of the mountains. Anxiously following in the wake of Tumbrul they entered the pass through which the Regent had been borne in his litter a short while earlier.

Barlak caught up with the trotting guide and he asked the reason for his pace which was hardly suitable for Her Highness.

'Cannot you feel it or is your skin as thick as your mail?' he retorted. 'There is something amiss, something beyond nature . . . I taste it in the air and I see it in the sky. We must . . .'

His next words were drowned in a stupendous roll of thunder, the pass ahead was filled with lightning glare and blue flame outlined the warriors' weapons. Before the growling echoes faded a white wall of swirling snowflakes descended before them.

They halted in astonishment. Not a single flake had alighted upon them yet a few paces ahead a snowstorm raged within itself.

'We must go back,' Tumbrul shouted. 'There is demon work here.'

'It is only snow,' remonstrated Alwald. 'Freakish weather is to be expected in such a mountainous wilderness and it will doubtless pass as quickly as it came. We have faced things a trifle worse than snow on our travels and lived to tell the tale.' The Princess gave him an approving look but Tumbrul raged.

'Only snow! Freakish weather!' He actually danced in his anger. 'You ox-brained poltroons, you stupid . . .'

Alwald's hand dropped to his richly decorated sword hilt.

'Call me what you will, you long-nosed maggot, but if your childish abuse includes Her Highness I am duty bound as a man of gentle birth to teach you manners with the flat of my blade.'

'Thou put it well,' approved the Princess.

'Look! Look!' screamed Tumbrul.

'Furthermore, I think an apology is the least one could expect even from a goblin . . .'

'The Maid take you!' retorted Tumbrul, so outraged he momentarily forgot what had caught his attention. 'I have told you before I am not a goblin.'

'Gnome, Potton, dwarf, boggard . . . I care not what you are, but I demand . . .'

'Demand what you will — we are doomed!'

Alwald and the others followed Tumbrul's terrified gaze to the curtain of flakes and became aware of pale shadows moving within the seething whiteness.

'Snow wraiths!' Tumbrul cried. 'Get back or it will be more than your bodies that you lose!'

Although his words meant nothing to them, there was no mistaking the menace that emanated from the indistinct forms. As one, the travellers turned — to see that twenty paces behind them a similar wall of falling snow blocked their retreat. Within it there were more moving shapes which as they watched became defined as skeletal caricatures of the human form . . . elongated heads with fang-filled mouths, arms that hung to knees, ribs protruding from drum-tight skin, dagger fingers.

There was no doubt of their hungry intent, their greed for sustenance, and yet as their victims stared at them they realized that they were without real substance. They imposed their shape upon the floating flakes in the same way that an eddy of wind will give

239

its form to the dust it stirs. Yet this insubstantiality did not lessen the fear they inspired. Here was a psychic threat that they recognized by inborn instinct from the First Time when men shared existence with beings since relegated to nightmares.

Ognam exclaimed, 'They cannot harm us as long as we are outside the snowfall.' But the hope conveyed in his words died as it was realized that both snowfalls were advancing to envelop them.

The warriors surrounded the Princess with Elmo fire still flowing from their weapons. Krispin seized the grip of Woundflame and gave a curse of pain. The metal was so cold that it seemed to *burn* his hand, an indication that they had unwittingly entered a realm of the strange.

Drawing the blade he ran to the snow curtain and aimed a stroke at the nearest of the wraiths within it. A cloud of vapour hid the effect of the blow but not the shriek that vibrated within their heads. A coldness beyond that of ice travelled up the blade to Krispin's arm and robbed it of movement.

It was Tumbrul's shouts that jolted them out of the paralysing fear inspired by the approaching apparitions.

'Up there, up there!' he yelled and began scrabbling up the lefthand wall of the pass. The others followed with terror-born desperation though Barlak only started to climb when he saw that Alwald was helping the Princess to find secure footholds. With his arm numb Krispin had the most difficulty until Gambal seized him by his useless limb and hauled him up.

Luckily for the travellers they had not ventured far into the pass and thus the walls were not high at this point, and after some frantic minutes they reached the top to find themselves on the edge of a great stretch of ice-streaked rock. Looking down they saw that the pass was filled with what appeared to be a blizzard though up here they were free from the unnatural menace.

'No time to rest,' panted Tumbrul. 'If the snow is made to fall here they will smell us out.'

He started over the rock that sloped steadily towards the distant snowline. The others followed swiftly thanks to the renewal of strength that the Wells had bestowed upon them, and as they climbed higher the cloud above lost its greyness and soon afterwards the west wind shredded it to wrack.

At last shortage of breath forced them to rest with their backs against an outcrop of reddish rock. For the first time Krispin was able to take notice of the scenery and he was overwhelmed by its grandeur; to the east rose the highest peaks of the Mountains of the Moon, to the south stretched a rolling wasteland of ancient rock, weather-sculpted into a petrified sea through which the pass snaked. The west and north provided a panorama of snow-mantled ranges descending towards a distant darkness that was the Shadow Realm.

Although he was accustomed to the high country of the Wald, Krispin had never experienced such vastness and majestic desolation, and he had the half-thrilling, half-frightening sensation of being on the very top of the world. Only once before had he known such exhilaration and that was when he flew over the Ranges of Dono Kara on the back of a great golden griffin.

When he had breathed enough thin air to be able to speak again he turned to Gambal to thank him for his assistance but he merely smiled and put his long forefinger to his lips to suggest that it was unnecessary.

'What were those hideous shadows?' asked Tana.

'Snow wraiths,' Tumbrul replied. 'They are elder beings who haunt the high places. Being without bodies they use falling snow — or mountain mist, I have been told — to take shape in order to hunt those who trespass here. As spirits they feed on the spirits of those they bring to their death. Normally they only haunt the snow peaks and what puzzles me is why the snow fell only in the pass. It was as though a weather witch conjured it to allow the wraiths to form where they could reach us.'

'And I have a good idea who that witch might be,' Gambal muttered to himself.

'Surely it is only the Magus Ysldon who knoweth I have been wakened,' said the Princess. 'He explained to me the sad state of my kingdom under the regency and why the Regent should wish me harm but even if my enemies guess I am back in Time Present how wouldst they know where to strike?'

'How indeed?' muttered Danya.

'Ay, how indeed?' echoed Alwald and like the others his eyes turned to Gambal.

For a moment Gambal lost his nerve. He knew that if he opened his mouth to protest his innocence — and the irony was that he was innocent — he would stutter like one deep in guilt. Help came unexpectedly from Krispin who, remembering Gambal's words from the prevous evening, said, 'It cannot have been him, Alwald, for it would be against his interest to betray us to his old master after ruining his plan.'

'So the spy has found a friend,' Alwald murmured.

Krispin sighed, recognizing that the goodwill

engendered at the Wells was evaporating now they were further from their influence.

'The problem with village folk is that they lose judgement as soon as they are fed a few patronizing words,' Alwald added.

Krispin remembered his feeling of warmth towards Alwald with sadness at its loss but it did not prevent him saying in a mock High Wald accent, 'I tugs me forelock in respect, Lord Alwald, and begs leave to say that us Toyheim folk did put great store on a kindly word as you say — so it must have been a kind word from the Reeve of the High Wald that fooled me into undertaking a quest with a spoilt . . .'

Despite himself Krispin was about to come out with a terrible insult but the Princess saved the moment by saying, 'Enough. This is no moment for petty rancour, Master Krispin. We have left the Wells but a short time and already have been emperilled yet thou wouldst bicker. I forbid it.'

In a sudden shift of mood Krispin felt like laughing, not at what the Princess had said but her manner of delivery — it was so like a rebuke from Jennet in the good old days.

'Do not bandy words on my account,' said Gambal, recovering his poise. 'All I will say is that no matter what you might think about the allegiance I once owed to the Regent, if it had not been for me you would now be entombed and Her Highness would have been a captive bound for an unhappy fate in Danaak.'

Then with a sense of timing that had been of such use during his term as Revel Master, he added accusingly, 'You all stood like statues when Her Highness's life was under threat — is that why you forget that it was I, Gambal, who saved her?'

243

Alwald was about to make a retort but when he saw the Princess glance with new interest at the innocent-faced young man he curbed his tongue.

'We must march not argue,' said Tumbrul, climbing to his feet and shouldering his clinking bag. 'We have a fair way to go.'

'Where?' asked Alwald.

'As it is no longer possible to risk the pass I can only take you through the mountains to where the ice river descends into Ythan.'

'I thank you for speaking up for me,' Gambal said quietly to Krispin as they moved off. 'But I regret it caused ill words between you and Lord Alwald.'

'They are not the first we have had, as you well know,' Krispin replied.

After they had ascended the slope for another half hour they found themselves on the edge of a plateau bounded by snow-covered mountains. Where their peaks habitually blocked the sun's rays from reaching certain areas winter ice lay in freezing shadow. Wrapping their cloaks more tightly about themselves the travellers continued to follow Tumbrul, ever watchful for unexpected signs of snow but to their relief the sky remained free from cloud. When evening drew on, their rotund guide won their approval by finding a dry cave in a fantastical rampart of wind-worn rock. Thankfully they lay down in the blankets and chewed dry traveller's bread and when the sentries were posted all drifted into sleep without words other than mumbled goodnights.

NINE

Toy Soldiers

The Pilgrims rose with the sun and after a mouthful of wine each they set out over frozen snow between ice formations suggestive of folktale castles and fabulous beasts. The cold emanating from these dazzling fantasies chilled them to the bone and they wrapped their blankets about themselves as extra cloaks.

'Are you certain this is the only route?' Alwald asked Tumbrul.

'Heh? Of course I am certain!' he retorted. 'I grew up in the Mountains of the Moon. My people . . .' His voice trailed off as uncomfortable thoughts assailed him. His people? Even the Magus Ysldon had been unable to answer his questions about them. Was he the only one of his kind left in the world? If so his loneliness would be beyond words – had such a fate been the real price of his treasure?

He tried to drown such thoughts in a surge of anger, a trick that had always worked for him in the olden days. Turning to Alwald he said furiously, 'If you do not have faith in me as a guide you can lead your friends through the pass yourself and ask the way of the snow wraiths as you go.'

'It was not for myself that I asked,' replied Alwald curbing his irritation. 'My concern is for Her Highness.'

'She is healthy enough after her long rest,' cried Tumbrul. 'She seems to have had no difficulty in keeping up with the party. But mayhap she sees you as her champion and you feel you must work for that privilege.'

Alwald flushed and turned away. It was true that while they rested at the Wells the Princess had called him her champion — and why not? Before The Enchantment a Lord of the River March had always been the King's Champion — and, in the tradition of folktales, he had been the first person the Princess had seen on waking which made him special in her eyes. He found pleasure in the thought though he reminded himself that his heart remained in the Vale of Mabalon with the Lady Demara.

Reaching the far side of the plateau, the Pilgrims found themselves climbing treacherous slopes and trekking in single file through twisting ravines whose floors remained frozen even in high summer. By midday they halted for a meagre meal amidst more ice formations that lay about them like the ruins of a dead city.

'How fine these mountains looked from the deck of the *Amber Star*,' Danya mused as he broke his hard traveller's bread. 'Little did I dream then I would soon be climbing their accursed slopes.'

'Heh, sailors are only at home on the sea,' said Tumbrul. 'To me there is nothing more beautiful than the Mountains of the Moon.'

'How didst they come by their name, Master Tumbrul?' the Princess asked.

'It goes back long before your kingdom was founded,' he answered. 'It was in the days when the Children of Yth roamed the world and the stars were still new in their courses. Then the moon fell in love with the earth and departed from the path that the All Father had decreed for him. Nearer and nearer he came to the face of his beloved while the sun burned bright with jealousy.

'The earth thrilled at the approach of the moon, her seas overflowed and the very ground trembled with expectation.

'Closer he came until they almost touched, and so eager was the earth for his caress that part of her rose to meet him. At this the sun became so enraged she began to burn the lovers with the heat of her anger. The seas of the moon turned to vapour which fell upon the earth in scalding tears, and parts of the earth began to flame so that to this day she is scarred by vast wastes of sand.'

Such is the power of story-telling that for a few minutes the party forgot their discomfort as Tumbrul described the anger of the sun.

'Then it came to pass that the All Father, who had shaped everything from his breath in the First Time, noticed the brilliance of the sun and heard the groaning of the earth, and he saw that the moon had left his ordained track. And so the All Father saved the earth, which was his most favoured creation, by sending the sad moon back into the sky and cooling the heat of the sun, and he decreed that in order that there would be no more strife between the moon and the sun, the moon would only travel through the sky at night when the sun had gone to her rest.

'But the moon has never forgotten his love for the earth, and sometimes he breaks the commandment and rises into the sky before the sun has gone or after she has dawned so he can look upon the earth in daylight . . .

'As for the earth her seas cooled and her forests returned and she was much the same as she was before though the part of her that had risen to touch her lover remained which in time was rightly named the Mountains of the Moon.'

'Bravo,' cried Ognam. 'That is a tale I shall remember. You are a born story-teller, Master Tumbrul.'

Tumbrul's memory stirred. He had a fleeting picture of a vast hall lit by a hundred lamps round its tapestried walls, tables smothered with platters of food and wine jugs, an old man with a beard to his knees sitting on a canopied throne and before him was a harper who was short, globe-headed and with a long sharp nose like the rest of the company.

'My people held saga-telling in the highest regard,' he said. 'Once I knew a thousand tales but . . .' He shook his head, impatient of his wayward memory.

'We should move on,' said Alwald, standing up. 'Summer days may be long but it would be good to be clear of the ice by nightfall.'

'There is more ice than you imagine, Lord Alwald, so your words are apt,' said Tumbrul, heaving his bag on to his shoulder and setting off along a trail that led upwards between two ice castles. When the way became too steep and slippery one of the warriors used his battleaxe to cut steps.

It was the middle of the afternoon when they

emerged on to a snowy plain where they paused to regain their breath after a long climb. Danya, who had the sharpest eyes of the party, noticed something glinting on a piece of flat rock that protruded from the snow. Wondering idly whether it was merely an ice crystal or something of greater interest he walked over to the rock and then cried out in astonishment.

'Come, look what I have found,' he called.

They drifted towards him, not really interested but polite enough to humour him.

'How in the name of the Mother do they come to be here?' the shipmaster muttered as they approached and then stared in equal surprise.

On the rock, as though spaced out on a table, stood rows of identical little figures, their garments and harness brightly painted. It had been the sunlight striking their tiny mail shirts that had heliographed to Danya.

Krispin picked one up eagerly and examined it with a professional eye as it lay on the palm of his hand.

'They are toy soldiers,' he exclaimed. 'Cunningly crafted.'

'One does not need to have served time as a toymaker to see that,' said Alwald. 'When I was a boy in River Garde I had several just like this − well, they were a bit chipped because they had been handed down from my great-great grandsire. My favourite had a blue shield and I called him Stalwart.' He stopped, remembering that Stalwart had gone for ever along with River Garde and everything else that he had treasured since childhood. Perhaps it was the memory of his toy soldier, or perhaps it was the workmanship that so impressed Krispin, that made Alwald pick up one of the miniature men-at-arms.

For a moment he gazed at its flesh-coloured face with its fierce moustache and eyes of tiny glass beads that stared back at him ferociously; then he gave a yell of astonishment as the toy soldier twisted in his hand like a fish suddenly coming to life after being taken from the net.

It fell to the snow where it floundered to its feet and stood brandishing its tiny spear. Krispin opened his hand in a moment of panic and his soldier, too, was struggling in the snow. On the rock a ripple of movement ran through the toy ranks. A faint clash of weapons reached the onlookers.

'What are they, and how did they come to be here?' demanded Tana in half-affrighted fascination.

'More gramarye,' Ognam said with a mock groan. 'I had hoped that we had left such marvels behind. At least we would have to be the size of mice before they could harm us.'

As he spoke a bodkin-sized javelin flashed through the air and its needle point buried itself in Krispin's cheek. As he felt the warm flow of blood he instinctively drew Woundflame from its scabbard and brought the blade down on the toy that had hurled the lance, striking the shoulder close to the neck and slicing the little body in two. There was no blood as it fell apart, only the white gleam of the bone from which it had been carved.

Tiny cries of rage rose from tiny throats and a flight of tiny javelins arced towards the travellers. The missiles fell short but they now realized they were facing something more malign than just remarkable toys.

'Serene Mother, they grow,' breathed Danya.

He was right. Even as they watched, the toys,

originally the size of a man's forefinger, visibly increased in height and breadth. They leapt from the rock as their expansion created a need for more space.

The whole company backed away, unable to take their eyes off the phenomenon. Soon the toys were double their original size and the strength of their battle cries grew in proportion. There was such menace in this occult manifestation that when their miniature foes suddenly charged across the snow towards them the travellers began a desperate flight. Had the enemy been of normal size they would have doubtless stood their ground but there was something unnerving in the fact that toys, normally associated with the happy hours of childhood, were animated by an urge to kill them.

'This way, this way,' Tumbrul shouted. Without question they followed him to where the terrain became a long downward slope out of whose covering of snow rocks reared like black fangs. The warriors, ashamed of their flight but equally demoralized by the toys, brought up the rear. When they looked back they saw that their pursuers had grown with such alarming rapidity it appeared they were chased by small children but children who gained stature even as they ran.

The superior height of the travellers gave them a good lead but this lessened when the toys finally became full-sized.

A cry of dismay rose as Tumbrul led the companions through a belt of rocks and they saw that the slope before them was rent from north to south by a broad chasm, an immemorial fault in the structure of the ranges that at no point was less than twenty paces across.

As the fugitives approached the edge, wary of

standing on the snow-powdered ice that overhung it, they could not see the bottom of its shadowed depths.

'Here we needs must make our stand,' declared Barlak. 'Here we will fight with honour against the demons.'

His men gave a shout of agreement and their weapons flashed in the cold sunlight.

'For myself I shall leap into yon crevasse rather than become a hostage of evil powers,' said the Princess quietly to Alwald. 'And to thou I look to give me the courage when the time cometh.'

'I pledge . . .' began Alwald.

'Very noble no doubt,' interjected Tumbrul, 'but not yet necessary as it may be possible to cross by that ice bridge.'

He pointed along the chasm and in the deep shade cast by a peak they discerned something they had not recognized until their guide had spotted it, a dim white rainbow that arched from wall to wall, a ghostly remnant of the winter freeze when the chasm had been covered by snow and ice. Lying half a league to the north it was a symbol of hope and the companions lost no time in setting off towards it. Luckily their pursuers were less at home on the frosted snow than they, and they were still out of javelin range when they entered the shadow that lay over the bridge and the desolate waste on either side.

Ice stalactites fringed its arch and, though massive where it joined the walls of the chasm, it grew more slender towards its gracefully curving apex where its width was no more than a couple of paces.

The companions approached it eagerly and Krispin panted to Barlak that the midsection might be severed with axes to thwart pursuit.

'Possibly,' grunted Barlak, 'but some of us will have to hold the bridge while the ice is chopped.'

The rearmost warrior screamed. They turned to see him with bright blood spurting from his mouth and his hands clawing the air as he sank to his knees. When he toppled forward they flinched at the haft of a javelin protruding from his back. His heart had been transfixed and the Dark Maid had beckoned, and now that the pursuers were so close there was nothing to be done but race to the bridge.

The Sun-in-Splendour warriors took up position in front of it with their shields locked while the others tensed to make the giddy crossing. Danya, the most sure-footed after a lifetime of balancing on rolling decks, mounted the bridge first to test that it was sufficiently strong for them to cross and kick away treacherous humps of snow.

The Princess followed but only edged several paces when she happened to look down into the abyss and vertigo clutched her. With a moan of terror she pressed her hands over her eyes and stood swaying. Alwald leapt on to the bridge and, with his soft-soled shoes sliding alarmingly, he hurried to her. Speaking soothingly as to a frightened child, he took her by the arm and led her across the narrow centre whose seeming fragility made his forehead damp with sweat despite the freezing air rising from the depths.

Tana followed, her arms extended like a carnival rope-walker.

As the toys approached, the others did not wait to cross one-by-one but jostled on to the bridge. Three warriors broke their shield wall and leapt forward in a suicidal attack to give their comrades enough time to get across. Their swords whirled and their axes rose and fell but within a minute they were sprawled on reddening ice. Although they had not managed to destroy any of the toys their valour had not been in vain; the rest of the party had either reached the opposite side or were safely on the bridge when the last defender collapsed from his wounds.

Hampered by the weight of his treasure sack Tumbrul was the last to cross. The leading toy soldier leapt on to the bridge and ran after him with his two-handed broadsword raised.

Danya, standing at the very edge of the chasm, aimed his crossbow as Tumbrul reached the middle of the bridge where his frenzied legs flew from under him and his sack struck the ice with a resounding clatter. At that moment Danya pressed the trigger against the stock.

The bolt struck the soldier in the chest and penetrated his mail to half its length. Brought to a halt by its impact he stood still while Tumbrul regained his feet and fled to the far side where all eyes were fixed on the enemy who remained as immobile as a statue. Why did he not falter? What sort of creature could survive a kraken bolt? Then with jerky movements the toy took one hand away from the grip of his broadsword and seizing the missile drew it bloodless from his body.

Realization struck Krispin. He had managed to destroy a toy with Woundflame but Danya's deadly bolt had no effect. The foe was invincible when it came to ordinary arms but Woundflame was a very special blade into which Weyland Weaponsmith had melded sword magic when he had forged it.

Knowing what must be done to protect his comrades he drew the sword whose normally tarnished blade now shone mirror bright.

On the bridge the soldier raised the bolt mockingly, let it drop into the depths and took a step forward.

Krispin mounted the bridge and, swallowing his in-born fear of heights, stepped over Tumbrul's sack and advanced with Woundflame raised above his shoulder.

'Come back, fool, you have no chance against witchcraft,' shouted Alwald with unusual concern in his voice. For the briefest of moment Krispin paused and waved Woundflame as though in answer.

Next instant the soldier swung his broadsword in a stroke that would have rent the finest breastplate made by the armourers of Nimos as though it was a linen shirt. But it was a stroke that failed to reach its target as Krispin parried and the blades met edge-to-edge with a screech of tempered metal. At the same time it appeared to the anxious watchers that white fire bathed both weapons before the broadsword shattered leaving only grip and hilt in its master's hand.

For a moment the soldier looked in disbelief at what remained of his weapon while Krispin, recovering his balance from the shock of the parry, swung his sword in a wide curve from right to left. The blade struck his adversary's gorget and continued its sweep. The soldier's head whirled away and plummeted out of sight; Krispin put his foot against the decapitated body and pushed it over the edge.

Infuriated by the defeat of their champion several soldiers ventured on to the bridge and the first advanced upon Krispin with raised axe and shield. Again the mysterious power of sword magic saved Krispin. He lunged and saw his point shatter the boss of the enemy's shield and send him sprawling on the ice. Filled with an awed confidence, Krispin followed up his advantage and aimed a blow which hurled the soldier into space. Then he shouted, 'Barlak, cut the bridge.'

'Then be ready to fall back,' came the reply but before the warriors could set foot upon the bridge Tumbrul burst through them and made a reckless run towards the centre where his precious bag lay. Beyond it Krispin was engaged in desperate combat but ignoring this Tumbrul reached out, slipped and went down on his knees.

'Back, dwarf, we have to cut the bridge,' roared Barlak.

'Dwarf, heh?' exclaimed Tumbrul. 'How dare you . . .'

As he spoke his hand moved towards the bag containing the treasure it had taken him a century to earn; his fingers had almost closed on the canvas when Krispin jumped back to escape the thrust of a halberd.

His heel caught the sack and it was enough to set it sliding towards the edge.

Wailing his despair Tumbrul lunged after it, his hand grasping it just as it slipped over the side. The sudden weight of silver upset his balance and he found himself poised above the abyss. His only hope was to open his hand and let the sack go — instead he clung grimly to his treasure.

The travellers watched aghast as his rotund body moved further over the drop, saw his free hand scrabble uselessly on the glassy surface, saw him fall head first into the depths still clutching his sack, heard his shriek echo on and on.

The Princess turned away with her eyes blinded by tears. Gone was the faithful servant who through the hundred years of her entrancement had cut her hair and kept her resting place pristine. Gone!

On the crown of the bridge, enveloped by the white vapour of his breath, Krispin continued to hold the enemy at bay. Shouting orders to a couple of his men armed with war axes, Barlak took up his position a few paces behind him where the bridge was narrowest. The heavy crescent-shaped blade of his axe descended and fragments of ice exploded under the impact. The others joined him, swinging their axes like demented woodcutters.

Krispin was heartened by the sound of the rapid blows as he waited for the next soldier to attack. His heart thudded against his ribs and his breathing was agony in the rarefied air — something that did not appear to trouble the enemy — and he doubted if he could fight for much longer. Despite its magical properties Woundflame was becoming heavier and heavier, and though he had now accounted for three foemen there were still nearly two score waiting their turn to challenge him.

'Serene Mother, preserve thy child.' He muttered the childhood supplication involuntarily as a soldier, with lowered spear and eyes blazing above the bronze rim of his shield, charged up the incline.

At that moment fate favoured Krispin. As the soldier came within lunging distance he slipped and fell forward. Woundflame flashed down to cleave the spear haft and the hand that held it. No blood spurted from the severed wrist, all it revealed was the whiteness of ivory.

'Be ready to jump, Krispin,' came the harsh voice of Barlak. 'We are almost through.'

Chips of ice struck Krispin's back as the axes continued to rise and fall. The soldier he had wounded was backing awkwardly down the bridge. He risked turning his head and saw that behind him the width of the bridge had been narrowed to a couple of handspans and there was a series of sharp cracking sounds as the remaining ice found the weight of the bridge intolerable.

Barlak stood poised to deliver the final blows while his men hastened back to the chasm edge. Behind them Krispin could see his comrades — it might be the last glimpse he ever had of them — and in that fleeting moment he wondered why Gambal had his arm outstretched to the sky. He steadied himself to face the next onslaught.

Barlak shouted to Krispin to come over but a line of soldiers was advancing towards him. The bridge shuddered beneath the added weight — shuddered and broke.

Krispin turned to see the section Barlak had been working on fall away to leave a gap almost too wide to jump. Disregarding the oncoming soldiers he tensed for the near impossible leap. Barlak leaned forward with arms outstretched to catch him.

Too late. The ice on which Krispin stood cracked and shattered into a thousand flying prisms and he felt himself plunge into the dark void.

TEN

The Valley
of Thorns

The highway that snaked out of the west, from the High Wald and past the decayed town of Lasgaad, crossed barren hills marking the rim of the Great Plain of Danaak by means of a shallow valley.

From a high vantage point the Regent surveyed it and said, 'From this day the Valley of Thorns will be a part of history. It will be spoken of as the place where Ythan's new era began.'

Urwen, the perpetual wind playing with her fiery hair so it streamed like flames from her head, gazed over the dun hills and said, 'My lord, surely mangonels are engines for battering fortifications and I do not see how they can halt a mounted army, no matter how accurate they may be.'

'Have patience,' said the Regent with a smile that his mistress recognized as boding ill for his enemies. 'Bors, is all ready?'

'All is as you commanded, Lord Regent,' answered the Companion of the Rose after toiling up to the Regent's rocky lookout. 'Two score mangonels are set on the high ground on either side of the valley and concealed with brushwood. I have ridden my drong along the road and I could not see anything but rock and scrub.'

'Excellent. According to the latest report from our scouts the Horde should reach the valley an hour from sundown. Be sure that all have entered before the signal is given.'

Bors nodded and said, 'They will need more than their Wolf-in-the-Sky before night falls.'

The Regent sat back on his portable throne while a long-haired page poured him black wine. Behind him stood his Avenger, with crossbow cocked and his face hidden behind his visor, and his personal bodyguards in their red surcoats, while near at hand a signaller waited with his coloured flags set out in a neat row on a flat boulder.

'I still do not understand,' said Urwen, touching his goblet with hers.

'Neither do those wretches turning the great capstan in the Nether World,' the Regent told her. 'At least ere long *you* will have your curiosity satisfied.'

Urwen smiled into the wind. Although she could not envisage what the Regent had in store for his enemies she was filled with admiration for his arrogant self-confidence; thanks to the Wells of Ythan he was once more the only man she had ever wanted to master her. She looked forward to the lowering of the sun and what might follow with almost erotic anticipation.

At the far end of the valley another signaller sat amid a bank of summer-dried nettles, a rank and painful place of concealment but one that gave him a fine view of the treeless terrain rolling westward and the highway that ran into its shimmering distance. The sun was too hot on Rulf's mail-clothed back and after

260

the exhausting journey from the capital — the only halts were for the harnessing of fresh relays of drongs at staging posts — he could not prevent his attention from straying from the task of watching the blank landscape. Disconnected pictures fluttered from his memory like birds appearing from a dovecot . . . his head sank forward and remembrance of his mother's humble cottage became a dream.

Rulf jerked awake and his heart thudded with terror. How long had he slept? Serene Mother, he was the 'eye' of the Regent and if an officer had seen him he would have been crucified at nightfall!

In panic he surveyed the land beyond the valley. Far off there was a grey smudge like the smoke of a grassland fire. Perhaps that was what it was. He watched the distant smoke for some minutes and then he sensed a vibration beneath him and he knew that what he was watching was not smoke but dust thrown high by the hooves of steppe ponies racing towards the hills.

He reached for his long staff on which a blue pennant was already fitted, ready to give warning that the Wolf Horde was in sight. Moving back to a bank of baked earth that would shield him from the sight of eagle-eyed barbarians he waved the flagstaff to and fro. It was acknowledged by a similar speck of colour on the brow of a hill a thousand paces to the east.

All along the valley mangonel masters gave quiet orders to their crews. Horsehair torsion ropes creaked as beams were winched down into the firing position and projectiles loaded into their 'spoons'. Then all eyes turned to the eastern end of the valley where the Regent's signaller raised a green flag commanding them to remain concealed until the next signal.

Among the nettles, Rulf watched in awe as the tidal wave of mounted barbarians flowed towards him, outnumbering his master's force by at least a score to one. The low sun appeared like a pale coin through the rolling cloak of dust that trailed behind them and now the signaller not only felt the tremor of hooves but their rumble was in his ears. And, although he was safe from observation, he crouched lower among the nettles as the leading riders entered the valley. These were standard-bearers holding tall poles decorated with wolf skulls, and leading these was a nomad a head taller than the rest whose crimson wolf-skull sceptre proclaimed him as the Wolf King himself.

Riding stirrup-to-stirrup beside him was a man whose long features and fair hair proclaimed him to be a man of Ythan rather than the Outlands – the traitor Affleck whose words had inspired the Wolf King's crusade to humble the Mother-worshippers and set the banner of the Wolf-in-the-Sky on the topmost tower of the Citadel.

Rulf watched as the riders streamed below him a score or more abreast, ready to raise the red pennant that would signify that the rearguard had entered the valley.

Then he saw it.

Glancing aside to make sure that the crucial pennant was fitted firmly on the pole he saw a black and greenish band a couple of paces away, a serpent with a bright crown-shaped marking on its head. It was this marking that told Rulf he was looking upon a basilisk. He knew that a movement on his part would bring the creature's deadly gaze upon him and with it venom that nothing in nature could withstand. He remembered tales of how pools would become poisoned once a basilisk had drunk from them.

And yet if he was to make his signal he would have to move, and move fast because the last riders were already past him. If the red flag did not show it could mean disaster for his fellow soldiers, even for Danaak . . .

The coils of the basilisk rippled slightly. The dust was settling at the mouth of the valley. Rulf took a deep breath and muttered, 'Serene Mother, into thy arms . . .' He raised his pole and waved the red pennant.

The movement caused the basilisk's eyelids to flick open revealing eyes shining like burnished copper — eyes it was believed could kill by their stare alone — and from its mouth spurted a jet of vile brown liquid that struck Rulf in the face. The features began to dissolve and Rulf fell across his carnival flags. The basilisk uttered a cry of triumph, not the hiss of a serpent but something akin to the crowing of a cock that was the terror of the wastelands.

Rulf's shriek and the horrible cry of the basilisk caught the ears of the nomads; many reined their mounts and swept the slopes on either side with their keen yellow eyes but all they saw was parched earth and tinder-dry brushwood and, reassured, they moved on.

What they had not seen was the groups of men positioned round the disguised mangonels, aimers watching the ends of the valley through their brass sights, loaders crouching beside neatly stacked casks, winchmen with their hands on levers ready to draw the beams back into position after firing, fireboys holding charcoal pots and the mangonel masters with eyes eager for the next signal.

'Lady Urwen, accept the honour of sending those barbarians to whatever demon underworld they may believe in,' said the Regent as the standard-bearers of the Wolf Horde approached the head of the valley. 'No woman in the history of Ythan has had such an opportunity until this day.'

She inclined her head. The Regent nodded to the signaller who reluctantly handed her a long pole to which was attached a large blood-red banner.

'All you need do is wave that,' said the Regent. Urwen nodded and, raising the flag, waved it briskly to and fro. The bright signal was seen by the mangonel masters down the valley. The order to fire was given and a score of black projectiles sped towards the rearguard and another score hurtled towards the leading ranks. A moment later ragged thunder filled the valley as the casks detonated; huge flame fountains marked where each landed, horses and riders were blown apart, the earth rocked under the multitude of explosions and dirty, fire-streaked smoke swirled over the sea of horsemen.

'Magic!' exclaimed Urwen. 'You are a magician!'

'Alchemy!' the Regent shouted above the din of the startled horde. 'Better than magic — it requires no magicians. Though he had no idea of its worth, old Leodore discovered it when he was seeking to improve fireworks. Sulphur from the Sulphur Isles, saltpetre from the western mines and charcoal from the Arkad Woodlands, ground together in a secret mill driven by the capstan in the Nether World. With this new weapon none can withstand . . .'

His words were drowned as a second volley of casks fell among the swirling tide of bewildered horsemen in the middle of the valley. Spouts of fire, earth and human debris gushed to the roiling clouds of smoke above; the ground trembled again and in between the explosions the screaming of mutilated men and ponies was a ceaseless obbligato.

The faces of the Regent and his party were rapt as they gazed down upon the destruction that had been unleashed less than a minute ago and which had already turned an army into a shambles. Here was power that had been undreamed of until the Regent had begun preparing the alchemic powder in secret chambers beneath the Citadel. In the past, casks of naphtha had been flung from catapults but they only burned on impact; these casks had the power of lightning bolts to destroy all about them in thunderous blasts, to hurl broken bodies high into the smoky air and leave fuming craters in the very earth.

A wolf skull on a broken staff landed within a few paces of the Regent. Urwen seized it and held it towards the Regent as though offering him victory but the din of the exploding casks drowned her words, and he made a sign for her to keep it.

Sweat ran in rivulets down the bodies of the men working the mangonels who were now ordered to fire at random into the lurid smoke that filled the valley – it had been made known there would be a bag of silver crowns for the team that fired off the most projectiles. As soon as a mangonel master released the retaining bolt and the cask hurtled forth with a ribbon of smoke trailing from its fuse the spoon arm was winched back into position, a cask was loaded, the fireboy ignited the hempen fuse and with a shudder of heavy timbers the engine hurled another load of destruction among the now obscured horde.

The master of one engine was about to pull the firing

bolt when one of the specially woven ropes that powered the spoon arm snapped. One end cracked like a whip across the face of the fireboy as he stood back from lighting the fuse. The crew leapt away in terror from the useless engine but too late. The cask exploded and the mangonel was blown to fragments along with the men who, moments before, had been shouting boasts of how they would spend the prize money. They were the Regent's only casualties in what became known in Ythan's chronicles as The Rout of the Horde — the kingdom's most spectacular victory since the days of Johan I.

When the first cask fell Affleck was blown from his horse. For a moment he lay on the sandy soil of the valley in stunned bewilderment. The standard-bearers had been skittled like himself, there was a smell of sulphur in the air, thunderclaps and flashes all about him and then a scream rose simultaneously from a hundred throats.

Gramarye! The word was like lightning stabbing through the fog of shock filling his mind. A curse had been called down upon the valley — a curse of wind, fire and thunder.

Affleck climbed to his knees and found he was dripping with blood — and with relief realized that it was not his but that of a disembowelled pony. Fifty paces away he saw the Wolf King swing into the saddle of a riderless horse, flourishing his axe and shouting words that were drowned by the boom and shriek of the onslaught. He was lost to sight when magical fire gushed nearby and choking smoke swirled between them. As scores of explosions turned the valley into a nightmare of flashes and ear-numbing thunder,

Affleck knew that the dream of the Wolf Horde capturing Danaak was over. Self-preservation was the priority.

Through rifts in the smoke he saw that the fiery curse was confined to the valley floor where panicked barbarians fought to control their stampeding mounts. He made a crouching run to the valley's sloping side and scrambled up it until he was in a belt of scrub and, sheltered behind this, he began to work his way westwards. Black objects – obviously part of the gramarye – arced over his head, each to be followed instantly by a crack of doom and the ship-like heave of the ground beneath his feet. Behind him brushwood crackled into flame as blazing fragments drifted from the inferno.

At last the explosions grew less frequent and in the intervals between them a drumming sound was audible above the continuous moaning from the valley floor – the surviving nomads were galloping back along the highway that led to the High Wald.

Must get a horse, Affleck thought but next moment there was a thunderclap close by and he was hurled down on to sun-baked earth. He held back a scream as pain surged from his broken leg; if he could hold on he could still crawl out of the accursed valley. And crawl he did until he reached a point where the valley opened out so he found himself looking over a flat landscape lit by the sun now poised on the rim of the world. He decided to rest where he was until night fell, and looking about saw several flags scattered by a rock and beyond them the corpse of a signaller. A leather waterbottle was attached to his belt and Affleck suddenly wanted water more than anything else in the world.

He crawled across to the body and had his hands on the bottle when a sense of danger made him look up. On a flat rock a couple of paces away he saw a great serpent with the mark of a crown atop its broad head.

Serene Mother . . . !

The basilisk opened its dreadful eyes.

Sunset. The slaughter was over. The smoke in the Valley of Thorns had thinned and mangonel crews stood by their engines gazing in awed silence at the carnage they had wrought. The valley floor was carpeted with the broken bodies of men and beasts, all mutilated but not all dead. The terrible carpet moved with the arm-waving of the wounded and the convulsions of the dying.

'Old Leodore sought to create life,' remarked the Regent as servants set up folding tables. 'The irony is that he has been far more successful in bringing death with his alchemy.'

'But it was you who put his alchemy into practice,' said Urwen, still holding the shattered wolf standard. 'None guessed your secret and in Danaak they took your delay in facing the wolfmen for weakness. Imagine the effect when news of your triumph reaches the city.'

The Regent smiled his bleak smile while the battlefield feast was prepared to celebrate the victory as it had been in days of old. Cooks brought up hot roasts and wine for the mangonel men from the waggons that had been hidden out of sight, while samite cloths and crystal goblets were laid on the tables for the Regent and his party. Musicians tuned their lutes, casting uneasy glances at each other as the groaning from the valley floor rose at times to an agonized crescendo.

'Lord Regent, shall I send out the mercy squads?' asked Captain Bors.

The Regent shook his head.

'The men are weary, Bors, let them feast in peace. Send one party only to seek the Wolf King. If he lives he will be flayed in the Square of Punishment, if he be dead his head will ornament the main city gate. As to the others, once the lads have had looting permission and the ravens have done their work, I want a barbarian skull set on a post at every hundred paces between here and Danaak.' He gazed along the valley which was illuminated by the sunset. 'By the look of things there should be enough.'

ELEVEN
The
Bargain

Tana screamed. The Princess turned her pallid face away. The men invoked the deity with oaths which were both prayers and blasphemies as with a cracking that reverberated throughout the chasm the centre of the ice bridge fell away, and with it Krispin. The only one not to witness the disaster was Gambal who was gazing upwards with a look of disbelief on his face.

Krispin felt the ice shudder beneath his feet; next moment he disappeared into the shadowed depths. His cloak streamed behind him and Woundflame flew from his hand as he plunged into the darkness with ice shards spinning about him and death only a couple of heartbeats away . . . then there was an agonizing wrench on his neck as his cloak became taut as though caught by a giant's hand. The descent continued but its impetus slowed and through terror and disorientation came the sensation of gliding downward rather than falling.

He felt the soles of his feet strike rock, his knees buckled and he pitched forward with his cloak tumbling over his head. The pressure on his throat

271

relaxed and his lungs fought greedily for the chill air. When his panting eased he freed himself from the enveloping folds of cloth; he tried to stand but fell back into a sitting position as much with astonishment as with physical shock.

In the grey light filtering down from the thin strip of sky he beheld an extraordinary figure above him, a *winged* man whose pinions shifted lazily to preserve his balance.

At the sight of the apparition Krispin wondered if he was dead and in the keeping of a Valk, one of the fabled servants of the Dark Maid entrusted to bear away the spirits of the slain, yet the pain in his neck and knees reassured him that he was still in the body.

'Well met, Master Krispin,' came a voice that, while familiar, he could not reconcile with the upright figure. 'This day it would seem the Serene Mother guided my wings in order to catch you.'

'I – I . . .' Krispin began hoarsely.

'Of course you do not recognize me,' said the stranger with a low laugh. 'The last time I was in your eyes I was a poor crouch-backed creature.'

'You are the Hump?'

'That is indeed who I was. Since then the wings that were hidden in the deformity that gave me my name burst forth and, as men say, I came into my own.'

'But we left you in the Domain of Olam. And where is the horsemaid Silvermane?'

'I took her back to the Arkad Woodlands from whence she came and there, alas, she suffers a mortal distemper whose only remedy lies in the Wells of Ythan. But of that, and your quest, we can talk by and by. First I must return you to your companions.'

As they had been speaking Krispin's eyes had

become accustomed to the murk that pressed upon them with almost a physical weight. Some distance away he saw the broken forms of enemy warriors who had toppled from the bridge.

'Our guide fell into the crevasse,' he said. 'I should seek him.'

'It would avail nothing,' said the Hump. 'No man could hold his life's spark after such a fall.'

Krispin nodded and made no mention of Tumbrul's treasure – let it lie with him for eternity. Then he added, 'But Woundflame I must find.'

The Hump said, 'I remember Woundflame well. I would not be here this day if it had not been for your wondrous sword. And if I am not mistaken it is close by.'

Turning, Krispin saw what appeared to be a phosphorescent cross. It was the sword with its blade half buried in ice, glowing as though to signal its position to its master. He hurried over and, seizing the grip, tried to withdraw it but it was embedded too deeply and he realized that it must have been the magical qualities melded in it which had preserved its highly tempered steel from shattering with the impact.

'I feel like the prince in the folktale who tried to draw a sword from a block of stone,' he said with a ghost of a smile. 'Would that I was pure of heart like the hero.'

'In this world can you be a hero and pure of heart?' asked the Hump joining him, but their combined strength was not enough to free the blade.

Suddenly a wisp of vapour rose from the ice.

'It is heating,' the Hump exclaimed. 'It melts the ice to free itself.'

Again Krispin seized the grip and with a loud hiss

and a gust of steam Woundflame came away, its point glowing redly.

A minute later the travellers beheld a winged man soar out of the chasm with his arms locked round Krispin's body. But, as he landed, another marvel attracted their attention. Across the space once spanned by the ice bridge the foemen were shrinking. Moment by moment they lost height and girth until they were finally reduced to their original minute stature; once more toy soldiers, they scurried ant-like until a blast of dark wind roared across the plateau and whirled them into the abyss.

It was the time for explanations. Stunned by what had taken place in the last hour, the party moved away from the chasm and when they reached a sheltering outcrop of black snow-crowned rock they sank down wearily. The loss of their comrades had left the warriors grimly silent but the sight of the Hump, his wings folded beneath his cloak, fired the curiosity of those who had known him. While a flask of apple spirit was passed round to revive them the Hump related his story in a few sentences.

'In my search for the Wells of Ythan something – my old instinct for wayfinding – drew me south to these mountains,' he said in conclusion. 'Am I right in believing that they are close?'

'We have come from there,' replied Alwald who, like the others, could not come to terms with this tall winged version of the man they remembered as a crouched drong-rider. 'You were on course for them when you saw us.'

'At first I doubted my sight when I saw you below me,' the Hump told them. 'But I did not have time to ponder it when I saw the bridge collapse and Master Krispin fall.'

'Never was an arrival so timely,' declared Krispin in heartfelt tones. 'If chance had not brought you here at that moment my bones would lie in that dismal crevasse until Time's end.'

'Chance?' mused Ognam. 'I think there might have been more than mere chance in it.'

'There was certainly no chance about the attack,' said Alwald. 'It seems to me some enemy with malefic powers is eager to prevent the return of Her Highness.'

'And it is not difficult to guess who that might be,' Gambal said sombrely. 'In Danaak the old Revel Master Wilk babbled in his cups about toy soldiers from the olden days that could be magicked into full size, and that the lore hag Mandraga had such a company.'

'I would gladly be facing corsairs in the Cold Sea rather than these mysteries, for at least I could understand enemies of flesh and blood,' grumbled Danya. 'What next will come to haunt us?'

'Mayhap nothing,' said Alwald with pretended optimism for the sake of the Princess and Tana. 'I wager our perils are behind us and once we leave the Mountains of the Moon . . .' His voice trailed away as his attempt failed. Like the others he was aware of what Tumbrul's death meant to them.

The gloomy silence was broken by the Hump announcing that he must resume his journey.

'I cannot tarry a moment longer,' he declared. 'With arrow poison in Silvermane's blood, every moment counts. It has warmed my heart to see you again, Lord Alwald, Krispin, Gambal and you Ognam. I shall never forget the time we journeyed together from

Danaak to the Domain of Olam, and would that I could spend longer with you but her life is in the balance and I must leave while I may.'

He nodded at heavy clouds rolling from the north and began to remove his cloak. The others watched with fascination as his membranous wings stirred as if with independent life. Krispin put his hand on his arm and said quietly, 'Spare me one moment, there is something I would tell you.'

'Your thanks have already been sufficient,' said the Hump, but seeing Krispin's intense face he allowed himself to be led out of earshot of the others.

'Hurry your words, Master Krispin.'

'Our guide is dead and the truth is we do not know where we are or what route to take to reach the river of ice that leads down from the mountains,' Krispin told him. 'With your instinct as a wayfinder you could lead us to safety.'

The Hump moved impatiently but made no reply.

'The hope of Ythan could end here in the Mountains of the Moon, not from the strange perils that have beset us but by simple cold and starvation. The Princess is the symbol that might free Ythan from the Regent. You know as well as I the evil of his works, even to the arrow that pierced Silvermane . . .'

'And that is why I must reach the Wells without delay,' he said in an angry tone and his pinions expanded as though eager to bear him skywards.

'Supposing the Guardian of the Wells will not let you take any water,' Krispin said.

'I shall worry over that when he says "no".'

'You cannot desert your old companions when it is within your power to save them.'

'I cannot desert Silvermane,' the Hump retorted harshly.

A snowflake spiralled between them and the world became a darker place. For a moment Krispin closed his eyes as though struggling with an inner conflict, then he said in a resigned voice, 'Do you trust my word?'

'More than that of any man I know but . . .'

'Then listen. Though the valley of the Wells is not far from here as the eagle flies, you might not find them because there are times when they appear elsewhere in the world. And if you do find them you may have difficulty persuading the Guardian of your need. He may look like a simple old man with his countryman's hat and staff but in truth he is a mighty enchanter. He has a special interest in the Princess Livia who is doomed in this desolation unless she receives help.'

The Hump said nothing and, drawing a deep breath, Krispin went on.

'On the other hand if you lead us from here I shall give you water from the Wells of Ythan. In my pack there is a flask of the water I brought away . . . for . . . for a purpose of my own. You may have it now if you agree. That way you will have no doubt about getting it and as there will be no need for you to fly to the Wells you will not be the loser as far as time is concerned.'

'Keep it until you are safe,' said the Hump gruffly. 'I trust your promise.'

'You will guide us?'

'To the best of my ability.'

'One thing more.' Krispin was irked by his own embarrassment. 'Mention not our agreement to my companions for none know I took the water by night.'

The Hump nodded and they hurried back to the others.

'Our friend will guide us to the river of ice,' Krispin announced. 'In all Ythan there is no wayfinder of his skill, as some of us learned in the past. Let us go forward while we may.'

'Knowing the need for you to fly on, may I say how we appreciate your noble gesture,' said Alwald and there was a chorus of agreement.

'Thou wilt not find me ungrateful,' the Princess added. Later she whispered to Tana, 'What a splendid royal courier he wouldst make.'

'Before the snow thickens I shall spy out the land,' said the Hump gruffly. His wings spread; their speed increased and with a sound that reminded Krispin of geese flying over the Wald, he soared directly upwards.

All except Krispin watched in awe as he dwindled to a dot above them; Krispin childishly bit at his thumbnail, tortured by the thought that he had bartered away Jennet's chance of a cure. On the other hand, he tried to console himself, if he had not done so there would have been very little likelihood of him returning to the Peak Tower with it.

Snowflakes commenced to fall with the grace of Fey dancers, and when the Hump swooped down through them he appeared momentarily like a gigantic bat.

'I have seen the way,' he said. 'To begin with we must cross this plain and head for those two peaks. Let us go before the snowfall increases, there are pregnant clouds above.'

With their packs in place and the hoods of their cloaks drawn up over their heads they were eager to follow the Hump; the thought of snow and what might take form in it filled them with apprehension.

As Krispin plodded with freezing feet over frozen snow he was prey to bitter thoughts. Once again he had been betrayed by the quest. It was typical that having risked the displeasure of the Magus Ysldon by stealing a flask of the miraculous water in the belief it would restore Jennet he had to agree to relinquish it a few hours later. He felt an illogical resentment towards the Hump for having accepted such an offer without pausing to think that in similar circumstances, if Jennet's life was endangered, he would have acted exactly the same.

'The Hump says we should reach the ice river within the hour,' said Alwald, falling in beside Krispin. 'He told me that when he flew to spy out the path he saw there was another chasm to cross but he will be able to fly us over one at a time. Who would have thought our old pilot was about to grow wings when we left him in the Domain of Olam? I really wonder what manner of creature he really is.'

'I doubt if he knows himself,' said Krispin. 'Did he not once tell us he was found by a caravan captain beneath a thorn in the Wilderness of Gil.'

Alwald nodded.

'What oddities we have met since we left the Wald,' he said. 'Sometimes I think we have entered a world of nursery tales . . . wizards, griffins and beings like Tumbrul, may the Mother keep him.'

'And a sleeping beauty,' added Krispin.

'At least she is not an oddity, and yet . . .'

'You feel there is something strange about her?'

'Yes. What it is I cannot fathom. I mean no

disloyalty by saying so, and after all the poor girl has been in a magical slumber for a century.'

'That is just it,' Krispin said. 'She does not act as I would have expected after such an experience. True she shed a few tears but on the whole she might have woken from a night's sleep. And she says so little.'

'It is as though she nurses a secret sadness,' said Alwald. 'And yet her entrancement has not robbed her of her royal mien.'

He glanced ahead to where the Princess walked over the hard snow with her guards flanking her; her expression was one of disdain for the conditions that made the others openly miserable, and despite being swathed in a sleeping blanket she retained a regal air. With her spun-gold hair, white skin and bright lips she might have been the Snow Queen from one of the childhood tales Alwald had mentioned.

'Breeding counts,' he murmured in admiration. 'It must be daunting for her to ponder on what lies ahead for her.'

'It seems to me the regaining of her throne is an impossible task,' Krispin said. 'The Regent is too well versed in putting down rebellion.'

'Mayhap, but I doubt not there are surprises in store for us.'

'Of that there can be little doubt,' Krispin agreed sourly.

'I must get back to her,' said Alwald.

'Of course. Are you not her champion?'

Alwald did not recognize, or preferred to ignore, the ironical note in his companion's voice. He merely answered, 'In a way. Before The Enchantment my forebears . . .' And he explained the office they had held.

'Then your duties will prevent you from returning to Mabalon.'

Alwald's features were bluish with cold but for an instant a blush suffused them.

'I cannot tell what the future holds,' he said quietly. 'I dropped back because I have never seen you wear such a gloomy countenance when you should be rejoicing that you were brought safe out of the depths.'

'You speak truly,' admitted Krispin. 'I should be savouring the fact that I can feel this accursed cold. The truth is, my thoughts were on someone else.'

Always you have Jennet in mind, thought Alwald. *Do you ever give Margan a thought? What would you say if I told you that I saw she was with child when I visited the Vale of Mabalon through the magic casement? Was it my duty to have told you or is it best for all sakes that you remain ignorant of the child who will grow up beside Demara's son Grim? Would that I knew the answers to so many questions. I long to see Demara again, I promise myself I shall return to Mabalon to be with her and yet . . . and yet was my feeling for my father's wife a youthful obsession that haunts me less now that I realize the unlikelihood of her returning my ardour?*

As he thought these thoughts he was filled with a sense of grief — grief for the lost illusions of youth. Without a word he hurried forward to join the Princess Livia.

In her tower chamber the Lady Mandraga lay back in her chair and gazed at the mirror suspended between its silver pillars. It bore little resemblance to the gleaming sheet of crystal it had been a short while ago; now it was disfigured by a crack running from side to side, it was spotted as though its silver backing had become tarnished and here and there the crystal itself was cloudy. It vindictively refused to reflect the face of the Lore Mistress as the beautiful woman that she had once been but showed her as the exhausted old woman that she now was.

The Lady Mandraga wondered how long it might be before the glass completely disintegrated under the weight of the spell she had used to force the inherent power in the crystal to show her distant events without the psychic link to the hand mirror that Gambal had destroyed. If it lasted one more hour that would be enough.

She raised a glass filled with a dark potion to her lips to bolster her flagging strength and her eyes wandered to the empty box that had contained a company of toy soldiers – soldiers that in their enchanted form Mandraga had furiously swept into a chasm in the far Mountains of the Moon after they failed to halt the Princess Livia. Since then the mirror had shown only brief glimpses of the party trudging in the white world of the high ranges.

'Weary yourselves and then I shall unleash Eskolth,' she said aloud. 'You will curse the days of your birthings when he becomes your bane.'

TWELVE
Evil
From Afar

It was amid the highest peaks of the Mountains of the Moon that the great ice river had its source, so high and cold and desolate that even the black eagles shunned it. Here it was born out of the ever accumulating ice that formed at this desolate height, and here began its immemorial journey of a few paces a day to the lowest slopes of the range.

The travellers heard it long before they beheld it. Fearful crackings rent the frozen silence and frequently started snowslides on the surrounding crests that added to their sense of peril. What elation had been felt over their escape from the demonic toys and Krispin's deliverance from the chasm was soon supplanted by the memory of Tumbrul's fate and the loss of several of the Princess's bodyguards whose numbers had been reduced by a half since they had set out. And as they followed the Hump across snowfields and through icy passes the cold leeched their strength and determination.

As the Hump had predicted, they reached a chasm towards the end of the long afternoon and beyond it they could see the source of the ice river between two peaks. One by one their guide ferried them across the gap and momentarily the novelty of being lifted into the air and borne over the black depths dispelled their gloom.

When most of the party were on the far side, Krispin felt a curious sensation of warmth against his thigh and when he laid his hand on his scabbard he was surprised to find that it was almost too hot to touch. He drew out Woundflame and to his amazed gaze saw that the blade was glowing.

'What can it mean?' asked Danya who stood beside him.

'I think it must be a warning,' replied Krispin. 'Mayhap the magic in the blade responds to some ill-wished threat.'

'Then it must be evil indeed for this has never happened before,' said Ognam.

'You next, Master Jongleur,' called the Hump as he landed beneath his outstretched pinions.

'I shall not be sorry to cross over,' muttered Ognam as their guide gripped him for the brief flight.

'As fast as you can,' Krispin said. 'There is something abroad that bodes ill for us.'

'Yet I have seen nothing,' the Hump told him before he rose.

'That means little,' muttered Krispin as with Danya he scanned the waste of frozen snow over which they had travelled. 'I learnt on the Amber Isle that malefic beings do not need to have substance.'

'Look!' It was the keen sight of the shipmaster that had caught a distant disturbance in the snow, not a wind-driven flurry but what appeared to be the instant formation of a shallow hole. As they watched another appeared in line with the first and then another.

Danya cursed with frustration and said, 'It is too far for me to make out what they are.'

'Could there be some natural passage under the snow that is caving in?' Krispin wondered.

'Not that,' said the Hump landing beside them. 'Footprints!'

They turned to him aghast.

'From above I saw they were enormous footprints, and they are coming this way,' he said. 'Quickly, Shipmaster, I shall take you over and then be back for you, Krispin.'

Krispin nodded and waited with Woundflame's blade glowing even brighter. As he watched he saw the depressions continue to appear in the snow with a regularity of something taking steps, an invisible giant on a ponderous walk, and Krispin had no doubt that was what it was. A childhood tale returned to him about a giant who lived in a high place and could smell out mortal men.

And it – whatever it is – has scented us, he thought. And it was with a surge of relief that he heard the hiss of the Hump's wings. A moment later he was whirled over the chasm to his companions who were staring at the approaching line of footprints.

'What size it must be to take such strides – at least as big as the stone giants of Olam,' said Gambal with bitter memory returning.

'But moving much faster,' added Ognam. 'Perhaps the chasm will halt it.'

'Let us not tarry,' shouted Barlak. 'The rearguard is to remain in case it crosses . . .'

His words were lost as a bull-like roar rolled over the snowfields. Never on the quest had Krispin and

Alwald heard a sound that held such menace and for a long moment the whole party stood as though overwhelmed while the imprints of the huge unseen feet approached the chasm.

Danya was the first to shake off the paralysing effect of the monstrous cry. Raising his crossbow he waited until a new print appeared and then aimed his last poison bolt exactly above it. The effect was more dramatic than even he could have expected for while the author of the mysterious footsteps was invisible it certainly had a physical body.

Another terrible cry, this time filled with unholy outrage, told Danya that his bolt must have found its mark, and as he watched he saw a pair of globular eyes materialize in the air high above the last footprint. Huge black pupils set in yellowish eyeballs, they were without a vestige of human intellect. Next to appear was a ring of jagged teeth, sunken nostrils, hands ending in horn spikes, an enormous penis . . . Then lips grew over the teeth, an idiot face linked the mouth and eyes, a forearm appeared joined to one of the hands and then an upper arm materialized to connect it to a massive shoulder. Within seconds an immense figure had become flesh before their eyes, a naked giant surrounded by an aura of malignancy warning the stunned companions that what they saw was merely the outward and visible form of an elemental that had been summoned from beyond the confines of the mortal world.

His fingers fastened on the bolt which protruded from the hide of his sagging belly and he plucked it out rather as a gardener removes a rose thorn from his hand. As he did so the obscene body began to disappear, the corpse-white flesh became transparent,

286

then only teeth and eyes remained as though suspended in the air and then they too were gone. A moment later depressions in the snow appeared again as the invisible ogre resumed his march towards the chasm.

'Twice my bow has failed this day,' said Danya with a curse. 'Mayhap the crevasse will defeat him.'

'Let us not tarry to find out,' said Ognam and with the others he ran in the wake of the Hump who was racing in the direction of the ice river. A third cry rumbled behind them, this time redolent of frustration as the enemy reached the chasm and found it too wide even for his great stride. Snow cascaded into the depths as he kicked it like a child in a tantrum, then the footprints began to appear in quick succession along the edge as he ran in search of a place where the crevasse narrowed enough for him to leap it.

Alwald caught up with the Hump who, seeing the distress of some of the companions, had slowed to a hurried walk.

'If that − that thing crosses over I dem − ask that you take to the air with the Princess Livia and fly her to safety,' he panted.

'I already had a mind to do that,' replied the Hump. 'But if we reach the ice river you all may yet escape if I was not mistaken in what I glimpsed from above.'

'What . . . ?'

'Save your breath, Lord Alwald. I could not be certain before which is why I made no mention of it − pray that I was not deceived by the ice glare.'

Alwald fell back beside the Princess. The Sun-in-Splendour warriors who made up the rearguard kept glancing behind them for a clue as to whether the ogre had managed to cross the gap. It came some minutes later when they saw a distant flurry of snow on the chasm edge indicating that the enemy had found a spot narrow enough to jump across. Immediately afterwards those with the sharpest eyes saw the prints of unseen feet appearing in such quick succession that it was obvious he was racing after them.

'Make for the ice boat,' cried the Hump, gesturing towards the expanse of white lying between the peaks. Without another word he turned, unceremoniously wrapped his arms about the Princess and soared away.

Ice boat? The companions looked at each other in puzzlement.

'Let us do as he bids,' said Alwald. 'There is naught else I can think of.'

They needed no more encouragement. The line of footprints was coming closer and they fled, stumbling and sliding and filled with panic, towards the river of ice. Only Barlak kept his head.

'Klem, Halbek, Jorg and Medok, you stay by me,' he snapped. 'That thrice-poxed walking dungheap is not going to put the old Sun-in-Splendour to flight, by the Mother. Spread out and when the footprints get close chop the whoreson's feet from under him.'

Soon the warriors could hear the crunch of frozen snow as the line of foot-shaped depressions approached them. Barlak watched, trying to judge where the next footstep would fall.

'There!' He pointed to a patch of snow. 'Axe him!'

Sword-in-hand he sprang forward, his men converging on the spot where, as he had predicted, the snow began to sink beneath the ogre's weight. War axes rose and fell and struck invisible flesh, and having delivered their blows the warriors leapt away. High above them eyes and teeth appeared as they had after Danya had fired his crossbow. For a brief instant the ogre was visible, a look of rage twisting his cretinous features, and then as he faded again a shadowy arm swung down and an almost transparent hand seized the warrior Medok by the shoulder and hoisted him into the air.

Medok's shriek halted the fleeing party. They turned and saw him rise as though levitating without support. For a moment he remained suspended, legs and free arm waving. His war axe fell from his hand. And then his arm disappeared . . .

The travellers stared in disbelief as blood rained on the snow. They groaned with revulsion as they realized that the warrior was being devoured before their eyes. Danya, hardened adventurer that he was, doubled up and vomited. The mutilated warrior rose higher, and his leg vanished.

'Save him!' screamed Tana. 'You men, save him . . .'

Her voice died to an incoherent moan as the body was suddenly headless. Medok's cries were replaced with the mindless laughter of something evil that could only rejoice in evil. And then all that remained of the warrior was a pattern of crimson stains on the snow. A footprint appeared beyond them. The ogre was on the march once more.

Even Barlak and his veterans were too shocked for any thought but that of flight. Panic drove the party before the advancing footprints. They ran as they had never run, often slipping on the frozen snow that was giving way to hard ice. When Tana fell and lay prone with her hands across her eyes Ognam ran back, pulled her to her feet and kept hold of her arm as they followed the others with stumbling steps.

Krispin raised his head as he ran and saw a long

white shape glimmering in a distant shadow cast by one of the peaks, a shape that had the lines of a sleek craft.

The ice boat. The Hump's parting words returned to his mind. But he had no time to think of what it might mean. A burst of shouting behind him warned that the ogre had caught up with them. He turned to see that Barlak had halted and was standing with his sword raised — a noble but hopeless gesture against the invisible menace. The booming laugh sounded above him and before he could realize what was happening he was snatched into the air.

The warriors moved forward in a hopeless attempt to save their captain; one was sent flying through the air as the ogre kicked him contemptuously out of the way. Alwald sprinted back with his sword raised and Krispin felt a familiar shock run up his arm from Woundflame's grip. And then he had the sensation that Time was stretching, a phenomenon he had experienced twice before thanks to the inherent magic in the sword he held.

Those about him moved more and more slowly, the running figure of Alwald lost its speed and took on a rare grace as moments passed between each step, and even the figure of Barlak no longer struggled violently but made languid arm movements.

Krispin knew he had to save Barlak and his companions with these long-drawn moments of respite that Woundflame bestowed upon him. His first impulse was to run with the sword and use it as he had against the enchanted toys, and then he understood it would have no more effect than Danya's kraken bolt. The enemy was not of this world, not subject even to the laws of magic, but an elemental force of destruction summoned from a void the mind of man could not imagine to annihilate them.

Woundflame had warned of this danger, Woundflame had slowed the passage of Time for him but the sword could do no more. And weaponless, what could he achieve against such an adversary?

It seemed to Krispin there were whispers and hissings in his brain, words just out of reach of recognition, and then with perfect clarity he *knew*.

He reached to his neck and pulled at the chain there so it cut deep into the skin and then snapped. He seized the medallion that it held – the Disk of Livia with its spirals of runic characters, the symbol of good against evil – and he threw it straight at where the ogre stood above his footmarks.

The disk travelled true. The mountains reverberated with an inhuman wail of agony and frustration. Captain Barlak fell to the snow *whole*. Krispin found that everything was back to its proper speed. For several moments there was a ghastly display of anatomical parts appearing only to vanish again; bloody teeth, soulless eyes, a beating heart . . . and then there was nothing left except footprints in the snow.

The mirror that hung in Lady Mandraga's special chamber shattered. Shards flew outward and before the Lore Mistress fell back in a bloody swoon she heard a distant wail above the crash of the disintegrating crystal – an echo from some accursed deep beyond the boundaries of the Three Worlds.

Mauve and purple shadows descended upon the Mountains of the Moon, darkness filled the deep valleys and only the highest snow crests glowed rose pink as the light of the sinking sun caught them. In the twilight that thickened between the two peaks the travellers stood gazing in bewildered admiration at the boat. Twelve paces in length, it was a mastless galley with a high curved prow and an equally high stern deck that was just large enough for the steersman to handle the long steering oar pivoted on the righthand side. What astonished the party — apart from the fact that it was the last object they expected to come across in this high desolation — was that the hull was carved out of sparkling ice.

'A tidy craft,' cried Danya and he swung himself over the low bulwark.

'It must be the gift of the Magus Ysldon,' said Princess Livia. 'Didst he not say he wouldst help us to journey by magic? If the pass had not been held by the wraiths we wouldst have reached it long since.'

'Yes, but how do we use it?' Alwald said. 'We began the quest in a Fey boat but for all its bespellment it needed water on which to sail.'

'An ice boat will sail down an ice river,' cried Danya who stood with his hands resting on the steering oar. 'Come aboard and let us see what will be. The Lord Magus told me I might handle a craft more remarkable than the old *Amber Star*.'

As they began to climb aboard Krispin took the Hump to one side, unslung his pack and took out the flask of water from Ythan's Wells.

'You fulfilled your bargain and brought us to the ice river,' he told the Hump who stood watching while his wings unfurled. 'Now it is my turn.' He held out the flask.

'I thank you, Master Toymaker,' said the Hump as he placed it carefully in his scrip. 'I can guess at what cost you do this, and if it did not mean a chance of life for Silvermane I would not take it. Once you are safely on your way I shall fly with it to the Arkad Woodlands where she rests in the Hermit's tower.'

'Sir Guide, I have heard thy story from Lord Alwald,' said Princess Livia. 'When the Empty Throne is no longer empty and I am queen in Danaak I command that thou present thyself at my court. Thy travail on our behalf shall never be forgotten.'

'May that day be soon, Your Highness,' said the Hump with a slight smile.

Alwald helped the Princess aboard where she seated herself in the bows with him and Tana.

'Now what happens?' muttered Gambal. 'What loons we shall look if this boat is just a sculpture.'

On the stern deck Danya seized the steering oar in his broad hands and swung it over. Immediately a shudder ran through the vessel and slowly at first its keel began to slide over the ice beneath it.

With his arm raised in a gesture of farewell the Hump watched it gather speed and then with his wings rising and falling rhythmically he ascended until he was caught in the final rays of the sun and for a moment was transmuted into gold.

In the gloaming the boat moved steadily over the ice between the peaks with Danya guiding it round enormous frozen humps that lined the edge of the ice river. A low grinding note caused by the slow but inexorable movement of the glacier filled their ears, and every so often there would be an awe-inspiring cracking as walls of ice high on the peaks broke away and hurtled down the mountains to shatter on the tumbled formations that fed it. To the relief of the travellers Danya navigated away from these and aimed the bows at the ice lying beyond the peaks, a broad expanse that ended in a ghostly line against the darkling sky.

'I could imagine that we are about to shoot over the edge of the world,' laughed Tana who as usual had managed to sit next to Ognam.

'Many a jest contains an uncomfortable truth,' muttered the jongleur eyeing the edge of the ice sheet with apprehension. 'Do you not think it would be prudent to slow down, Shipmaster?'

'I can only steer,' was his shouted reply. 'She makes her own speed.' A moment later he added, 'Hold hard for I cannot tell what lies ahead.'

The vessel raced on and for a moment the companions had the breath-freezing illusion that it was about to fly into space. Then the bows dipped and they found they were looking down a smooth steep sweep of ice that curved like a ghostly highway between dark tiers of mountains.

Stars appeared like scatters of diamonds above and before them, causing the ice river to gleam with reflected starshine and give the travellers the sensation they were sailing among the constellations.

Danya laughed with exhilaration as he held the steering oar and guided the craft down the Mountains of the Moon towards the marches of Ythan.

Book Three

Truth can only be what truth is perceived to be, thus truth is legion.

Time is what we perceive time to be. Though it may be measured by celestial rhythm, it can vary according to each man's experience. A day of pain can be likened unto a week, a day of bliss may pass in seeming minutes.

A man and an ant see the sun. It is the same sun they see yet is man's perception of the sun the same as that of the ant?

A butterfly lives as many days as a man lives seasons, yet do both measure time equally?

A baby sees a diamond as a pretty bauble, a merchant as his fortune, a holy hermit as a Tear of the Mother. What is a diamond but a bright pebble from the earth.

Therefore, possessed of such conceits, who dare write a history? Indeed it is my belief that folktales contain as much truth as a scribe's chronicle.

– the Sage Omgarth

ONE

The Law
of the Axe

'It be true I tell you,' cried the ragged forester facing the Wish Maiden on the watchtower of River Garde, her favourite place since the capture of the castle. 'The Wolf Horde returns and it has been defeated.'

In the early morning light the Wish Maiden's white banner streamed and cracked in the endless steppe wind. Wode, who had been gazing over the River of Night at the drab grassland beyond, turned from the parapet and asked, 'Tobin, how do you know this?'

'I saw them coming down the track from the White Virgins, hundreds upon hundreds of them.'

'But how knew you they had been vanquished?'

'I only had to watch with my eyes, Master Wode. They had the look of defeat, they smelled of defeat. Half were without weapons or horses, and a great many had been hurt — blackened they were as though they had been caught in a fire. And not a single wolf-skull standard to be seen. I cannot guess what happened, but if you ask me all they want is to get back to their cursed Outlands.'

Wode rubbed his hands together.

'It seems we took River Garde at just the right moment,' he said to the Wish Maiden. 'If we had waited we would not have had the excuse . . .'

'Tobin, this news has brought me joy,' she interjected. 'You must be exhausted after travelling so fast through the forest, go down to the kitchens and enjoy the best fare the castle can offer.'

He ducked his head, the nearest to a gesture of obeisance a Waldman could make, and hurried down the steps.

'If he speaks true we must be prepared in case they would plunder us before they cross over the River of Night,' said Wode.

'If the wolfmen do go back to the Outlands, our men will want to return to their old lives in the forest and on the river,' said the Wish Maiden. 'Our days here will be over.'

'Never!' said Wode vehemently. 'The castle is ours.'

'But by what right?'

'By the most accepted right of all – the right of conquest.'

She smiled at him.

'Oh, Wode, I may be the Wish Maiden but you see some things in a bolder light than I. Yet to keep a castle one must have servants and guards, and those who guarded it before were nearly all killed when the Wolf King murdered Lord Grimwald. How could we . . .?'

'We will hire our garrison.'

'And where will the money for that come from?'

'Taxes,' said Wode.

At noon, Tobin's words were proved when watchers on the castle walls saw the first of the dispirited Wolf Horde. Wode had prepared for River Garde to stand siege; every follower of the Wish Maiden was in position behind the battlements, massive stones were piled high to drop on attackers and cauldrons of smoking oil were ready to be poured through gargoyled spouts in deadly rain. But the straggling groups of nomads moved sullenly past the castle without giving it a glance.

Using the Eye, a mechanism with a bowl-shaped mirror mounted on the tower, Wode watched as they crowded on to the bridge that was the only link between the Wald and the Outlands. Crudely rebuilt after he and the Wish Maiden had fired it, the ramshackle structure swayed alarmingly as those with ponies led the exhausted animals across.

In the crystal eyepiece he saw that Tobin had been right in his description of their hurts. All the shuffling wounded showed signs of having been burned with their black hair singed and their garments scorched, but what elated him was the expressions of defeat on their normally impassive faces. There was nothing left of the eagerness with which they had followed their king to wage a holy war on Ythan, and he guessed that the euphoria which followed their invasion of the Wald had been replaced by disillusionment − they had been abandoned by their Wolf-in-the-Sky, the deity in which each wolfman had placed fanatical trust since babyhood.

'To have inherited such blind faith is why the barbarians can never hold what they conquer,' Wode declared. 'Believing you are favoured by your particular totem gives a tremendous advantage in the heat of battle but it is no help in administration and disastrous in defeat. Look at that shaman by the bridge . . . *Serene Mother!*'

He pointed to where a figure dressed in wolf furs

and holding an auroch-gut drum was haranguing the weary men waiting for their turn to step on to the bridge. A nomad with half his face a mask of blackened flesh drew forth a hunting knife and disembowelled the holy man with no more effort than a butcher trimming a carcass. Those about him laughed and patted his shoulders while the shaman writhed at their feet.

'Why did he do that?' gasped the Wish Maiden.

'The shaman must have been doing what priests have always done when the god they serve fails his followers − rant that the fault lies with the people through their lack of faith.'

Through the afternoon the trickle of barbarians became a flood and the Waldmen stared in amazement at the silent spectacle of their erstwhile enemies. None of the nomads spoke except to curse the congestion on the bridge or the drivers who tried to cross in the leather-canopied waggons they used as wheeled homes when wandering the steppeland. When several of Wode's scouts entered River Garde through the castle's underground passage they told of abandoned loot and bodies lining the trail that led through the forest from the mountains.

When the Wish Maiden saw one of the young Waldmen draw back an arrow to fire at the nomads milling round the bridge she laid her hand on his arm.

'Do not give them the honour of being our enemy any more,' she said. 'Let them only remember our contempt.'

Her words were taken to heart when out of her sight several Waldmen loaded a mangonel with a bucket taken from the castle latrine and fired it so the foul contents landed amidst those hurrying on to the bridge.

The bespattered victims did not even look back at the castle.

Unnoticed by his companions, Fulk the Woodcutter left the rampart where he had been watching the exodus. Taking his newly-honed axe he slipped out of a postern gate on the far side of the castle and set off through the forest to a point where he could watch the path down which the defeated army was retreating. He took up position behind the broad trunk of a spreading oak and waited with deadly patience.

At the same time a forester hammered on the gate of the Peak Tower with the news that the Wolf Horde had been defeated and within a matter of hours the only nomads left in the Wald would be the wounded who had fallen by the wayside.

The Lady Eloira, who had known and trusted the man since his childhood, gave orders for her cook to prepare a celebrative banquet for her retainers. Then with her steward supporting her she ascended the steep steps to the terrace on top of the tower that gave them a view over the magical cloud stretching to the distant mountains.

The old Reeve was grateful for the steady hand of Hans holding her arm. She had felt the weight of her many years before she used the magic inherited from her ancestors to enter the body of Jennet's doll; since then she had felt frail as well as old. When the great bear had sent the doll spinning far out over the cliff Eloira had opened her eyes to find herself in her bed in the Peak Tower with her maid sitting beside her. It was as though she had wakened from a dream too vivid to be endured.

'Oh mistress, you have come back to us,' Gill cried with tears rolling down her cheeks.

'The spell I cast is over,' Eloira murmured, 'but it has taken its costly toll. Never have I felt so *drained*.'

It was days before she was able to walk about the castle as before, for though it had been impossible for her to come to physical harm through the destruction of the doll, Eloira's body reflected the impact on her mind caused by the experience. Now, as she gazed towards the White Virgins, she summoned all the strength that was left to her.

'Ever since I conjured that mist to keep the Peak Tower safe from the barbarians I have dreamed of this day,' she declared. 'Yet now it has come I feel not joyful. While it has lain over the forest I have failed in my duty to Jennet. I fear that she escaped the bear only to find herself once more in the Witchfinder's power.'

Hans looked puzzled, 'Dear lady, do not blame yourself. You were not to know that the man you took in out of compassion would repay you in such a vile way.'

'And though we may no longer be under threat from the Wolf King, the Regent still remains in Danaak like a spider in the centre of his web and sooner or later the Witchfinders will come to the Wald,' she continued. 'The quest I sent Alwald and Krispin upon seems but a hollow undertaking now and for all I know I may have been responsible for their deaths — or worse.'

Hans looked anxiously at his mistress and was dismayed at the way the weight of her years seemed to have become too heavy a burden for her.

'And on account of me Piper has set out for Danaak. Alack, what hope is there for a Fey of the open Wald in that iron-girt place!'

'Lady, lady, you do but torture yourself,' cried Hans. 'Remember the words you said to me when my Janis was taken by the Dark Maid and my heart overflowed with grief? No? You told me that I must think no further ahead than midnight, and that next day was to be lived without thought for the one that followed. Now I beg you to do the same. Enjoy this day when we are freed from fear of the wolfmen and have no other thoughts until tomorrow.'

'How much easier it is to give advice than take it,' sighed the Lady Eloira. 'But you are right, faithful Hans. I must remember that I am Reeve of the High Wald with responsibilities to others. So let us be rid of this cloud that has lain heavy upon us for so long.'

'And that has given us protection with its heaviness. The warrior grumbles at the weight of his shield until it blocks a spear thrust.'

'You are full of wisdom today, old friend,' said Eloira with a ghost of a laugh. 'Now to work.'

Remembering the last time he had seen his mistress make an incantation in this place, Hans watched anxiously while she unrolled a vellum scroll and, walking to the parapet, began to intone words in Old Ythan. After the first couple of faded lines her voice gained strength and for a short while she was the Reeve of old.

Thunder muttered among the distant peaks and Hans felt the atmosphere about him change so that − as he told the cook later − the air felt strange as it did before a thunderstorm.

Sanus, sanus, avili carsum mosni lupa.

As Eloira continued sheet lightning made silhouettes out of the White Virgins. A wind shrilled through the large bronze astrolabe mounted in the centre of the terrace; high above, an eagle that had drifted lazily on a zephyr was suddenly hurled across the sky.

Hans seized one of the corroded bands of the astrolabe to keep his balance as the wind became a gale and with her hands clutching the top of the parapet the Reeve watched it sweep over the lake of opaque vapour and shred it to flying tatters.

Still as a statue Fulk remained behind the great oak that shaded the broad forest track and which was destined to become known as Fulk's Oak. He stood with his axehead between his feet and his hands lightly on the haft while his eyes scanned the nomads who continued to make for the bridge. And with every group that appeared round the bend in the track, with every single wolfman who rode an exhausted pony or limped with his long-handled war axe as a support, he hoped to recognize a certain nomad whose good-looking features had been branded in his memory — his daughter's pagan lover.

He knew that the young man had not gone with the main army into Ythan, that he might already have crossed the River of Night. But he reasoned that the nomads who had remained in the Wald would be leaving with the rest of the Horde and while there was the slightest chance of encountering him he was not going to leave his post. Of his daughter he refused to think.

Late in the afternoon he heard distant thunder and the trees shivered as a vast wind flowed over them, and between their flailing boughs Fulk saw that the cloud that had hung for so long over the High Wald was rent. Within minutes it was replaced with clear sky and a hush descended upon the forest again, broken only by groans of the walking wounded or unanswered pleas for help from those who collapsed in the bracken bordering the pathway.

The sun sank low. Night shadow raced across the Wald. The Constellation of the Griffin seemed to burn brighter than usual and nomads still came though now the groups were further apart and there were more lonely stragglers.

Fulk took advantage of gaps in the sorry procession to exercise his aching limbs, and he cursed the darkness until the full-blown moon sailed into the cloudless sky and made every forest leaf appear as though wrought out of pewter. Now long periods passed without a barbarian in sight and the woodman felt despair burgeon within him as he began to accept that his hope of retribution had been a forlorn one.

Fewer and fewer figures appeared in the moonlight yet he could not force himself to leave in case the next should turn out to be the one who had destroyed his idyllic existence with his daughter. When none came Fulk still waited, waited until the moon was overhead and the track bright with his cold light. Then, cursing his star-crossed fate, he raised his axe and was about to leave when he heard voices coming towards him. He froze in the deep shadow and waited.

Round the corner came two barbarians, one mounted and one on foot. The rider, taller than most of his kind, wore a wolfskin cloak while on his head the mask of a huge wolf acted as a helmet. The retainer limping beside his stirrup carried a staff on which was mounted a wolf skull painted crimson. It was this emblem that told Fulk he was looking at the dreaded Wolf King himself. He suddenly knew that while he had not been able to find the barbarian who had stolen his daughter's heart and virginity, fate was presenting him with an opportunity to avenge himself upon the whole accursed race. Without hesitation he stepped into the middle of the track.

The sceptre-bearer shouted at him in his uncouth tongue and then hobbled forward to defend his master. Fulk saw that he had been wounded in the thigh and, apart from his dagger, he had lost his weapons.

Fulk waited with a calmness that surprised him. It was like taking stock of a tree that he was going to bring down; he knew exactly the stroke he would make.

When the barbarian endeavoured to stab him he merely stepped back and with an easy stroke buried the blade of his axe in the enemy's chest. The man collapsed to his knees making a ghastly noise in his throat and Fulk had to put his foot against his ribcage in order to loose his weapon.

Meanwhile the Wolf King had climbed from his saddle and stood, a fearsome figure in the moonlight. He too appeared to have lost his weapons and for a moment Fulk was reassured by this, but only for a moment.

A low, intermittent and horrible sound issued from his throat.

Growling!

Was it a trick of the silver light that made his face change to a replica of the animal mask on his helmet?

He dropped on to all-fours and Fulk suddenly realized that the stories that had been told about the leader of the Horde were true — he was a werewolf.

The enormous creature swished his tail and a howl that held all the hate of the world issued from his dripping jaws. His eyes, glowing like twin amber lights, blinked and then he sprang in a huge curving leap that would enable him to tear the throat of the peasant who had dared to stand in his path.

For the rest of his days Fulk was to remember the terror of the beast hurtling towards him yet he could not recall judging the blow or even making it – it was a reaction inspired by a lifetime of axe work and required no thought.

With even more strength released in his body than when he felled the pine opposite the wall of River Garde, Fulk swung his axe in a sideways arc. The blade caught the man-wolf on the side of the neck. Such was its sharpness and the power of the blow that the head flew into a clump of ferns while the decapitated wolf fell at the woodcutter's feet.

TWO
Taloon

The ice boat was melting.

All through the night it had glided down the ice river and when that extraordinary highway ended among the foothills it had continued over sloping meadows until it came to rest several hours before dawn. Despite the exhilaration of the descent, exhaustion claimed the travellers and when the hull slithered to a stop the only one awake was Danya. Wearily he relinquished the steering oar and grinned as starshine illumined the huddled forms of his friends. In the bows the Princess Livia lay with her head against Alwald's shoulder, Tana had assumed the same position with Ognam once the jongleur had begun to doze, the warriors sat on the thwarts with their bearded chins on their breasts while the others rested against the bulwarks.

Danya stretched.

'You were right, old Magus,' he said aloud. 'It was a remarkable passage and one that will never dim in memory.' He yawned, rubbed his cramped arms and allowed himself to slide down to the deck where moments later he was submerged by a black wave of sleep.

At dawn they awoke, looked about them with dazed eyes and, remembering the headlong rush of the craft through the night, marvelled. Their craft now lay in a swale covered with a profusion of tall white lilies. Behind them reared the Mountains of the Moon and it was hard to believe that a few hours earlier they had been breathing the thin air of their highest peaks.

Beyond the lilies' voluptuous heads lay one of the rivers fed by the glacier's melted ice and beyond that stretched a deserted plain.

'Ythan! There lies the beginning of your kingdom,' said Alwald to the Princess.

'And exceeding dull it looks,' she said with a shrug. 'Hast thou an idea of how we travel hence? This craft will not last the day.'

Her words were true. The warmer air of the lower regions was melting the ice boat and water was rapidly filling the hull. Krispin, who had wandered off through the shoulder-high lilies to relieve himself, returned with a look of excitement on his face.

He seized Alwald by the arm and said, 'Come and see what I have found.'

Alwald suffered himself to be led to the river.

'There!' cried Krispin.

Tied up to the bank was a white barge with a large white horse tethered nearby.

'The Magus has provided it for us,' he added.

'How do you know that?'

'Alwald, I have seen that craft before.'

'How can that be?'

'In The Mage's Tower I saw it in one of the magic casements. It was moving through lovely countryside and that horse was pulling it. I swear it is there to carry us on the rest of our journey.'

Alwald looked doubtful.

'Mayhap it is a trap. I have to think of Her Highness's safety.'

'That is unlikely if I saw it through the casement some time ago.'

'In that case you can board it first.'

'As your lordship wishes.' Krispin went to the barge and ran up the gangplank, drawing Woundflame as he did so, then disappeared into the large cabin amidships.

Alwald waited and when a couple of minutes had passed he became anxious and hurried over to the elegant craft.

'Krispin! Krispin?' he called.

A moment later Krispin appeared with a roll of hot bread in his hand and a grin on his face.

'What in the name of the Mother have you been doing?' Alwald demanded. Krispin waved the roll at him.

'Breakfast is laid out for us – ale, hot bread, wild honey, delicious bacon, eggs, smoked fish . . . Bless Ysldon, he thinks of everything.'

'I shall call the others,' said Alwald who now caught the aroma of newly cooked food. 'Your Highness,' he said some moments later, 'I have found the means for you to continue your journey.'

As soon as the weary travellers boarded the white barge they felt a sense of peace and contentment steal over them. When the tow rope attached to the harness of the white horse became taut and the vessel moved forward with Danya's hand on the tiller the Princess

311

said, 'The Magus Ysldon hath given us more than a means of travel, he hath given us the comfort of enchantment.'

Krispin, sitting near the stern with his legs dangling over the side, pondered on her words. As the lily-grown banks slid past them it seemed that they were travelling much faster than they could have expected from such a leisurely form of transport. He guessed that to travel by barge into the heart of Ythan — where he presumed they were heading — would normally take weeks yet whenever he surveyed the landscape he was aware of changes in it. This sense of speed was contradicted by Dobbin — a name inspired by Princess Livia's memory of her rocking horse — plodding along the margin at the usual pace of a towing horse.

As ever there is much that I do not understand, he thought. *And at this moment I shall not tax my poor brain with it. No doubt Ysldon knows what he is about and* . . . Further thought was lost in a prodigious yawn. There was indeed the comfort of enchantment in the air.

An hour later Krispin glanced over the stern and saw that the Mountains of the Moon were no more than a white line on the horizon. He looked again at Dobbin moving peacefully beside the river and shook his head in bewilderment. Seeing this, Barlak said, 'Be not surprised, Master Krispin, this is not the first time that my lads and I have known such progress. Do you remember I told you how the Magus Ysldon sent us from Haven to the Mountains of the Moon and somehow we reached our destination in one march. There is the same feel in the air as then.'

'How right you are,' said Ognam who had come to the stern to tactfully escape the attentions of Tana.

312

'There is something unreal about this journey. Have you noticed that if you look closely at the river bank it is slightly blurred as though seen through an ill-cast piece of glass?'

Krispin peered at the blue-flowered rushes within a couple of paces of the barge's gleaming side and nodded in agreement.

'There does seem to be a slight mist over everything,' he said. 'And never have I seen a golden mist before.'

'It is the mist of enchantment,' said Danya from where he stood at the tiller. 'And after steering that ice boat I am ready to accept anything that the Magus may devise. He has proved to be a good friend to us and who am I to question such a sorcerer?'

'Indeed. Let us savour this tranquillity while we may for if the rest of the quest has been anything to go by it will not last for long,' said Ognam, raising a brimming wine cup that he had found on the cabin table and which was immediately replaced by invisible hands.

As if to emphasize the words of his friends Krispin looked up and saw that the landscape had altered again and they were entering a valley guarded by a ruined castle that had been built on a high bluff. The countryside was now luxuriant with groves and sweet meadows; well-fleshed cattle waded hock-deep in the river to drink and in the distance ribbons of smoke marked a village of thatched cottages. It was exactly the scene that Krispin remembered when he had drawn back a curtain from one of the magic casements in The Mage's Tower.

Ognam began to play a gentle melody on his jester's staff and the charmed journey continued.

*   *   *

313

Time lost meaning for the Pilgrims aboard the white barge. After their inland voyage they would have been hard put to say whether it had lasted for hours or days. And when reality returned they found that the barge was on a vast sheet of shimmering water. There was no sign of Dobbin and according to Danya the craft was moving of its own accord.

'There is no point in me remaining at the helm when it knows its course,' he said. 'Mayhap a current draws it to its destination.'

The others looked about them like those awakening from a dream-filled slumber. The strange golden haze that Krispin had noticed enveloping them was gone and there was no doubt that they were back in what Ognam called 'the real world' though none knew what part of the real world this might be.

The opposite shore of the lake appeared ragged with trees. When the dazzle on the water was lessened by a passing cloud the travellers saw they were of gigantic proportions. Above serpentine roots writhing down the bank their pale grey trunks soared as straight as pikes, though their branches drooped and grey-green leaves hung down in weeping strands. Large sombre-feathered birds glided among them and the sigh of the breeze through their heavy leaves had a melancholic quality despite the bright day.

In the bows of the barge Tana gave a sudden exclamation of astonishment.

'Ognam, I know those strange trees — I know where we are.'

She cupped her face in her hands as tears began to flow.

'And where are we, lady?' asked the Princess gently.

'Taloon. The Lake of Taloon.'

'Her father's palace was built on the shore of this lake,' explained Ognam. 'It was part of his demesne.'

'But surely the Lake of Taloon is hundreds of leagues from the Mountains of the Moon . . .' began Danya and then stopped as all realized the vast distance they had travelled with such ease.

Between her sobs Tana murmured, 'Oh, will my home still be standing, will my parents be living?'

The barge swung to the right and cruised parallel to the shore. Krispin noticed that here the water was thick with livid weed whose scarlet flowers lay on the surface like spatterings of blood. It seemed that they drew back on their own accord at the approach of the vessel.

A short time later the companions crowding the bows observed that some distance ahead, where the line of trees ended, a series of terraces descended to the water's edge. Above them was a long elegant building whose domes and turrets gave it a fantastical air. At the sight of it Tana wept openly and all guessed that this must be the home from which she had been absent so long. No one quite knew what to do to comfort her and then Ognam simply patted her shoulder as though she was a troubled child. The girl gave him a look of gratitude and, like a child, wiped away her tears with the backs of her hands.

As the barge approached the palace, Ognam remembered how Tana had described it when they talked in her subterranean prison beneath The Mage's Tower. There had been a yearly festival when scented oil was poured on the surface of the lake, he recalled. Now he saw that the terraces were just as she had described them with rows of statues and ornate urns mounted on the balustrades from which dark vines cascaded to the terrace below. But everything had a greenish tinge and the edges of the stonework were no longer clean cut but blurred and Ognam realized that the whole area was overgrown with creepers. Raising his eyes he saw that the palace bore the marks of decay and held the silent and forlorn air of a place long deserted.

'Alas, as I feared, I have returned too late, far far too late,' said Tana quietly.

The barge ran alongside the lowest terrace and Krispin leapt ashore to secure its lines to rusted mooring rings.

'If this be our destination Ysldon hath kept his word to help us reach it,' said Princess Livia. 'But from now on I fear we cannot look to his magical help. And I must protest that this remote ruin seemeth an odd place to rally followers to our cause.'

'As to that we shall have a better idea when we have explored,' said Alwald.

A couple of the warriors ran out the gangplank and the Princess was about to step ashore when Ognam raised his hand and nodded towards Tana.

'Thou be right, Jongleur,' she murmured. 'It be her homecoming, though not a happy one I think.'

Having heard the story of Ognam and Tana from Alwald, the Princess smiled at him and added, 'It seemeth that your interest in that lady groweth again. Be that so?'

'Sadly, no, Your Highness,' Ognam replied. 'But we have all shared much together since we sailed the Cold Sea and what touches one touches all.'

'Thou art a wise fool,' said the Princess.

'If I was wise I would not be a fool,' said Ognam and he followed Tana across the plank.

As the others disembarked – the Princess's guard with weapons drawn – Tana stood on the terrace and said, 'We used to have such masques here. Coloured lanterns were strung along each terrace and the musicians played in an anchored barge so their music came across the water and there was a real fountain spurting wine for the guests.'

'Hast thou no idea why your father's palace should come to this sorry pass?' asked the Princess.

Tana shook her black locks.

'I do not know how many seasons have come and gone since I was taken as a host—, since I was taken by magic to The Mage's Tower.'

'And thou knows not why that was?'

'All I knew was that my father fell foul of that terrible old sorcerer and spite must have been the reason for my abduction.'

The Princess leaned closer to Tana.

'Didst he ever . . . thou know?'

'Never.'

'Then he was a fool. When I was younger – before The Enchantment I mean – I used to sometimes daydream that I was held captive by some bold and handsome brigand who wouldst rather have his lusty way with me than accept my ransom.'

'I think my captor was addle-pated and had forgotten the use of his natural wand – thank the Mother. Once I was installed in my grotto I am sure he never gave me another thought. If Ognam had not rescued me I could have remained there for eternity, though little gratitude I showed him for it, alas.'

The party walked up the steps from terrace to terrace and the only sign of life was black beetles scurrying into the creeper that carpeted the paving. On reaching the colonnaded wall of the palace Tana's sadness returned.

'I remember dancing here as though it was but yesterday,' she said. 'But now all those merry folk are for ever gone . . .'

The Princess took her hand.

'Lady, it is a shared grief . . .' she began.

'Halt, strangers!' cried a hoarse voice and from the deep shadow within the colonnade emerged a score of crossbowmen in a variety of uniforms with weapons cocked and raised.

'Who are you to threaten us?' demanded Barlak.

A man stepped forward who by the badge on his military garb was in command. Looking at Barlak's scowling warriors he guffawed, 'Where did you find those weapons? Such antiques went out of service a century ago.'

'Potton-spew, would you like to step over and test if their edges have lost their sharpness with the passage of time?' growled Barlak.

'Sweeten your mouth, soldier, unless you want to test the sharpness of our bolts,' retorted the man. 'How did you get here?'

'We are honest travellers and we came by barge,' said Danya in a reasonable tone.

'I see no barge.'

As one they turned to where the white barge had been moored and saw only water with blood-red blooms floating upon it.

'Curse magic both high and low — you can never depend upon it,' Krispin muttered.

'By the code of chivalry and the rules of war I demand to see whoever is in charge here,' declared Alwald.

'Fear not — or rather fear a lot — you will see him all right,' said the man. 'He can recognize the Regent's agents no matter how they are disguised — even if they are disguised as carnival clowns,' he added with a contemptuous glance at Ognam. 'I doubt not you are more comfortable in a Witchfinder's robe.'

'You are much mistaken,' said Alwald. 'Who can I explain to?'

'Commander Mandal.'

THREE
The Liegeman

While their companions waited under the threat of the crossbowmen, the Princess Livia, Tana, Alwald, Krispin and Barlak were escorted to a vaulted chamber lit by shafts of the sunshine struggling through grimy stained glass. Tapestries drooped in rags on the wall and it was obvious that for many years it had been the sole domain of spiders and mice.

As Tana entered she looked about her with an expression of sad wonder and said, 'This used to be my father's hall of audience.'

Seated at a table was a broad, military man with cropped hair whose manner of outward calm was belied by his restless eyes. A soldier stood beside the table with a parchment map unfolded.

Alwald and Krispin exchanged a puzzled glance. Was this the man who had commanded the Regent's army when they had been in Thaan? And, if so, why was he in this derelict place with such an ill-assorted band?

'Explain your presence in my palace,' said Tana in regal tones that could not have been bettered by the Princess.

The man behind the table stood up, nodded to the escort to wait at the far end of the hall, and said, 'Lady, I am Mandal, one-time Commander of the Host and the future bane of the Regent . . . *Serene Mother!*'

His startled exclamation came when Princess Livia moved into a ray of white light that dramatically illuminated her features against the dimness of the hall.

'It cannot be,' muttered Mandal. 'Forgive me but for a moment I was startled by your likeness to the portraits of the Princess Livia.'

'I am the Princess Livia,' said the Princess quietly.

For once in his authoritative life Mandal found he was without words.

'And I demand that this lady be treated with the courtesy befitting her royal blood,' declared Alwald.

'Please be seated,' said Mandal, gesturing to a carved chair close to his table. The Princess looked at its dusty seat with distaste and Mandal's lieutenant, to his own surprise, found himself placing the map upon it. It was not just that she was the most beautiful woman he had ever seen, there was something in her bearing that as a military man he immediately respected.

'You say that you are the Princess Livia — the same lady who was placed under an enchantment?' said Mandal.

'Yes. As thou canst see I have been awakened.'

'Then you have escaped from the Regent?'

'I do not understand thy question.'

'I have had secret information from Danaak that the Regent found the legendary sleeping princess and holds her in the Citadel.'

'Of that I know nothing, it is a hundred years since I last beheld Danaak.'

Mandal's fingers furrowed his short hair in perplexity.

'The likeness is remarkable,' he muttered.

'So it should be,' said the Princess. 'I grew weary of sitting for portraits, and then my father sanctioned only the finest copies.'

Mandal said, 'I should like to hear your story from beginning to end.'

The escorting soldiers brought up equally dusty chairs for the others before being dismissed.

'It could be argued that thou should make the explanations but, as I sense we share a common cause, I shall comply,' said the Princess. 'The first part of the story should be told by Lord Alwald who undertook the quest to awaken me.'

'If it is the wish of Her Highness I shall do my best but it is something that cannot be related quickly,' said Alwald.

Mandal nodded and turned to his lieutenant, 'Ulrik, see if you can find some wine among the stores, but first pass the order to the sentries that no one is to leave. Should there be a traitor among us we do not want him running to the Regent with word of this . . . yet.' He turned to Alwald and said, 'Begin.'

An hour and then another passed as Alwald recounted the adventures that led up to the discovery of the sleeping princess. The only time Mandal's expression changed was when the narrative reached the point where the Pilgrims stayed in the beleaguered city of Thaan. His lips tightened and his sombre gaze rested upon Alwald as though seeking his inner thoughts but Alwald continued calmly until he reached the events

323

in the cavernous resting place of the Princess. Then Barlak was told to continue with an account of the journey to the Wells of Ythan.

The hall darkened as the sun threw her last rays over the Lake of Taloon when the warrior ended with a description of the Princess's awakening.

'So, like the Princess, you had remained under a glamour for a century,' said Mandal thoughtfully. 'I know something of military history so can you tell me who was the commander of the White Eagle Legion before The Enchantment?'

'That would be Old Farting Noll . . . Commander Nollkin, sir.'

'And do you remember the name of the horse he always rode?'

'He never rode a horse, sir. He claimed he got a better view of the battlefield from the saddle of a drong. The name of the drong was Hero.'

Mandal nodded and turned to the Princess.

'And what happened when you left the Wells of Ythan, lady?'

The Princess graphically recounted their ordeals as three times some form of sorcery was used to put supernatural dangers in their path.

'It would seem that the Regent, or rather some person versed in the art of conjuration with his interest at heart, didst all in her power to destroy me and my companions.'

'*Her* power, lady?'

'We believe it to be the Lore Mistress.'

'And now you have arrived at this ruin on the Lake of Taloon,' said Mandal. 'Is it not a coincidence that you should come to the one place where the downfall of the Regent is being planned?'

'I doubt coincidence,' said the Princess. 'It was the Magus Ysldon who set us on the journey to Taloon and I believe he knew more than he told us when he provided us with the white barge. Though he be the Guardian of the Wells he doth roam beyond the Valley of Yth in different guises to collect knowledge of the kingdom.'

Mandal picked up the wine cup that had remained untouched during the recital of the Pilgrims' adventures. From start to finish his features betrayed not the slightest hint of what he thought and Krispin wondered uneasily if he regarded their arrival as some devious plot by the Regent. Although he had relived the quest as Alwald told it, he knew that to an outsider — to someone who had not seen the magic and travelled in the weird realms that they had known — it would seem like a sagaman's romance.

'A wonderful tale,' Mandal said as though to confirm Krispin's fears. 'And well told. I would not be surprised if that jongleur who is in your party had not passed on some of his skill. What would interest me is if you could produce proof of what you have told.'

'I could describe in detail how the Red Death came to Thaan,' said Alwald, irritated by Mandal's attitude.

'Or how the city's great mirror burned your war engines,' added Krispin. The Princess turned to them inquiringly, not aware of the role the man opposite had played in the siege of the heretic city.

'I have no doubt you could for then we were on opposite sides of the wall,' said Mandal mildly. 'All I shall say is that it was not my plan to catapult the Death into the city, that order came from the Regent. And, should you not have heard while you were in outlandish regions, the result of his decision was that my entire army was lost and I was imprisoned. That may give you an inkling of my present feelings towards my Lord Regent.

'You may wonder at the way I asked for some evidence of this amazing narration but mayhap you will understand shortly,' he continued. 'The Regent has more wiles than a drong has ticks and there is much more at stake than you might guess.'

While he spoke Krispin bent and unbuckled the pack at his feet, removing a leather tube which had been crafted for him in Mabalon.

'Is this proof enough?' he asked, and from the slender case he drew out the light wand. Immediately it replaced the dusk that was thickening in the hall with brilliant light.

'So that is the wonder you stole from the eidolon, Master Toymaker,' said Mandal. 'I am satisfied.'

He stood up and to the surprise and consternation of all he drew his sword. The blade flashed dangerously in the cold light of the wand. Instinctively Krispin's hand reached for Woundflame's grip only to touch the empty scabbard, all weapons having been confiscated before they were admitted to the Commander's presence.

Mandal walked round the table and stood directly in front of the Princess. Holding the blade horizontally he offered it to her and said formally, 'If you will accept and honour me as your liegeman I shall accept and honour you as my liege sovereign and I shall not rest from your cause until you have claimed and won the Empty Throne.'

Princess Livia took the sword in both hands.

'I accept thy devoir,' she said and handed the sword

back, adding, 'but I wouldst be happier if I knew why thou offered it.'

'And I shall tell you,' said Mandal and he related how, after the survivors of the Thaan campaign had been massacred for fear they carried the plague he, the Commander of the Host, was thrown into the Cage high on the wall of the Citadel. 'All my life I had served the Regent and my reward for carrying out his commands was to be left to die for the amusement of the mob,' he said bitterly. 'But looking out on the world through the bars of the Cage I gained a view on life that I had never had before. Until then I had thought of naught else but military matters and my own advancement but now I understood the ills that beset Ythan.

'And there was an old hag with me who had been accused of witchcraft and because she admitted it she escaped the cauldron for the mercy of the Cage. It is strange, death has been my trade yet I cannot forget her dying hours . . .' His voice trailed off as memories of his humiliating captivity returned too vividly.

Recollecting himself, he explained how the imprisoned alchemist Leodore arranged his escape and how the two of them followed a secret passage through the Nether World. On the way they released the conspirator Lord Odo from his dungeon and took him with them.

'The passage, which was doubtless intended as an escape route in olden times, came out in a mausoleum in the necropolis,' he said. 'And there we found two fugitives, Garn and Aldis, living in it − ghouls such outcasts are called − and they befriended us. We stayed hidden in that great cemetery until Odo regained a little of his physical strength though his mind has

327

remained on the borderland of madness. And it was during that time while we lived as ghouls that I determined to avenge myself, the old woman believed to be a witch because she concocted love philtres, and my brave lads who died unnecessarily, on the Regent.

'It had occurred to me that if I could return Odo secretly to his family I would be given the support to raise a rebellion against the Regent. The tomb-dwellers helped us greatly and thanks to their skill at thiefcraft we were able to acquire a couple of drongs and leave the city in secret.

'Alas for my plan. On the second night of the journey Odo died in the belief that a rat was devouring his brain. We buried him by the roadside but when we finally arrived at his estate his sons disbelieved our story. They feared we might be spies from the Guild of Witchfinders.

'Neither Leodore the Alchemist nor I could risk returning to Danaak so on his advice we went on to the Lake of Taloon where he knew of an abandoned palace where we might shelter.'

'Did he know the reason for it being abandoned?' interrupted Tana.

Mandal shook his head and said, 'I wish I had an answer for you, lady, but it is a mystery that none seem to be able to unravel. When we came here we lived as wild men for the first few days and I must give Leodore credit for the fish traps he devised to sustain us.

'Our fortune turned when a troop of cavalry on a routine patrol came here and I recognized men who had served under me. To prevent my tale becoming tedious it is sufficient to say that when I made myself known to them they agreed to serve me again. They were disillusioned with the regency after their comrades' fate in the Raven Pass and they recruited disaffected soldiers from other companies, hence the diverse uniforms of my little army. As the word spread, men who had never handled anything more warlike than mattocks began travelling by stealth to Taloon to join us.

'Having studied military tactics I knew that I needed more than deserters and peasants behind me if I was to advance upon Danaak without my campaign becoming yet another petty revolt doomed to be suppressed. All I could offer was revenge and that was not enough. I needed something that would shake the populace out of the lethargy resulting from three generations of suppression, a symbol that would remind them of long-lost liberties and inspire the hope of regaining them.'

Mandal paused and his words seemed to hang in the air as all understood his meaning.

'Now, thanks to your Magus or chance or the workings of providence, our paths have crossed at this crucial time,' he said. 'If you are to gain your throne, Princess, you need an army behind you − if I am to have an army that will overthrow the Regent I need you to inspire men to join it by the thousand.'

The Princess looked calmly at Mandal.

'And if the return of Ythan's blood royal and your military skill combine to bring down the Regent and those who have supported him, what then, Commander?'

'You would be enthroned, Princess, and resume your ancient rights which would protect and benefit the commonweal.'

'And you?'

Mandal smiled for the first time.

'I have no ambition outside my profession. I would ask to be Commander of the Host once more.'

'So be it,' said the Princess Livia.

FOUR
Two Visions

Grand Johan tolled in the belfry of Danaak's Great Shrine with a solemnity that portended some grave and unusual event. Inside the vast building, smoke from acolytes' censers rolled down the altar steps like a pale herb-scented fog. The steps leading up to the arched entrance were flanked by Companions of the Rose awaiting the arrival of their master, and beyond them Witchfinders made sure that members of the Guild of Acclaimers were in position.

Before long, dignitaries of the city began to be ushered to their places by fresh-faced novices, and then a hush fell within and without as the Witchfinder-General entered, escorted by two lines of black-cowled figures who, despite their religious appearance, were known to be his bodyguard. When he had seated himself on his gilded chair to one side of the sacred flame that burned before the towering symbol of the Serene Mother there came a blaring of ivory trumpets as members of the Regent's Council and the courtiers from the Citadel appeared and were shown to their special boxes.

The one box that remained empty was the one reserved for the Lady Mandraga and there was whispered speculation when the Lore Mistress failed to appear.

The next fanfare was drowned by delirious cheering from the Guild of Acclaimers as the Regent arrived by a passage that led directly from the Citadel escorted by six Companions of the Rose and his silver-masked avenger. Despite the fact that they were within holy precincts the burghers stood and applauded their master who the day before had returned from his triumph over the Wolf Horde.

When he took his place on a chair with twice as much gilding as that of the Witchfinder-General, the sonorous voice of Grand Johan fell silent and through an archway appeared a dozen boys dressed in white robes – known by the irreverent as the unholy virgins – who advanced with prancing steps to sprinkle rosewater and petals in the path of a priestly procession. As each member of it appeared through the arch he displayed more silver and gold embroidery on his robe than the last. When Archpriest Mattan appeared, his vestments contained more precious thread than samite and he glittered like an enormous jewel.

The priests took up position before the altar and each bowed in turn to the Archpriest who bowed in reply, bowed to the Regent and then to the symbol of the Serene Mother. When this ritual recognition of each other and the deity was finally completed, when the Seven Major Adorations had been intoned and the priests had bowed to each other at their conclusion, the Archpriest declared, 'I have summoned you to the temple of the Serene Mother to give you tidings of a miraculous vision that has been granted to me.'

He paused dramatically as a murmur like a distant sea surge filled the shrine and, his features hidden by his hood, the Witchfinder-General permitted himself a sardonic smile.

'A week ago I knelt in a night-long prayer vigil for the success of the Lord Regent against the pagans – a prayer that has been most graciously granted – when a few moments after the midnight gong had sounded I beheld a light floating above the altar.'

There was a ripple of movement as a thousand necks craned to see if the mystical light was still there.

'And as I watched I saw it grow until its light shone all about and its centre was too dazzling for mortal eye, and then from the light came a voice of surpassing sweetness. And lo, the voice spoke of the sin of Ythan for ignoring the testament of King Johan XXXIII. And summoning my courage I said, "If we sin we sin in ignorance for I know nothing of such a testament."

'And the voice told me to go into the Citadel and there in a certain place where the ancient scrolls are kept I would find one that had been sealed since The Enchantment.

'And the voice continued, "Mattan, beloved and faithful servant, take that scroll and see that its instruction is followed as is ordained by the law and thus bring a righteous benefit to the kingdom." Slowly the light faded and I heard no more.'

Archpriest Mattan paused as though too overcome by memory of the miracle to find words but he made a visible effort and continued, describing how, when he had recovered from this divine visitation, he went to the Citadel and there with the help of the Lore Mistress he discovered the scroll just as it had been described. He held up a yellowed parchment.

333

'In my hand is the last testament of King Johan XXXIII and it reads thus: "As the whereabouts of my beloved daughter Livia are unknown at this time and I sense the approach of the Dark Maid I hereby declare that if no legitimate claim is made to my throne for one hundred years after the disappearance of my daughter the said Livia, I do decree that on or after the hundredth anniversary of the aforementioned disappearance all entitlement of my House shall be void and whosoever shall have the safekeeping of Ythan at that time shall be accorded the title of King and shall be crowned with due ceremony so that the kingdom may prosper under the rule and protection of a new Royal House. Signed in the belief that the Serene Mother will grant that this, my final mortal wish, will be duly honoured, Johan." '

Silence followed the Archpriest's words and all eyes turned to the Regent who sat as though stunned, then the Archpriest approached him and, bowing low, proffered him the document with its faded lines of writing.

'I find this impossible to believe,' the Regent declared. 'Has this been authenticated?'

'By the Lore Mistress herself. The signature has been verified against existing signatures of King Johan,' replied the Archpriest. 'But what makes it inviolate is the fact that it was brought to my humble notice by divine will, Your Majesty.'

As the Archpriest spoke the last two words Grand Johan pealed a paean of iron-throated jubilation and outside the Great Shrine the Guild of Acclaimers cheered their throats raw.

A subtle change had come over the quest, if the

situation that the Pilgrims found themselves in could still be called that. After the momentous meeting with Mandal very little was seen of the Princess or Alwald. Most of the time they were closeted with the Commander and his lieutenants planning the strategy of rebellion and the means of informing the followers of the Pilgrim Path that their Princess was looking to them for support.

When the story of Barlak's warriors spread, the soldiers never tired of questioning them, usually on what it was like to serve under a real king, how the pay of a hundred years ago compared with the pittance each soldier received today and other such military topics.

Tana wandered about the empty palace, re-peopling it in her imagination and giving way to hysterical tears when her grief overwhelmed her. Then Ognam would reluctantly follow the sound of crying until he found her and endeavoured to calm her.

'Oh, Ognam, it was my dream to return here with you to find it as I remembered, and how proud I would have been to present you as my saviour,' she said on several occasions.

Looking at her sad, beautiful face Ognam left unsaid the cynical thoughts that sprang to his mind.

Krispin, Gambal and Danya felt that they were no longer needed, especially as Alwald in his new role of the Princess's Champion had little time to speak to them other than to make routine greetings when they met by accident. Krispin became increasingly depressed by the memory of giving his flask of Water of Life to the Hump. Seeing him in this frame of mind, Danya slapped him hard on the shoulder and said, 'Lad, you began the quest in the High Wald along with Lord

Alwald so you should be in there with him and Mandal instead of moping like this.'

'I expect they do not consider a toymaker would be able to contribute anything of value,' he said.

'Nonsense and you know it. You are the last person who should undervalue himself. Your craft should have nothing to do with it.'

That's where you are wrong, he thought. But he did not explain how, when Alwald was in conversation with Commander Mandal, he had overheard his fellow quester refer to him as 'the apprentice'.

'I shall go for a walk, Shipmaster,' he said and, slipping Woundflame's baldric over his shoulder, he set off along the lakeside towards the grey trees that lined it. As he walked by the margin he noticed that the pale waterweed with its red blooms moved as though animated by a will rarely associated with flora. It reminded him of the Upas groves in the Shadow Realm and he shivered.

At last he seated himself on one of the serpentine roots of a grey tree and watched a heron flapping lazily over the surface.

The quest is over for me, he thought. *The Princess has been found, Alwald is happy to be her champion and Commander Mandal will lead her army. I am not a soldier and it is time for me to return to the High Wald. Why am I not delighted by the thought? It is something that I have dreamed about for most of the quest. Is it because I no longer have the cure for Jennet, or because with Toyheim razed I have no home to return to, or is it something to do with the quest after all?*

As he sat pondering by the ever-stirring weed he became aware of a thin sweet sound that immediately transported him through time and distance to the bank of a forest mere where he had lain beside Jennet. He turned and there, just as he remembered him, was a small, grey-cloaked figure playing a bone flute.

The music and the recollections it inspired brought tears to Krispin's eyes. Was it those tears that made the piper appear insubstantial as though the edges of his form were blurred? When he moved there was a certain transparency about him.

The Fey lowered his pipe.

'There is no need to be afraid, Krispin Tammasson.'

'I am not afraid – this time,' Krispin responded.

'Much has happened in the world of men since I last saw you,' said Piper, seating himself on a root opposite. 'And life is changing for me also. I am dying, Krispin. Dying.' His voice, as soft as a breeze passing through a leafy tree, faded.

'Sir, you look well enough.'

'Ah, you know nothing of the Fey. What you see is my shadow.'

'But I was told that Fey . . . good people like you . . . are born without shadows.'

'We do not have shadows as you know them, figures of shade cast by the sun. Our shadows are reflections of ourselves, our second self if you like, and it is possible for us to inhabit them briefly and travel outside nature's confines. This I am doing now while my body dies in Danaak.'

'But cannot you be healed? There must be skilful chirurgeons in the capital.'

'There are iron gates in the capital and iron bars, and I am behind them and such are the eternal bane of us forest folk. But I did not come in shadow to discuss my fate . . .'

'But if iron has such an effect why did you go to Danaak?' interrupted Krispin.

'To seek Jennet.'

'Jennet!'

'Listen and I shall explain about Jennet and why I have sought you out in my closing hours.' And the Fey recounted to a white-faced Krispin how Jennet had been abducted from the Peak Tower, of the distress of the Lady Eloira, and how he had set out in search of her.

'Do you believe she is in the hands of the Regent?' demanded Krispin, aghast.

'I know,' said Piper. 'She is held in the Citadel.'

'Is she harmed?'

'No more than captivity harms. She is not ill treated because the Regent and the Lore Mistress may use her likeness to Princess Livia to their advantage.'

'Are you sure? Have you seen her?'

'I have and it was my undoing. When I reached Danaak I presented myself as a pipe-player to the Revel Master for I had little doubt that my music would gain me entrance to the Citadel. My plan worked and I was given quarters there but already Danaak's iron gates were sapping me. I knew I must hurry if I was to be of help to the maid and so I garnered all the clues I could from my fellow entertainers and the servants I piped for. One night I set out to find her.'

'And you succeeded?'

'Yes. We Fey are not conspicuous and I managed to reach the chamber in which she was held. The door was locked but I saw Jennet through the spy hole, and that was when I was caught. If I had been in the forest I could have protected myself with Fey magic but in iron-gated Danaak such power was lost.

338

'I was examined by the Witchfinder who realized there was something strange about me — from the arrogant human viewpoint — and I was thrown into an iron-barred cage in the Regent's menagerie of freaks. No words of mine can describe the horror of that place, of the suffering of those creatures both human and animal whose ill destiny it was to be born without conformity to their kind. The least of their torments is to be forced into perverse mating for the gratification of their master. My only piece of luck is that since my capture he has not visited the gallery as he had set forth against the Wolf Horde, and I have been spared his vile attention in my latter days.'

Krispin was too overwhelmed to speak.

'Looking over this tranquil lake I must confess that I find it hard to leave the beauty of the world but that be the fate of both man and Fey sooner or later, and the menagerie has taught me that there is as much ugliness as there is beauty just as there is equal darkness and light. I have used what little of my Fey powers that remained to seek you out in shadow, to warn you of the danger that hangs over Jennet. This danger is that the Regent will likely decide to use her body — her dead body — to end the legend of the sleeping princess.'

Speechless, Krispin merely stared at the Fey with anguished eyes.

'With that knowledge, Krispin Tammasson, you must decide what you must do.'

'I — I shall go to Danaak,' Krispin muttered.

'I expected nothing less. Perhaps a human will succeed where a Fey has failed, for iron is a blessing rather than a bane to your kind, and doubtless you have gained much that will stand you in good stead from your questing. Now my time is short and I have little strength left to remain in shadow. When the earthly span of a Fey is ended it is our belief that some inner part of us awakens on a star. It is my fancy that I might find myself on one of the stars that makes up the Griffin . . .'

His voice was softer; the breeze was dying in the leafy tree.

'Tell me, Lord Fey, why you imperilled yourself on account of Jennet?' asked Krispin. The reply came in a whisper.

'I learned that there is about her something of unique value.'

To his dismay Krispin found that he could see a pattern of branches through Piper's fading form.

'Tell me who she is,' he cried desperately.

'You may learn all you wish to know when you return Woundflame . . .'

The Fey was gone. His words died on the air but Krispin had a curious sensation that within his head he could hear the distant music of a pipe.

FIVE
King
Death

As Krispin returned to the palace along the lakeside
he was so preoccupied by his chaotic thoughts he was
unaware of Gambal until he laid his hand on his
shoulder.

'I would have a word with you,' he said. And then,
as he looked closer at Krispin's stricken face, he added,
'You look as though you have seen a ghost.'

'Mayhap I have,' said Krispin with an attempt at
a wan smile. 'Say on, Gambal, for I have little time.'

'Then you are lucky for some of us seem to have
too much since we came here.'

Krispin nodded his agreement.

'Today I was thinking back to the Mountains of the
Moon and how it was your Disk of Livia that saved
us from the invisible evil that trod the snowfield. And
because you had worn it for all the quest and must
be missing it, I want you to have this.'

From his neck he removed a chain to which was
attached an identical medallion and handed it to
Krispin.

'Is this a true one?'

341

'I cannot say that it has magical properties as yours did but it is no forgery. The Regent gave it to me so I could prove my credentials to you and Lord Alwald when you were in the Citadel dungeons.'

'But how came he by it?'

'From some poor wretch of a Pilgrim who had been discovered by the Witchfinders,' Gambal answered. 'Now it is correct that you, who have proved yourself on the Pilgrim's Path, should wear it.'

'I thank you, Gambal, for I must admit that I was grieved at the loss of my own disk,' Krispin said as he dropped the chain over his head. 'But now I must hurry to Mandal and tell him that I am leaving.'

'You are what?'

'I must go to Danaak immediately.'

Gambal's expression showed his astonishment.

'And you think Mandal will allow you.'

'Remember he is the Princess's liegeman now and if he makes difficulties I know at least she will understand. If I thought otherwise I would slip away without a word but I want to bid farewell to Alwald and the rest of you in a proper manner. We have come a long way together for good and ill and I sense we may never meet again.'

'Then good fortune attend you,' said Gambal. With a calculating frown that was at variance with his normally innocent expression he watched Krispin hurry along a vine-carpeted terrace.

Minutes later, two of Mandal's guards ushered him into the hall where, in splashes of garish light from the stained-glass casements, he sat at a table with the Princess, Alwald and several of his newly appointed staff.

'Master Krispin?' he said, looking up from the parchments spread out before him.

'I have come to bid you farewell,' said Krispin.

Alwald jumped to his feet.

'I cannot believe my ears,' he exclaimed. 'You talk of deserting now! It is impossible.'

'Why?'

'Because . . . because . . .' Alwald thought desperately for a reason. 'Because we started the quest together and that is how we must end it. And besides, when we left the Peak Tower it was understood that you were to be my esquire and . . . and as such you cannot quit without my permission.'

'As to the quest, it ended with the revival of Her Highness as far as I am concerned, and as to your second objection I suggest you take me before a Court of Chivalry though it seems to me that until a moment ago you regarded me as an apprentice rather than as anything as elevated as your squire.'

Alwald blushed deeply as he realized that Krispin had overheard the remark about his trade.

'Dear Krispin, sit thou down and tell me why thou wouldst leave,' said Princess Livia.

Calmed by her words Krispin told about Jennet, her resemblance to Her Highness and her present plight.

'You say she is as beautiful as me?' asked Princess Livia in a certain tone of voice that even Krispin recognized.

'Your Highness, I said there was a . . . resemblance. Never did I mention the beauty – you are a lady of the blood royal and Jennet is a lass from the High Wald.'

'If there is a *resemblance* it could explain a spy's rumour that reached us about the Regent having found

343

the sleeping princess,' said Mandal thoughtfully. 'If you feel you must go, Master Krispin, we cannot do aught but wish you well.'

Krispin looked at him with surprised gratitude.

'I suggest you can save a lot of time by crossing the lake in a boat and then travelling south until you strike the old Thaan highroad that leads directly to Danaak. You will need help when you reach the city, especially if you are to enter the Citadel, so go to the necropolis and find Garn and Aldis who befriended us. Tell them you come from he who gave the token and I swear you will be well aided.'

'The token?' repeated Krispin.

'Yes, it was all I had to give when Leodore and I left. It had been given to me in the Cage by the poor old woman. It was a coin on a chain and it had a spiral of strange characters engraved on either side, probably a witch charm.'

'Was it like this?' asked Krispin and he held out the disk that Gambal had just given him.

Mandal nodded.

'Garn will recognize it,' he said.

Some minutes later, when the Princess and Alwald had left with Krispin to make his farewells to the others, the lieutenant Ulrik said to Mandal, 'Commander, is it not dangerous to allow that young man to enter Danaak. If the Witchfinders get hold of anyone it is inevitable that they will confess everything they know and then more.'

'If Krispin should have the misfortune to be captured it would do us no harm if he told about the Princess. On the contrary, such testimony would be accepted — the Witchfinders have great faith in confession through torture — and would weaken the

344

Regent's claims that he had found the sleeping princess. You will remember that Omgarth, in his treatise on warfare, stated that to sow words of dissent among the enemy is more effective than a siege.'

A path of reflected moonlight lay across the smooth face of the Lake of Taloon as Krispin descended the terraces to where a rowing boat was moored. He had found his farewells to his fellow Pilgrims more distressing than he had expected and it was at his insistence that he set off without the final pain of watching them get smaller and smaller as he rowed away.

As he was stowing his pack in the bows of the small craft he was aware of a figure emerging from the shadows.

'Fear not,' came a familiar voice.

'Gambal?'

'No other. I would come with you.'

'But why? There is no reason for you to risk entering Danaak.'

Gambal believed he had a very good reason. As things were he had little chance of coming to the attention of the Princess. Above all, he needed her notice so that if she became Queen of Ythan his fortunes might revive. And the only way he saw of achieving this was to go with Krispin to Ythan where he might perform some noteworthy exploit. Aloud he said, 'The Citadel is like a maze on many levels. You would have no chance of finding your Jennet there unless you had the help of someone who knew it as you once knew your village. When I was Revel Master I made a point of exploring every back staircase and every ancient passage. I shall be your guide.'

For a moment Krispin hesitated. On their journeying he had never been as close to Gambal as to the others and there was still a shadow of mistrust in his mind despite Gambal's overtures. Then he realized the truth of Gambal's words and reminded himself that the only thing that mattered was to rescue Jennet. For that he would take the Demon Omad as a guide.

Without a word he seized Gambal's hand and moments later their oars left arabesques of silver on the dark water.

Excitement seethed in Danaak early on the morning when two young men — travelling journeymen just out of their apprenticeship by their appearance — mingled with the crowd approaching the city's great caravanserai. They passed the scrutiny of Witchfinders who kept permanent watch on the city gates and were soon eating a long-promised breakfast in the Golden Drong, one of the many inns catering for the men whose lives were spent on Ythan's far-flung caravan routes.

'The place has hardly altered,' said Krispin who with Alwald had stayed in the caravanserai when they first came to Danaak seeking the Lady Merlinda. An age ago it seemed though in fact they had come in at the beginning of spring and it was now just past high summer.

'And yet there is a different feel to it, like the days that lead up to the Feast of Fools,' remarked Gambal. He turned to the young drab who was placing hot bread, pottage, grilled Green River pike and mead on their table and asked her what was afoot.

'Oh sirs, you must have been on a far journey not to know. Why, the Lord Regent is to be crowned King

346

of Ythan in the Great Shrine at the next sickle moon,'
she replied. 'Already they be hanging lanterns in the
squares, and there will be free meats and wine and
music. It will be like ten feast days rolled into one —
and I shall be run off my feet in this place.' And she
hurried to a noisy group of drong drivers who had just
returned from the Crystal Ranges.

'I wish we could get the news to Mandal,' said
Krispin. 'He must announce the return of the Princess
before the Regent claims the Empty Throne.'

Gambal nodded gloomily.

'It does not augur well but I am sure Mandal will
have the news soon enough. He has plenty of old
comrades in Ythan to keep him supplied with
information.'

When they had finished their meal they pushed their
way through the crowded alleys where they were less
likely to encounter Witchfinders. Gambal was
unusually ill at ease since they had entered the city and
Krispin could guess how much he feared recognition.
The punishment he could expect from the Regent if
he was apprehended would be unimaginable.

Hurrying through the poor and squalid areas of the
city they realized that while the prospect of the
coronation was welcomed by those who prospered
under the rule of the Regent, those who suffered under
the régime saw the enthronement of their master as
their ultimate tribulation. The new dynasty would
merely perpetuate the tyranny that condemned
thousands of citizens to being pittance moilers,
denizens of underground slave shops, unpaid
conscripts, tax-serfs and child labourers so that those
favoured by the Regent might profit.

Thanks to Gambal's sense of direction they finally

found themselves beneath the high wall of rain-worn stone that completely encircled the necropolis. Guards patrolled it in an effort to keep its outcast population within this boundary, and whipping posts had been set up at regular intervals to mete out summary punishment to first offenders. An outcast caught a second time was sent in one of the slave caravans to distant mines, but avoiding the guards had become a highly developed art among the ghouls.

After following the wall for half a league — and disappearing into the slum alleys opposite it whenever a patrol appeared — Krispin and Gambal reached a spot where part of the wall had collapsed. The work of ghouls on the other side, as yet it had not been repaired by the armed masons employed to maintain the barrier between outcast and citizen. It took only a few moments for the pair to scramble up the slope of debris and leap through the gap.

They found themselves sprawled amid tall ferns and when Krispin straightened up he gave a cry of amazement. Before them was a broad avenue of mausoleums still awesome despite a century of neglect. The dark creepers that clung to their marble and the self-sown trees that rose about them inspired a pleasantly melancholic atmosphere which had not been apparent when the tombs were regularly scrubbed and their rows of mourning trees were kept as uniform as a parade of elite guards.

'I have heard it said that in Danaak the dead are housed better than the living,' said Krispin. 'Now I can believe it.'

They began walking down the avenue and, though many eyes watched them, they had the impression that the place was deserted. Krispin tried to pick out the landmarks Commander Mandal had described that would lead him to the tomb inhabited by Garn and Aldis, the fugitives from the House of Mistress Joy.

'He told me to make for a figure of Grief on a tall pillar,' said Krispin. 'Their mausoleum is in an avenue that leads from it and, being the tomb of some hero, has a sword and helmet carved on the lintel.'

Gambal gazed over the panorama of statuary, memorials, columns, urns, massive tombs and domed mausoleums amid a wilderness of extravagant vegetation, and he sighed deeply.

'Come on,' he said. 'Let us seek Grief on a pillar.' But Krispin was standing stock still, gazing up at the Citadel that reared above the north end of the necropolis, its walls greened at this point by ivy that was rooted among the illustrious dead. The sun flashed on the guards' armour and yellow banners hung from casements and fluttered from scores of flagpoles in honour of the forthcoming coronation but all Krispin could think of was that somewhere within those soaring walls was Jennet. And with a surge of panic he realized that with every passing moment she was a moment deeper in danger, and it might take all day or even longer to find Mandal's wretched ghouls.

He threw back his head in desperation and bellowed, 'Garn! Garn!' But the only reply was an echo rolling back from walls of lichened stone and a swirl of startled crows.

'Well, that should bring every ruffian and cut-throat,' said Gambal. He was about to say something else but the sound of wheels on ancient paving made them both spin round. Jolting down the avenue towards them was a chariot drawn not by horses but young men in sweat-drenched rags. Other men armed

349

with a variety of makeshift weapons — an iron railing spear, a sword wrenched from a statue, a funerary vase club — ran on either side of the chariot which, Krispin learned later, had been found in the sepulchre of a royal general.

The young charioteer appeared equally bizarre in a cerecloth cloak with a chaplet of metal flowers round his brow. But what held the eyes of the two companions was his passenger, a gap-toothed fellow who peered with one eye — the other was covered by a black patch — through hair that did not appear to have been trimmed for years and was only equalled for its greasy tangles by his beard. His cloak was fashioned from a purloined altar cloth of brilliant purple and he wore a gilt crown that an enterprising ghoul had removed from a holy statue. In his right hand he held a skull sceptre-like while his left grasped a wine jug.

The skewed wheels of the chariot rolled to a stop a few paces away from Krispin and Gambal, and the running escort immediately formed a threatening circle about them.

The ludicrous man rose to his feet with his bacchic belly quivering, while the charioteer cried, 'Trespassers, tremble and make obeisance to my master.'

'And who might he be?' asked Gambal with studied politeness.

The man answered in a drink-roughened voice, 'You be cursed outsiders if you do not recognize King Death.'

SIX

Name
Magic

Like currents intersecting at the turn of the tide, two very different waves of disquiet suddenly swept Ythan, creating maelstroms of fear and elation where they crossed. The first wave spread out from Danaak in the form of heralds racing their drongs over the highways radiating from the capital to announce that, as the result of divine intervention, the Lord Regent had graciously agreed to comply with the last testament of King Johan XXXIII and ascend the Empty Throne. Shrine gongs were ordered to be sounded in thanksgiving and jubilation was to be expressed. Celebrations would be supervised by the Witchfinders while on the great day compulsory services were to be held in the shrines where all would have the honour of swearing allegiance to the new monarch.

The news carried by the other wave was not announced by dusty heralds or with obligatory fanfares – it was carried by stealth, by whispered words in market places and by strangers at the door after midnight.

'The Princess has awakened,' was all that was said

and if there was a lack of evidence it was made up for by hope.

Followers of the Pilgrim Path who had kept alive the legend of the sleeping princess since The Enchantment now passed messages that emanated from Livia from one to another; the word was that Commander Mandal was planning the campaign that would restore her and all were called upon to play their part when the signal was given. In manors that had done nothing but decay since the rise of the Regency, antique weapons were brought from cellar to grindstone; in impoverished hamlets gaunt peasants lashed scythe and sickle blades to poles, and in slave workshops daggers were secretly beaten from discarded pieces of metal.

The word spread to certain captains in the army, captains who had served under Commander Mandal or had lost brothers or comrades in the Raven Pass. And the word spread to the men who served under them.

High in the bitter Ranges of Dakkakan Master-at-Arms Radalf paraded his small company that had been patrolling the bleak area in the endless conflict with outcasts. It was work the men hated in an area they hated – fanatical wretches and constant wind that scattered campfires and filled their eyes with grit.

As the master-at-arms stood in front of them the wind tore at their pennants with invisible fingers, and above its howl he cried, 'Slinger Kallas, what is the penalty for desertion from the army?'

'Crucifixion, sir!'

The men glanced surreptitiously along their ranks to see if there were gaps.

'Spearman Strak, who is the chief of the army?'

'The Commander of the Host, sir!'

'So would it be desertion to follow the Commander of the Host? Well, Kallas?'

'Commander Mandal was put in the Cage, sir.'

'Nevertheless he was our commanding officer. Word has reached me that he is no longer in the Cage. To take orders from him, in my opinion, is not desertion but if it were I would still risk it because Mandal is the finest general Ythan has seen since The Enchantment. I am therefore going to travel to his headquarters to receive my orders from him. If any of you are minded to come with me, take one step forward and fall out, the rest may continue patrol work in the hills.'

The whole company took one step forward and fell out.

The Witchfinder-General inclined his cowled head as the Regent entered a vaulted chamber in the subterranean hell beneath the Citadel which he referred to as the Nether World. In the light of several lanthorns the Regent saw that a young man was manacled to a wooden frame and a scribe stood at a lectern with vellum and inkstick ready.

'One of my watchers was suspicious of him when he entered by the Unicorn Gate,' said the Witchfinder-General. 'He has admitted he was a messenger sent by Mandal to a group of Pilgrims here in Danaak. They will be arrested within the hour and we will make an example of them in the Square of Punishment tomorrow. It is the message he carried that I deemed you ought to hear.'

'I see you are using the Hook to encourage his

frankness,' said the Regent, looking at the victim on his frame.

'I congratulate you on devising it,' said the Witchfinder-General. 'Infinite pain without insensibility. This one could last for hours yet. To work, Yooth.' A fat man wearing a leather apron and traditional executioner's mask — the operation of torture instruments came within the compass of the Executioners' guild — advanced out of the shadows but the Regent waved him back.

'My turn,' he said with his unexpectedly high laugh which gave an illusion of good nature. He leaned over the foot of the frame where a bloodied cord was attached to a windlass and began to turn the handle.

'My son, tell us the message you carried to Danaak,' said the Witchfinder. The eyes of the victim opened and he looked about him stupidly, then the slack of the cord was taken up and a shriek burst from his mouth that could be heard beyond the massive oaken door of the chamber. The scribe finished shaving his inkstick and held it poised to record the confession.

The Regent stopped turning and the terrible cries died to a bestial slobbering.

'What message did you bear for Commander Mandal, my son?' the Witchfinder-General repeated.

The blood-caked lips strove to form words but it was only after the Regent resumed his turning that the captive began to scream out what was required of him: 'I was told to say, "Princess Livia . . . lives and . . . has returned . . . to claim the Empty . . . Throne. Be ready for the signal . . . to rise on . . . her behalf." And then I had to . . . tell them to pass on the message . . . and the watchword.'

'And what was the watchword, my son?'

For a moment the only sound was that of desperate breathing and the Regent gave the windlass half a turn.

'Phoenix.'

'Is this message true?' demanded the Regent. 'Have you seen the Princess yourself?'

'I have . . . seen her.'

'Describe her.'

When the half-shouted, half-mumbled words ended the Regent turned to the door.

'I think if the cord was to be knotted it would be a mite more effectual,' he said.

'It is true − he described her perfectly,' the Regent declared. 'Somehow those accursed Pilgrims joined Mandal and he will obviously use her as the figurehead for his rebellion.'

He was in the Lady Mandraga's apartment. She lay under a rug of zaar fur on an ivory couch; if in the past her features had reflected the burden of her years they now reflected her weakness. Her attempts to destroy the Pilgrims in the Mountains of the Moon by enlisting malefic powers had exhausted her, and since Krispin had banished the final entity she had summoned with his Disk of Livia she had been in a state of collapse.

'It must be made known that you have the true princess in your keeping,' murmured the Lore Mistress.

'And how do I do that? Does Archpriest Mattan have another convenient vision?' In his agitation the Regent strode up and down the room and Mandraga's mute fled in terror.

With each turn he took, a new thought struck him.

'And my doubts about the Witchfinder-General are

not lessening,' he said. 'I have heard from one of the Guild who has no love for his master that he burns to increase his power over the kingdom.'

'The Witchfinder-General is already one of the most powerful men in the kingdom and he knows he can go no further,' the Lady Mandraga said. 'It mayhap be a charge inspired by spite rather than substance.'

'I think not. Do you remember the wording of King Johan's testament that your forger penned so well? It was to the effect that whoever had care of the country one hundred years after the disappearance of Princess Livia should ascend the throne. At the time I thought you had worded it well but now another thought strikes me: Who traditionally takes over the rule of the kingdom when a regent dies?'

'The Witchfinder-General.'

'So if I were to die he would gain the right to claim the throne,' said the Regent.

'You have survived more bitter enemies than he, my son. Forget not that it was he who warned you about the Princess.'

'She is as much a threat to him as she is to me.'

'She need not be. Your answer lies with Jennet.'

'A dead princess will prove less than a live one.'

'I do not mean for her body to be displayed — I mean for her to be your queen, then it will not be difficult to make the people believe that it is Livia who is the pretender.'

'But Urwen . . .'

The Lady Mandraga closed her eyes to hide the anguish that showed in them. It was the first time she had known the Regent to succumb to the weakness of sentiment.

Painfully she propped herself up on the couch.

'You purged your enemies on your return from the Wells of Ythan, you have just had one of the most resounding victories in Ythan's history and you are about to be crowned king,' she said. 'The destiny of Ythan turns to you and your future House, and yet when it comes to safeguarding all of this your first thought is for your spy-mistress who would even kiss your monstrous hand when she thought it set her ambition one pace forward. When you could have any woman in the kingdom you wished you behave like a love-struck youth.'

The Lore Mistress leaned back. At last she had said it. She waited for the explosion of wrath, feeling too weary to care.

It did not come.

The Regent asked mildly, 'Could she go through the ceremony?'

'She is still as childish as she was when the Witchfinder Mordan brought her to me. She spends most of the day gazing through the bars of her casement and she has asked for toys and a doll. But as a child she is obedient and she could be led through the marriage ceremony as though it were a game – Mattan would know how to arrange that. And if it should appear that there is something odd about her it will be put down to the ordeal of her awakening.'

'Yes. With such an ordeal behind her it would be understandable if she did not live very long after becoming queen.'

'She must first bear you a child,' said Mandraga. 'Your House will be doubly secure with a royal bloodline – or what will be regarded as such.'

'I shall go and make myself known to her,' said the

Regent. 'One consolation is that she is as beautiful as the original.'

When the Regent explained the necessity for him to wed the daughter of Johan XXXIII, Urwen held back a flood of recrimination with professional self-control. She bowed her head in a pretence of acceptance and announced that she would go into retreat in the sanctuary attached to the Great Shrine until the coronation was over.

'Then I shall spend half my wedding night with you,' said the Regent coarsely.

'Be not too sure of that,' she answered sombrely.

Two days after Urwen left the Citadel, the taster provided for Jennet took ill with agonizing cramps in his stomach and did not survive the next day.

SEVEN
The
Nighthawk

Day by day, rumours of the miraculous return of Princess Livia continued to spread across Ythan. At night, mysterious bonfires blazed in high places and in Danaak scraps of parchment were pinned to doors with the legend, 'The Princess returns.' One morning the priests of the Great Shrine were horrified to see that it had been painted in ox blood across their holy doors. Witchfinders were more in evidence than ever before and their black coaches rattled over the cobbles night and day taking suspects to the Citadel.

At the same time those who supported the Regent and who expected to prosper even more when he became king prepared enthusiastically for the coronation. Hired musicians played in the squares, at dusk the Green River reflected a thousand coloured lanterns and at midnight rockets showered silver and gold stars down upon the city. The contrast between these celebrations and the atmosphere of pending rebellion gave Danaak the unreal suggestion that it was two cities superimposed upon each other.

In the caravanserai returning merchants, drong

drivers, pilots and caravan guards all had tales for
eager ears; the townsfolk of Valgaad had massacred
all Witchfinders and tax-gatherers, the Princess had
been seen in a dozen different locations, a battle was
being fought between Mandal's followers and a legion
of the Regent's élite troops, mutiny had broken out
among the slaves in the Arkad Woodlands and a
mighty disembodied voice had spoken from a black
cloud above the marshes of Dulmere, though what it
had actually said no one could declare.

At length a whisper even reached the High Wald and
the Lady Eloira celebrated the success of her two
Pilgrims — for she had no doubt that the astonishing
news was due to Alwald and Krispin — with a flask
of her favourite green-tinted wine in company with
faithful Hans.

'You are too well dressed for outcasts, too well fed
for escaped prisoners,' said King Death. He was
enthroned on an aventurine sarcophagus in the largest
mausoleum as befitted the lord of the necropolis. On
either side of the chamber stood his bodyguard with
their bizarre assortment of funereal weapons and
coffin-lid shields; his tatterdemalion courtiers squatted
on the floor with their eyes fixed greedily on the
clothing and packs of the two captives.

'We claim to be neither,' Krispin.

'Then what are you? Spies? Witchfinders? Or are
you grave-looters? My justice is equal for all three —
a cosy little tomb with the entrance sealed.'

'We came to find two of your people, sire,' said
Gambal tactfully. And he went on to tell their story
in part truthfully.

'And is it true — have you seen the Princess?'

'We have seen her entranced and we have seen her awakened,' said Krispin. 'And we know that at this very moment she prepares to take her rightful throne.'

'Can you prove this?' demanded King Death.

By way of reply Krispin removed the Disk of Livia from his neck and held it up. A young woman wearing a faded spider silk shroud snatched it and after looking closely at its spiral of runic characters said, 'I believe him. This is just like the one Commander Mandal gave to Garn. Aldis showed it to me afterwards.'

Reluctantly she handed back the medallion.

'In the streets and marts of Danaak we have heard rumours of the Princess,' said the King. 'As the Regent is the cause of most of us living in this land of the dead, we longed for proof. You are messengers of that proof so you are more than welcome, and when you have shared a bumper of wine with me you will be escorted to Garn's tomb.'

'There is no time . . .' Krispin began but Gambal cut him short.

'. . . like the present, is what my friend was going to say,' he said. 'Your Majesty bestows a great honour upon us.' But even Gambal flinched when he saw that the wine cups had been crafted from skulls.

Sometime later a tipsy guard — a constant supply of smuggled wine was the meed of King Death's servants — led them down a series of tomb-lined paths to the mausoleum that the two runaways had made into their home. Here the Disk of Livia once more proved its worth and Krispin explained that they wanted to enter the Citadel by means of the escape passage on a mission for Commander Mandal. The name of their late guest won over the two ghouls and after Aldis had insisted upon giving them bread Garn prised up the slab behind the sarcophagus.

'You will need this,' he said, offering them a refurbished votive lamp. Krispin thanked him but, unbuckling his long pack, he took out the leather cylinder containing the light wand and Woundflame which he had been unable to wear publicly in the city.

'I have explored the tunnel myself,' said Garn. 'It is useless to enter the Alchemist's Tower because the entrance to that has been bricked. Go on further to the end of the passage and you will come out in a wine cellar.' He laughed. 'I have become a regular supplier to King Death since Commander Mandal appeared out of the ground.'

'I thought he was a dhrul at first,' said Aldis with a laugh.

Garn looked grave.

'I must give you a warning,' he said. 'While I was hiding behind a tun one night I overheard two servants talking — scared bowelless they were. It seems that there is a monster lurking in the dungeon passages beneath the Citadel. Several turnkeys have been found with their throats bitten through in dark corners and the servants said it was a blood-drinker. Mayhap it is some poor demented prisoner that escaped from his cell and is taking his revenge, or mayhap it really is some horrid creature from a lair deep in the Nether World. Be on your guard.'

Krispin nodded and, remembering how his sword had dealt with night-walkers in the Wilderness of Gil, he drew comfort from the rough feel of its grip.

A minute later he and Gambal descended into the sour air of the tunnel with the brilliant light from the wand playing on crumbling stonework and the fronds of nitre that hung from the roof. They moved cautiously forward until they reckoned they must be passing beneath the ancient ramparts of the Citadel.

'What is that smell?' asked Alwald, pressing the back of his hand against his nose.

'Blood, shit and despair,' replied Gambal. 'Do you not remember the perfume of the dungeons.'

'I do now,' said Krispin. 'You do not suppose Jennet . . .'

'She is too valuable an asset for Ratland, as the citizens of the Regent's secret city call the dungeons. Did not your shadow man — the Fey — tell you that she is in the tower where Mandraga has her apartments?'

Krispin nodded.

'It is just I fear that if they want her dead as proof that the Princess did not survive her awakening they would let her languish to death in such a place.'

'Never. Much more cunning assassinations are devised in the Citadel,' said Gambal with tactless enthusiasm. 'For a body that must remain unmarked by violence the usual way is a bodkin thrust up the nostril or a tiny Salamander spider dropped into the ear, or . . .'

Not wishing to hear more, Krispin hurried along the passage. Before long they reached the gratings in the floor that looked into dungeons and here Krispin returned the light wand to its case to avoid the danger of some turnkey noticing it. Sometimes lantern light shone up through the grilles and frequently they heard groans or mumbled prayers rising from unfortunates forgotten by the world. It was with relief that they reached the recently displaced slab in the roof that told them Leodore's tower was above them. Heeding

363

Garn's advice they continued for another twenty minutes until they found that the passage ended in a small door of corroded metal.

Holding their breath, and flinching at every rusty protest from the hinges, they pushed it open and found themselves behind an enormous tun just as Garn had described. When they were sure the place was deserted they emerged and Krispin again produced the light wand. In its radiance they saw they were in a vast undercroft with a dozen such tuns lining its circular walls.

Ever foresighted, Gambal produced a fragment of chalk from his scrip and marked their tun so that in emergency they would know where to find the hidden door. Then they mounted the steps to the doorway leading out of the undercroft and emerged in a high corridor faintly illuminated by rushlights set at intervals on wall brackets.

'Do you know where we are?' whispered Krispin.

'Er — yes,' replied Gambal with some hesitation. 'As we are in the cellar area beneath the kitchens we need to . . .'

He broke off as the deep fast-repeated note of a gong echoed thunderously down the passage.

'The Mother curse it!' cried Gambal. 'We have the Luck of Omad. That is the Nighthawk Gong.'

'And what is that?'

'Every so often that gong is sounded along a stretch of passageways and all servants and guards quit it if they value their lives. Then it is sealed off and a nighthawk is released so it can kill any spy or thief that is in hiding.'

'What are nighthawks?'

'Strange savage birds that are reared in the Nether

World to become eager for human flesh. They are trained to fly along tunnels and round cellars, and they are never ever allowed to see daylight because it is said that if they see bright light they pine and die. Let us get back to our passage and shut the door behind us.'

'I agree to that,' said Krispin and as they hurried back towards the undercroft they heard the beat of pinions. Turning they saw in the rushlight a huge winged shadow swooping towards them. Shielding his face with his left arm, Gambal drew his knife but remembering his companion's words Krispin wrenched the light wand from its leather tube. In the burst of brilliant light that filled the passage he saw a monstrous creature hurtling at him with its long jaws agape. It was unlike any bird he had ever imagined. Instead of feathers its wings were composed of tough grey membrane and pointed teeth glittered where a true bird had its beak.

This sudden apparition had the effect of momentarily paralysing the companions with the sheer ferocity of its appearance but the light had an even more dramatic effect on the nighthawk. It dropped to the flagstones, leathery wings trailing as with ungainly steps it was drawn towards the wand, its jet eyes glittering with ecstasy. A soft mewling issued from its throat.

Even on the ground its terrible V-shaped head was level with Krispin's heart and in his imagination he could almost feel the impact of the crocodile jaws upon it.

Bedazzled and becharmed by the light, the nighthawk continued its ungainly advance until it was only a couple of paces from the outstretched wand.

At that moment Krispin swung Woundflame and laid open the monster's breast.

Gambal and Krispin watched with grisly fascination as the wings flapped deliriously, spinning the heavy body round and round while pale blood pumped from the wound. At last it lay still and as Krispin forced himself past it he shuddered as he looked down upon the still-snapping jaws that had been capable of tearing him apart. It was some time before either was able to speak and then Gambal said, 'One advantage of the nighthawk being released is that we will not meet another soul unless he be an intruder like ourselves.'

Jennet sat on the edge of her bed combing her spun-gold hair. A doll sat on the patchwork quilt beside her, a present from the terrible old woman whose face she sometimes saw at the spyhole in the door staring at her for minutes at a time. Of all the frightening things that had happened to Jennet since she had meekly followed Master No-Name out of the Peak Tower, she found that wrinkled face at the spyhole the worst, perhaps because its gloating expression struck a sinister chord with something that remained on the edge of her earliest memories — something that she never got into focus for fear of what it might reveal.

Her aversion to the old woman included the doll she had given her. It was a horrible doll and completely different to Dolly who had been the gift of the Lady Eloira . . .

Jennet looked up and nearly screamed. At her open casement a head and shoulders was suddenly silhouetted against the waning moon. Two hands gripped the bars and then came recognition — the girl flung herself to the window.

366

'Krispin! Krispin! Krispin!'

She knelt on a chest beneath the sill and pressing her face against the grille she managed to touch his cheek with her lips.

'Krispin! Krispin! Are you real?'

'Of course I am real.' And as though to prove it he moved his head so that their mouths met in the gap between the rusting bars.

For a minute they remained thus, and then Jennet drew back to look at him.

'Do not be frightened, little Jennet,' he murmured.

'Of course I am not frightened. I have never been happier. There is no need to talk to me like a child.'

'But . . . but the doll and . . .'

'I have been in my right mind ever since I was brought to the Citadel. It was coming back in patches before then but I was very confused. Dear Kris, as you can see I am captive here and I thought it best to continue to act like a child. Tell me how you found me, how you got here.'

'I climbed up a ladder,' he replied softly. 'Workmen who had been hanging lanterns between the towers left it on the roof and Gambal found it.'

'But you are scared of heights . . . Who is Gambal?'

'My companion. Listen, Jen, you have not been hurt . . .'

'Tell me where you have been . . .'

'What about Lady Eloira . . .'

For a minute both hissed questions at each other and then found reassurance in another kiss.

'You are in danger out there. If you are seen . . .' said Jennet when lack of breath parted them again.

'Gambal is keeping a lookout.' He tugged at the

bars. 'If only I could have brought a file. I shall get Garn to steal me one and return tomorrow night.'

'Now tell me everything that has happened to you, from start to finish.'

Holding her hands through the bars Krispin began with the agreement that he had come to with the Lady Eloira to try to discover who they really were in return for him undertaking the quest with Lord Alwald. The Constellation of the Griffin was dipping towards the horizon when Krispin reached the point where he had entered the Citadel and Gambal had guided him to the roof.

'Someone comes,' she cried. 'Get down out of sight.'

She ran back to the bed and threw herself upon it, cuddling the hated doll.

There was the rattle of locks, a mute servant opened the door and the Regent strode in.

EIGHT

'Livia! Livia!'

The sun striking the rippled surface of the Lake of Taloon bombarded the grey trees on its northern shore with sparkles of reflected light. Beneath their weeping leaves, Tana walked slowly along the margin where waterweed writhed with the petals of its crimson flowers opening and closing like tiny mouths in the heat of high summer. Though the scene was tranquil the face of the young woman was one of deep suffering and it was with unseeing eyes that she looked across the expanse of water that had once brought her pleasure in the gay days of her girlhood.

'Weep not for the past while there be a life ahead for thee,' came a gentle voice and turning Tana saw the Princess Livia. Although she still only wore her simple white robe, the sun striking her spun-gold hair gave a haloed effect that emphasized her beauty more effectively than the most expensive gown that the best tailors and seamstresses of Danaak could produce.

'Your Highness, I do not sorrow for the past,' said Tana. 'It is the departure of Ognam that weighs heavy on my heart.'

'Few jongleurs have ladies like you to regret their going, but I know that passion hath no rules. Ah, well I knoweth it.'

Despite her grief Tana's interest was reflected in her expression.

'Yes, Lady Tana, before the spell was cast upon me I had a secret lover, a real lover and not one of those mincing courtiers whose endless flattery and protestations of adoration were made in the greedy hope of winning the richest prize in the kingdom. If I had a choice of becoming Queen of Ythan or returning to my beloved there would be no question — no crown could compensate for the joy of his arms.'

For a moment she stood lost in thought, her fingers absently stroking the heavy grey leaves that trailed beside her.

'But that be long past,' she said, recollecting herself and smiling. 'It was *almost* the scandal of the day but luckily my father did not notice — the wine of Ronimar had been his solace since the Dark Maid took my mother. The Magus Ysldon was my help and strength when . . . but no matter. Love, scandal, heartbreak, joy — it was a hundred years ago. Now must I heed the advice I gave thee — look to the future and prepare to be queen if it be the Serene Mother's wish.'

'I have heard that, now the Regent is to be crowned at the sickle moon, Commander Mandal is preparing to leave Taloon to strike at Danaak. Though it is but a ruin of what it was, I shall be doubly grieved when I leave this place.'

'Lady Tana, if I taketh the Empty Throne I vow that I shall have this old palace returned to the state in which thou knew it. There will be music and lights and feasts again, and I shall come and stay with thee to escape the Citadel for thou knowst not how dull court life can be. All those intrigues and petitions and laws to be passed!' She made a face of mock despair and Tana heard herself laugh.

'To liven my life I shall find Master Ognam and appoint him Court Jester, and then mayhap thou wilt repay my visits to thee.'

'And Lord Alwald? What will be his appointment when you wear the crown?'

'It is still *if* I wear the crown, but as for Lord Alwald . . . we shall see. I be fortunate to have such a fair youth as my champion.' And now she laughed so merrily that Tana joined in and all sad thoughts passed from their minds.

'And verily I should like to find the winged man who became our guide in the Mountains of the Moon, what a wonderful royal courier he would make,' the Princess continued. 'Dost thou think it be true that he loves a girl who is half-horse? Thinkst thou what might result . . .' And their laughter was renewed.

Krispin was exhausted emotionally and physically by the time he and Gambal raised the slab in the sepulchre shared by Garn and Aldis.

'Thank the Mother you be safe,' cried Garn as Krispin's head appeared through the aperture in the floor. 'I was about to come seeking you.'

'It has been a long night,' said Krispin wearily.

'As it has been for those awaiting you,' came a familiar voice.

'Alwald!'

Krispin ran round the massive tomb and embraced Alwald and then Ognam in the feeble lamplight.

'How I have missed you both,' he cried. 'But what are you doing in the City of the Dead?'

'We could not imagine how you would manage without us,' said Ognam mock seriously.

'It is true,' said Alwald. 'I must confess that after you had gone I realized that . . . well . . . things were not the same . . . we have been a-questing together for so long that . . . *Gambal*!'

He cried the name in obvious relief as Gambal appeared.

'What are you doing here? We thought you had des. . . left us.'

'I decided to come with Master Krispin,' replied Gambal. 'My knowledge of the Citadel has already been of use.'

Alwald stepped over to Gambal and seized him by the hand.

'It is true that I have greatly mistrusted you,' he said, 'but it is also true that you have since proved your worth. Let the past bury the past. There are great things afoot and we must play our part as comrades.'

'Let us drink to that,' said Gambal. While the Pilgrims had been speaking Aldis had filled her assortment of cups with wine purloined from the cellars of the Citadel. After a toast had been raised — 'To the restoration of Livia!' — Krispin demanded to know how Alwald and Ognam had found them.

'When Mandal learned that the Regent was going to be crowned at the sickle moon he knew he had to bring his plans forward,' Alwald explained. 'He wanted a messenger to go to Danaak, which was just the opportunity we needed to follow you. The errand was to involve the lord of the necropolis — that dreadful fellow who calls himself King Death — in the revolt. After he had agreed to help — at a price — he brought us to find you. Now tell what news of Jennet.'

The companions seated themselves with their backs against the cold walls of the mausoleum. While Aldis served bread and dried meats, for day was breaking over Danaak, Krispin related how he and Gambal had entered the Citadel and, thanks to the latter's knowledge of its mazelike passages and stairwells, had reached the roof and thence found their way to the Lady Mandraga's tower.

'And no one stopped you?' asked Alwald wonderingly.

'Only once,' said Gambal. 'A servant met us on a flight of steps and was suspicious until he recognized me. "Why, Master Gambal," he said. "I have not seen you for ages." I guessed that few must know about my betrayal of the Regent so I said, "I have been on our master's business." And he wished us goodnight.'

Krispin went on to describe how he was able to reach Jennet's barred window by ladder.

'Thank the Mother, her mind is clear as it ever was,' he said, 'but to her captors she pretends to be childlike still. While I was at the window the Regent came and I ducked below the sill but I could hear his voice. He spoke to her as he would have spoken to a child, telling her about some game they were going to play.'

'A game?' said Alwald.

'At first I could not understand, indeed I thought it might be some perversity he was planning until I realized he was preparing her to take part in a marriage ceremony at his coronation in the Great Shrine.'

'The coronation?' said Ognam looking puzzled. 'A marriage ceremony during the coronation.'

Alwald cursed as the Regent's plan became suddenly clear.

'The only way to stop him is to rescue Jennet,' said Ognam.

'Of course,' said Krispin impatiently. 'If I can get a heavy file I shall free her tonight.'

While Krispin and Gambal rested in the mausoleum during the day Garn went to a market where he acquired a file, and Alwald visited the caravanserai to hire the drongs to take Jennet to safety after Krispin had released her.

An hour before the midnight gong, when there would be few about in the Citadel's kitchen passages, he and Krispin made a second journey along the escape tunnel and found their way to the roof where lines of coloured lanterns twinkled their loyal tribute to the forthcoming king. Here, to Krispin's infinite relief, the ladder still lay in the shadows and a minute later he was level with the barred casement. But no light shone. There was no reply to his whisper and when the waning moon peeped from behind a cloud he saw that the room was empty. Every trace of Jennet was gone.

At last I feel like a soldier again, thought Mandal as he rode his drong at the head of the column travelling down the abandoned highway that led from Thaan to Danaak. *Mayhap this enterprise will succeed, mayhap not, but if the worst comes to the worst I shall die in a befitting manner, not an object of ridicule in the Cage.*

'You look thoughtful, Commander,' said the Princess Livia who rode beside him on a white drong. She wore the lightest armour that could be found. Her breastplate had been painted white and on this was emblazoned a black rose, the ancient symbol of Ythan. She had no use for a helmet, letting her golden hair stream behind her in the restless wind that swept the Plain of Danaak.

Looking at her with admiration he did not try to conceal, Mandal was reminded of a pagan shield maid, a goddess of battle.

'I was trying to put myself into the mind of the Lord Regent,' he said. 'By now his spies will have told him we are on the march and I am puzzling how he will counter us. As yet there is no word of an army being sent forth but instead of comforting me it makes me wary. Our enemy is the father of deceits.'

'Mayhap he knows that, thanks to the followers of the Pilgrim Path, there be bands of rebels marching on Danaak from the four corners of the kingdom and he hath not enough troops to block them all.'

'It is true that since he lost his main army on the Thaan campaign he has not had time to conscript another,' said Mandal thoughtfully. 'If I were Regent I would avoid battles. But what would I do instead?'

'He may not have the army that thou once commanded but he had a victory over the Wolf Horde.'

'A deserter from the city guard told that he used fire magic.'

'The days of magic are over,' said the Princess. 'But what is that in the distance?'

Squinting against the noonday glare, Mandal could make out a distant smudge on the highway, a dust cloud that could be caused by marching men. He raised his arm to halt the column which was made up of outcasts and peasants but mostly deserters in an amazing array of uniforms. Under the orders of his lieutenants the force spread out on either side of the road and archers and slingers took up positions ahead. A few moments later a scout arrived on a lathered drong and saluted Mandal.

'It is the Black Storm Company, sir,' he reported. 'Their banners are furled but they are in fighting order.'

'Then we can only wait,' said Mandal. He turned to the officers who sat their drongs in a tight group behind him. 'Ulrik, take the skirmishers and attack from the west the moment you hear the trumpet. Alin, how many lancers do we have?'

'Only thirty, sir, all deserters from the Winged Spear Company.'

'Enough. I want them to charge the banners and the officers that will be with them.' He turned to the Princess. 'Your Highness, I should be more easy if you went to the rear of the column.'

'Then thou must remain uneasy,' she said angrily. 'A fine example I would be to my subjects if I turned my back on the enemy the moment they appeared. Remember, Lord Mandal, I am of the blood of Johan the First who took Ythan by right of conquest.'

'I am unlikely to forget it,' he replied drily and nothing more was said as they watched the Black Storm Company approach.

Before long the Princess's archers took arrows from their quivers and planted them beside their right feet, ready to be plucked up for rapid fire. Their object was not individual accuracy but to disable the approaching force with a deluge of arrows. The slingers would take care of those foolhardy – or courageous – enough to continue the advance.

When the standard-bearers were just beyond bowshot the company halted, the furled banners were shaken out and the Princess gave a cry of surprised satisfaction when she saw that the normally plain yellow banners of Ythan now bore the emblem of the black rose.

The commanding officer spurred forward with his sword held hilt foremost while the troops began chanting 'Livia! Livia! Livia!' as she rode out to accept their allegiance.

In the high chamber that gave him a view of his city the Regent sat back in his ivory chair and accepted a goblet of wine from one of his long-haired pages.

'The desertions mean nothing,' he said to Captain Bors. 'I would be thrice mad to go forth to meet the rebels. Only by my doing so would their increasing numbers avail them an advantage. No, they will come to besiege Danaak like ants drawn to a honey lily, and like the ants they will find that while the honey is sweet the trap is bitter. The more men Mandal has the more mouths to feed and the more to voice discontent when the victory is not quick – and Danaak could stand siege for years. Are the blacksmiths ready to weld the gates when the rebels are sighted?'

'They are, my lord.'

'And the mangonels?'

'One at every twelve paces on the walls, as you ordered.'

'Excellent, Bors. I only hope they do not arrive in the middle of the coronation, the noise would spoil the chanting. Now come with me to the menagerie. I am told that there is a new curiosity there, a little pipe-player who casts not a shadow. He is said to be close to death so I should like to see the phenomenon before it is too late.'

'Master Krispin, you must eat something,' said Aldis to the young man who lay listlessly on a ragged pallet in the mausoleum. 'I know how you worry about your lady, but you will be of little use to her if you starve your strength away. Garn went specially to the Street of Butchers to steal the meat for your broth . . .'

'Aldis, you and Garn could not have been more kind than if we were blood kin,' Krispin said, 'but I am not ill.'

'But you soon will be. You do not sleep and when you do you grind your teeth and you refuse food . . .'

'Do not scold, I will have your broth. I do not mean to be ungrateful but I cannot get Jennet out of my mind for a moment. A few nights ago I was actually talking to her and now I have no idea where she might be or what has happened to her. She may be dead for all I know.' He put his hand across his eyes in his misery.

'Broth!' said Aldis. 'And try not to fret. If the Regent is going to marry her she will not have been harmed . . . yet. Most like she has been taken to some apartment more convenient for her to be groomed for the ceremony. Her gown will have to be sewn and jewellers will probably be making her a crown at this very moment.'

Krispin picked up a horn spoon but put it down as Ognam and Gambal hurried down the steps.

'Good news,' cried Ognam. 'We have come to an agreement with the Guild of Mendicants.'

Krispin looked bewildered.

'What have beggars . . .?' he began.

378

'You wanted to get into the Great Shrine for the ceremony,' said the jongleur. 'Master Gambal found the way for this to be done.'

'I remembered from my time as Revel Master that there is an ancient tradition that at certain state ceremonies a score of mendicants attend to symbolize that all are included from the highest to the lowest,' Gambal explained. 'We went to the guild master and he has agreed to allow us and some of King Death's most stalwart guards to join the mendicants for the coronation day and thus be admitted to the Great Shrine.'

'That is indeed wonderful news,' said Krispin. 'But how did you persuade the guild master to help.'

'Silver has a silver tongue, as the saying is,' laughed Ognam. 'We used the crowns that Commander Mandal had provided for such purposes.'

NINE
The Sickle
Moon

According to Mandraga the Lore Mistress, the Kings of Ythan were traditionally crowned at sunset on the day of the new moon and she insisted that the Regent should uphold the tradition when he suggested bringing the day forward. He wanted to do this in order to be an anointed monarch by the time the rebels reached Danaak so their treason would be even more heinous in the eyes of those who supported him.

He was mollified when reports came that it would be unlikely for Mandal to reach Danaak before the coronation and the preparations went ahead as planned. The mixed tensions of the populace were symbolized by the ever-increasing number of lanterns that were turning the Citadel into a Fey palace and the setting up of hundreds of mangonels on the city ramparts.

In the dungeon hall beneath the Citadel, whips were constantly in use to force the prisoners chained to the huge capstan to turn it faster so the machineries below would grind and blend more and more ingredients of the alchemic powder that had exploded the Wolf King's dream of conquest.

The last to learn of the forthcoming coronation was the little custodian of the Regent's collection of life-sized automata. As he worked his daily way along the gallery of sheeted figures with oil, feather and duster he informed each of his mute charges of the momentous news.

'Our master is going to be a king,' he said as he slipped the covering from the mechanical dancer. 'Oh yes, our master is going to wear a crown. "Your Majesty" I shall have to say if he ever visits us again. Remember the last time he and his red-haired mistress came? Oh yes you do. Who could forget how he had Merlinda beheaded for her amusement?

'Poor Merlinda! I mean no disrespect to you when I say that she was the most beautiful of you all, and she had the best mechanisms. Oh yes! Remember how I used to walk with her up and down the gallery . . .'

Tears came into the custodian's eyes as he remembered her delicately carved hand in his, the rustle of her gown, the way he had set her mechanism so that as they promenaded she turned her head to him so realistically.

'It was Merlinda's ill fate that she had been modelled on the real Lady Merlinda who was once the Regent's favourite until he wearied of her and she was sold to a pleasure house,' the little man told the mechanical dancer for the hundredth time. 'Urwen was jealous of her even though it had happened long ago, and jealous that the Regent'd had her likeness made. That was why she was destroyed. Oh yes, yes, that was why the executioner's axe fell upon her pretty neck. We shall never forget Merlinda, will we? No, never. Nor the

Regent. Oh yes, we shall never forget what the Regent did.'

He ran a brush over the dancer's hair and then went to the next automaton.

'Our master is going to be a king,' he began as he took the sheet from the mechanical lute player and began polishing the mirror-like metal of his graceful body.

In a small chamber in an equally remote part of the Citadel another man sat also polishing silver; on his aproned knees lay a silver mask that in appearance was similar to visors worn by the Companions of the Rose, its main difference being that its eye-holes were much larger and the outline of an ironically smiling mouth had been graven upon it. It was the mask of the Regent's Avenger, the unknown crossbowman whose sole purpose in the event of an assassination attempt upon the Regent was to fire his terrible triple-barbed bolt at the member of the company most likely to benefit from his master's death.

The Regent had found this the most effective protection from attacks in public and with the tang of revolt in the air he now rarely moved without his avenger shadowing him. The mask was not to provide protection but anonymity; if the identity of the avenger was known it would be possible to approach him with bribes.

Now the nameless guardian hummed a tuneless note as he burnished the mask for his appearance at the coronation where he would take his stance two paces from his master. The fact that he had to remain nameless was compensated by the sense of power he enjoyed when, with his fingers round the trigger of his cocked weapon, he surveyed an assembled company and, following the prior instruction of his master, singled out the man or woman he would kill in the event of an outrage.

There was a knock at the door and he immediately donned the mask. Outside stood a Companion of the Rose.

'The Lord Regent requires you,' he said with the cold formality the Companions used to those who served the Regent outside their order. The avenger nodded and picked up his weapon whose bow had been reinforced with rare unicorn horn to give it the power necessary to drive an iron bolt through the finest armour.

As he walked along the torch-lit passages to his master's apartment the avenger embarked upon a familiar guessing game: Who would be today's potential target?

In the Great Shrine Archpriest Mattan gazed about him with sombre eyes from beside the sacred flame while priests and vergers made the final preparations for the most significant ceremony to be held since The Enchantment. The Lore Mistress had instructed him in the ancient ritual to be employed and, having rehearsed it several times, he felt confident that the Regent would find no fault. It was the following marriage ceremony — as yet a closely held secret — that made him anxious. The Lady Mandraga had warned him that he would find the bride childish and in need of strong guidance throughout the short rite.

From the arched passage leading to the Citadel, a number of workmen under the supervision of a Companion of the Rose carried in the Empty Throne and placed it directly in front of the altar. More than anything the sight of this ancient piece of furniture impressed upon him the significance of what was about to happen. Generations of Ythan's kings had been crowned upon that unembellished seat and now, in a matter of hours, it would play its symbolic part in the birth of a new dynasty. What would be the effect upon the kingdom and, more to the point, the priesthood?

Again Mattan wondered if he had complied too easily with the Lore Mistress's scheme to change the regency into a monarchy, yet what would it have availed the Shrine to have opposed her and, he quickly reminded himself, the Regent had kept his word to destroy the heretics of Thaan which had indeed strengthened the influence of the True Faith. He guessed that immediately after the coronation the Regent would ask for an interdict to be put on the rebels, and that would give him an opportunity for bargaining . . .

His thoughts were interrupted by the chief verger.

'Lord Archpriest, do we have to have those loathsome mendicants directly in front of the Empty Throne?' he asked. 'I mean, it ruins the whole effect.' He stood nervously sucking his lips.

'Alas, brother, it is tradition that the mendicants do occupy the prime position,' Mattan answered. 'Originally it was to signify that in the eyes of the Serene Mother all are equal but, if you consider it a moment, it does have one great advantage − if that space was free there would be so many on the Rolls of Entitlement claiming places there we could only satisfy a small number while earning the enmity of the rest. Would you like to inform the Lady Ingarda that there was no place for her when she already knew that the Lady Hesta had a place?'

'Never,' muttered the chief verger. 'But those ghastly beggars . . .'

'Make sure there is an incense brazier close to them to cloak their stink and strew sawdust where they will stand.'

Biting his lips now, the chief verger hurried away and, sighing, the Archpriest went to ensure that a new spider silk cushion had been placed on the Witchfinder-General's gilded chair set a few paces down from the Empty Throne.

In her tower apartment the Lady Mandraga rose late and immediately drank an elixir that would give her the strength to carry out her duties as Lore Mistress in the Great Shrine in a few hours' time. Already Grand Johan was sending its brazen note across the city at decreasing intervals as custom required and, without even looking from her window, she could sense the suppressed tension of the people.

As her mutes dressed her in her robes of office and set her sparse white hair the old woman savoured her triumph. Not only would the Regent be enthroned this day but he would marry the double of Princess Livia just as she had desired, and the thought of Urwen's discomfort in her retreat inspired such a rare smile that the mutes jumped back in alarm.

When the Regent was ushered into the apartment Mandraga could not prevent herself from inquiring after the Lady Urwen.

'Sulking, as you would imagine,' replied the Regent sourly.

At last your infatuation is ebbing, thought the old

woman but she did not allow her features to betray her elation.

'You have made yourself an adversary there, lady,' the Regent added.

'In that case we must see that her potions are removed,' replied the Lore Mistress. 'Reliable tasters are hard to find.'

The Regent frowned but merely said, 'And what of my bride?'

'She is prepared. The little fool has not stopped weeping since she was taken from the tower to the Chamber of Brides.'

'A reluctant bride will add interest to my nuptial night,' said the Regent.

'You may not be disappointed after she has drunk the bridal draught. The Lady Urwen is not the only one with potions.'

The Regent gave one of his old genial laughs.

'Lady, you forget nothing,' he said.

'What news of the rebels?' she asked.

'They approach the trap. As we have offered no resistance they will be over-confident, doubtless thinking that the people will fling open the gates for them.'

'And there is no danger of revolt in the city?'

He shook his leonine head.

'After my return from the Wells the Witchfinders took good care of those who had uttered against me, and to emphasize the lesson they are holding executions in the Square of Punishment. Besides, most of the rabble will soon be too drunk on free ale to raise a prick let along a rebellion. The only question that remains is what is to be done with the real Livia if she comes into our hands alive.'

'I shall tell you what is to be done,' said the Lady Mandraga signalling a mute to pour wine. 'No question of her true identity must be allowed. Whether alive or dead when we get her, she must be taken in secret to the limepit, then a corpse that has some little resemblance to her must be put on display in the main square. There is a servant wench newly come to the Citadel who will make an excellent stock, especially if her hands are uncovered. Believing that Mandal had used her as an impostor none will doubt that the true daughter of old Johan is your queen.'

'Lady, you forget nothing,' the Regent repeated and raised his goblet in a toast to the Lore Mistress.

'That is why a new dynasty begins this day, my son,' she replied.

As a mountain trickle flows into a beck, and a beck flows into a stream, and a stream joins a river, so men and women joined Mandal's rebel army as it flowed down the ancient highway to Danaak. When they passed villages the road was lined with ragged crowds who cheered themselves out of breath at the sight of the beautiful princess high on her white drong with the sun flashing on her armour.

'Let us pray the Mother that you get such a reception in Danaak,' said Mandal who rode beneath her black rose banner. 'With such a ragabash army, to have to take Danaak by a frontal attack would be a desperate business.'

The Princess looked over the farms, vineyards and orchards that now stretched into the distance on either side of the highway.

'We must be close unto Danaak now,' she said. 'I would fain not be late for the coronation.'

It was in the early afternoon that her sharp eyes picked out a spire-like object on the horizon.

'That is the main tower of the Citadel,' said Mandal. Behind them a ragged cheer echoed along the column as the news travelled from rank to rank.

TEN
The
Crowning

The sun was descending over the western plain when Mandal sent his herald to the main gate of Danaak. His army was deployed in a great semi-circle just beyond arrow range, its black rose banners fluttering fitfully in the summer breeze.

From the vantage of a turret above the gate the Regent, already wearing his cloth-of-gold coronation robe beneath his cloak, watched as the rebel herald spurred his drong forward until he was beneath the walls.

'I demand herald's rights,' he shouted. 'I demand the safety of my person from weapons of metal, wood and bone while I deliver my message, and I demand safe conduct to my lines when that message is delivered in accordance with the ancient courtesies of warfare.'

'No weapon of metal, bone or wood will harm you,' replied Captain Bors ritually through a speaking trumpet. He paused as Grand Johan boomed its summons to the Great Shrine and then continued, 'Say on, herald.'

'I demand these gates be opened for Livia, the only

issue of King Johan XXXIII, so that she may enter and claim the Empty Throne of Ythan as her birthright.'

'Is that all?' demanded Captain Bors.

'It is enough,' replied the herald. 'Your watchmen will see that other columns approach from the east and the south. Danaak will be surrounded, so for the sake of its people accede to my lady's lawful demand.'

Captain Bors turned to the Regent who nodded.

'Your so-called Livia is naught but a whore painted and dressed by the disgraced Mandal as an excuse for his treason,' he shouted, his voice magnified by the trumpet carrying down to the city streets. 'Tell your master to take the poxed drab back to the wayside brothel where he found her and let her prove her birthright to the caravaneers at a copper groat a time.'

There was a ripple of laughter from the men who stood by the canvas-shrouded mangonels.

The herald pulled round the head of his drong in disgust.

'One moment more, herald,' cried Bors. 'If one member of that rabble I see out there takes but one step forward it will bring the wrath of the Regent upon your heads.'

Seated on his drong beside the Princess, Mandal watched impassively as the herald rode back. Turning to his lieutenants he ordered in the casual voice he affected on the battlefield, 'Give the signal for the scaling ladders to go forward. Master Archer, see that they have covering fire when they near the walls. When the first ladder is in position sound the trumpet for the general attack.'

On the city ramparts the covers were snatched from

the mangonels and the crews took up their positions with the same disciplined speed as they had at the Valley of Thorns.

The smell!

Krispin was almost sick with the stench of beggars' rags about him, and what made it worse was the certainty that he smelt equally foul. Alwald and the master of the Guild of Mendicants had insisted that if their plan was to succeed they must change their clothing for genuine mendicants' clothing, lice and all, while bandages with horrific stains were wound round their limbs and dirt was smeared on their faces.

Alwald was unable to restrain his laughter while Krispin and Ognam, in company with a number of King Death's ghouls, had to submit to this vile transformation.

'It is all right for you,' Krispin had muttered bitterly. 'At least you can do battle in a clean shirt.'

'As Champion to the Princess Livia, I could hardly greet my royal mistress smelling like a decomposing drong,' Alwald declared and relapsed into gales of mirth. But before they parted to play their different roles the two Pilgrims from the Wald clasped hands for a moment.

Limping and supporting themselves on crutches, the mendicants duly presented themselves at the Great Shrine where vergers, holding nosegays to their nostrils, ushered them to their traditional place before the altar steps where braziers of smouldering incense were hastily positioned about them.

Ognam, always the actor, whined for alms and received a blow on the head with the verger's rod of office. Then, with a disgusted-looking Companion of the Rose keeping watch nearby over them, they were left alone.

By the time Mandal's rebel army had taken up position in front of the city gates the Great Shrine was filled with those favoured to watch the crowning of their master. Then, as tradition dictated, when the sun's disk touched the horizon, the ceremony began.

Archpriest Mattan led the Regent in from his special entrance to take up position with his avenger two paces beside him in front of the altar while priests chanted a paean to the Serene Mother. To one side of the altar, still strengthened by her elixir, the Lore Mistress leaned on her crutch with the supposed testament of King Johan XXXIII ready to be declaimed at the appropriate moment. In a side chapel opposite the raised floor on which stood the Empty Throne the Lady Urwen watched the proceedings with a mourning veil covering her face.

When the Archpriest had assured himself that everyone was in place, especially the acolyte holding the samite cushion on which lay the electrum crown of Ythan, he raised both arms in an invocation to the deity and the coronation began. He had only uttered a few words when there came what most thought was a roll of summer thunder and for a moment it seemed a tremor ran through the fabric of the Great Shrine. As the litany continued a brief smile of satisfaction was seen to cross the Regent's face.

As the trumpet note echoed against Danaak's walls the Princess Livia, with Barlak and Danya beside her as her bodyguard, watched as hundreds of her followers raced forward to where scores of crudely constructed scaling ladders were being raised against the ramparts over which Mandal's archers sent hissing flights of arrows. A wild cheer reached her as the first men reached the crenels.

Suddenly a number of black, keg-shaped missiles rose from behind the battlements. Each trailed a grey line of fuse smoke. The first landed among the men jostling to get on to the ladders and then the world went mad with flame and thunder. Bodies were hurled high into the smoke-choked air as more and more casks exploded among the rebels, each marking its moment of bloody glory with a fuming crater.

'The retreat! Sound the retreat!' the Commander bellowed at the trumpeter but there was no need for such a signal. While the main body of his army looked on aghast, men − some of them with their clothing ablaze − staggered out of the smoke that now hung in front of the gates like a roiling black curtain.

'This is not war,' gasped Ulrik.

'You can be sure that it is from now on,' said Mandal grimly as he set about moving his forces out of mangonel range.

'By the authority placed in me by the Shrine of the True Faith and as the mortal representative of the Serene Mother, I declare you King of Ythan and Sovereign of all who live within its borders,' intoned the Archpriest. Censers swung, a golden gong resounded, the sacred flame leapt high as he advanced to the kneeling Regent, placed the crown upon his head and, taking him by the hand, led him to the Empty Throne which was flanked by a dozen Companions of the Rose. A great sigh rose throughout the shrine as the new King seated himself upon it, and under his filthy cloak Krispin's hand closed on the grip of Woundflame.

The Regent turned his head in the direction of the Lore Mistress and for a fraction of a moment he allowed his eyelid to close in the universal sign of recognition.

Weighed down by his glittering robes, the Archpriest moved to the steps in front of the throne but, suddenly aware of the effluvium reaching him from the mendicants, despite the barrage of incense, he retreated to a less noisome position.

'What you have seen here is the outcome of divine intervention − of a miraculous vision that had been granted to me, unworthy though I be for such an honour,' he cried in his rich voice. 'But the miraculous does not end with the acclaiming of His Majesty. You will have heard rumours that the Princess Livia who has lain entranced since The Enchantment has been awakened. Those rumours are true.'

A great stillness descended upon the shrine.

'Where the rumours are untrue is in the claim by the traitor Mandal that the painted strumpet he parades is the Princess,' Mattan continued after a dramatic pause. He then went on to describe how, while on a pilgrimage to a distant shrine in the Mountains of the Moon, the then-Regent was led by the grace of the Serene Mother to the place where the Princess Livia lay in her magical sleep. The drastic effect of her awakening brought on an illness from which she had only just recovered which explained why she had made no public appearance.

'Now it is with indescribable joy that I tell you that His Majesty, in recognition of her royal blood and out of the love he bears for her, will take her to be his wife and Queen of Ythan. The nuptial ceremony will now take place.'

Amid a hubbub of questions and exclamations echoing through the shrine the new King rose to his feet. The tumult died as the Lore Mistress, preceded by a beautiful boy scattering drops of red wine from an ewer as tradition demanded, crossed in front of the altar to the archway leading to the Citadel.

The sound of lutes and dulcimers filled the air and a group of women in vestal robes appeared escorting Jennet who, clad in a gown of blue samite fantastically decorated with river pearls, walked slowly with her head bowed. In her hands she carried a sheaf of white lilies symbolizing purity. The Lore Mistress took her hand in her gnarled fingers and, whispering in her ear, led her towards her bridegroom.

The tension leading up to this moment had been coiling within Krispin like a clockwork spring but it could not coil a moment longer. Flinging off his cloak, he drew Woundflame from its swaddling of rags and cried the agreed signal at the top of his voice, 'A rescue! A rescue!'

Immediately his fellow mendicants drew forth hidden weapons which were mainly crutches to which they had surreptitiously fitted blades while kneeling in supposed supplication for blessings upon their enemy. At the same time the great doors of the shrine burst inwards and a horde of yelling outcasts led by King Death swarmed through to race down the centre aisle.

The Companion of the Rose close to the mendicants raised his unsheathed sword and aimed a blow at Krispin. He parried and lunged, and Woundflame's blade vanished to half its length into the red surcoat.

397

He reeled backwards amid a clatter of falling braziers. Krispin leapt towards the King.

The Regent's Avenger took in the scene through the eyeholes of his silver mask. It was a situation for which he had been preparing himself for half his lifetime. He turned, raised his crossbow and fired his bolt straight into the heart of the Witchfinder-General.

Under the regency Danaak was like an ancient house that while appearing sturdy from without had long been decaying within. The mortar that bonded it flaked with distrust, fear corroded its bolts and hatred spread rot through its timbers. And now the heirs of its greed-inspired squalor joined in the destruction of its crumbling fabric.

Like rats emerging from rain-flooded sewers, the ghouls of the necropolis left their tombs while Grand Johan had been booming his prelude to the coronation. Already there were exultant looks on pallid faces — here was an undreamed-of opportunity to riot and loot and above all wreak revenge upon those who had forced them to become outcasts. When the bell became silent signifying the beginning of the ceremony hundreds poured over the walls of the necropolis to race to the city ramparts. Others crowded into Garn's mausoleum where they dropped down into the tunnel to jostle in an endless cursing procession to the undercroft where Gambal waited to direct them.

The ghouls running through the streets with their cries of 'Livia! Livia!' had a galvanizing effect upon the ordinary folk of the city. Word spread that the Princess — *their* Princess — was beyond the gates. At last they could see a dream enshrined in legend coming true; at last they could bring down the usurper. While most hurried with the ghouls to the city walls, others who had lost family and friends to the Witchfinders formed into spontaneous gangs and combed the city for their black-robed enemies.

On the ramparts the men who had manned the mangonels stood easy, looking down with satisfaction on the scores of craters and their edgings of scorched and shattered bodies. Jeering the rebels who were retreating under a pall of dirty smoke, they dismissed the commotion in the city behind them as part of the enforced jubilation — until the mob surged up the stairways. Few had time to draw their swords before they were flung through the crenels; those who did put up resistance were soon overwhelmed by the sheer press of hostile humanity.

Only Captain Bors held his own against the rabble. With his back to a mangonel he swung his bloodied sword in scything strokes that laid a mound of bodies before him. Then a tattered figure mounted the mangonel and struck the side of his head with a cobblestone. He spun round with his sword raised — and saw that the attacker poised above him was a young girl. He lowered the blade and next moment he was overwhelmed and flung to the flagstones. The ghouls descended upon him, their knives rising and falling, rising and falling, until they resembled the monsters from whom they got their name. When they stood back exhausted one of their number severed the corpse's head and mounted it on a spear. For the rest of the night it was paraded from one drinking den to another.

The light was fading fast when Alwald and his specially picked band from the necropolis reached the main gate. The blacksmiths who were about to weld the massive iron portals fled and the guards, having no wish to die for a cause already lost, pelted after them. In a matter of moments the great crossbars were pushed back and the doors groaned apart to the endless chant of 'Livia! Livia! Livia!'

The famous scene of the Princess being welcomed into Danaak by her champion was to be portrayed by generations of artists as one of the most heroic moments in the history of Ythan.

ELEVEN
The Gallery
of Toys

The unbelievable had happened. The Regent stood
paralysed at the sight of the ghouls led by the bizarre
figure of King Death surging down the aisle towards
him. Shrieks filled the vast building as the panic-
stricken congregation fought to get out while more
outcasts fought to get in. Courtiers rushed into the
passage that led to the safety of the Citadel. Priests
and vergers fled into the numerous sanctuaries. A thick
fog of incense smoke billowed from overturned
braziers and abandoned censers, and the sacred doves,
driven into a frenzy of fear by the noise, battered
themselves against wall and pillar. White feathers
floated down like snow upon the mad scene.

From the side chapel the Lady Urwen ran forward
and, seizing the Regent by the arm, endeavoured to
drag him away while the Companions of the Rose
stepped forward to make a living wall between him
and the oncoming ghouls. At Urwen's touch the
Regent came to life and hurried with her to the
passage.

Glancing once over her shoulder Urwen saw that the

Companions of the Rose were falling under the weight of their attackers who had to step over those who had fallen to the guards' disciplined swordwork. Beyond them she had a glimpse of Jennet being dragged away by a filthy mendicant with a crimsoned sword in his free hand.

Good, she thought. *I hope he rapes her to death.*

Moments later they passed through another arch into the Citadel and the Regent slammed shut the bronze door and shot its bolts.

'The Companions . . .' she began but he seemed not to hear her — or the sound of knocking behind them. The Regent pushed aside the panic-stricken men and women who had fled the shrine and alarm gongs were sounding when he reached the Great Hall. Here more Companions of the Rose had assembled to defend their master.

'The walls are manned and the gates sealed,' one reported.

The Regent nodded.

'In the Citadel we can stand siege for a year if needs be but that rabble will soon lose its fire and then by the Mother there will be a bloody reckoning,' he said. 'Take word to Bors on the ramparts to turn the mangonels round and fire casks into the old quarter. That will give those who would welcome Mandal something to consider.'

'With respect, the streets are filled with rebels and no courier could get through,' said the Companion.

'Then use signal lamps,' cried the Regent. 'Where is the Lore Mistress?'

No one spoke.

'Did she not come through?' The Regent's voice suddenly trembled.

'Mayhap she did but I did not see,' Urwen answered.

'She has most likely taken refuge in one of the sanctuaries,' said the Companion soothingly. 'Now that you have escaped, the mob will soon leave the shrine to start looting and then we will be able to escort her back to the Citadel.'

The Regent's ruddy face changed to enraged purple. For a moment Urwen expected him to strike the Companion.

'You will fight your way into the shrine if necessary . . .' he began but his words froze as a Witchfinder staggered out of the shadows.

'The prisoners are killing the turnkeys,' he cried and tears rolled down his pallid face.

Without waiting for orders a number of Companions hurried in the direction of the staircase that spiralled down to the Nether World.

'Where are the Citadel guards?' demanded the Regent who seemed to have forgotten the Lore Mistress.

'They are manning the walls,' the Companion replied as though explaining something to a child. 'It is routine when the alarm gong sounds.'

'What is that?' demanded the Regent as the sound of shouts and iron ringing on iron reached them. All eyes turned to the far end of the hall to see scores of ghouls appear through its arched entrance. Without a word the Companions formed a line from wall to wall.

'I suggest you go to a place of safety, Your Majesty,' said the leader. 'I cannot say how long we can hold them as it would seem they have broken into the armoury.'

Without a word the Regent turned and, taking

Urwen by the wrist, hurried to the opposite end of the hall. They were ascending the staircase to the Regent's Tower when the sound of fierce fighting reached them from above. They turned into a corridor and had gone half its length when shouts echoed after them.

'They are everywhere,' wailed Urwen.

'The game is not over yet,' said the Regent. 'There is a secret passage . . .'

He pulled her to the end of the corridor after which she had a confused impression of going down staircases and through deserted galleries, and all the time the distant cries of ghouls rang in her ears.

'This is his great night, oh yes it is,' the custodian of the Regent's automatons told his mechanical charges as he removed their coverings. He had lit the chandeliers and their light reflecting on his pebble glasses created the illusion that his eyes were glowing.

'Everyone in Danaak will be celebrating the crowning of the new king,' he continued. 'So we will celebrate too, oh yes we will. But not his coronation. Never! Never! Instead we will celebrate the memory of our dear Merlinda. Timbal will play her favourite music on the lute, and we shall dance the pavan that she performed so beautifully — or some of us will.' He looked meaningfully at the winged lion, his least favourite automaton. The monologue continued as he went from figure to figure winding clockwork and setting the hidden levers that would control their movements when he set their mechanisms in motion.

He had just completed his adjustments to the drummer when the door at the far end of the gallery swung open and the Regent and Urwen entered with their chests heaving.

'Your Majesty . . .' he began in his fawning voice and then realized that there was something dreadfully wrong.

'Out of the way, Prince, the Citadel is in the hands of rebels,' shouted the Regent as he strode down the gallery without a glance at the figures he once referred to as his toys.

'There is an entrance to the tunnel beneath the Alchemist's Tower,' he told Urwen as they passed into the chamber beyond.

The custodian hurried to the door, turned the key in its massive lock and then flung it away. Moments later he heard the Regent cursing and he ran the length of the gallery to the antechamber where he saw his master tearing down a tapestry that depicted a rustic scene with a father playing with his little son and daughter.

'Your Majesty must have forgotten that you had the entrance to the tower bricked up to punish old Leodore,' laughed the little man, all subservience gone. 'Oh yes, left to starve he was.'

As though to emphasize his words the wallcovering came away to reveal an expanse of roughly mortared brickwork.

'You fool!' screamed Urwen. 'You sealed the escape route. How could you forget you had done that? We are trapped.'

'There is another entrance in the wine cellars,' the Regent mumbled.

'Then let us hurry.'

At that moment a drum began to beat slowly.

'What is that?' cried Urwen.

'That, lady, is the drummer,' the custodian answered. 'The last time you heard him he played a roll before the axe fell upon Merlinda's neck.'

Urwen shuddered and clung to the Regent's arm as they returned to the gallery to find a semi-circle of automatons waiting. There was something menacing about the silent figures and the drummer's measured rataplan that halted them; then with whirrings and clickings of hidden mechanisms the metal figures advanced with arms outstretched and metal fingers open.

The Regent attempted to run past them but the mechanical knight sent him sprawling with a blow from his mace. As he tried to regain his feet, his erstwhile toys closed about him with their metal fingers – those terrible *sharp* metal fingers! – plucking at him.

Moments later he began to scream and Urwen saw that their hands had become red as they tore away fragments of his golden gown – and then continued tearing. And all the time the drumbeat continued, a rhythmic counterpoint to the frenzied cries.

Holding her hands to her ears Urwen stumbled the length of the hall to the door to find it immovable.

Locked!

Now it was her turn to scream as the automatons straightened up from what appeared to be a red mound – a mound only vaguely human in shape – and with their arms outstretched marched towards her in time to the drum.

TWELVE

Into
the Darkness

After the delirium of the night a curious malaise hung over Danaak. Men were exhausted from fighting and celebrating, and from the changes that had suddenly taken place in their lives. Prisoners who had awoken in the dungeons of the Citadel without ever again expecting to see the light of day had slept beneath the stars, outcasts who had lived in dread of the Regent's troops found they were free to walk the streets, and burghers who owed their prosperity to the Lord Regent fled to their country estates when rioters burned their mansions overlooking the Green River.

To most, the night remained a disconnected series of vivid events: the sound of Grand Johan pealing a welcome to the rebel army when the ghouls captured the Great Shrine, the radiant Princess Livia entering her city on the traditional white drong, the obligatory celebration that suddenly became a genuine celebration, and the wild rumours, each more bizarre than the last, claiming that the Regent was dead.

In the Citadel, now uncannily quiet after the ghouls had rampaged through it, the alchemist Leodore descended the staircase that was once used by the Regent when he went to see the wretched captives he referred to as his pets. Now the Nether World was abandoned. The gaolers and members of the Guild of Executioners had been slain, or were in flight far beyond Danaak's walls, after the prisoners, inspired by the news that Princess Livia's army had surrounded the city, had mutinied. And as they had raced along the torch-lit passages releasing their fellows they learned a great truth — once they realized their strength they were many times stronger than those who had dominated them by fear and custom.

Leodore held a lanthorn in his shaking hand. The destruction he had witnessed through the powder he had invented to provide pleasure burdened him with guilt and it was only the thought of his 'daughter', as he privately considered the homunculus who had become lost in the labyrinthine Nether World, that gave him the strength to begin his subterranean search.

Stepping over the body of a turnkey, he found himself in the hall where the great capstan stood motionless at last. Several prisoners — mercifully dead — hung in chains from its beams.

'Titi,' Leodore called. 'Titi.'

The echoes mocked him in corridors and galleries where only yesterday the smoky air had been filled with the cries of the oppressors and the oppressed.

'Titi, Titi!'

'*Titi . . . Titi,*' mocked the echoes.

Nearly all the flambeaux had burned out and shadows leapt wildly as Leodore crossed the hall with his lanthorn. He paused, summoned up both breath and courage and plunged into the first dungeon-lined passage. His cries of 'Titi! Titi!' faded as he went deeper into the Stygian maze. Then there was silence and the old alchemist was never seen again.

In a long gallery lit by large casements providing views of Danaak's gabled roofs, Mandal, now reinstated as Commander of the Host, held a council of war or — as the Princess had insisted — a council of peace. He sat with his lieutenants, the Princess and her friends including Jennet round a table at the far end of the room chosen because it contained fewer reminders of the regency than other chambers in the Citadel.

Krispin still could not get over Jennet's likeness to the Princess. It was as though they were twin sisters. 'I think I am looking in a mirror when I look at thee,' the Princess told her but there was something in her tone suggesting that she did not enjoy the experience. Perhaps it was because Jennet, radiant after being reunited with Krispin, had an inner beauty that outshone that of Livia. Jennet knew how to be tactful and to Krispin's disgust plaited her hair so that, in his words, 'she looked like a milkmaid'.

Messengers were continually admitted by the guards at the doorway and soon Krispin was thinking that war was a far simpler matter than peace. Fighting had broken out between the outcasts of the necropolis and the outcasts who had returned from the Wastelands, fires were still burning in the merchants' quarter, the Guild of Mendicants demanded a huge sum for the assistance given to Krispin and his band, King Death sent a petition for a place in the new court, the price of bread had doubled . . . the list seemed endless.

'There are too many items for us to deal with separately,' said Mandal. 'Only when Her Highness has been enthroned and becomes Her Majesty will the

409

people be truly united and life in Danaak return to normal. Until then it will be chaos.'

'Then let her be crowned at once,' declared Alwald.

'Who will perform the ceremony?' asked Gambal. 'Has not Archpriest Mattan set out for a far hermitage where he can lead a life of contemplation?'

'There will be plenty eager to fill his vestments,' said Ognam.

'That doth not answer the immediate question — who will conduct my enthronement?' said the Princess impatiently.

'I will.'

Although the voice was not loud it seemed to fill the gallery. All looked to the far end where the guards sought to bar the way to an old man in black with a broad-brimmed hat and a long staff in his hand. Ignoring them he stepped into the gallery, and when they reached to halt him they were flung aside by an invisible force.

'Magus Ysldon!' cried the Princess, rising to greet him. 'Thou art ten times welcome at this time.'

'You would not think so by the way your sentries behave,' he replied as he seated himself at the table and looked round the assembled company with glittering eyes. 'I think we can take it that the quest is now completed — or as much as a quest can ever be completed. It is no longer a time for derring-do but wise governing. For generations, my dear Princess, your hoped-for return has been linked with a revival of Ythan's Golden Age and that is what your subjects will expect. But let us have you crowned before you have to face such problems.'

'How did thou get here, Magus?' the Princess asked.

'I certainly did not walk from the Valley of Yth,'

410

he replied. 'I still have some conjure magic left and now that you have won your throne without the use of gramarye as was required, I see no objection to giving a demonstration of my remaining powers. Let us see . . . a mild theurgical show on your behalf will make the right impression on your subjects while they are in an excitable mood.

'In the days before The Enchantment the emblem of both king and kingdom was a black rose on a yellow banner. After The Enchantment the standard was plain yellow with the symbol removed to signify that the country was without a sovereign – apart from the surcoats of the Companions of the Rose. I think the time is appropriate for the rose symbol to be revived.'

'A splendid idea,' said Mandal with a hint of impatience in his voice. 'However, to replace every banner in Ythan will take some time and meanwhile . . .'

Ignoring him, Ysldon walked to the open casement and looked out over the city above whose buildings fluttered hundreds of plain yellow flags which had been hoisted to acknowledge the Regent's coronation.

'The good thing about being a High Magician is that you can dispense with spoken spells, wands, pentagrams and such trappings,' he said as he returned to his seat.

It was only then that the company saw that every flag that flew in Danaak was emblazoned with a black rose. And even as they gazed in wonder they heard a murmur from the streets below that swelled into a roar of amazement and satisfaction.

'That should give them something to think about until, as Magus Royal to your late father, Princess,

I place the crown on your head,' said Ysldon carelessly.

'One moment, Lord Magus,' said Mandal. 'If it would not be asking too much perhaps you could use your powers to extinguish the houses that are burning and then . . .'

Ysldon held up his hand.

'In the past Ythan depended on High Magic which finally became its bane,' he said. 'If you are going to have a happy kingdom the people must rely on themselves, Princess. Conjuring such as you have just witnessed is just a little fun, but more than that I shall not do.'

'I do not wish to be crowned in the Great Shrine,' said the Princess. 'Not after what hath happened there.'

'Quite right,' said Ysldon. 'You must distance yourself from everything that has the taint of the regency. I suggest your coronation takes place at noontide in the open air.'

'But where, Magus?'

'The Square of Punishment.'

'What? How can I be crowned in that ghastly place?'

The Magus smiled at her sudden anger.

'If you are crowned there you could not have a better way of reassuring your subjects that the days of evil are over for ever, that the destiny of Ythan has swung from the shadow to the light.'

'But the gibbets!'

'Gibbets can be removed. I might even magick a monument to those who have fallen in your cause — another bit of fun, you understand.'

The Princess nodded.

'If I am to appear in bright sunlight a white robe will look too pale,' she said. 'Perhaps something in blue . . .'

'Blue is my favourite colour,' Jennet told her impulsively. 'It is said to suit our colouring.'

'That brings me to something very important,' said Ysldon. 'Mistress Jennet, I want you to return to your homeland. There is danger in having someone who resembles the Princess so closely in Danaak, it will always excite conjecture and there are those who make mischief out of conjecture.'

'Oh Jennet, I should hate to see you go when we have only just met,' said the Princess, 'but mayhap the Lord Magus speaks wisely, and for your sake as mine.'

'I should like nothing better than to live in the High Wald once more,' declared Jennet. 'That is . . . if Krispin accompanies me.'

'Well said. And what say you, Master Krispin?'

'For me the quest is truly over,' Krispin replied. 'I want for nothing more than to go back to the Peak Tower and return Woundflame to the Lady Eloira. Then, mayhap, I shall find a cottage where I can go back to my craft.'

'And I shall help you both on your way,' said Ysldon. 'Tonight I want to hold a feast in your honour, Master Krispin, and you, Lord Alwald. If it had not been for you both the Regent would be wearing a crown and Her Highness would still be a-slumber in the Mountains of the Moon.'

The feast given by Ysldon in honour of the two questers was even more lavish than the one he had provided at the Wells of Ythan, and Krispin guessed

413

that while he might have been one of the most remarkable sorcerers in Ythan's history he derived simple pleasure out of playing host.

It being a hot night the casements of the feasting hall were open and frequently the sound of singing reached them from the streets below and several times there was the now ritualistic chanting of 'Livia! Livia! Livia!'

When the platters were finally removed and new flasks of wine provided, the Princess said, 'It is important to me and my kingdom that when I am crowned my coronation will be so splendid it will be talked of when we are all gone. It must remind people that it marked the end of tyranny. Not only must the ceremony stay in men's minds but the entertainments that will accompany it, and to that end I appoint thou, Master Gambal, as my Revel Master not only for the heroic way thou led the outcasts into the Citadel but because I understand thou hast had some experience in the post.'

A hot joy filled Gambal. Revel Master again! And at the beginning of a new reign! Who could say to what heights it would lead on to! And by his wits alone he had done it! But he let none of this almost savage satisfaction show. He bowed with due humility and gracefully accepted.

'Captain Barlak, I have had no opportunity to thank thou and thy men who served me so well and it is my wish that thou will continue to do so,' the Princess said. 'Therefore I appoint thou the Royal Bodyguard and so that there will be no link with the previous guards I declare that thy surcoats will be black and thy badge a white rose — the black is for the earth beneath which you lay so long and the white is for the snow of the Mountains of the Moon where we faced such dangers together.

'Shipmaster Danya, thou lost thy ship the *Amber Star* in my service. Wouldst thou another ship or can I compensate thee in a different way?'

'Your Highness, it has been in my mind to quit the sea since I lost my crew on my last voyage,' Danya replied. 'I should like to settle with a waterfront tavern in the Port of Gysbon where I could still swap tales with bluewater sailors. When thinking on it before I thought to name it the Quest but, if permission be granted, I should like it to be known as the Queen Livia.'

'So be it,' said the Princess. She turned to Ognam. 'Sir Jongleur I shall never forget thy merry tune we danced to at the Wells of Ythan, and in the days that lie ahead I doubt not there will be times when merriment is a much needed commodity. Therefore I wouldst be glad if thou became my jester.'

'You honour me,' said Ognam and the bells on his motley tinkled as he bowed.

She will turn to me next and what shall I answer? thought Alwald. *For so long my one wish was to return to the Lady Demara in Mabalon. And I cannot deny that I loved her almost to a point of madness, but now I am not sure. To expect her to return my love after the love she had enjoyed with my father was but youthful yearning. And yet . . . and yet I still see her in dreams and I still hear her laughter but do not all men carry such an image? Here I can be of service to Livia who is of my age — apart from the time she was entranced — and who some day may seek . . .*

His thoughts were interrupted by the Princess speaking his name.

'Lord Alwald, I offer thou naught because thou art already my Champion. Thy exploit in opening the gates to me will be told in folktale and saga. I knowst of thy wish to regain thy castle that I hear is held by a person called the Wish Maiden, and her followers, who claim thy domain by right of conquest over the Wolfmen — a problem we shall solve by silver or arms in the fullness of time. But, now, I beg thee to follow the ancient tradition of thy family and remain the Queen's Champion.'

'I could ask for no greater honour,' replied Alwald and his pulse suddenly raced as he felt her hand clasp his beneath the table.

'Your Highness, I have a boon to ask,' said Mandal. 'It is not for myself, for I am content to be Commander of the Host. It is for the two outcasts, Garn and Aldis, who befriended me in the necropolis. They are runaways from a bawdy house where Garn happened to strangle a Witchfinder.'

'That is enough to recommend him,' laughed the Princess. 'What would you ask for them?'

'That you take them into your service. To begin with they would make excellent pages.'

'Then send a message to their tomb,' said the Princess with another laugh. 'I wager I shall be the first queen to be served by ghouls.'

More wine was served and Ysldon's eyes shone brighter than ever.

'And now Master Krispin,' said the Princess. 'Didst thou think I had forgotten thee? Tell me, what would thou take back to thy High Wald that would reflect my gratitude for thy questing?'

'Answer Her Highness in your speech of farewell for the time for parting is close upon us,' said Ysldon.

Krispin stood up and as Jennet gazed at him in the candle light she marvelled at how he had changed from a youth to a man since she had last seen him. She smiled as she remembered how smooth-faced he had been and now he had a beard that matched his auburn hair. And, as he began to speak, the love that she had always felt for him rose within her like a crescendo.

'Your Highness, I ask nothing for myself for I have learned the curious thing about a quest is that it contains its own reward,' he said. 'But there is one thing I would take back to the High Wald and that is a royal charter for a village to devote itself to the crafting of toys. My village of Toyheim was destroyed by the Wolf Horde and is no more than ashes but I have a dream that toymakers may come together once more in the High Wald and build a new village in memory of the old.'

'After I become Queen my courier will carry such a charter to thee,' declared the Princess.

'As to a farewell speech I can only say that it will be impossible to forget you and the times we have shared,' Krispin continued. 'Looking back I feel I have been living in a land of folktales with giants and griffins and the sleeping beauty.' He paused while there was laughter. 'But mayhap it is the other way round, and what we have experienced will become folktales in long years to come. Who knows, some clever story-teller may yet make a tale out of the Red Death.

'For myself I must say that I do have a deep regret that one of the fellowship of the quest is not with us this night.'

'The Hump,' said Alwald.

Krispin nodded.

'Not only was he a good comrade who led us across the Wilderness of Gil to bravely share our dangers in Thaan, but without him we should never have found our way in the Mountains of the Moon. He left us to return to the Arkad Woodlands with a possible cure for Silvermane who lay dying from the wound of a poisoned arrow.'

'What was this *cure*?' asked Ysldon with an expression of bland inquiry.

Krispin swallowed and then said, 'It was water that I took secretly from the Wells of Ythan.'

'Such theft was no secret from me,' Ysldon declared and then he burst out laughing at Krispin's expression. 'And now you wonder if the stolen water was effective and what has happened to the crouchback who grew wings.'

'Just so, Lord Magus,' answered Krispin.

'Then behold.' Ysldon waved his hand towards the shadows in the far corner of the hall and as the company turned their eyes in that direction they saw a yellow disk begin to glow. Soon other points of light appeared behind it and they realized they were looking at a magical representation of the moon sailing in a starry sky. As its luminosity increased they made out the jagged backdrop of a forest and — was it more than imagination? — a moist woodland smell filled their nostrils.

In the foreground, brightly lit by the moon's cold radiance, was an ancient tower and while they watched an oblong of yellow light appeared as a door was opened. Three figures came out — a man in a hermit's gown; the Hump, with his wings unfolding above his shoulders; and Silvermane, limping slightly as she walked on her delicate hooves. In the moonlight she

418

lived up to her name as her long hair and silky tail appeared like liquid silver.

The Princess leaned over to Jennet and whispered, 'I swear she be quick with child and I would guess her winged lover is going to take her to her own people.'

Jennet nodded wisely, though to her eyes there was little to suggest that the horsemaid was pregnant and she guessed that Livia had a more worldly instinct than her in such matters.

For a moment the three figures stood together outside the tower, hands were clasped in farewell and then the Hump placed his arms round Silvermane and with his pinions rising and falling he soared up until they were no more than a graceful shadow against the night sky.

The stars went out, the moon dimmed and the vision ended.

'I hope that satisfies you,' said the enchanter.

'We are well satisfied,' said Krispin. 'But I can say no more because my heart is too full at the thought of parting.'

Toasts were drunk to Krispin and Jennet and then Ysldon said, 'My ancient heart, too, is full, Krispin Tammasson, for we shall not meet again. When I return to the Wells of Ythan I shall never leave them, for the time has come for me to seek the truth they hold in their depths. For the last time, I salute you and Lord Alwald who succeeded where hundreds failed. Now join hands with Jennet and walk down the hall into the shadow.'

When Krispin stood up to obey, Alwald came up to him and without a word they embraced. Then he and Jennet walked away from the table into the darkness. And next moment there was only darkness.

*   *   *

Krispin and Jennet continued walking with their fingers locked as they had when they were children and gradually the blackness lessened to starshine and they saw rearing against it the silhouette of the Peak Tower.

THIRTEEN

The Dark Maid

The reunion was over, the story of the quest had been twice told and after the excitement of the night before the Lady Eloira sat in her solar with Jennet, talking of her abduction by the Witchfinder Mordan.

'I can remember the wolfmen attacking the guards at the pass,' Jennet said. 'I think it was the shock of seeing them again that started to bring my mind back into the present. And I certainly remember when Dolly started talking, but after we were chased by the bear everything got hazy again. It was not until I was in the Citadel that I was really myself once more though I deemed it best to continue to be childish.'

'I thank the Mother that Krispin managed to reach you,' said Eloira, raising her glass of greenish wine while Smoke her big grey cat purred on her knee.

'It may sound strange but I was not surprised, not really. I cannot explain it but I somehow knew he would find me. The worst time was when I was moved from the tower before he came back with a file.'

'I should have thought the worst time was in the

Great Shrine when you were about to be married to the Regent.'

'The terrible old woman — the Lore Mistress — she tried to drug me but as she thought she was only dealing with a child she was easy to outwit. For the same reason I was able to steal a knife which is why I knew that I would never be the Regent's bride. I hid it in the sheaf of lilies I carried and it would have been for him or for me before I had to make my vows. But dear Krispin was there.'

'Where is he now?' asked Eloira. 'There remains something important to be done.'

'He is looking at the collection of toys from the Choosing at Toyheim. Now the quest is over he wants nothing more than to start making his rocking horses and mechanical dolls again. He has this dream about a new toymakers' village . . .' And Jennet went on to tell the Lady Eloira about the royal charter the Princess had promised.

There was a knock on the door and Krispin entered, carrying Woundflame.

'Your pardon,' he said, smiling. 'I lost the measure of time in your attics looking at my Jennet doll which you selected at the last Choosing. I think I could improve upon it now.'

'There will be plenty of time for toys,' said the old woman getting to her feet. 'Jennet, my dear, please bring that lamp.'

She led the way down from the solar and across the courtyard to a bronze door set in a rockface behind which was the sepulchre where generations of her forefathers lay in their armour.

Krispin gave her the sword to hold while he struggled with the massive key.

'The blade does look blunt and tarnished and the hilt is no better,' she said. 'No wonder young Alwald did not want it.'

'You should have seen it when its magic flowed in the blade,' said Krispin. 'It shone like new-minted silver and its edge lived up to its name though that is something I have no wish to remember.'

The door grated open and they entered the still air of the tomb. With Jennet nervously holding the light they passed between the slabs on which lay skeletal figures in time-dimmed armour to an altar at the far end.

'I did not see that before,' murmured Krispin pointing to a scroll.

'Piper left it there in safe-keeping for you,' said Eloira. 'But first let me replace the sword.'

She raised Woundflame so that its point was above the altar and declaimed, 'Spirits, note well that I, Eloira, Reeve of the High Wald, return this blade wrought by Wayland Weaponsmith and wielded by Rusthal when he won this demesne by right of conquest, and here may it remain until it be needed to serve the kingdom of Ythan again.'

Carefully she lowered it until the sword fitted into a notch cut in the stone and remained upright like a pagan cross. Then she handed Krispin the scroll and they made their way into the living world. Back in her solar she explained how Piper had left the vellum without telling her of its contents before he set out for Danaak.

'Once the Citadel was taken I searched for him but in vain,' said Krispin. 'In the Regent's unspeakable menagerie I found a bone pipe in a cage but that was all.'

The Lady Eloira sighed.

'He said there was such in that scroll that might be disturbing and that if you were content with your lot to let it be. He had been seeking your origins on my behalf as part of our agreement.'

'If it tells whether we be kin or not then I must open it,' Krispin declared.

Jennet laid her hand on his arm.

'Be you sure that you really want to know?' she asked. 'And does it matter now that all who knew us in Toyheim are dead? Whether we be brother and sister or not, it makes no difference to the love I hold for you.'

'It does matter to me,' said Krispin grimly and he broke the seal. As the vellum unrolled they saw that it was covered in small spidery writing and Krispin cried in frustration, 'Dame Norbet had little success in teaching me my letters. I cannot read this Fey script.'

The Lady Eloira offered to read it to them and when they gratefully accepted she began:

Greetings, Krispin Tammasson.

The task laid upon me was to seek out the truth about you and the girl Jennet, as you had been brought up as brother and sister by the toymaker you knew as Father Tammas. I have not enough vellum to repeat how I set about this: suffice it to say that Fey lives are much longer than your span and that we have an abiding curiosity in the affairs of mortals. Many an old one of my race I sought out, and as a Fey I had a key to knowledge denied to ordinary mortals, such as that held by the ancient spirit of the forest and the Tablets of Eon, long hidden in caves beneath the White Virgins. And while there were gaps in the story that

424

I have failed to fill I have garnered enough knowledge to assure you that you have no blood tie with each other . . .

Krispin heaved a great sigh of relief and tears misted Jennet's eyes with the realization of what this meant to them both.

Krispin, your parents were neighbours of Jennet's in Lasgaad and from the time you could both walk you were constant playmates. When the Red Death came and claimed ycur family, Jennet's father and mother took you into their home and when they sickened they sent you both with Jennet's nurse to the Wald where the plague had not reached. When the nurse realized that she too was carrying the distemper she left you, with all the money she possessed, at a woodcutter's cottage. When this had been spent and he could no longer earn due to the ravages of the plague he abandoned you in the forest.

It was your ill fortune to arrive at the lair of a forest dhrul who took on the shape of a kindly old woman living alone in a pretty cottage to which she lured her victims . . .'

'Goody Goodheart!' exclaimed Jennet turning pale as the words released memories long buried. 'She was kind at first. We were starving and she gave us food, and being small we did not know what the word dhrul meant. Then she would not let us leave the cottage and Krispin . . .'

'I killed her,' said Krispin tonelessly. 'She wanted our hearts, but I managed to kill her in my desperation.'

'Listen,' said the Lady Eloira and she continued to read:

You escaped by turning her own knife upon her, and

425

no doubt you have always thought that you brought about her death, but a dhrul, even in the shape of an old mortal, cannot be slain by ordinary weapons. In time Goody Goodheart recovered to prey on lonely forest folk until some foresters banded together and visited her with silvered axeheads.

You may remember wandering in the forest until Tammas found you and, as you could remember nothing of what had happened before the ordeal in the cottage, he wrongly assumed you were brother and sister. You are free to wed. The blessing of the Fey be upon you. If you do not wish to risk your happiness read no further but lay down this scroll.'

'Shall I continue?' asked the Lady Eloira. 'Piper was most mysterious about this scroll and what is writ must be the reason.'

'Please read on,' cried Jennet. 'How could anyone stop at this point?'

'As you will,' said Eloira. 'I must confess to great curiosity myself.' She picked up the scroll.

What I write now concerns Jennet and her likeness to portraits of the sleeping princess. I have thought from the moment I first saw her such a resemblance could not be happenstance, nor is it.

I learned that, before The Enchantment, the Princess Livia, left much to her own devices by her father, fell in love with a musician at the court in Danaak, so much so that she went through a clandestine marriage ceremony with him when she found she was carrying his child.

Thanks to the discreet aid of the Magus Royal, Livia had the baby in secret just before the entrancement was laid upon her. Afterwards, the musician took the child and lovingly brought him up in a far part of the

426

kingdom. *After The Enchantment he feared his son would be endangered if it was known he had royal blood. He finally settled in Lasgaad and lived modestly as a maker of musical instruments.*

In due course Livia's boy grew up, married and had a son who, late in life, became Jennet's father. Jennet is therefore the rightful inheritor of the Empty Throne unless it should come to pass that Livia is found and awakened.

The danger that this could bring upon Jennet from the Regent far outweighs any pride she might gain from announcing her royal lineage. If you some day read this scroll my hope for you both is that this secret is never revealed and with this thought in mind I have becharmed this scroll. Written by the hand of Piper the Fey.

The Lady Eloira laid the scroll upon a table and the three looked at each other in amazement.

'My lineage matters little now that Livia will be on the throne,' said Jennet. 'And I shall be content to be a toymaker's wife, but I would be grateful if you would read it to me once more.'

'Certainly,' said Eloira, but when she turned to the table all she could see was a handful of withered leaves.

'Do you know what I want to do?' Jennet asked Krispin when they left the solar.

'I have no idea, Your Highness,' he replied.

'I want to go back to the mere where we saw the crystal bird. What happened there meant so much to me, and this time you will not be plagued by the thought that I am your sister.'

Hand-in-hand they set off down the road that led in awe-inspiring curves from the Peak Tower.

*　　*　　*

That evening, the Lady Eloira apologized that she was too tired by the recent excitement to attend supper. Instead, she sat in her room and carefully wrote her testament in which, as the last of her line, she bequeathed the Peak Tower and its lands to Krispin Tammasson on the understanding that when he encouraged toymakers to come to the High Wald he would reintroduce the traditional ceremony of the Choosing.

She called for her steward Hans to witness her words. Then she poured wine for them both and, sitting opposite each other before her perpetual fire, they talked together like two old friends rather than mistress and servant.

Later that night the Lady Eloira awoke to see a young woman in dark robes and her face made mysterious by a black veil.

'Ah, I have been expecting you,' she said. 'Many may fear you but you come for me as a friend.'

The figure inclined her head.

Eloira ran her fingers through the soft fur of her cat who had leapt up to purr to her. Then she arose. The figure, smiling behind her veil, advanced and took hold of the old woman's hand.

'You have given much in your life and you are weary,' she said softly. 'Now it is time for you to rest.'

'There is much I shall miss,' said Eloira.

'But not for long. What do you remember from the time before your birthing? It is not as some fear, my lady.'

'I have one question,' said Eloira. 'Those I have loved most in life you took long ago. Will . . . will they . . . will we meet?'

'That I cannot answer, for as yet we have not crossed over but you will learn soon enough. Are you ready, my lady?'

'I am ready.'

For a moment the Lady Eloira looked back at the bed on which her body lay and then she followed the Dark Maid.

Epilogue

That year autumn lasted late and golden and fruitful, and many swore that it was a reflection of the change that had come over the kingdom since Queen Livia had ascended the Empty Throne. But now the first snow of winter had dusted the trees of the High Wald and weatherwise foresters predicted that soon the pass between the White Virgins would be closed.

In the Peak Tower a fire burned brightly in the chamber that the Lady Eloira had used as her solar, and which was now the favourite place for the new Reeve of the High Wald and his bride to spend time together. Seated gratefully by the fire was the last courier who would be able to enter the High Wald that season and Krispin and Jennet, after receiving the royal charter promised by the Queen, plied the man with wine and questions.

At first he replied formally as was the way of royal couriers but as Jennet never let his goblet stand empty his tone became that of a gossip − as was the way of royal couriers.

'Master Ognam? Why, he disappeared,' he said in reply to Krispin's question. 'Her Majesty was furious I can tell you because she wanted him for her Court Jester — right comical he was with his tumbling and stories and those songs he wrote himself. But one day he disappeared. Afterwards some drong drivers said they had seen him on the old highway that used to lead to Thaan but only a fool would set out for a dead city.'

'Fool he is, a fine fool,' said Krispin. 'I wager he travels to Thaan.'

'But why, when he could have done so well for himself in Danaak?' asked Jennet.

'I suppose he never forgot the children he led into the Drakenfel.'

'The Queen's Lady-in-Waiting, the Lady Tana, was in a terrible state after he left,' the courier went on. 'She wanted to go in search of him but Her Majesty would not let her, so instead she got permission to go to her old home on the Lake of Taloon.'

'The Thaan road passes by Taloon,' said Krispin.

'Ay, so it does.' The courier grinned and then looked with mock surprise at his refilled goblet.

'And my other old companions — how do they fare?'

'Lord Alwald is everywhere with Her Majesty. Of course he is the Queen's Champion but even so there is gossip. And Master Gambal thrives. As Revel Master he excelled himself at the coronation and now he practically runs the Citadel. If you want anything done see Master Gambal, is what folk say.'

'And tell me, did they find the Lore Mistress?'

'Some think she escaped down into the dungeons before they were sealed, and others that she magicked herself to some far place.' He shrugged.

That night as Jennet lay in Krispin's arms she said, 'I know you miss your Pilgrim friends . . .'

'It would be strange if I did not,' he said lightly. 'Mayhap we will meet again.'

'And when do you think that might be?'

Krispin ran his fingers through her golden hair covering their pillow.

'When the crystal bird returns.'

'But the Magus Ysldon told you it comes only as a harbinger of change. Surely now that Livia is queen everything will stay peaceful.'

Krispin looked to the window which framed the Constellation of the Griffin and sighed.

'There is something that nags at the back of my mind,' he said. 'You remember I told you how High Magic ended and the days of the sorcerers are over?'

'Yes.'

'I fear it may not be true. In The Mage's Tower I traded the Esav — the jewel I brought from the City Without a Name — for the knowledge to find Livia. The Mage wanted the Esav because, he said, coming from the stars it could renew the magic of this world.'

'So?'

'If magic be used again everything would be repeated as before.'

Jennet laughed.

'Kris, you always had strange fancies.' She put her arms round him. 'Forget the Esav and let us work our own magic tonight.'

In the Citadel, Queen Livia sat late on her throne with Lord Alwald standing beside her. The candles had burned low since her council had retired after hours of useless talk following the news that the Red Death had laid his bloody mark on a town in the south.

'I feel so helpless,' she murmured. 'The people expect too much. In my father's day there was the Magus Royal who took care of plague and pest.'

'Yes, but Ysldon told us that magic became the bane of the kingdom.'

'Then I wish I had that bane to banish the Death. And give us a better harvest. And punish the rebels in the Eastlands.'

At that moment Garn appeared in the green and silver attire of a page. His bow was a little awkward, but he was learning.

'Your Majesty, there is a stranger without who asks for an audience with you,' he said.

'At this late hour?'

'He says he has come very far to offer you a rare favour — a panacea for all Ythan's ills.'

'Did he tell you his name or what he wants?'

'I dared not ask him because he is such a strange old man,' Garn confessed. 'But he did say that Lord Alwald would know him as The Mage.'

A selection of bestsellers from Headline

FICTION

RINGS	Ruth Walker	£4.99 □
THERE IS A SEASON	Elizabeth Murphy	£4.99 □
THE COVENANT OF THE FLAME	David Morrell	£4.99 □
THE SUMMER OF THE DANES	Ellis Peters	£6.99 □
DIAMOND HARD	Andrew MacAllan	£4.99 □
FLOWERS IN THE BLOOD	Gay Courter	£4.99 □
A PRIDE OF SISTERS	Evelyn Hood	£4.99 □
A PROFESSIONAL WOMAN	Tessa Barclay	£4.99 □
ONE RAINY NIGHT	Richard Laymon	£4.99 □
SUMMER OF NIGHT	Dan Simmons	£4.99 □

NON-FICTION

MEMORIES OF GASCONY	Pierre Koffmann	£6.99 □
THE JOY OF SPORT		£4.99 □
THE UFO ENCYCLOPEDIA	John Spencer	£6.99 □

SCIENCE FICTION AND FANTASY

THE OTHER SINBAD	Craig Shaw Gardner	£4.50 □
OTHERSYDE	J Michael Straczynski	£4.99 □
THE BOY FROM THE BURREN	Sheila Gilluly	£4.99 □
FELIMID'S HOMECOMING: Bard V	Keith Taylor	£3.99 □

All Headline books are available at your local bookshop or newsagent, or can be ordered direct from the publisher. Just tick the titles you want and fill in the form below. Prices and availability subject to change without notice.

Headline Book Publishing PLC, Cash Sales Department, PO Box 11, Falmouth, Cornwall, TR10 9EN, England.

Please enclose a cheque or postal order to the value of the cover price and allow the following for postage and packing:
UK & BFPO: £1.00 for the first book, 50p for the second book and 30p for each additional book ordered up to a maximum charge of £3.00
OVERSEAS & EIRE: £2.00 for the first book, £1.00 for the second book and 50p for each additional book.

Name ....

Address ....

....

....